# the sacred art
# of stealing

# the sacred art of stealing

## christopher brookmyre

An *Abacus* Book

First published in Great Britain in 2002 by Abacus

Copyright © 2002 Christopher Brookmyre

'The Sacred Art of Leaving' written by Billy Franks © Billy Franks 2001
From the album *Sex, Laughter & Meditation*. Lyrics reproduced by
kind permission. Title artfully stolen. *www.billyfranks.com*

'Unemployed Boyfriend' words by A.P. Alexakis, music by Everclear.
From the album *Songs From An American Movie Volume 1:
Learning How To Smile*. Lyrics not reproduced, but any excuse to plug
the details of a magnificent record. *www.everclearonline.com*

The moral right of the author has been asserted.

A CIP catalogue record for this book
is available from the British Library.

ISBN   0 349 11554 0

Typeset by Palimpsest Book Production Limited,
Polmont, Stirlingshire
Printed and bound in Great Britain by
Clays Ltd, St Ives plc

Abacus
An imprint of
Time Warner Books UK
Brettenham House
Lancaster Place
London WC2E 7EN

www.TimeWarnerBooks.co.uk

*For Marisa*


Debts of inspiration: Billy Franks and Art Alexakis.
Seek out their music. You may be inspired too.

# prologue: consumer services

Was there anything quite so under-rated in this shallow, plastic, global-corporate, tall-skinny-latte, kiddy-meal-and-free-toy, united-colors-of-fuck-you-too world, than a good old-fashioned, no-frills, retail blow-job?

It was one of the very few consumer transactions left in which you really did get what you paid for, no more and no less. No packaging, no marketing, no fake smiles, no on-the-door greeters, no aspirational lifestyle kudos; just functional, dispassionate cock-sucking for a pre-agreed flat fee.

All those uptight assholes who took *way* too much pride in telling you they never paid for it in their lives – they didn't know what they were missing. And this was because they didn't understand the nature of the transaction. They thought paying for it was undignified, that it somehow diminished them as men. What kind of insecure loser did you have to be to believe that, when, in every other aspect of your life, paying someone else to render you services was what underlined your status? Yeah, sure, you could pump your own gas, wash your own car, shine your own shoes; you could roll dough and make your own fucking pizza. But who the fuck wants to do that when you've got money in your pocket? Having to do that shit yourself because you *don't* have money in your pocket – *that's* undignified; *that* diminishes you as a man. Paying for it didn't mean you couldn't get it any other way – it meant

1

that you could afford the convenience option, same as any other service.

And talk about denial! 'Never paid for it.' Yeah, right. Maybe not directly, asshole, but you fuckin' paid for it, make no mistake. Sneakier than a stealth tax, and just as unavoidable, there's a traceable dollar outlay connected to every time she unzips your fly, whether she be your wife, your mistress or a one-night stand. And this isn't just about steak dinners and hotel rooms, either. This is about that thousand-buck suit on your back, your health-club subscription and your stylist's fee, too. Even if you're a rock star backstage at the Hollywood Bowl: that seventeen-year-old with the doe-eyes and the awe-struck look is still playing an angle, and she ain't leaving without a piece of you bigger than the one between her teeth. Whether it's a noseful of your best pure, or the cheque she'll get when she tells all, one way or another, that blow-job is coming at a cost.

Of course, there were also those who claimed it didn't turn them on unless the girl was genuinely into them; presumably the same deluded jerks who thought that no broad had ever faked an orgasm while *they* were fucking her. Sure. Like every girl who ever went down on them did it because she found them irresistible. Were there really that many chicks out there with a fetish for pot bellies and beer breath? Come on. Even your ever-doting wife has to feign her interest now and then. So if feigned interest is what you need, a hooker could fake it better than most. But that's only for those sensitive-flower or pretty-boy ego-tripper types who actually thought it made a fucking difference whether the bitch gives a shit.

What these clowns didn't grasp was that you were paying for their disinterest as much as their attention. That

2

bored look was an integral and essential part of the retail blow-job experience. Jeez, it was an insult to your intelligence for her to expect you to believe she was enjoying it, so there was an invaluable honesty about the nature of the transaction if she looked like she couldn't care less. There was no have-a-nice-day fake sentiment bullshit. Blow-*job*, understand? Not blow-hobby. She wasn't doing it because she liked it, she was doing it because she needed the dough and you were going to give her it once she'd made you come. Two blocks down, the girl flipping burgers at Mickey D's would be looking even more bored for even less green, but it didn't make your Big Mac taste any different whether she had a fucking smile on her face.

This was raw, honest, old-school, pre-globalised capitalism. You need her services, she needs your money, and nobody is pretending there's anything else going on. No branding, no mission statements and no customer loyalty card. You want No Logo? Go get yourself some professional head.

And if the chance presents itself, go get yourself some Third-World head, especially. Shit, it was only natural that there had to be some kind of benefit to balance out the negatives about being stuck in fucking Mexico. The whole place stank like a busted sewer, the beer tasted like anaemic piss, and just driving as far as the fly-ridden corner store was like entering a stock-car race – but goddamn if the skanks weren't a whole different quality.

It was kind of reassuring to know that there were still places in this culturally colonised and strip-malled world where you could find a hooker who wasn't about to put every cent you gave her straight into her arm. Unfortunately, those places also tended to be the most economically deprived. That wasn't to say you couldn't

3

toss a rock down a Mexican red-light street without it bouncing from crack-whore to smack-head like a pinball; nowhere was isolated or backward enough to be immune from that most successful example of globalisation. Jeez, there was probably some junkie bitch selling her ass in the middle of the Sahara fucking Desert right now. But the thing about south of the border was that there were girls down here who were selling it simply because they were dirt poor from the day they were born, and hadn't needed any drugs to put them on the street. There was something satisfyingly pure and natural about that, and at the basest level it was far more of a turn-on if the girl didn't have track-marks up her arms or eyes like an insomniac panda.

They tried harder down here too, though maybe that was because he was an American and likely to be splashing more money in reward for good service. Whatever the reason, they definitely put more effort into it, and not that embarrassing fake enthusiasm either: just professional dedication, care and diligence. So much for the Protestant work ethic. These girls gave you their best every time, and they were Catholic to the last.

All of which made such exquisite distraction hard to resist when he was stuck in this dump with nothing to kill but time. When he was younger and keener, he'd have been more disciplined about it. He remembered the rules, some he'd set for himself and others he'd learned from guys who'd been around the block, and one of those was not to get laid until the job was over. A hard-on kept you sharp, kept you focused, kept you ruthless. Bloodthirsty, even. But now *he*'d been around the block enough to know when it was okay – even advisable – to cut himself some slack. He didn't have a fix on the target yet, for Christ's sakes, and what was the point of hanging out in fucking Mexico if you couldn't bang Mexican skanks?

The phone rang, its pre-historic bell-tone seeming to shake the rickety bedside table, the sound probably loud enough to be heard downstairs in the lobby. This was the best hotel in town, but that wasn't saying much when the town was Hermosillos. It was standard practice to stay someplace anonymously low-key on this kind of business, and he'd never minded hanging out in flea-pits, but all things were relative. In this neck of the woods, a hotel was classed as ostentatiously swanky if it had a phone in the room, and that was something he really couldn't do without right now.

It also had clean sheets (they smelled of cheapo detergent, but that they smelled of detergent at all was worth a star above the front door), an *en suite* and a colour TV, for what that was worth. Cool if you were into Mexican wrestling or soccer, both of which accounted for all but two channels, the remainder offering Spanish home-shopping and, inevitably, MTV. The most useful in-house facility he'd installed himself. She was named Conchita – at least that's what she was calling herself – and so far she was proving far better value for money than the room rate, even minus his Diners' card discount.

The girl seemed less startled by the phone than he was, probably because it hadn't been five years since she'd heard one sound like that. She knelt up and began moving across the bed, intending to answer it. Sweet gesture, but it wasn't a secretary he needed.

'What are you, expectin' a call or somethin'?'

'Pardon, *señor*.'

She didn't speak English, but it was still pretty clear she got the point.

'Well I guess this'll be for me, then, huh? You just keep talkin' into that pink receiver down there, sweetie. And don't mind me, I can concentrate on two things at once.'

Conchita went back to work as he lifted the phone, cradling it against his ear as he lay back on the pillow.

'Hey. Who's this?'

'Miguel.'

'Yo Mickey. What's up?'

'Pack your bags, Harry. You're in the wrong place.'

'I'm in the—? Bullshit. Says who?'

'Come on, how long you been there? Nearly a week? You like Mexico so much you wanna hang out some more?'

'Well, your mother's still givin' good head, so I figure why leave?'

'My mother was born in Texas, fucko. She ain't never been to Mexico.'

'Yeah, right. Not since she carried you 'cross the Rio Grande in a shawl, leastways.'

'Whatever, *Javier*. We got a new lead. Vancouver.'

'A new *lead*? What the fuck is that? A lead is something you put on a dog. Tell me you got a mark or don't waste my time.'

'Nunez was seen, man.'

'Who by?'

'What the fuck does that matter? He was seen, and that's good enough for Alessandro, so it's good enough for you to get on a fuckin' plane, okay?'

'Alessandro.' Harry spat the word, managing to keep a laugh out of his voice. At least Miguel couldn't see the smirk, but there was no question he'd be picturing it anyway. Miguel didn't rate the kid any higher than Harry did, but his position required him to be more circumspect

6

about it. He let the pause drag on a few seconds, allowing Miguel to assume it meant acquiescence. It didn't.

'You're booked on flight—'

'I ain't goin'.'

'Harry, the—'

'Nunez is in Hermosillos, Miguel, trust me on this.'

'Fuck trust, Harry, we're dealing in proof. We got a witness sighting in Vancouver, and what have you got, 'cept cheap burritos and cheaper blow-jobs?'

'Hey, just because they're a bargain don't mean they ain't high quality.'

'I'm serious, man. We need a result on this, fast.'

'Sure, but you ain't gonna get it sendin' me to Vancouver when the dude's in Mexico, are ya?'

'What makes you so sure?'

'Come on, how long I been doin' this?'

'Alessandro Estobal don't wanna hear about instincts, Harry. You know what he's like.'

Meaning naïve, ignorant and rash.

'Believe me, Mickey, Nunez will go to what he knows. That's what people do when they're feelin' scared and insecure. You're shittin' your shorts an' lookin' over your shoulder the whole time – you think you'd decide that was a good moment to head into the great blue yonder? Fuck no. Vancouver! That little prick wouldn't know what street Canada's on. He ain't been further north than Barstow in his life. He ain't gonna go to a city he's never been and where he don't know nobody. He'll wanna be somewhere he thinks he knows the lie of the land, some-place he associates with being safe and sound. Home. Hermosillos. Remember that accountant a few years back? The one who—'

'The skimmer, yeah. Rounding down the figures and

syphoning the difference into his own little pension fund.'

'That's the guy. Everyone said he'd gone to fuckin' Lichtenstein, or Switzerland, or Disneyland fuckin' Paris. Where'd I find him? Hidin' out in mom's basement, back home in Incest, Alabama.'

'Well you ain't found this one in his mom's basement, and Alessandro's gettin' antsy. He wants you on a plane.'

'That would just be a waste of everybody's time and money, Mickey. Yeah, I could fly to Vancouver and hang out there for as long as it takes to demonstrate that this so-called "lead" is bullshit, and meantime I'd be checkin' in with my contacts right here in Mexico. Then after that I'd have to get on another fuckin' plane to come straight back down to Hermosillos and check into the same fuckin' hotel I'm sittin' in right now. Shit, it's all the same to me, but it sounds like a lot of bills to pay just to teach Alessandro the comparative values of bein' antsy and bein' patient.'

'Yeah, like I'm gonna tell him that. Give me somethin', Harry, you know? Say you need two more days, tell me you got some kinda fuckin' scheme in motion here.'

'Of course I got a— Oh fuck me, Jesus, baby, aw, yeah. Fuckin' A.'

'What did you say?'

'Aw, shit, sorry, Miguel. I just came.'

'You fuckin' *what*? You tellin' me you're gettin' head while you're fuckin' talkin' to me on the fuckin' phone?'

'Don't sweat it. Your mom says hi.'

'You fuckin' asshole. Unless you got it in her ear, she can hear every goddamn thing you're talkin' about.'

'Relax, for Christ's sakes. She doesn't speak English. First thing I asked her. Hey, try this. Listen up.' Harry held the receiver away from his ear and caught Conchita's eye. 'Babe, this is a freebie, right? That's what we agreed, yeah?'

8

'*No ablo Iglese, señor.*'

Harry cradled the phone again. 'Voi-fuckin'-la.'

'And it didn't occur to you that she could be lying? You know, hookers have occasionally been known to be less than honest.'

'No shit. Okay, she comes up to me in the hotel bar, she's fishin' for trade. I ask her does she speak English. She knows I'm fuckin' American and that the desired answer is obviously yes if she wants to seal the deal, but instead she lies and says no, just in case I happen to impart some top-secret information. Gimme a fuckin' break. This is Hermosillos in the hot summer, Mickey, not fuckin' Berlin in the Cold War.'

'So do I go tell Alessandro you're too busy gettin' your cock sucked to bother with his orders?'

'Tell him whatever the fuck you like. Tell him I'm bein' an asshole if it makes your life easier. But I'll be expectin' everybody to eat some crow when I finish what I came here to do.'

'What? You mean if it turns out you're right, you ain't gonna be your usual modest, unassuming, light-under-a-bushel self?'

'Fuck you.'

'He'll put it out to contract if you're not gonna be a good doggy.'

'Suits me. Let some other prick freeze his nuts off in Canada. Be my guest.'

'I think they have summer up there too, Harry.'

'Well at least the weather'll be nice for fuckin' sight-seein', cause that's all there's gonna be for anyone to do. Shit, I *insist* he puts it out to contract, how about that?'

'Sounds cool to me.'

'I don't see what the big fuckin' hurry is, either. Nunez

is gonna be a long time dead. Or does Alessandro think the Respectometer is countin' down every minute the guy who stiffed him is still alive?'

'Alessandro's young. That kinda shit matters more when you still got to prove yourself to everybody.'

'Problem is he thinks it's the *only* way of provin' himself to everybody. You ask me, the kid puts too much stock in fear as a personal motivator. What, does he think Nunez gipped him because he wasn't scared enough? Nunez gipped him because Alessandro was bein' cheap. He's a major-league fuckin' gangster, for Christ's sakes, head of the fuckin' Estobal family. Nunez was nothing *but* scared: scared of the Estobals, scared of the cops. He's lookin' for an exit at every turn, so it's no wonder he took the first one offered. But Nunez would have relaxed a little if the kid had made it more worth his while. Alessandro needs to learn that you can terrorise people into doin' somethin' on the cheap, or even for nothin', but it's not good business. Just because somebody's afraid of you doesn't mean they won't fuck you if they get the chance; whereas you can trust someone a lot more if they know you're their meal-ticket.'

'There's a lotta things he needs to learn. What can you do but wait?'

What can you do but wait. For what, Miguel wasn't saying, but they both knew it wasn't for the kid to wise up. Sooner or later, Alessandro was going to get himself dead; understanding that was kind of a long-term strategy among the wiser heads in the Estobal organisation. There was no appetite for a coup from within – not yet leastways. It would be too messy, too weakening, a further advertisement to predators that the big beast was ailing. So meantime it was the job of guys like Miguel and Harry to make sure the kid didn't damage the operation too much before

10

he inevitably fell off the end of his way-too-steep learning curve.

Alessandro had been The Man's only blind spot, maybe worse than if he'd been his own son. That way he'd have been close enough to notice the flaws, and no doubt influential enough to iron them out. But The Man never had a son, and so his nephew twinkled all the brighter as his golden boy, the anointed. The kid got things too easy, things he didn't earn, whether they be power or possessions, and as a result he didn't know the value of any of them. He confused fear with respect, obedience with loyalty, and egotism with ambition.

The Man had been a survivor. Well, apart from the lung cancer, obviously. But he'd known that the secret of survival was to get up in the morning and ask yourself what the world could teach you today. The kid didn't think the world could teach him shit. Kids don't though, let's face it, but the smarter ones grow out of it. The smarter ones survive. It's called natural selection. The Man was aware of his limitations too, another vital strategy in the game of staying alive. He wasn't any kind of brainbox. Shrewd and streetwise, yeah, but not clever, and he knew that, so he was able to play to his strengths and avoid exposing himself on his weaker fronts. Alessandro, unfortunately, reckoned he was some kind of fucking genius, and that in itself was his biggest weakness. Christ, he thought he'd pulled a master stroke with this Nunez caper, and look how that'd turned out.

'I always figured we'd get burned by these little art-fags,' Harry said, after a pause he reckoned long enough for both of them to have silently acknowledged the meaning of Miguel's last remark. 'They're sneaky and they're smart.'

11

'They ain't that smart.'

'Don't kid yourself. They're fuckin' smart. Or maybe it's just I can't get my head around 'em. I can't suss how they think, and that makes them unpredictable. Nobody saw Nunez's little flanker comin', did they?'

'No. Or else we wouldn't be havin' this conversation.'

'Exactly. We can't under-estimate guys like that, and I think it should be pretty fuckin' obvious to all and sundry that we definitely can't trust them. The sooner this is over and put down to experience, the better.'

'Hmm.'

'What do you mean, hmm? What the fuck is hmm?'

'Something you're not gonna like. Not one itty bit.'

'Well I just had a blow-job. This is about as relaxed as I'm gonna get for handlin' bad news.'

'I was supposed to tell you this once you got to Vancouver, but as you ain't goin' . . .'

'I sure ain't.'

'The game's changed. Alessandro's got a new plan for gettin' us out of this hole. Nunez still gets smoked, that's a done deal, but it ain't the end of it, and you sure don't put five million bucks down to experience.'

'So Alessandro has a new plan. Why do I feel like it just started raining?'

'Don't worry, it won't be you who gets wet. It's goin' down in fuckin' England – can you believe that? Some place called Glasgow.'

'Who the fuck's gonna do a job for us over there?'

'Innez.'

'Felipe Innez? The guy's hardly been out of East LA. He'd get culture shock in Vegas.'

'Not Felipe, Harry.'

'Well who the . . .' And then it hit him, the truth behind

the hmm, the thing he was not going to like, not one itty bit.

Zal Innez.

'Aw fuck. No. No.'

'Uh-huh.'

'But he's in jail.'

'Gets out of Walla Walla in less than three months.'

'Sounds like a long time for matters to stay out of our hands.'

'What we need ain't goin' nowhere in the meantime, believe me. It'll be under big-time lock and key. Besides, Alessandro might not be patient, but he knows something this big requires the long-term view.'

'He's fuckin' nuts.'

'Who? Innez or the kid?'

'The kid. Nuts, as in dumb, as in deluded if he wants anything more to do with Innez, to say nothing of the freak-show that comes with the package. The kid's nuts, but Innez is just plain crazy. Craziest motherfucker we were ever stupid enough to get involved with. He's also smart, devious, resourceful, entirely unpredictable and easily the last person anyone with two fuckin' brain cells would want to bring into this already fucked-up situation. He *lives* to deceive. That's his nature, his *raison* fuckin' *d'etre*.'

'It's a shame, really. With a better upbringing, Innez could have channelled his talents into a proper, structured criminal career. That's probably why Alessandro reckons he's the one guy who can pull this off.'

'Nah. Alessandro just wants to own him because Innez makes him feel inadequate. Innez is ten times smarter than the kid and the kid doesn't even have the brains to see that and leave well enough alone. Innez will fuck us, you mark my words.'

'Dunno, Harry. I think you're over-estimatin' the guy, especially since he's spent the past three years gettin' his ass fucked on D Block. I reckon Walla Walla will have taught him a thing or two about respect.'

'Oh, I don't doubt it'll have taught him a thing or two. So when he gets out he'll be all the things he was before, plus a shitload tougher.'

'We've got an angle on him, Harry, believe me. He'll do as he's told. Even the kid can learn from his mistakes sometimes.'

'What's the angle?'

'Ah-ah. All in good time. But it starts with teachin' Innez what happened to the last guy who didn't do what he was told, so you'd better hurry up and find the sonofabitch. You're gonna need a camera too, one of them Polaroids.'

'A camera? What the fuck . . . aw, shit.'

'Yep. Make it messy. That was the kid's exact words.'

'Oh, it's gonna be messy, Miguel. Alessandro's makin' damn sure of that.'


Hermosillos, Harry thought, driving through the nighttime streets of what passed for downtown. Jeez, what a bleak, ugly shit-hole. Heavy industry, hard grind, low pay and the sweaty stench of bovine resignation. Places like this were the reason alcohol got invented. Once you clocked off at the end of the day, there was nothing else to do but drink, fuck and fight, with the first playing an essential role in encouraging participation in the latter two. Shit, it wouldn't surprise him if the first heroin pedlar to hit the town had got a civic fucking reception.

It wasn't desperate; he'd *seen* desperate, and the smokestacks in those towns weren't spitting up anything but birds. In a way, this was arguably something worse.

Desperate meant people would try anything to get out of the shit they were in. Round here, they were *settling* for the shit they were in. Work, drink, fuck, fight, sleep, repeat. Like they knew there was worse shit they could be in, but they'd no spark left to try and find better.

This was where Nunez had come from. Sort of. Geographically, leastways. Like most of those little art-fags who made a big deal of their 'roots', he was quite definitely from the right side of the tracks. Because even in a grim industrial shit-hole like Hermosillos, those factories have owners, and you can't rack up that much soul-crushing misery without it generating serious coin for somebody. Nunez's father owned the steel plant, and this was where he had been brought up. Of course, the family hadn't stuck around long once they had the money to be elsewhere. Who would? These days the home and hearth was in Guadelahara, with Nunez Senior only flying in now and again to keep tabs on what was now one of many interests in the north of the country. Nunez Junior had his studio on the Baha California, a couple of hours south of Tijuana by road.

When Nunez went to ground, however, Harry knew he wouldn't go back to Mama. Too obvious, even if he thought Papa's wealth might be able to buy some protection. Hermosillos was the next best thing. Nunez knew the place, maybe better than he knew anywhere else in the world; and besides, it was remote, anonymous and forgettable. Who, he probably figured, would want to try looking for him in a gloomy concrete maze like that? And if he kept his head down and his mouth closed, how would they find him?

How indeed. Well, problem is, people see things, hear things, *notice* things, whether you've got your head down

15

or not. And maybe you can keep your own mouth closed, but you can't shut everybody else's, especially in a town where money is guaranteed to loosen lips. That said, time was marching on, and despite his reservations over Alessandro's impulsiveness, Harry knew there was a fine but important line between exercising patience and just sitting around with your thumb up your ass. There was also a more blurred distinction between giving someone time to get results and being jerked off by some prick who thinks you're a sucker, and it was getting clear which side of this border his so-called informant was currently residing.

Harry parked his car on the street and walked into a bar, Hermosillos' idea of an upmarket joint with nightclub pretensions. These extended little beyond there being a postage-stamp dancefloor surrounded on three sides by couches, a shitty sound system playing nothing but Ricky Martin and Gloria fucking Estefan, and the fact that the place stayed open until the last drinker fell down. The principal evidence of the establishment's status among the clientele was that it was just about the only joint in town where you could find a guy not dressed in snakeskin boots, skin-tight denims and a cowboy hat. Oh, that and the fact that there were women inside who might *not* be hookers.

Martinez was sitting on one of the couches, talking to two girls who looked just about old enough to drink and just about young enough to be impressed by a loser like him. The little pretty-boy runt was probably having himself some sort of *Scarface* fantasy, pretending he was something other than a small-time hood in an even smaller-time backwater, who didn't even have the sense to appreciate when he was out of his depth. He pretended not to notice Harry as he walked in, which Harry didn't like one fucking bit.

16

Harry bought himself a beer and walked over to the snitch's table, at which point Martinez 'suddenly' looked up and affected the air of unruffled nonchalance he'd been preparing for the past three minutes.

'Harry,' he said, gesturing with an open hand to the stool opposite, not bothering to even sit up straight. 'Have a seat. How's it hangin'?'

'Lose the bitches, Luis. We need to talk.'

'Hey, that's no way to speak to a lady, man. You loosen up a little, maybe they treat you right later, you know what I'm sayin'?'

The girls might have been young, but they read the situation far better than Martinez. They got up right away and headed quickly for the bar, leaving him to his Señor Geniality act.

'Listen, you little fuck, I'm payin' you to get me information, not sit here drinkin' cocktails and sniffin' around jailbait muff. It's been, what, nearly a week and you haven't given me jack.'

Martinez kept up the unruffled front, though he dropped the old-time buddies grin. 'You're payin' me to keep my eyes and ears open, man. That's what you said, that's what I'm doin'.'

'Oh that's what you're doin'? And in all this time you ain't seen or heard nothin'? Is that what you're sayin'?'

Martinez shifted on the couch, slumping slightly to an even more slothful (and as far as Harry was concerned, even less respectful) posture, the right side of his face contorting a little. Harry couldn't decide whether it was supposed to be a smirk or a shrug, but he knew what it was intended to convey. The little fuck did know something, he just wasn't ready to give it up.

'Money for lookin' and money for talkin' – that's two

different kinds of money, man. The first kind is sort of a retainer, you know?' He had a sip from his cocktail and slumped back again. 'The second kind is more expensive.'

Harry took a long gulp from his beer, keeping his eyes on the weasely fuck the whole time. He knew there was only one thing to do.

'How much?' he said, putting the bottle back on the table.

'Two thousand.'

Harry nodded. 'I can live with that. Two thousand pesos it is.'

'Dollars. Two thousand American dollars.'

Harry laughed. 'Yeah, right. You been watchin' too many movies, kid. It's not Jimmy fuckin' Hoffa I'm lookin' for. Two thousand bucks. Get a job.'

'This Jimmy Hoffa I don't know about. But I know Nunez is who you want, and that's the price, man. Makes no difference to me if we don't do business. This guy's got enemies, maybe someone else wants him bad enough to pay what's right. I can wait.'

The arrogant little fuck – probably wished he had this on videotape: me playing hardball with the big American gangster.

'Don't kid yourself, Luis. Me needin' your help is a gift from the fuckin' gods, okay? That's why you've been stringin' this shit out, because you know that once I'm gone, it's back to pimpin' your sister or whatever the fuck else you do when Santa Claus ain't in town. I'll give you a grand and you'll be fuckin' grateful, okay?'

'Fifteen hundred.'

'I said a grand. But if you wanna barter, how about I also throw in a promise not to beat the shit out of you? There, that's my final offer.'

18

'Twelve hundred.'

'Is that with or without me deducting what I've been paying for you to sit on what you already know for I don't know how many days?'

Martinez finally sat up. 'A grand it is.'

'Okay, start talkin'. I'll give you two hundred now and the rest if and when it turns out to be worth it.'

'No way, man. Up front, all of it. Yeah, like I'm gonna see you again once you've found Nunez.'

'I only got two hundred on me.'

'Then come back when you have a thousand.'

'I can only get you the peso equivalent at this short notice. There an ATM someplace in this dump?'

'Opposite the railway station,' Martinez said, sitting back. 'I'll give you directions.'

'The fuck you will. Come on. I'm tired of this shit, I'm tired of you and I'm tired of this fuckin' town. Get your ass into my car. I want this over with.'

Martinez feigned a bit of reluctance and climbed languidly to his feet. Yeah right, like he wasn't coming in his pants at the thought of holding that much money. Harry walked briskly to the door, Martinez picking up the pace too, like he was suddenly afraid of being left behind. His keenness evaporated when they reached the car, however.

'No fuckin' way, man. I'm not gettin' in there. How do I know you won't just put a gun to my head instead of payin' me?'

Harry sighed. 'Yeah, like you're worth a bullet. What good are you to me dead? I put a gun to your head and say talk, you know if I pull the trigger I'm only gonna have to go through all this shit again with some other lowlife. Gimme a fuckin' break and get in the car.'

Harry drove them to the station and told Martinez to

19

stay where he was while he lifted the cash. He bent down and folded the notes into his left sock, in full view of his passenger. Having left the engine running, he didn't want him getting jumpy enough to switch seats and bail if he thought there was anything hinky about the deal.

Martinez looked expectantly at him as he climbed back in, like he was just going to hand it over there and then.

'Okay. Let's roll,' Harry said, pulling away and ignoring him. He hung a U-turn across the plaza and then took a right at the traffic lights.

'The bar's back that way, man.'

'Yeah, I'm gonna hand you a wad of bills in a crowded public place. You're not the only snitch in town, Luis.'

'Where we goin'?'

'I'll tell you when we get there. Until then, shut up unless you want to tell me where Nunez is right now.'

'Not till I'm holding the money, man.'

'That's what I figured.'

Harry drove on in silence until they were out of the downtown area and into the industrial belt, well away from streetlights and sidewalks.

'This'll do,' he said, pulling into an empty parking lot outside a warehouse. He stopped the car and put the inside light on, then bent down, removing the bills from his left sock.

From his right he palmed a flat-handled knife.

Harry placed the wad of bills on the dashboard and sat back. 'All yours,' he said. When Martinez reached forward to grab them, Harry stuck the blade into his thigh and clamped his left hand over his mouth. He drew the knife across slowly, his arm pinning Martinez's torso to the seat despite his panicked writhing.

'Now you listen to me, you little come-stain. I just cut

your femoral artery. That's how the Romans used to commit suicide, did you know that? It should take about a half hour. So here's how it's gonna be. Either you can tell me where Nunez is and I can drive you to the hospital, or else I can sit here and watch you bleed to death. What do you say?'

Harry took his hand away from Martinez's mouth but kept the blade in his thigh. He gave it a twist, eliciting a loud yelp, but there was nobody around to hear it.

'Clock's ticking, Luis.'

Martinez spilled everything he knew just as fast as his hyperventilating little lungs would let him, after which Harry pocketed the bills, withdrew the blade and opened the passenger-side door.

'Get out.'

'You said you would take me to the hospital, man.'

'Phone a fuckin' ambulance, asshole,' Harry said, kicking him out of the car. He pulled the door shut and put the car into gear, swinging it around until he was alongside Martinez, who had by this time got to his feet and begun limping towards the main road. Harry pushed a button on his armrest and slid the window down.

'I hope you make it, Luis. I really do. And if you survive, I hope you just learned an important lesson about who not to fuck with. *Adios.*'

The 'house' was about fifteen minutes outside of town, close to the main road south for ease of a fast getaway. It looked like Nunez had placed his trust in secrecy rather than security, as the place was an anonymous, run-down pre-fabricated shack, definitely not capable of keeping out the Big Bad Wolf if he decided to huff and puff. Harry had driven past along the narrow road and parked out of sight,

21

then doubled back on foot to where he could get a clear view. No lights on, no surprise. Little sign that the place was occupied by anything other than rats and roaches, apart from the large, indistinct shape of a black tarp at one side of the building – the side obscured from the road.

Harry got his things from the boot, cursing Alessandro for this Polaroid crap. 'Make it messy.' What an asshole. Like people wouldn't be afraid enough once you told them they were dead unless.

He stalked silently through the sparse bushes and the dust, making his way to the tarp by the light of the moon and the glow of passing headlights from the main road. There was no sound other than those of engines and tyres on asphalt a couple of hundred yards away. Harry made it to the tarp and crouched beside it, reaching into his bag for a narrow flashlight. His hand could feel cold metal under the tarpaulin, confirming his assumption that it concealed a vehicle, most probably a dark blue 1999 Toyota 4x4. He pulled himself under and switched on the torch, the sheet hiding the light from view. It was a blue Toyota, sure enough, but he checked the number plate just to be completely thorough.

Mark.

He made his way slowly towards the front of the house, tentatively testing his weight step-by-step on the boards of the wooden porch, rocking back when he heard the beginnings of a creak. The doorframe looked like it wouldn't withstand being heavily pissed against, let alone a good kick, but he opted to pop the flimsy, cheap-motel-style lock instead. If for whatever reason it turned out Nunez wasn't around, it would kind of remove the element of surprise regards lying secretly in wait if he came back and discovered his front door was missing.

Harry crouched on the porch and placed his gun on the floor before taking a tiny, plastic-handled awl from his pocket. Gently inserting the awl into the lock with his right hand, he gripped the round aluminium doorknob with his left, whereupon the knob came away in his fingers and the door swung a few inches ajar. Harry scrambled for his gun, almost falling flat on his face through a combination of sheer surprise and sudden loss of balance.

There was no movement from within, and only blackness to be seen through the narrow gap, but not all of his senses were to be deprived. It was hard to tell what struck him first, the smell or the sound of the flies, but there was no question which hit the harder.

'Jesus.'

Harry barely swallowed back the impulse to gag. It was a discipline learned hard from being around a lot of dead people, two of whom he'd had to dissenter and re-bury, but this particular stench tested it to the limit, and he was still on the porch. He bent down to his bag and pulled out a cloth intended for wiping away fingerprints, tying it around his nose and mouth like he was about to pull a Wild-West hold-up. Then he took hold of his flashlight again and reluctantly nudged the door open with his foot.

The flashlight barely penetrated the blackness, picking out only tiny areas as it passed, like he was viewing a dot-matrix image one line at a time. Harry turned around and pointed it at the wall just inside the door, eventually finding a light switch. Unfortunately, it worked.

The shack consisted of a single bed/living room, with a kitchen area in one corner and a separate toilet at the back. The sink, two-ring stove and worktop in the 'kitchen' constituted the only furniture, other than a fold-down sofa-bed draped with a single linen sheet. Other points of

23

interest included a careless scattering of empty food cans and pizza boxes, a canvas bag containing male clothing, a pair of men's shoes, a half-drunk Jose Cuervo bottle, a copy of *Hustler*, a brown suede jacket, several dog-eared paperbacks, and Nunez's head in a glass jar.

Oh yeah.

It was just sitting there at the end of the bed, on a pillow, for Christ's sake, like it was the Hope fucking Diamond. Bruised, slashed, swollen, discoloured and immersed in fluid, but still recognisably Nunez, staring off to one side with that goofy look corpses always got after a few days underwater.

And *everything* around the place was streaked with blood, like they'd used a fucking garden sprinkler: walls, floor, trash, clothes, everything. The only thing spared, in one respect, was the sheet covering the fold-down bed; spared as in the streaks, not the blood. It was more kind of smeared.

No. Blotted.

If there was a mercy, it was that there didn't seem to be as many flies as the noise suggested. Probably amplified by his imagination, though he'd have expected the sound to be tuned out a little once his brain got busier with all the shit his eyes were throwing at it.

Harry approached the bed hesitantly, then thought better of touching the sheet with his bare hands. He retreated outside to retrieve a pair of latex gloves from his bag. In truth he was motivated less by forensic considerations than by a skin-crawlingly bad feeling about the blotting. He returned inside, less than briskly, he'd have to admit, took a deep breath and pulled the sheet away.

Immediately, he found himself clouded by a zillion flies, disturbed from their all-you-can-eat glutathon under the linen. He closed his eyes and swung his arms around in an attempt to ward off at least a few thousand of them. If he thought he'd done well not to gag when the door opened, then he deserved some kind of award for keeping his dinner down at this point. The smell worsened, accompanied by the relatively harmless but nonetheless revoltingly unpleasant sensation of several dozen insects crawling through his hair.

After a few seconds of flailing, the intensity of the aerial assault reduced, the majority of the flies returning to the feast, and he felt confident enough to open his eyes again.

'Fuck me.'

It looked like the rest of Nunez had been put in a blender. The bed was covered from top to bottom in rotting flesh, bones sticking out from the mass here and there, as well as the odd internal organ. The lungs were the most noticeable, sheer size meaning there was more of their shape still recognisable after the attentions of the Beelzebub First Airborne Squadron. Other than that, it was pretty difficult to guess what any particular fly-crawling lump used to be, especially as there didn't appear to be any skin remaining. Had that been the flies too, or . . . Fuck, who cared?

Harry had seen some funky stuff in his time – but this? This looked like serious serial-killer psycho shit. Nevertheless, certain habits died hard; maybe after a while they became a reflex. Harry picked up the suede jacket and patted down the pockets until he found what he was after: Nunez's wallet. The credit cards were still there, as well as some small bills, but there was a clear plastic window where his driver's licence should have been.

Standard proof-of-hit procedure.

'Motherfucker.'

Somebody had beaten him to it, by a few days, too.

'Make it messy.'

Alessandro. Fucking Alessandro. He'd put it out to contract from the word go, the double-crossing little prick. Perhaps that was even why the kid had wanted to send Harry to fucking Vancouver – maybe he secretly had Hermosillos covered. Son of a bitch.

But if so, then why did nobody know about it? Why did they wait until this afternoon to phone him? Harry was no pathologist, but he'd seen enough to guess Nunez had been dead for at least two days. And what was it Martinez said? 'Nunez has enemies.' Harry had assumed the plural referred collectively to the Estobals, but maybe they weren't the only ones Nunez had screwed.

Shit.

Ah well. Either way up, the job was done, and that was the main thing, for now at least. He could take his Polaroids and get the fuck out of this toilet. However, he couldn't help feeling a little deflated. That was the problem with the free market. He knew he was good at what he did, and everybody likes to feel special, but something like this reminded him that in the grander scheme, figuratively speaking, he was just one more hooker on a very long street.

# I

# all your bank are belong to me

Give a man a mask, and he will tell the truth.

**Oscar Wilde**

## so much for the afterglow

Angelique could taste sweat on her tongue as she pressed a palm to his chest. It had run off his top lip, her mouth mere centimetres below, sharing the same hot, stale air; or maybe they were close enough to be just exchanging spent breath. Their feet were entwined at the ankles, sinews tightening as they pulled against each other, her heels and shoulder blades like four narrow casters as she arced to raise the weight of both their bodies from the floor. They stayed locked in place for a moment, both of their gazes flitting back and forth from each other's eyes to the tangle of their bodies, as though they were both verifying that the other grasped the significance of what was finally passing between them.

She was giving in; *had* given in. She'd been vulnerable, she knew, but it had still been her call to get into it at a time like this. Distracted, weakened by this creeping diminishment to her sense of self. So here he was, for once able to slip through her defences in ways she had so easily repelled before.

He knew it, too. After all this time together, there was no way he could have missed it any more than she could have hidden it from him. She reached for his face with her free hand, but he brushed her away at the wrist with an ease that both acknowledged and dismissed it as no more than an obligatory and half-hearted gesture.

Stewart sighed with a disappointment that blatantly invited query.

Angelique let her body go limp and felt the energy suddenly dissipate from his, too.

'What's wrong with your face?' she asked, taking no pains to mask her own irritation.

'I can tell you're not really into this.'

'What, just because you're on top?'

'You know what I mean.' Stewart took his weight on one elbow and rolled off of her. He sat up, supporting himself with his right hand. 'If you're not giving me your all, I know I'm just kidding myself.'

'And is that such a crushing blow to your male ego?'

'No, but I'm honest enough to know that it's a waste of both our time.'

This was fair comment. Angelique pulled herself into a sitting position, wiping sweat-dampened hair from her brow. 'I'm sorry. I'm like a half-shut knife at the moment. I wouldn't even have come here today if it wasn't that I thought it might kinna jump-start me, you know. Clear my mind, just concentrate on something physical.'

'I know what you're saying. I've done the same myself a few times, but in your case I don't think it's working. It's like half of you's somewhere else.'

'Bit of a catch twenty-two. I thought being here would help me blank out all the shite, but I'm bloody useless here because I *can't* blank out all the shite.'

'Best thing for you in this state would be just to work on your kata.'

'If you can't fuck you can always have a wank, is that what you're saying?'

Stewart laughed. 'Sensitively put, as ever, but yes. If you're concentrating on just your form and movement, that might help because it's more basic; plus it's just you you've to worry about. At the very least, if you keep at it long

30

enough you can knacker yourself. That usually helps flush my mind out anyway.'

'Thanks. But I think the best thing for me in this state would actually be to call it a day. I feel like I'm just grinding gears. Sorry.'

'No use pushing it if it ain't happening.'

'What about you? Are you . . .'

'I'm gonna do some work with the bags for a while. You might be only half here, but even that half's still deflecting my kicks like my legs are made of balsa.'

'I don't deflect—'

'"Just redirect", I know. But hearing you say that a hundred times hasn't made me any faster.'

'You still haven't quite forgiven me for that time you broke your clavicle, have you?'

Stewart smiled, self-consciously raising an instinctive hand to the once-injured collar bone. 'It's myself I haven't forgiven for trying a move that was equivalent to a rhino attacking a hummingbird. The lesson's learned, but the theory's still a sight easier than the practice.'

Angelique felt like she could stay under the shower all day. Bad sign. It was the buffer zone between mental states, as much procrastination as ablution, allowing time to prepare for the condition of higher alertness that was imminently demanded, or as often merely the opportunity not to think about it for a few more minutes. There were times when she wished she could remain in that protective stasis, specifically that first moment when she turned and let the warm water flow through her hair and down her back.

These were never happy times.

Even when she was pretending otherwise – lying, denying – this was the place where she couldn't hide from

31

herself, the place where she would always get found out. Angelique was more resilient than most, fuelled by high levels of self-discipline and low reserves of self-pity. She could put on a public face and convince enough people she was okay that she might almost believe it herself, like a tabloid editor looking at the results of a loaded-question phone-in poll. But she knew that when the shower started feeling like a refuge and she wished it was a suspended animation facility, it meant she was suffering from a psychological condition referred to in the medical journals as 'all fucked up'.

This morning's abortive exercise had seemed an appropriate course of therapy, intended to take her mind off of . . . well, there was why it hadn't worked. She couldn't say what her mind was specifically and problematically *on*, and that was very much symptomatic of this current malaise. There'd been plenty of times when a session at the dojo proved the perfect respite from whatever happened to be worrying her, when she'd channelled all her concentration entirely into the physical, to the exclusion of all peripheral concerns. She could lose herself in the exertion, in a place beyond pain and fatigue, worrying only about her opponent and the four walls that confined their combat. As Stewart said, sometimes the exhaustion simply cleared your mind; and better than that, sometimes it helped reduce your worries to the basest facts, allowing you to see only the issues and not the long shadows that anxiety cast around them.

This morning, though, that just wasn't applicable. Worry wasn't the problem. Worry, at least, was a sign of knowing what was wrong, and of feeling sufficiently exercised about the possible outcomes. Worry was a sign of giving a fuck.

In this state, she'd been lucky to walk away uninjured.

She and Stewart were careful about pulling blows during these sparring bouts, with mere contact to specified spots read as a point scored, but it was a sign of mutual respect that they each expected the other to avoid certain attacks (sometimes strategically depending upon it), so a lapse in concentration could have highly damaging consequences. Stewart had been her Judo instructor when they first met, and he still ran police classes in it, but in recent years they had combined their martial arts knowledge over countless one-on-one sessions, two obsessives grateful to have found someone else in no imminent danger of getting a life. Their sparring was an indistinct mish-mash of different disciplines, partly as a valuable means of practice, and partly to level the odds a little: Stewart had an insurmountable advantage if it was restricted to Judo; while Angelique held the upper hand if it was restricted to anything else.

She'd never lost until today, though inevitably there'd been some close-run things over such a proliferation of encounters. However, it wasn't simply loss that was indicative of Angelique's state of mind – it was the nature of her defeat: the ease of it, and not for him.

It would pass, she knew. She'd get through it, come up smiling on the other side, put it down to biorhythms or whatever lie best obscured the true source. But what seemed even more certain was that it would be back, perhaps even sooner than before, and the spiral would coil that bit tighter. The first time she'd felt this way, it had forced the unpalatable acceptance that she had walked out of Dubh Ardrain having sustained more damage than just a few cracked ribs. Then, when it returned, it drove home the even less welcome understanding that she still hadn't recovered. Now, this third time, she was left to wonder if it meant she never would.

Dubh Ardrain: her finest hour, or at least that was the official line if anyone enquired about the police's efforts in averting a potential catastrophe. Internally, she'd been made to feel that her contribution was not received with quite the same unqualified gratitude that her bosses were happy to accept from the general public. She'd endured police politics long enough to have become thoroughly divested of any naïve idealism she might ever have had about the nature of the job, but it burned a new layer of cynicism deep into the soul that the closest thing to an official plaudit she'd received for what she pulled off at Dubh Ardrain was the phrase 'disciplinary action would be inappropriate'. Hey, don't get all gushy on me guys, it's embarrassing.

There was something about all official debriefings that made you feel your efforts were the absolute least you could have been expected to do, and that you were teetering on the brink of a negligence charge or due diligence lawsuit for your sloppy and indisciplined actions. Yes, it was true that they had to dispassionately examine all of the events in order to learn from what took place, but did that process really require an absolute excisement of the bigger picture? The death toll could – would – have been in the thousands, and yet they were talking about structural damage and reconstruction costs. She had averted a grand-scale atrocity assisted only by one civilian, a brief element of surprise, gross complacency on the part of the terrorists, and a jam factor rating in the ionosphere. In the process of doing this, certain things got blown up. Expensive things. Logistically-complicated-to-clear-up- and-reconstruct things. But ultimately replaceable things. Material things. On September 11th 2001, did anybody shed a tear over the loss of several million dollars' worth of aircraft? Aircraft don't have mothers, don't have husbands, don't have kids. Neither do power plants.

What they do have are owners, but she wouldn't kid herself that the financial implications were what truly concerned the stuffed shirts she'd had to answer to after the fact. Angelique had little doubt that if by a miracle someone had been able to prevent the attack on the Twin Towers, then he or she would still have found themselves staring at a row of unearned epaulettes afterwards, being asked 'Why didn't you . . .' this, and 'Did you not consider . . .' that.

All her decisions were minutely deconstructed, her alternative options laid out under the full glare of the retrospectoscope, her choices evaluated in an air-conditioned room with fresh coffee and chocolate digestives. As far as she could observe, lead and shrapnel were not complicating their deliberations.

Maybe it would have been better if they had been. She'd certainly kept a cooler head at Dubh Ardrain than at the inquiry. Angelique had had to pull herself back from the brink several times during the various interrogations, but inevitably one accusatory hypothesis too many sent her into meltdown.

'Everybody's Jim Baxter from the fucking Broomloan, aren't they?' she'd railed, getting to her feet. 'It's a sight different down on the pitch. Try and bear in mind that I was shooting terrorists while you were shooting ten over your fucking handicap.'

'Please sit down, DI de Xavia. You have to understand, we're not necessarily criticising you, we're just trying to build up an accurate picture of what happened.'

Not *necessarily*. That really was the clincher.

'Go and fuck yourselves.'

35

Ah, that coldly calculating careerist streak, seizing with two firm hands her big chance to impress the men who mattered. Also recognisable – and fortunately interpreted – as spitting the dummy. Slack was cut her way over the histrionics, she would have to concede. Calm words from wise heads, indulgences sought by senior allies, allowances made, outburst overlooked. It was perhaps unfair, then, to accuse them of ingratitude, when saving several thousand civilian lives had scored her just about enough points to swear at the top brass and still keep her job.

*Disciplinary action would be inappropriate.*

And the Volvo you drove here in, pal.

Angelique wasn't lacking in approval from her rank and file colleagues, naturally. Those closest to the front line had understandably the keenest appreciation of what she had achieved, and they weren't shy about voicing support. However, under these circumstances, the back-slapping and the words of solidarity merely added to the sense that she was under a cloud. Support was what you got when your reputation was on the line, and however well meaning their sentiments, that was increasingly what it felt like. Instead of a story to tell, it felt as though she had a case to answer.

She wasn't looking for adulation or acclaim. That was not the root of her disaffection. It had been her own choice to remain anonymous when the media sought 'the hero of Dubh Ardrain', their normal hunger for such a figure rendered ravenous just days later with the events of September 11th. More than ever, people wanted to believe that their own forces of law and order could protect them from terrorism; and more than ever, the forces of law and order wanted them believing it, too. In a time of barely precedented despair and panic, they didn't just want a hero, they wanted a superhero, and Angelique knew better than most that they didn't exist. Dumb luck and sheer coincidence had given her the drop on the Black Spirit and his scum, nothing more. It wasn't down to professional intelligence, security infrastructure, public vigilance, individual ingenuity, or any of the things that people so desperately needed to believe were at work for their protection. One single coincidence changed everything, and without that, the UK would have had its own Ground Zero. It was in the police's interests to suggest otherwise, but she wasn't prepared to be party to the deception.

Her decision was also motivated partly by the more personal desire to protect her privacy, and to a greater degree by the professional desire to be able to work undercover again if required. Seeing her name and face splashed all over the papers wouldn't just preclude that, it would sentence her to an inescapable role in police public relations. Having so long resisted senior officers' desires to sideline her into the window-dressing role of a visibly Asian and female figurehead, she was buggered if she was going to be Strathclyde Police's ethnic posterchild now.

Not that giving them what they wanted would have spared her the Star Chamber treatment, right enough. If anything, it would have been twice as harsh, cutting her down to size in case she started believing the hype they would be selling the public about her. They were scheming, two-faced, self-preserving, Machiavellian, intransigent, conservative, deceitful, hypocritical bastards; in essence, boasting all the properties necessary to attain and carry out the work of high-ranking polis politicos. This was not a revelation. So why, she was forced to ask herself, was she bothered by the responses of people she so little respected?

The answer was the same reason her closer colleagues'

words of congratulation rang hollow, too. She didn't need their approval any more than she needed the Star Chamber's criticism. What she needed was to feel that someone understood what the hell she had been through at Dubh Ardrain, and to grasp that it hadn't been just an exceptionally eventful day on the job. The epaulettes wanted to hear explanations for the multi-million-pound damage bill. Her colleagues wanted to hear tales of baddies, bombs and kicking ass. Nobody wanted to hear about night sweats, vomiting, insomnia or breaking down in tears in the M&S food hall.

It was easy, at first, to tell herself she was all right. She'd come out on top, after all: saved the day, wiped out the bad guys, unmasked the Black Spirit, and all at the meagre personal cost of a shotgun blast to her Kevlar-protected chest. The morning after, she felt like she could do it all again, and this time single-handed; whatever doesn't kill you makes you stronger and all that.

The morning after was Sunday. Tuesday was September 11th. What she was about to experience was already in the post, but the events in New York and Washington upgraded it to Special Delivery.

The resilient feeling had been, she now understood, merely the survivor's post-traumatic euphoria: an enhanced sense of vitality brought on by having come so close to death. In Angelique's case, it had also served to maintain her adrenalin levels at the all-time high they had reached during her battle with the terrorists. However, sooner or later, the adrenalin and the euphoria had to wear off, as did their physical and psychologically analgesic properties. You could take Ibuprofen to replace the former, but the latter had to be endured cold turkey.

Terror and revulsion were the principal, overwhelming

emotions, buffeting her like a sparrow in the tail-wake of a 747 as the magnitude of what she had escaped finally made itself felt. It was as though she was involuntarily subjected to an all-sensory playback of what had happened, containing everything her mind had censored at the time in order to get her through it. Each memory, vivid even in taste and smell, came with a payload of suppressed fear that had to impact before any sense of relief was possible. What had seemed at the time discrete actions, physical sensations, deductions, objectives, strategies, responses and reflexes, now became unified and compounded, each moment's fear and horror multiplied by the last within the vast and dreadful context she could not previously afford to contemplate.

And as though it wasn't enough to be mercilessly ravaged by this belated understanding of just what she had avoided, she also had to cope with the delayed comprehension of the acts she had carried out – and the scenes she had witnessed – in the process. Blood featured prominently in this palette, lavishly strewn across an array of images demonstrating vividly the human body's inability to share space with more robust or tensile substances. Death had come in many and various forms, most of them messy, and the majority had come at her prompting.

There were few people on this earth who would be mourned less or who had it coming more than terrorists, but that didn't alter the fact that there were now indelible images of horror, suffering and fatality imprinted upon Angelique's mind. Her conscience might be clear, but she would still have to live ever after with the knowledge of what her hands (and feet) had wrought.

But then, they'd no doubt say, that's what counselling's for, right? And these days, in the new touchy-feely polis, you could get it if you'd witnessed a particularly traumatic parking violation. The doors of the tea-and-sympathy professionals were always open. Angelique, however, didn't want the practised solicitude of strangers, taking care of her little emotional problems for the greater convenience of the Constabulary. What she wanted was those she worked with – and worked for – to realise that a price had been exacted from her by what she had done in the line of duty; to appreciate that she had literally put her life on the line at Dubh Ardrain, and had done dangerous, frightening, painful, sickening and downright horrible things that day. She needed her fellow officers – including those superannuated, Freemasonic stuffed shirts – to understand this, not some glorified social worker.

Their lack of empathy was not entirely down to indifference, she would have to concede. She was now paying a price for having presented that bullets-bounce-off-me front for so long, putting her well down the list of people anyone expected to need a sympathetic ear. In the beginning it had been a necessary form of self-defence in the face of those who'd been reluctant to accept her. They didn't have to be racist or sexist to take a look at a skinny Asian female and think 'positive discrimination', or worse, 'passenger'. So if the cliché was true that a non-Caucasian or a woman had to work twice as hard for half the credit, then in this profession she had to come across four times as tough as everyone else and do a quarter of the complaining.

It wasn't just the rigours of the job that had to be met with this shield of impenetrability, either. There were the slights, innuendos and blatant insults of colleagues to deal with too, these falling into two categories. The first were those who were, they would claim, testing to see whether

40

she could 'take a bit of ribbing' (though she must have missed the meeting where these wanks were appointed official character judges) and stand up for herself without going off in the huff. The attainment of official 'all right' status in their estimation required that she 'didn't make a big deal' about her ethnicity. That this was precisely what *they* were doing was an irony they were tragically inequipped to grasp, so there seemed little to be gained from pointing it out. These weren't bad people, just immature and inclined to unknowingly wear their insecurities on their sleeves. To some of them, she had 'proven' herself, and requisite respect was accorded henceforth; to others, her ball-busting image made her a 'character', and thus the role became expected of her.

The second category were those who genuinely resented her and whatever their individual bitterness perceived her to represent. These might never respect her, but the don't-fuck-with-me attitude at least conveyed that try as they might, they wouldn't be able to hurt her.

They often did, though. The shield *was* penetrable and the image was merely that: a projection, a façade. It was a mask that had proven invaluable in integrating with her colleagues, but since Dubh Ardrain, she'd been using it to conceal a growing alienation from them.

She wasn't kidding herself. It was a textbook symptom of post-traumatic stress to feel apart from those who hadn't shared the event, and thus proof that some form of counselling was indeed required; but it was also why the only 'counsellor' worth a damn was Ray Ash. He was the one person who could truly relate to her, beyond rehearsed platitudes, practised compassion and sympathetic prompts, because he'd been there. They had stalked, hidden, run and battled side by side in those tunnels, chambers and pools, through the firefights and explosions, through the fear, the anger and the killing. Unlike Angelique, the closest thing to combat training Ray had had to prepare him for the ordeal had been playing *Quake* on his computer. Despite this, he seemed to be the one handling the aftermath better, which made him an even more valuable source of comfort.

Comfort, however, wasn't therapy, and while it made her feel better at the time to talk to Ray, she knew it wasn't entirely constructive. It wasn't particularly fair, either. Angelique represented the worst thing that had ever happened to Ray and his family, so she had to bear in mind what she was bringing back every time she showed her face around his house. Plus, as a single woman, there were only so many times you could reasonably ask a married man out for a drink.

And there was the rub. Ray had bounced back because of what was waiting for him when the bullets stopped flying and the last of the rubble hit the ground. The experience had given him a hard-earned and uniquely focused lesson in what truly mattered in his life. If Ray ever felt troubled by the horrors he had witnessed or the deeds he had done, then he only had to cast a glance at his wife and children to put it into perspective. Not only did he undoubtedly value what he had all the more for having come so close to losing it, but his family constituted the whole of the here, the now and the future, providing a compelling motivation to leave Dubh Ardrain in the past.

What did Angelique have to return to, by comparison? Only a job that she now understood, in her mother's told-you-so words, would never love her back. These days, in fact, it was starting to feel like an abusive relationship, all the worse for being the only one she had.

God knows she'd endured some trials of late, but was

there anything quite so awful as having to admit to your-self that your mother was right? Um, yes, obviously: having to admit to your *mother* that she was right. Fortunately, Angelique's current depression hadn't reached the self-harm stage, so she had thus far resisted that particular act of humiliation.

She reached limply for the shampoo, reluctantly begin-ning the process that would all-too-soon leave her with no further need to stay in the shower. Oh well. At least she could now point her befuddled mind towards a specific reason for not wanting to get out of the cubicle today: *diner chez sez parents ce soir*, the one prospect that could almost make her come over all nostalgic about Dubh Ardrain.

The job would never love her, she could agree with her mum about that now. Where they continued to differ was over the theory that nothing else would matter if she could just find someone who did. Her mum talked about it as though it was that simple, like some domestic appliance she had pointlessly resisted purchasing: satisfaction guar-anteed, and the procurement no more problematic, merely a matter of deciding to do so.

Just do it, as the child-labour sweatshop adverts said. If you build it, he will come; and prematurely, going by Angelique's experience.

'Is there still no-one on the horizon?' was Mum's preferred oh-so-reluctant-but-I-have-to-ask-because-I-care phrase for dredging up the subject, usually accompanied by a wilting smile, already offering sympathy in anticipa-tion of the unfailingly disappointing reply.

'Not that I can see without a fucking big telescope, Mummy,' she took great pains not to reply.

In fact, Angelique considered her mother's choice of words unwittingly apposite. If there was a right guy for

43

her in this world, then the horizon was exactly where she'd expect to see him, it being a place you can never actually reach. There hadn't even been a particular *wrong* guy in a while either, meaning that these days the only physical entanglements she got to enjoy were in the dojo, and that was in no danger of leading anywhere. Stewart was considerate, friendly, attractive, quite beautifully built and tantalisingly single, but Angelique was sadly one penis short of being his type.

Perhaps she should try a lonely hearts ad:

```
Embittered, disillusioned, increasingly shrew-
ish and expertly violent female workaholic
seeks horizon-dwelling male to make nothing
else matter. Must be n/s, gsoh, tolerant of
unsociable hours and unintimidated by
prospect of sleeping with someone who has
now killed more people than she has had
sex with. Please reply to Box 999, quoting
code DSPR8.
```

She'd phone it into *The Herald* today, then she'd at least be able to tell her mother she was making an effort.

Her brother James had also suggested a remedy for her melancholy, which Angelique had rather miserably failed to conceal during the 'celebration' dinner his wife Michelle had cooked the previous night. His cure sounded more modestly plausible than Mum's, but he'd offered no greater clues as to where it might be found. 'You need some fun in your life,' he'd said.

Give that man a pipe and deerstalker. Then, for his next case, he could deduce that the identity of the lifeless corpse discovered in the Rangers eighteen-yard-box was Bert

Konterman. James might be right, but like ditching Bible Bert, just because it was screamingly obvious to the whole wide world didn't mean it would solve everything at a stroke. That said, again like ditching Bible Bert, it was still bound to be an improvement.

Where the comparison ended was in the execution. All Big Eck had to do was stop writing the useless bastard's name down on the team sheet. Angelique getting some fun into her life seemed a less straightforward proposition, especially feeling like this, today of all days.

Stewart was waiting for her when she came out of the changing room. He was still in his gee, and looked to have worked up quite a sweat during her self-imposed limbo in the shower. The smell was more noticeable to her now thoroughly washed, conditioned, deodorised and perfumed person. Pheromone rush; far from unpleasant, but liable to induce instinctive longings that were unlikely to be satisfied any time soon. In his hand he held a pen and a clutch of folded-up papers.

'Thought you had melted in there.'

'Wicked Witch of the West Enclosure.'

'I thought your seat was in the Govan?'

'Yes, but it doesn't scan, does it?'

'True.'

'Shower's hard to leave sometimes, you know?'

'Yeah, but there's usually two in it before I feel that way.'

'Slut.'

Stewart smiled, but he didn't exactly look happy-go-lucky. Angelique's own personal raincloud was evidently starting to sprinkle more liberally around the periphery.

'Look, you doin' okay?' he asked, his voice soft and serious. 'You seem . . .'

'Wabbit?'

45

'To say the least. Do you want to grab some lunch or something? Have a blether?'

'Thanks, Stewart, but I think I'd be better off on my own just now, instead of inflicting myself on innocent bystanders. What's that you've got there?' she asked, before he could make any well-intentioned but needlessly masochistic attempt to insist.

Stewart unfolded the sheets and flicked through them, pulling one to the front.

'It's annual registration stuff for the association. I just need you to sign the bottom unless any details have changed. You haven't moved in the past year or anything?'

'No.'

He began scanning the form, tapping panels with the pen. 'So, name, address, phone, date of . . . ah.'

Angelique sighed, bereft of any appropriate verbal response.

'Well I suppose that would explain a lot,' Stewart said with a small wince. 'Thirty today. I guess I won't be wishing you Happy Birthday, given your demeanour.'

'Not unless you want another broken collar bone.'

Okay, so yes, that did explain a lot, but not everything. Perspective was still required. Angelique didn't believe there was a *good* time to turn thirty, just like there wasn't a good time to concede a goal, but this felt bloody close to the half-time whistle. It was difficult to believe that merely seeing those two digits on a birthday card would have made her feel quite so mortal if it wasn't coming on the back of so many blows, figurative and literal, to her sense of self. Maybe she was wrong, though. Maybe turning thirty made you feel this way even if you'd spent the past year on a yacht in the Caribbean. Perhaps the process was as unavoidable as age itself: the approach of thirty prompted a harsh evaluation of where you currently stood in life, what you had done so far and what you still needed to do; and she'd have found herself asking the same questions, with the same jaundiced answers, even if Dubh Ardrain had never happened.

One thing she was definitely right about was that she needed to be alone right now, and in Angelique's experience, there was nowhere better to do that than in the immediate vicinity of 50,000 other people. It wasn't as daft as it sounded: this was football we were talking about, and if you went there unaccompanied, there were times when the heart of a crowd could seem like the most isolated place in the world. Not all of those times involved being two-nothing down, either; nor did it have anything to do with being the only brown face in a sea of white (apart from the ways in which it had everything to do with being the only brown face in another particular sea of white).

Even with 50,000 people around her watching the same spectacle, feeling the same emotions and wishing for the same outcome – maybe even because of all that – it was possible to seem removed from all human intercourse. This was because no matter whether there were 50,000 of you or only one, you were still just helpless spectators gambling your emotions on the outcome of a contest between other people. Maybe it wasn't the same if you were there with your ten best mates (and maybe it was exactly the same), but Angelique felt like her contact with everyone around her was completely suspended until certain events had resolved themselves, and that could mean the outcome of a fifty-fifty ball or the duration of an entire match.

Sometimes she could lose herself in the game, and sometimes she could just lose herself. It didn't need to be a classic, in fact it didn't need to be any bloody good at all, she could still drift somewhere entirely alone, as though she was looking down on the stadium, the players and herself. Her thoughts could be consumed by plays, tactics, required substitutions and desired retributions; or her mind could empty itself entirely, to be suddenly startled by some incident that yanked her back to the game. Either way, when the final whistle blew, it felt like her brain was a PC being rebooted, with only the most essential elements initially restoring themselves, allowing a precious window of clarity and perspective before all the old clutter got loaded up again.

She had always gone to the football alone, even before the season-book tyranny had made it impossible for specific people to sit together at less than nine months' notice or for a duration of less than twenty-odd home games. Angelique, however, couldn't actually cite any friends from whom she was separated by this, and though she was on nodding (and occasionally hugging) terms with the guys who sat round about her, they were not 'acquaintances' beyond the shared knowledge of which team they supported and their vocal opinions on certain of those paid to wear the jersey. Those she sat with every other Saturday (or at least every other Saturday she was off-duty) knew nothing else about her, while the majority of those who knew a lot about her knew nothing about where she sat every other Saturday.

This was because Angelique de Xavia was a Rangers supporter.

No, it's okay.

Not *that* kind of Rangers supporter. Not the Catholic-hating, right-wing, BNP-supporting, anti-Irish, monarchist, triumphalist, boorish, arrogant, ignorant, sash-wearing, bowler-hatted, Crimplene-trousered, UVF-tattooed, flute-playing, King-Billy-portrait-on-the-mantelpiece, only-started-going-when-Souness-arrived-but-swear-I-was-there-in-the-early-Eighties, snaw-aff-a-dyke-when-the-team's-no-winning, couldnae-name-a-non-Old-Firm-player, Union-Jack-waving, Scotland-hating, Nazi-saluting, pipe-bomb-hurling, squeeze-the-toothpaste-at-the-top-end and fart-in-a-crowded-lift kind.

Obviously.

Not the kind who would take all the worst traits and features perceived of individuals within a very large group and then indiscriminately attribute every last one of them to every last person within it. No. That kind of person would be a bigot.

Very few of Angelique's friends, and even fewer of Angelique's colleagues, knew she was a football fan at all, far less a Teddy Bear. She'd even managed to keep it from James during her younger years, until the enormous temptation to silence his Celtic-supporting self-righteousness finally proved irresistible. Ironically, they had got on better since this adolescent revelation, though not necessarily on Old Firm days, and it had unfortunately come at the price of him referring to her ever after as 'the Kampala Loyal'.

As an adult, however, she found herself enormously reluctant to volunteer any aspect of this information, different reasons applying to different groups. Outside of work, she kept it from her social circle not because she was in any way ashamed of it, but because she couldn't be arsed with the disclaimers, explanations, apologies, clarifications and all-round ideological delousing routine that the mere mention of being a bluenose would entail in smug-liberal, aspirationally-intellectual company. Inside of work, she shunned football talk entirely, because she detested its capacity for engendering a shallow camaraderie, and simply would not demean herself by doing anything that made her look like she was trying to be one of the lads. It was also a cheap route to acceptance and approval: even the Celtic supporters on the job would have no doubt felt they could 'relate' to her more if they knew she (follow) followed the game, and that pissed her off. If they overlooked her other qualities but suddenly decided she was 'all right' because of the team she supported, or simply because she supported a team at all, then she didn't want their approval.

For that reason, staying quiet about it at work was easier than staying quiet elsewhere, as it felt like a matter of moral principle. However, it was her acute sense of moral principle that could also make her feel most frustrated about keeping her mouth shut on her own time. As a police officer, nobody had to tell Angelique about the abominations that could be carried out by certain of the pond-life who aligned themselves with the name of Rangers Football Club, and as a season-ticket holder, nobody needed offer her any further insight into the less palatable sentiments, opinions, beliefs and ideologies that could be heard around Ibrox on match days. She accepted that in mainstream popular perception, the worst images of Rangers fans were the ones that had stuck, however unfair and unrepresentative they might be (footage of 50,000 well-behaved Bears going to the game, watching it and then going home again not constituting much of a TV scoop, especially if it happened every week). She accepted that constantly singing a song about being 'up to our knees in Fenian blood' was not a PR coup in a part of the world where the word 'Fenian' was by most people's understanding a crudely pejorative term for Catholics, regardless of whether an informed minority more accurately considered it a reference to early-twentieth-century New York politicos and their subsequent followers. She accepted that the half-wits holding their right arms straight out in front of them at shoulder height during away games should not be surprised if onlookers described them as presenting a Nazi salute (as opposed to a gesture of solidarity with Ulster Loyalists: an important distinction, one being a bunch of thuggish, right-wing ethnic supremacists and the other being German). She accepted that a degree of reassurance would therefore always have to be imparted to people if she happened to mention this little sporting enthusiasm of hers, and she accepted that this was an unavoidable downside of following a huge, wealthy, high-profile and enormously successful club (St Mirren fans, for example, were not generally required, whenever they announced their allegiance, to apologise for the racist abuse of Ruud Gullit when Feyenoord played at Love Street in 1983). Being a fair-minded and morally principled person, as well as one who understood that the sufferings of a misunderstood football fan were unlikely to inspire a Thomas Keneally work, she could accept all of these things.

What she could not accept was that the same rules, values and assumptions did not seem to apply to those plastic-Paddy motherfuckers across the city, who could loudly trumpet their Sellickmanthruanthru credentials at the slightest provocation without fear of the same potential ostracism. Their support included just as many bampots, glory-seekers, bigots and extremists, and their club had just as many skeletons rattling in its closet, but in polite company Celtic fans did not seem to be held individually accountable for these shames and embarrassments the way Rangers fans were. In fact, if anything, it was

51

presented as evidence of some kind of lefty integrity and sympathy for the underdog (ignoring the fact that in Scotland, Celtic were actually the club forty-first in line for ratified underdog status). Nonetheless, whenever James told someone he was a Tim (about three minutes after meeting, on average), nobody ever asked if this meant he was an IRA-supporting, Provo-loving, Proddy-hating, terrorist-sympathising wannabe Irishman who'd never been inside a football stadium prior to Fergus McCann, sang songs glorifying child-murderers, condoned the club's thirty-year cover-up of the Celtic Boys Club child abuse scandal, backed the board's decision not to offer Jock Stein a seat because he wasn't a Catholic and always put some cash in a bucket 'for the boys' at the end of a night in the pub.

When she pointed this inconsistency out to James, he explained her travails as a consequence of Rangers being 'the establishment club'. Given that half the current Scottish cabinet held Parkhead season tickets and that every actor, rock star, comedian and public figure of any other stripe was these days proclaiming their life-long love for 'the Bhoys', it was difficult to work out who this 'establishment' actually included. Unless, of course, all those camel-coats in the Club Deck constituted a shadowy coterie who secretly ran the country. Hmmm. Maybe that explained why the bastards were usually too busy to stay for the full ninety minutes.

Ironically, as unfair and frustrating as she found all of this, Angelique would have to admit that it suited her in a way, by maintaining throughout adulthood the special status supporting Rangers had held in her younger life. It had always been her private, personal secret, like a vice, all the more thrilling for its being clandestine. Or rather, not so much a vice, as there was nothing immoral about it, but in fact a subversion. Going to a school full of Celtic fans, she was the one who could genuinely call herself a rebel.

Angelique had decided that she was a Rangers supporter when she was at St Mary's Primary in Leeside, before she even knew who or what Rangers were, before she knew anything about or had taken any interest in football. All she knew was that the people who hated her also hated Rangers, and they seemed to hate them for a lot of the same reasons. They were the others: different, alien, to be closed ranks against, to be defined as apart from, to be despised. So if the weans who were always tormenting the wee darkie lassie with the funny name felt so strongly about these 'Rangers', then the wee darkie lassie with the funny name reckoned she should be on their side. Then, having decided this much, she endeavoured to find out who her newly sworn allies actually were.

It never became an open stance, as she didn't need to give the wee neds any further reason to single out the school's most conspicuous target for abuse, but instead constituted a comforting private defiance, like giving them two fingers under her coat. From then on, hearing on a Saturday night that Rangers had won or Celtic had lost made her dread Monday morning that little bit less. Their victories were her victories, Celtic's defeats the defeats of every wee shite who had ever called her 'the Chocolate Button'. Soon enough she was starting to look at the back pages of the newspaper first, and becoming more excited about *Scotsport* on a Sunday afternoon than *Glen Michael's Cartoon Cavalcade*, which preceded it. In time, naturally, the prospect of actually going to a game became as tantalising a notion as it seemed unattainable.

By the time she was in Sacred Heart, James had long

been going to Celtic matches with his pals, something that she always considered to have bought him an easier ride from the school bampots. Apparently it mattered less that you were 'a darkie' if, first and foremost, you were a Tim. Playing for the school team gave her brother a certain kudos too, an option not available to Angelique, even if the status it afforded wasn't one she would have particularly valued. In accordance with the same physical education policies that forced girls to play a uniquely joyless variation of basketball, dispensing with backboards, dribbling, skill and any sense of fun, she had to make do with hockey at a competitive level, despite playing football with the boys every interval and lunch hour, and despite being more use than most of them too. This participation inevitably led to her having more friends among her male classmates than among the girls, but could hardly be said to have earned her anyone's respect, other than that she quickly ceased to be the last player picked.

With her own secondary school status confirmed, Angelique was able to take advantage of the same freedoms allowed James by her parents, freedoms they would most definitely not have granted if they knew that she was going to do the same thing with them. James getting permission to go to Parkhead had come at the end of a prolonged and tempestuous struggle, and even then only amid many promises of friends' fathers, uncles and older brothers being in attendance. Angelique knew that a request to go on her own to a Rangers game would be met with much the same response as a request from Idi Amin to pop round for Sunday dinner, so she had to resort to a degree of improvisation, or fibbing as it was more commonly known. Reminding Mum and Dad that James, at the same age, had been allowed to go all the way to

Aberdeen with his friends for a football match, the imminently twelve-year-old Angelique ascertained permission to visit the much nearer Paisley with her friends for a trip to the much less dangerous Kelburne Cinema. The cinema bit was a lie, as was the friends part, but she did go to Paisley, for her first live glimpse of the Rangers in action.

They were utterly rank. They lost three-nothing, to goals from Scanlon, McDougall and Jarvie, this coming on the back of a dismal run that had the pundits making jokes about an upcoming relegation four-pointer with Partick Thistle. But for Angelique, standing atop the broad sweep of the Caledonia Street terracing, they might as well have been winning the Cup Winners Cup in Barcelona: they were her team and she was finally watching them in the flesh. Defeat, in fact, made it all the more imperative that she go and see them again as soon as possible, which she would continue to do, alone and in secret, for many years to come.

Thinking back to that cold, dark day in Paisley, Angelique stopped and paused a moment at the top of the staircase, taking a look around the steadily filling stadium before she made her way to her regular seat. She thought about the girl she had been back then and wondered what she would have made of the woman who had turned thirty today. Would she have been impressed with her career, her abilities and achievements? Almost certainly: the young Angelique had no end of admiration for those who stuck it to the neds, the bullies and the hard men. Would she have been disappointed that she was still living alone and there was no muscle-rippling beau in the picture? A little, though she never had any dreams of being swept off her feet. Would she have considered, then, that the latter was worth sacrificing for the former? Unquestionably. But then what did a pig-headed twelve-year-old full of piss and vinegar know about disillusionment? At that age, she still had a stubbornly defiant appetite for slaps in the face, still filled with redoubled energy at the taste of her own blood. For Christ's sake, the silly cow thought a three-nil cuffing from St Mirren was a fun day out.

This was pitiful, she thought, as she made her way down to her seat, precisely the sort of sentimental and pointless navel-gazing she'd have mercilessly scorned in anyone else not so long ago. Jesus, that it should have come to this: musing wistfully on the things she wished she could tell her younger self, in anyone's book a hopeless admission of failure and regret. Instead, it might be more constructive to wonder what her younger self could still tell her, shrill, hectoring and direct as it would no doubt be.

'Quit feeling sorry for yourself. You think you've got problems? I'm watching us getting horsed at Love Street, Graeme Souness is still three years from showing up and Cammy Fraser's in the bloody team, but do you hear me complaining? Show some spine, woman.'

Aye, those were the days. Not an era one would naturally feel nostalgic for, in terms of the team on the park and the comparative dearth of silverware, but like the start of any relationship, it was the memory of that time that still sparked the most tingles. In fact, if there was any consolation for some of the club's recent shortcomings, it was the glimpses afforded of the time when Angelique first started going, especially towards the end of the season with Celtic romping to the title. A goal or two down with fifteen minutes to go, she could find herself sitting in a half-empty stadium, surrounded only by the die-hards, all of them having spent the game watching in hope rather than expectation, as it had been once upon a time.

Angelique fancied them today, though, due to some

solitary, worn-looking remnant of optimism her mind had managed to uncover amid the piled-up gloom. It was Aberdeen, for God's sake, and the last time they'd won here, Fred West could still have entered a full team for *Family Fortunes*. Or maybe it wasn't optimism, but sheer bottom-rung desperation. She knew it meant she was at a pathetically low ebb if she was relying on a football match to lift her spirits, but today she would settle for a sclaffed one-nil winner in injury time after ninety-three minutes of total dross, because she really needed to feel that some tiny little thing was going her way.

The teams took the field, the sight of the light blue jerseys causing the stadium to instantly fill with sound. Angelique got to her feet and added her voice to the din, feeling the buzz of hope, fear and anticipation that went all the way back to that first match in Paisley. This, above all, was what she needed right now. At the absolute, barrel-scraping least, the next couple of hours were hers to retreat to a place where all that other shite couldn't reach her.

The teams changed ends and took position either side of the halfway line. The goalkeepers kicked their posts and threw spare gloves into the back of each net. The referee looked at his watch then blew his whistle. Barry Ferguson played the ball to Shota Arveladze, and Angelique's emergency pager went off before the Mitre had left the centre circle.

# witness accounts:
# andy webster (19)

Christmas had come early.

Well, actually, with there still being three weeks to go according to the calendar, it was fairer to say that Christmas was at least no longer cancelled this year. Hallelujah. Sing Hosannah. Three more weeks, three more Saturdays including today, ascendingly the busiest of the year and therefore incomparably vital to the high street economy. Three more pay-days, no longer threatened with destruction of literally Biblical scale. Santa could saddle up again after all.

A cut in interest rates in November had been gratefully welcomed by the retail sector as it approached its most lucrative annual trading period, with the benefit predicted to reach even the remotest ancillaries. Andy considered his own ancillary business to be tangential rather than remote, and while not anticipating the trickle-down effect of this development to be substantial in his case, nor denying that it wouldn't hurt either, he nonetheless didn't consider it quite as exciting as his counterparts in the mainstream of the sector. Realistically, what the hell did he know – or care – about interest rates? His was an operation with zero borrowing requirements and, fortunately, very few overheads. On the other hand, it was a business subject to other uncontrollable variables that the rest of the retail sector did not have to worry about. M&S, for instance, while fretting about consumer confidence and whether they had correctly pitched their 'brand' in a rapidly evolving marketplace, did not have to worry about being moved along by the polis. The Gap might be ideologically besieged by the anti-globalisation movement and precariously subject to the damoclene whim of a sartorially fickle youth culture that could at any moment decide drainpipes were the new baggy, but it had never seen its earnings wheeched away by pubescent neds with Kappa tops and Stanley knives. And throughout November, the rest of the retail sector had been toasting the Bank of England and greasing the rollers on their registers' cash-drawers in anticipation of some serious pre-Yuletide turnover, because the rest of the retail sector were not having their pitch queered by some relentless Yankee Bible-thumper with a microphone and a battery amp.

Andy busked on Buchanan Street, near the corner of Gordon Street, as a means of generating some extra beer vouchers and in an attempt to ensure that when he finally paid off his student loan, it would be with his wages rather than his pension. He worked his spot most Saturdays and a few afternoons a week, the exact number a variable dependent upon his lecture schedule, essay arrears and whether the prevailing north wind was accompanied by lashing rain rather than merely threatening to freeze-weld his left hand to his fretboard. Having tried a few pitches between Argyle Street and Gordon Street, he had eventually settled for a stance just north of the latter, admittedly outside the busiest stretch of the pedestrianised area, but for that less prone to polis interference on the basis of obstruction.

He stood with his back to the weathered sandstone of a former bank turned mobile phone 'boutique', figuring the cellular vendors to be on relatively precarious ground if they wanted to complain about unsolicited and intrusive noise. Thus far this had proven an astute piece of thinking, though the solidity of the stone and some state-of-the-art double-glazing were probably playing a substantial part. A less qualified measure of his judgment was that the location more or less directly faced the McLennan Building, a faux Greek, Victorian-built mansion house named for its architect but known principally for the financial institution that had commissioned, built and occupied it ever since. Andy didn't know quite what to call it these days – the Bank of Scottish Presbyterian Austerity had merged with the Grim Northern Building Society and he wasn't sure which category the resulting behemoth fell into – but the practical upshot was that it was now open on Saturday mornings, which meant even more traffic than the cash machines already generated.

The downside, of course, was that wherever there were cash machines in this world, there were also *Big Issue* sellers, proximity to whom was often nothing short of Busker's Bane. Andy had nothing against the poor bastards, but business was business, and the harsh fact is that if you've got a spare pound coin rattling in your pocket and your avaricious consumerist bingeing has prompted a minor twang of conscience as you head back towards the multi-storey, then you're more likely to give it to the *bona-fide*, badge-carrying homeless guy than the hippy-looking student bastard who's clearly doing well enough to own that twelve-string he's rattling out *No Surprises* on. Fortunately, Andy's pitch was a good twenty or thirty yards across the flagstones from the bank, sufficiently outside the nearest *BI*-vendor's sphere of influence to garner gratuities from those who hadn't reached him yet, and possibly even to benefit from the belated guilt-pangs of those who had thought about buying a copy then changed their minds and hurried on past.

So in fact, very little was hard and fast about the micro-economics of busking. You could never entirely predict how those random variables were going to come into effect, how that butterfly beating its wings in the Amazon would affect what fortune blew up from Argyle Street: maybe that half a percent cut in interest rates would indeed be finding its way into his guitar case; or maybe it would mean some random bloke, who happened to like Green Day, would spend that bit more on lingerie for the wife and have nothing left but coppers in his pocket when he passed Andy singing *Time of Your Life*. It was all swings and roundabouts. Sometimes, for his own relief, he would divert from the standards and belt out something a little less universally familiar, which was normally at a cost of no bugger knowing it and no coins being forthcoming, but which could also have the unexpected upside of a punter being surprised and delighted to hear a busker singing what he or she personally regarded as an overlooked treasure. *Closer to Fine* by The Indigo Girls had a high strike rate for this phenomenon, though there had once been an ugly incident involving a rather uptight female who accused him of insinuating that she was a lesbian after he broke into it just as she was approaching his pitch.

One random factor, however, had proven all snake and no ladder, turning the vicinity into a pedestrian no-stopping zone more effectively than even the most vomit-streaked, Buckfast-chugging jakey (and without the inevitability that he would eventually fall asleep or get bored and fuck off). For the last three weeks, the centre of the concourse between the bank and the cellular dealership had become the al fresco pulpit of this voluble Jesus-junkie with a mountain-man beard and a raging case of verbal diarrhoea. He had been there every Saturday morning and a few weekdays too, spouting endlessly into his microphone and waving a Bible in his other hand. This had the standard outdoor-evangelical effect, seen in pedestrian precincts the world over, of causing the shoppers to hurry past, blanking out all sound and vision inside a sensory exclusion zone whose footprint sadly extended to cover Andy's spot. True, the guy usually jacked it in around lunchtime, but by that point he had already laid waste Andy's earnings for more than half the day.

He wasn't some wild-eyed, ranting, fire-and-brimstone loony, though the build on him was intimidating enough to deter Andy from any attempt to tell him to fuck off. Instead, he just stood there and wittered inanely but unceasingly, causing Andy to think of him as the Less-Than-Manic Street Preacher. The guy could literally talk for hours, and despite his taking up position bang in the middle of the thoroughfare, there was no chance of the polis cutting him short, in accordance with whatever unwritten law excused any anti-social conduct as long as its perpetrator had a firm grip on the Good Book. In the case of the LTMSP, it was a firmer grip than he had on reality. The guy just opened his mouth and let all manner of junk fall out. He didn't even look like he was bothered whether anyone was listening, just kept yakking away with a faraway stare, his eyes focused somewhere in the middle distance: he was looking into the banking hall but was probably seeing another dimension. Andy tried hard to tune him out, but even in the middle of singing and playing, he couldn't help but pick up random snatches of this gibberish, wondering whether the bits he missed either side could possibly contextualise it in a way that rooted the guy *somewhere* in the vicinity of planet Earth.

Underpants as a metaphor for Jesus's love, for fuck's

sake. 'Jesus and your underpants: you take them both for granted, but what would you do without them? They do things for you that you'd only notice if they weren't there, but shouldn't you think about that now and again? About that comfort and security, that support and warmth that all seems natural because it's always there? Uncomplaining, unconditional, too. But shouldn't you say thank-you now and again?'

Andy had briefly considered that the guy might be taking the piss before remembering that these guys were never, ever, *ever* anything less than entirely serious, sincere and officially certified 100 percent irony-free. Plus, as it was all delivered in that pious, over-sincere and affectedly humble tone, it sounded much the same as any other vacuous homily. The Parable of the Holy Underpants wasn't any less poignant than the drivel you could hear on Radio Scotland's 'Thought for the Day' on any given morning. Yesterday it had been the Reverend Misery O'Dreich delivering the obligatory annual whine about over-commercialisation and the 'true spirit of Christmas'. Andy had been close to phoning in and demanding a right of reply, pointing out that the Yuletide traditions of exchanging gifts, stuffing your face, getting ripped out your tits and having intoxicated sex with highly inappropriate partners had been around in these parts for a long time before Christianity. He'd even go as far as to predict that one day, somewhere around Salisbury Plain, archaeologists would uncover a cache of parchments depicting nothing but human arses, drawn during a winter-solstice piss-up 3,000 years before Xerox patented the first photocopier.

Faced with a depressingly under-commercialised festive run-up, it was fair to say Andy had constituted a less than receptive audience. On the basis of what he'd earned over the previous three Saturdays, a few photocopies of his own arse looked like being as much as he could afford to present his friends and family with this year.

But lo, in this season of miracles, something wonderful had come to pass. He'd turned up at close to half-eleven, having written off the majority of Saturday morning and equally discounted any prospect of knocking off early to catch the last home game of the year at Brockville. Crossing West Nile Street he looked ahead and saw, to the east, fuck all. A wide, empty space where the LTMSP had previously infested himself, some of the shoppers still walking around rather than over the spot as though something in their subconscious warned them to avoid it. Feeling a euphoric rush of seasonal cheer, Andy bought a flashing Santa hat from the greasy-looking punter who sold fag-lighters the rest of the year, then strapped up and launched full-throated into *that* Slade number he'd sworn he'd never play.

He had just about made it to the bridge part when, strumming quieter in anticipation of building up the volume for the last verse, he heard the shiver-inducing sound of an amplified voice. With a tangible degree of relief he realised that he recognised it, and the good news was that it was neither live nor American. It was the spoken intro to *One Step Beyond*, the extended album version. The bad news was that it was already boomingly loud, the source wasn't even in sight and it hadn't reached the music part yet.

In front of him, Andy could see heads turning *en masse* towards Royal Exchange Square as the quintessential Madness instrumental hit that signature saxophone riff. With any luck it would be a promotional car or a float, advertising a bar, a panto or maybe a pre-January sale. Knowing he had just been rendered invisible, he pocketed his plectrum and stood on his guitar-case to see over the shoppers, most of whom had stopped in their tracks to gawp at what was coming. It was neither car nor float, and if it had a promotional purpose then it was presumably to sell anti-hallucinogens.

There were five people – he'd guess male, but it wasn't easy to be sure – moving into the concourse in a human train, doing the walk/dance made famous by Madness videos and subsequently tarnished by the infamously ill-advised musical interlude in *The Breakfast Club*. It was a stomping, stop-start gait of knees, fists and elbows, its participants close enough for their joints to dovetail as they moved in near-perfect synchronicity. Their coordination would have been spectacle enough to attract attention on a Saturday morning, even in Glasgow, but they were kind of hard to miss visually too. All five had their faces identically made up as the weeping clown, inhumanly green of complexion, blue crosses over each tearful eye, and a beaming, cheerfully malevolent grin stretching almost ear to ear. They all had curly red hair, probably wigs, and they were uniformly dressed in multicoloured baggy overalls, a broad yellow T shape across the shoulders and down the trunk, bordered on both sides by bands of green and blue.

The one in the middle was carrying the boombox over his left shoulder, three of the others bearing luminous yellow rucksacks, the accommodation of which made their choreography all the more impressive. The one at the front was excused any manner of porter duty, presumably because he was smaller than the rest by an average of two feet. A further reason for his lack of encumbrance was made clear as they proceeded down Buchanan Street, when he was picked up by the dancer behind him and tossed, somersaulting, into the raised arms of the one pulling up the rear. Upon the short one being replaced, backmost, on terra firma, the group about-faced as one so that he was in the vanguard once again.

This little stunt was performed a couple more times as they marched up and down in front of the bank, amused shoppers forming into a wide circle, the radius of which left Andy hopelessly outside. Cutting his losses, he lifted the paltry sum his first two verses had accrued, and made his way over to watch what he hoped would be a brief performance.

'I think it must be McDonalds daein' a publicity stunt,' ventured one voice, but Andy knew otherwise. The hair, the overalls and the smile were all wrong, and it would have been a short career in the Evil Global Marketing Corp for the exec who suggested Ronald McDonald should have tears on his cheeks. The iconic showman they were made up as might have been famous for his greasepaint, but he was definitely no clown. Standing a little closer, Andy was surprised to observe that they were not only wearing identical make-up, but that they were in fact wearing the same face, the ginger curls attached to what were presumably latex masks. It looked an expensive get-up for street performers, which augured well for a non-financial motive.

The song reached its echoing, shuddering conclusion, the performance with it, all five figures coming to a staggered halt like a gradually braking steam engine. This drew warm applause from the gathered spectators, several of whom were vocally of the opinion that it was 'a lot better than that robotic mime shite ye usually get doon Argyle Street'. Andy grudgingly joined in, clapping a little more enthusiastically when he saw that the troupe weren't collecting any cash.

Some of the shoppers moved on, but others stayed in place awaiting whatever antics might follow. In keeping with the law of pedestrian curiosity, the crowd was soon

66

swelled by others who hadn't seen or heard anything yet but wanted to investigate whatever it was everyone else had considered worth standing around in the winter cold for. Fucking magic, Andy thought. They weren't even doing anything and they were pulling more punters than he could in a month.

The five of them had remained stock still since the end of the song. It had only been about twenty seconds, maybe less, Andy estimated, but the sense of unknowing and anticipation fairly seemed to stretch it. Then the one in the middle flexed a finger and music once again began sounding out from the stereo: a low, rapidly pulsing bass synth.

'Aw fuck, they *are* gaunny dae that robotic shite efter aw.'

Andy doubted it. He allowed himself a knowing smile, recognising the track: *Faith Healer*. There wouldn't be any pumping ska action from here on in, though it would be interesting to see what they *did* have in mind. The guitar crept in quietly, and with it they one by one became reactivated, as though sparked in turn by the electric signal carrying the chords. Then, like some ropily stop-motion animated creature, they began juddering forward, tracing a wide circle around the edges of the crowd. Having reached their starting point again, they turned and began moving towards the bank's wide stone front steps, the crowd parting to let them through.

'Mibbe it's a protest or somehin'.'

'Aye. That bank probably supports a foreign government that oppresses clowns. Geezabrek.'

'Naw, you know whit I mean. Mibbe they're sayin' the bank are clowns.'

'Fuck off. They'll huv a hat roon in a minute, you wait an' see.'

But so far, happily, a hat was still not forthcoming. They snaked jerkily up the steps towards the glass double doors, the short bloke stopping one step before the top and kneeling down. The next two stepped over him, vying in separate directions to grasp one door each, which they pulled open in time with a crescendo on their portable soundtrack. The rearmost two stepped over the little guy and continued inside, the last one revealing the wee man to be now facing the crowd, once again on his feet. He bowed with a flourish, retreating backwards into the building as he did so, then the first two stepped in front of him and pulled the doors closed like a final curtain.

Outside, the crowd were bereft, a sense of sudden disappointment palpable throughout the throng. It was as though the aliens had landed, shaken their thang, and then fucked off into the mothership before anyone could ask them how Elvis was getting on and whether that shot from Peter Van Vossen had reached the Horsehead Nebula yet. This only lasted for the briefest moment, however, after which the shoppers, as one, seemed to suddenly remember that they still had to get that teasmaid for Auntie Senga, and stepped back into their stride as if they'd never stopped at all.

Andy, delighted to see the spell broken but disappointed by the lack of resolution, returned to his spot and felt inspired to pick up where they, rather than he, had left off. With an energetically speedy strum, he broke cheerfully into *Boston Tea Party*, blithely heedless of the fact that the people in the vicinity most likely to know it had just disappeared into the bank.

# witness accounts:
# michelle jackson (26)

Michelle was trying to look busy behind a PC at the centre of the bank's imprudently open-plan Customer Information area, determinedly ensuring that none of the current assembly of customers would catch her eye even if they stripped naked and began daubing each other in woad. With an unaffectedly concerned expression compressing her features, she was pretending to examine a screen full of meaningless figures while she awaited the results of a search engine running in a minimised window. She was looking up hangover cures, rated a pragmatic internet-search priority ahead of UK Employment law (to see whether it outlawed being forced to work on the Saturday morning after the office Christmas do), EC Human Rights law (to see whether it outlawed being forced to work on Saturday mornings full stop), and the address of the Exit website, given the strong likelihood that she may have to kill herself if a certain incident at the party went public.

Saturday bloody morning – it just wasn't right. Who cared what time you got back during the week; what bloody use is a Tuesday afternoon to anybody? Never mind the Sabbath; in this part of the world, as far as Michelle was concerned, Saturday was the day of rest, especially when you'd been seriously shanting on the Friday night before. Their union had been sold a dummy over the whole issue, due to the complexities and potential pitfalls of the merger. The building society lot already worked Saturday mornings, which gave the new management collective a hefty foot in the door on the issue, but naturally the main bargaining plank had been guarantees of 'no forced redundancies'. The bastards knew that going to work on a Saturday morning sounded a lot better than having no work to go to at all, though right then, unemployment was sounding pretty bloody attractive.

There was only about fifteen minutes left until closing time, but the sense of 'so near and yet so far' was a merciless torture. It was a miracle she had made it this far, but having survived three hours made her feel less that she was on the home straight than that she was running on fumes. Her head felt as though someone had removed the inner-membrane of her skull with a Brillo pad and then siphoned off approximately three-quarters of the insulating fluid that normally kept her brain from banging against the sides. Minor movements caused her eyes to close as they involuntarily responded to flashes of white light that were unfortunately emanating from the wrong side of her lids, and though there was by this point nothing left in her stomach to throw up, she knew that the dry boak was but one waft of a chip-poke away. These, however, were only the chemical aspects of her sickness, ordinarily survivable with the assistance of lemonade, Ibuprofen and a good eight hours watching chick-flicks on her bedroom's wall-mounted telly. What Michelle was suffering was a phenomenon far, far more terrible. The truly debilitating hangover, the type that exacerbated all physical symptoms while simultaneously rendering their alleviation irrelevant, was resultant not of mere over-indulgence, but also of word or deed committed thereby.

Oh, yes.

*That* kind of hangover: a uniquely cruel symbiosis of toxicity and regret, whereby physical pain and emotional fragility get together and multiply themselves by the power of each other. Guilt times headache, nausea times embarrassment. But even within that Stygian sub-stratum of individualised suffering, there was still an upper and a lower tier. There were those occasions when, even with the smell of your own spew sticking two accusatory fingers up your nostrils as you *very* gently tip-toed past the bathroom, you could retain sufficient presence of mind to tell yourself that your enfeebled condition was causing you to fret way too much about behaviour or remarks that everyone else was probably too pissed to notice and definitely too pissed to remember. They were the hangovers clinging on to the bottom rung. Below them – way, way below them, in fact, far enough down to barely be able to make out the ladder above – were the ones when all consciousness was the enemy; where the moments of respite from pain or nausea only allowed deeper contemplation of the hideous effluence polluting your memory and obliterating all sense of perspective.

Regret did not seem a big enough word. Regret was what people felt when their house burned down or they failed to take Stalingrad. Something new had to be coined to cover getting stocious on Bailey's and giving the new Financial Services Advisor a hand-shandy – *no, Michelle, the whole truth: in the unforgiving bitchy gossip stakes, if it passed your lips for even a second it's a . . .* – okay, blow-job in a draughty hotel stairwell.

Oh why oh why oh why oh why oh why oh why oh why . . .

She was in a very dark and lonely place, and it was utterly inhumane that she should be required to interact

71

with other human beings – or even customers – at such a time. She needed a period of solitude and convalescence, at least the length of the weekend, before having to face anyone, far less her fellow staff, to say nothing of *him*, Grant Kelly. Thus far she had been spared this ultimate horror, but only because he'd been in meetings all morning and she had ducked behind the desk each time he popped out into the main body of the bank to greet his next client.

He had come to the bank after the merger, having previously worked in a nearby Great Northern branch that got 'rationalised'. They hadn't spoken much in the three months he'd been there, so she had no greater impression of him than that he seemed friendly, if a little over-confident in a self-conscious-and-trying-too-hard-to-make-up-for-it kind of way. He was also better looking than most of the other guys in the bank, but definitely not to the extent suggested by the cluckings of her female colleagues. That said, there was no denying that his being sought after by her peers had rendered him more desirable when the musical migrations of the after-dinner retro-Nineties disco left the two of them seated together.

Like most other things around here, what happened next was essentially the fault of the merger. As a result of the ongoing uncertainty, indecision, upheaval and general chaos, organising this year's Christmas party had been overlooked until so late in the year that they could only get a booking for the first Friday night in December, by which point her mind and body were not quite warmed up for full-on Yuletide saturnalia.

It was a catastrophic case of intoxicated flirting leading to reckless sexual bravado, creating a rising balloon effect whereby flirting became face-off and the price of backing down seemed to get higher and higher. It was as though part of her was flattered to be the subject of his attention, but a greater part of her was determined to be an opponent rather than a subject. He was talking big and so was she, his charm and self-confidence simultaneously making her fancy him but also piquing her desire to somehow get one over on him. You had to be there: it made sense after two vodkas, six glasses of wine and Christ knows how much of that sickly Irish alcoholic phlegm. She'd been expecting his self-conscious side to come to the fore and that he'd decide he was out of his depth, forgetting that guys, even when they are out of their depth, would never admit it. Somewhere in her inebriated mind she was telling herself she was Madame Verteille. Shame Laclos never included any tips about getting come-stains off of black Lycra.

Oh God oh God oh God oh God.

She was going to end up like that poor lassie in London whose boyfriend relayed her sperm-swallowing 'yours was yum' email all round the internet; twenty-first century communications technology rendering the planet not so much global village as global schoolroom full of sniggering male virgins and bitchy female hypocrites.

It was some kind of cruel, sick karma, her payback for KB-ing Alasdair Young at the school valedictory night ten years ago. She should have danced with him, snogged him and eventually married him. All right, by now she'd be suicidally bored, stuck in a loveless marriage with a dull husband, at least three weans and a cluttered semi in Bishopbriggs – but at least she wouldn't have been around to wank off Grant Kelly on the Central Hotel emergency stairs.

Michelle looked up furtively, the hourglass icon on her screen still stubbornly refusing to become a cursor arrow

73

and the effort of focusing on the statistics proving more than her headache could tolerate. The people in the queue were too intent on the teller windows to notice her anyway, but it was probably best for the customers that they didn't catch her eye. Her psychological condition was intermittently veering between pathetically needy and snarlingly misanthropic. If someone did manage to ask her a question, she guessed the odds would be 3/1 that she'd successfully answer it, with 11/4 that she'd burst into tears and 7/2 that she'd grab them by the throat, yelling, 'Okay, okay, I admit it, I knuckle-shuffled the FSA. Are you satisfied, you FUCKING BASTAAAAARD!'

It looked a stellar line-up, with the group directly in front of her not so much a queue as a posed tableau of 'The Ascent of Man' in Rangers colours. 'We are the people' was their motto, in which case Michelle was glad not to be. Behind that lot were assorted female shoppers, some sporting a bored husband as a logistical accessory, this group mercifully but precariously separating 'The People' from two further anthropological anomalies of a more verdant hue. These two were modelling the Garngad Winter Collection, following the tradition of bampot-couture that stipulated the colder the weather, the fewer layers one must wear outdoors. With the mercury struggling to break zero, the fashionable Tim-about-town wouldn't be seen dead in anything heavier than a gossamer-thin replica Celtic jersey. The People had at least had the sense to wrap up warm, though they were unlikely to be troubling the *Paris Match* fashion desk either.

Everybody seemed calm to the point of subdued, though it was always possible that Michelle's beleaguered brain was filtering out a lot of her sensory input in order to better concentrate on things that aggravated her discomfort and paranoia. So while the people in the bank seemed muted, the uniquely irritating sound of saxophone music from outside was going through the double-glazed windows and directly into her ravaged skull.

Fucking buskers and street performers. A plague on the lot of them. Inconsiderate bastards. Didn't these people drink?

Eventually, the sax-assault ceased, but it was followed by the depressing sound of applause, which meant whoever it was would only be encouraged to reprise their crime. And yup, sure as shit, the music soon started up again, some other tuneless racket that she could swear was getting louder. And louder.

Michelle could hear rhythmic clapping too, more morons unwittingly complicit in adding to her personal torment, while the music continued to get not only louder, but definitely closer. She returned her attention to the screen and tried to maximise the search engine window. The system appeared to have hung, possibly coming out in sympathy.

'Aw heh, whit dae these clowns want?' said one of The People loudly, ostensibly to his mate but beneficently intending a wider radius to share his wit. 'Hih-hih-hih. Ye gerrit?'

Michelle looked up to see what the joke was. If the saxophone music was precisely the last thing she needed to hear right then outside of a Primary Five recorder concerto, then this visual assailment, in a garish palette custom-designed to grate on her optic nerve, was brutal enough for her to take personally. And just in case the colours weren't distressing enough on their own, they were compounded by the kaleidoscope effect of one of the clowns tumbling across the floor, doing handsprings and somersaults.

Given the audacity with which they had marched in, to say nothing of their choreographic prowess, they had to be something more than street performers, which augured poorly for them buggering straight off again. However, as Head of Customer Relations, Michelle had been told nothing about any publicity stunts, and she would almost certainly have demanded an explanation if she had been physically capable of standing upright and focusing on any of them long enough to ask.

She did have just about enough stamina to look to Fraser the security guard by way of prompting him to intervene, but by this time some of the idiots in the queue were acceding to the performers' entreaty to clap along with the music, causing Fraser to grin idiotically at the unfolding spectacle. Eventually he noticed her glare and took a step towards the clown with the ghetto-blaster, who anticipated the objection and held out the machine, which Fraser accepted with guileless enthusiasm.

'Two minutes, mate,' the clown said to him winningly. 'It's for Children in Need. Cheers.'

But of course. Any act of anti-social insanity was immediately sanctified by the magic word 'charity'. As someone once said, if Hitler had invaded Poland 'for Spina Bifida' then everyone would have let him get on with it. And Children in Need, along with Comic Relief, were the two charities Michelle was least well disposed towards, and not due to any ideological conflict or lack of sympathy with their aims. It was because, wherever she had worked, the most miserable, curmudgeonly, right-wing bastards who never stopped muttering about dole cheats, asylum seekers and scrounging single mothers, would convince themselves they were the soul of giving because one Friday afternoon a year they dressed up in a fucking chicken outfit and cheerfully harassed their colleagues to 'chuck it in the bucket'.

The floor-show was therefore now unstoppable. The performers had a dwarf with them (Michelle didn't know the politically correct term these days, but in her current mood anything above 'short-arse' should be considered solicitously polite) and he was tumbling back and forth between two of the troupe, placing his foot in their interlocked hands and executing balletic mid-air somersaults at each end. Most of the customers were, depressingly, lapping it up. As well as clapping every other bar, many were also raising their hands at the prompting of the clowns each time the song got to a line that went 'Can I put my hands on you?'. A few others were, of course, utterly rigid, petrified of any direct interaction and quite clearly hoping they weren't going to be embarrassed into parting with any money.

Michelle's colleagues smiled smugly as they looked on from behind the bullet-, collecting bucket-, embarrassment- and direct interaction-proof glass that divided them from the unwashed. This sturdy frontage had been expensively installed at the same time as their new security system, with senior management less concerned than the front-line staff about the fact that the top of the booths stopped a good five feet shy of the ceiling. 'You'll only need to worry if you see some men entering the bank with black balaclavas and a large trampoline,' had been the heidbummer's glib assurance.

This was no idle recollection, but a thought provoked by the sight of the dwarf running, rather than tumbling, towards his waiting assistant, then being punted over his head and on to the top of the booths, from where he proceeded to perform a deep theatrical bow. Even the previously mortified members of the queue were moved to applaud this feat, with more of them joining in the raising of hands as the lyrical cue came around again. Perhaps it was Michelle's hungover condition and resulting tetchiness that was setting her apart from the other onlookers, but her reluctance to be engaged by the spectacle caused her to see what was otherwise being deliberately obscured by artifice. There had been no trampoline required, but there was now a man standing on top of the security barrier. There were no balaclavas to be seen either, but there were five people in masks taking up position in the banking hall. And though nobody had drawn a gun, the customers already had their hands in the air.

The force of the revelation caused her to voice her thoughts before she realised she was speaking aloud.

'This is a robbery,' she said.

The clown nearest Michelle turned around and pointed at her, placing a finger to his nose with his free, surgical-gloved hand in the gesture people made to indicate a correct answer during charades. Then he raised both of his hands dramatically and boomed out: 'Alakazammy, stairheid rammy!'

At this, the dwarf dropped down behind the barrier, almost every eye in the bank focused on him. By the time his feet hit the desk, he had produced what she would guess to be a machine-gun from beneath his overalls and was pointing it at the teller staff. Michelle, like everyone else on the other side of the glass, then looked around the floor of the bank and saw that four more weapons were now being trained on them. The clown nearest the entrance was covering the security guard, his back to the double doors. He reached with one hand to the stereo and turned the volume down, though, perhaps significantly, not off altogether. The rest were making eye contact with as many staff and customers as possible, gripping their guns in one hand and putting fingers to their lips with the other. Nobody had let out more than a startled yelp or an 'Oh God' anyway, but the calm subtlety of the gunmen's actions proved disarmingly effective in reducing the room to near-silence.

'As the young lady here accurately surmised,' announced the clown closest to Michelle, presumably the leader, 'this is a robbery. So those of you with your hands in the air, please keep them that way for now, and those of you without, please forgive this temporary breach of your right to individual free expression and stick 'em up where we can see them like everybody else.'

The teller staff had already done this in immediate response to the dwarf's weapon, though it was impossible to know whether any of them had kept sufficient presence of mind to hit the emergency button first. There was one of these under each till; pushing it sent out an automatic call to the police and engaged a number of automated security measures, but crucially did not sound any alarms, which would only update the crooks on the state of play.

The man spoke confidently but not loudly, with an incongruous air of pleasantry in his tone that suggested not only a lack of aggression but even that there seemed no need for it. His accent was American, but with confusingly occasional Glaswegian inflections, like he might be a local guy putting it on, or possibly a Radio Clyde deejay.

'Thank you,' he continued, having ascertained that there were no dissenters. 'Sincerely. Your cooperation in this is greatly appreciated, and I can tell we're all gonna work pretty well together this afternoon. There are a few preliminaries before we get started, so can I ask you all to kneel down on the floor just now. That's good. And the staff

79

behind the counter, if you could all please join us out front here, that would be just tickety boo.'

Michelle got up from her seat on unsteady legs, her head swimming from the change in altitude. She flopped down on to her knees, feeling for a moment like she might be about to faint, but disappointingly retained consciousness, probably due to a restorative rush of blood from her rapidly draining arms.

'Rest your hands on your heads once you're down,' the leader suggested, noting a few strained faces. 'We don't need you to look like a Pentecostal choir, and I sure know how much *I* hate getting pins and needles.'

While the staff were escorted out through the code-locked security door, at the other end of the hall the still upright Fraser was being relieved of his keys as he continued to hold the ghetto-blaster in both arms. The gunman instructed him to kneel down and place the stereo carefully on the floor, then fastened Fraser's hands behind his back with a white plastic strip. This done, his captor pressed a button on the machine to shuffle the track, after which Bach's *Air on a G String* began piping softly through the room. Michelle's colleagues filed out into the banking hall and took their own places on the cold tiles. With their hostages compliantly immobilised, the gunmen proceeded to remove their canvas backpacks and place them on the floor in front of the main counter.

'Are we sitting comfortably?' the clown-in-chief asked. 'Then I'll begin. Firstly, to make matters a bit less formal, allow me to introduce this afternoon's robbers. My name is Mr Jarry, and my associates are Mr Dali here; Mr Chagall next to him; behind the counter is Mr Ionesco, who performed those impressive acrobatics; and finally we have Mr Athena over there by the door.'

Each of the men either nodded or waved by way of acknowledgement as their names were mentioned. Michelle was reminded of those ghastly meetings at the start of a package holiday, where the reps patronisingly introduced themselves to the holidaymakers before warning them sternly against interacting in any way with the indigenous culture. She half-expected Jarry's next line to be, 'And if there's anything they can help you with today, don't be afraid to ask.' It wasn't, but the comparison still improbably held up.

'Sadly, places for today's performance are limited and there are a few restrictions in force,' he said, pacing along to where a tearful but determined-looking woman was protectively cuddling a mercifully sleeping baby. 'This programme is unfortunately unsuitable for children, Madam, so if you wouldn't mind, please make your way over there and Mr Athena will let you out in a few minutes. Sorry,' he added softly, offering her a hand to help her up. The woman looked around, incredulous at her good fortune and apologetically guilty towards those left behind.

'Jarry' then bent over two elderly ladies, again extending a forearm to assist each one in turn to her feet. 'Without meaning to be patronisingly ageist, I suspect our proceedings today will not be to you ladies' taste. You are, of course, welcome to stay if you feel otherwise.'

'Naw, son, we'll away before the Gordon Street branch closes,' one of them responded matter-of-factly.

'Awfy polite, wis he no'?' Michelle heard the other one remark as they shuffled towards the exit.

'Now, anybody here suffering from asthma or a heart condition?' Jarry asked. Almost every hand in the room went up, causing him to laugh out loud. 'I'm Brian and so's my wife,' he remarked. 'Okay, I'll ask again. Anybody got either of those things and able to prove it?'

This time only four hands appeared, one of them that chancer Arlene Fleck who carried a ventolin inhaler every day, but was known only to require it when she was being asked to explain her latest negligent calamity. Two further inhalers were produced, along with a bottle of pills clutched near-triumphantly in the hand of one of the press-ganged shopper-husbands. His euphoric relief was no doubt cut short when it became apparent that his missus was being allowed to accompany him.

'Is that everyone?' Jarry enquired.

Michelle looked towards the eternally mousy Caroline Reilly, whose protective instincts towards her unborn child seemed insufficiently developed for her to overcome her chronic fear of causing a fuss. Michelle nodded silently at her, beckoning her to respond, but the poor woman looked paralysed. Caroline was the kind of woman who, when she finally went into labour, would silently endure any amount of pain rather than inconvenience the anaesthetist in case he or she had more important things to do. Michelle put a hand up. 'This woman is five months pregnant,' she said, her voice still appallingly gravelly, a testament to her success in avoiding conversation all morning.

'And unfortunately it is our policy that pregnant women may not ride this attraction,' Jarry responded.

Michelle helped Caroline to her feet, knowing she'd need the prompt as much as the support. Jarry helped Caroline step past a couple more kneeling colleagues then looked back at Michelle. 'No such exclusions apply to the hungover.'

'Don't do me any favours,' she muttered, kneeling back down.

Jarry nodded to 'Athena', the clown at the main entrance, who allowed the lucky ones to file out then locked the double doors closed behind them. Upon the same unspoken command, 'Dali' and 'Chagall' slung their weapons around their shoulders and set about securing trembling hands behind nervous backs with more white plastic strips. Jarry paced up and down watchfully as his comrades busied themselves. The smile might be painted on the latex, but his voice suggested he was grinning underneath, too. All she could see of his true face were the eyes that peered out through the mask, and those appeared to be either twinkling with mischief or dancing with gleeful but genuine insanity.

'Thanks again, ladies and gentlemen, you're all being truly adorable. I'd just like to reassure you at this point that we have no desire or intention to harm any of you, and that you do not stand to make any financial loss whatsoever from today's proceedings, so there is really no incentive for impulsive heroics. Even in the unlikely event that one of you *is* able to overpower the five of us today, I can assure you that the only material outcome would be a grudgingly unreflective reward from the bank followed by several weeks harassment from the right-wing press who would be desperate to make you their have-a-go-hero. Or indeed heroine,' he added, acknowledging the imbalance of female staff. 'So think about what's worse: being taken temporarily hostage by us polite bank robbers or being besieged in your own home by uncouth tabloid journalists? You know it makes sense.'

Michelle couldn't be sure whether the sense of raw terror was dissipating or whether it was just that she'd spent the whole morning feeling like she was going to throw up and had therefore just about grown used to the sensation. The initial vertiginous sense of being overwhelmed by such unexpectedly dramatic events seemed to be giving way to pragmatic appraisal of a situation that was, while still in many ways bizarre, ongoing and very much a practical reality. A voice in her head told her that at least it put her worries over last night's indiscretion well into perspective, but the mention of tabloid newspapers reminded her that there was no such thing as perspective when it came to things like that. This just meant that come Monday morning, there'd be *two* big stories for everyone to talk about.

On the plus side, maybe they'd kill her; or even better, kill Grant before he could get the chance to blab. With this thought, it suddenly occurred to Michelle that Grant was not present. Her head turned involuntarily towards his office, the movement immediately homed in on by Jarry. The chief clown directed his gaze at the previously over-looked office door, which now seemed the more conspic-uous for being closed. Michelle bowed her head and looked at the floor, equally angry with herself for giving Grant away and for the unworthily flippant sentiment that had preceded this. She was unaware of having written any of this down on a flipchart, but evidently may as well have done.

'Don't beat yourself up about it,' he said. 'Believe me, it's better we get everyone where we can see them now, than a nasty surprise leading to an accident later. Mr Chagall?'

Chagall finished fastening the pair of hands he was working on and walked purposefully but unhurriedly towards Grant's office. Michelle attempted to assuage her guilt at her unwitting betrayal with the hope that his being overlooked would at least have allowed him the chance to hit the alarm button, but her optimism was tempered by the appreciation that these guys were clearly not engaged in any kind of smash and grab attempt. They had just let several hostages walk right out the front door, so they were hardly intending to keep the situation a secret. Whatever they were up to, they were getting dug in for the long haul.

She watched with a slight degree of surprise as Chagall turned the handle and gently pushed the door, realising that she had been expecting him to kick it open. Too many movies. What was the need for over-wrought aggression when you had four more machine-guns backing you up? He disappeared out of sight, but returned again quickly and unaccompanied.

'When he got there, the cupboard was bare,' Chagall reported. This time the accent suggested either an American trying to sound like an English toff or an English toff trying to sound like an American. 'However, I don't think whoever it is went off to play Bruce Willis. There's an *FHM* shrink-wrap in the bin, but significantly no *FHM*.'

Jarry turned back towards Michelle. 'How many are we missing?' he asked. It was only as he did so that she realised she couldn't remember whether she'd seen Grant's last client leave.

'One,' she answered.

'Mr Ionesco,' Jarry called out. 'Have you finished your sweep of the staff-only area?'

'Not quite.'

'Well can you prioritise the male toilet, please?'

'You got it.'

A few minutes later, a ghostly pale-faced figure emerged from the code-locked security door, the armed dwarf at his back, but it was not Grant. Fortunately, the startled client was dressed in a suit and tie, so the gunmen didn't realise they were still missing a member of staff. Michelle doubted this would allow Grant to, as Chagall put it, 'play Bruce

Willis', but at least it meant she was spared eye contact with him, so maybe this hostage situation had a plus side after all.

In the meantime, the clown crew had started to move more urgently into action. Athena was placed on patrol duty, which consisted of little more than standing in place with a finger over his trigger guard and his eyes on the huddled hostages while his comrades got busy elsewhere.

Chagall and Dali took a canvas bag over to the front entrance and removed from it a roll of masking tape and two cans of spray-paint. One of them placed a six-inch strip of tape at waist-height on the centre of each of the glass double doors, then set about spraying them with white paint from top to bottom. His pal, meanwhile, had already set about similarly covering the windows. After that, the taller and heavier Chagall gave Dali a leg up in order to spray the lenses of each of the banking hall's five CCTV cameras, which they presumably knew could provide an outside feed as well as recording to tape.

Jarry went back behind the counters and systematically cleared them of all cash, doing so neatly and without disturbing any documentation. The customers wouldn't know it, but he was being as good as his word regards their own money being safe: their deposit slips remained in place for processing, so the bank would still have to credit them with the money he was stealing.

The dwarf, Ionesco, was nowhere to be seen, which meant he could be rifling the floor-level cupboards behind the counters, but more probably that he was up to something in the downstairs admin area, such as trying to gain access to the basement. There was a further, more extensive office suite upstairs, looking out on to the banking hall through a windowed mezzanine level, but it was

86

closed on Saturdays (senior staff not having to drag *their* hungover arses to work at the weekend) and Michelle hadn't seen Athena pass the keys to anyone. There was nothing of value up there anyway, other than better-appointed staff bogs. The basement, however, was where the vaults were located, housing the main safe and the branch's 200 safety deposit boxes. If anyone had hit the alarms, the doors to both of these would have locked automatically.

Jarry emerged from the security door a few minutes later, carrying only his weapon, his ill-gotten gains presumably awaiting a more substantial supplement somewhere in the back office.

'Mr Dali,' he called out, 'how's the view?'

Dali peeled back one of the stickers from the double doors and crouched down to have a look through the gap in the paint.

'Just uniforms so far,' he replied, yet another American accent, this time one that suggested the face beneath his mask was black. 'I make four . . . no, wait, five, currently observing Headless Chicken protocols. They're movin' people back 'cause they can't think of any other way to be of use until the bossman shows up. So far one squad car, no Armed Response Units. Early days.' Dali rolled back the tape to re-cover the gap, then stood up straight again.

'They'll be there soon enough,' said Jarry. 'If you're all done down here, you should get yourself ready.'

'Sure thing.'

Dali walked briskly over to the counters where he crouched down and began checking the unseen contents of another canvas bag, while Jarry turned to address the hostages.

'For our next trick, we're going to need some volunteers

from the audience. Specifically, we're first going to need one Thomas Peat, who I believe has the position of duty manager today.'

Tom didn't have to identify himself, the sudden flush of colour on his liberally freckled skin making it extremely obvious which member of staff was now very much regretting having so successfully sucked up to the boss in order to secure this ironically uncoveted responsibility.

'Come on, don't be shy,' Jarry told him, helping him to his feet. 'I hate to put you on the spot, but I'm afraid one of these naughty children tripped your automated alarm systems, and we're gonna need you to give us a hand opening the vault.'

'I – I can't do that,' Tom stuttered, possibly the first time he'd spoken those words in this building. The guy was a walking mission statement, the living embodiment of the bank's ad-slogan-cum-corporate-philosophy: *Of course we can help.* 'I mean, I want to help, I'm not refusing,' he added quickly, either fearful of consequences or automatically reverting to type. 'But if the security system's been activated, I can't over-ride it locally. I mean, obviously I can key in my password, but that won't do anything because, see, it's the—'

'Remote Authorisation Delayed Double-Key System,' Jarry interrupted, 'as developed by Berkley Security Solutions for Pacific Western Bank in 1998. The safe is locked automatically and can only be reopened when the manager or duty manager's password is co-authorised at head office, after which there is still a six-hour built-in delay before the bars roll back.'

'That's right,' Tom added with sheepish redundancy.

Jarry continued, as though reading from a manual. 'The system is advertised to staff as being intended to protect them in the event of being taken hostage, as any information or cooperation that could be forced out of them would be rendered futile.'

Michelle remembered hearing something along these lines when the system was installed. Like just about everyone else, she hadn't paid much attention at the time, as nobody expects to see the thing in action for real, far less to be able to anticipate a flaw the experts have missed. Under the present circumstances, it seemed safe to assume that there was a pretty big one, and she guessed Jarry was about to point it out.

'Hate to be the one to break this to you, Thomas, but the Remote Authorisation Delayed Double-Key System is intended to protect *the money*, which is why so many banks across the world have implemented it. Its purpose is to buy time while the cops take position outside, encouraging the bad guys to give up on the dough and instead turn their attention to helicopters and non-extradition destinations. In a hostage situation, it prevents staff like your good selves from being able to unilaterally sell out the bank's passwords and access codes for something as trifling as their lives, but does not offer any protection against the robbers then threatening to kill their hostages if head office doesn't authorise the code and open the goddamn safe.'

It was not the most comfortable moment for Dali to stand up again, holding the most frighteningly elaborate shotgun Michelle had ever seen. By comparison, the identical compact weapons all five clowns were carrying looked puny and artificial. It had two vertically stacked barrels, the top one tipped with a sight-finder, a pump-action grip enveloping the lower, these both jutting from a formidable-looking steel trunk. However, the most disturbing part was the extendable shoulder-rest, currently folded forwards over the top of the weapon and accommodating a grey cylinder through each of four circular holes. Michelle knew bugger-all about guns beyond the fact that they went bang and that it was better to be behind them at that point, but she had been reluctantly dragged to enough macho movies to recognise that this one was going to be firing something bigger than bullets.

'But don't worry,' Jarry assured them, sounding more insanely jovial than ever. 'We're not here to threaten anybody. We just need Thomas to log us onto the network.'

# mental siegality

Andy was having fun watching the polis panic. It was enormously gratifying to see Shiftit and Liftit, the same glib
plods who always took so much pleasure in giving out that
super-confident and highly patronising 'make no mistake,
we're in control' patter, haplessly floundering now that
they were required to cope with something a wee bit more
strenuous than the everyday harassment of innocent
buskers.

The first sign that something was amiss came when he
saw some would-be customers turn back from the bank
steps and start running down Buchanan Street. He couldn't
hear what they were shouting, as he was continuing his
spontaneous Vambo tribute at the time with a predictably
head-turning rendition of *Ain't Nothing Like a Gang Bang*,
but the shoppers they encountered generally stopped in
their tracks; apart, of course, from the ones who started
running in the other direction for a gawk at what was
happening. A nimble piece of footwork flipped Andy's
guitar-case closed, and though he was able to step on to it
again without missing a strum, the same could not be said
for his vocals once he got a look inside the bank. Either
the Cleminson Clones had enlisted the bank's customers
in a mass rendition of the Hokey Cokey or they were
holding the place up. Flashes of gunmetal at waist height
suggested the latter.

The well-known busker-busting double act of boys in

blue came stomping up from Argyle Street a few minutes later, by which time a group of people had surprisingly been allowed to leave the bank. Shiftit and Liftit were talking frantically into radios as they ran, in a gait that suggested they were trying to give the appearance of haste without actually running as fast as they ought, probably praying the whole time that someone else would get there first.

If so, they were out of luck. Having heard confirmation of the circumstances from the exiting party, the pair found themselves in (Andy hoped temporary) charge of a situation they were conspicuously inequipped to deal with. Thus bereft, they were deploying the catch-all default plod tactic of randomly shouting at members of the public, which may not achieve anything constructive but was principally intended to give the impression that they knew what they were doing. There was a lot of arm-waving too, the general purpose of which appeared to be warding people away from the bank, but could also have been an attempt to fly; both possibilities proving equally ineffectual. Two coppers, a three-way junction, a broad pedestrian precinct and several hundred highly motivated Christmas shoppers, predominantly Glaswegian: it was exactly as it sounded.

Ever the opportunist, Andy resumed strumming and began singing *Police and Thieves*, segueing into *My Daddy Was A Bank Robber* and finally completing his Clash crime medley with *I Fought The Law*. He made about a tenner before Shiftit and Liftit remembered the one thing they *were* effective at and breathlessly told him to shut the fuck up. However, before they could formally or physically move him on, the cavalry noisily arrived, requiring them to report the progress of their hand-waving activities to a superior.

Two vans and four squad cars converged on the concourse, one of each from Gordon Street and the rest bludgeoning their way through the pedestrian precinct from West Regent Street. There were more plods on foot too, running towards the scene from all directions.

From one of the squad cars emerged a wee middle-aged guy with a dreadful comb-over, wearing a charcoal coat that was bigger than him. It enveloped him as rigidly as a tortoise-shell, and looked like it would remain standing on its own if its inhabitant extricated himself and walked away. The fact that none of the other polis were laughing at him indicated that he must be the ranking officer. He convened a brief pow-wow featuring much stiff-armed pointing, though it took a keen eye to spot whether any fingers actually made it beyond the expansive reach of his sleeves. Heads were nodded and cars were returned to, after which a more effective cordoning operation got underway. Vehicles were slewn across the three approaches, with the gaps either side soon plugged by red-and-white-striped plastic barriers produced from one of the vans. Shiftit, Liftit and their extended family took position around these roadblocks, eagerly grasping the opportunity to play to their undoubted strengths: viz, looking imperviously stern and telling people to go away. The barriers, however, were having the familiarly paradoxical effect of attracting people towards them in order to see whatever it was they were being excluded from. Crowds were building up on three sides of the now empty concourse, like they were waiting for someone to sink a final putt somewhere in the middle.

Andy was forced around the corner on to Gordon Street, where he backed himself into a disused doorway that afforded him both a slightly elevated view and space to persist with his musical commentary, figuring that with the polis otherwise engaged, it was unlikely he'd meet any further official objection.

The Coat was standing nearby on the empty concourse, a squad car between him and the crowd. He had a few other plain-clothes officers in attendance, but though discussion was taking place, it was clear that they were in a holding position, most definitely waiting for something.

The something arrived ten minutes later via two more squad cars, sirens audible for a while before they were able to part the sea of curious onlookers and reach the end of Gordon Street. Four men got out of each vehicle, kitted with body armour and bearing automatic rifles. None of them had to ask anyone to get out of their way as they marched around to join The Coat.

More talking, more pointing, and not a few frowns when the armed response cops noticed that they couldn't see into the bank, the windows and doors having been deliberately obscured. Nonetheless, four of them soon broke off from the group and took position, two each side, next to the barriers across Buchanan Street. They crouched on the pavement, weapons pointed at the front doors, and instantly had a greater impact in moving the audience back than any number of requests from Shiftit and Liftit. One glimpse of the hardware being pointed into the building was enough to spark a widespread contemplation of what might be pointing back out, and the entire throng took several collective steps backward.

The second unit remained grouped around The Coat, perhaps preparing for some specific tactical deployment, but quite probably, like everyone else, at a loose end until it became a bit clearer what was actually going on. One of them was looking up at the surrounding buildings, though Andy doubted The Coat's weighty sleeves would allow

him to point that high even if he did want people positioned there. Then from one of the slewn squad cars there
came a plain-clothes officer holding up a mobile phone,
indicating there was a significant call on it for the attention of The Coat. The ARU guys turned around with great
interest in whatever the plain-clothes bloke was saying, at
which point the entire group was suddenly engulfed in a
cloud of white powder.

Andy heard a series of muffled thuds and saw several
more such clouds rapidly appear on the concourse. The
first two scored direct hits on crouching armed officers,
and then four more landed around the remaining pair,
anticipating their attempted evasions. They did at least
manage to home in on the source and point their guns
towards the roof of the bank, but by the time they had
done so they were enveloped in billowing dust, from which
they emerged spastically, covering their eyes as they staggered. Andy looked up with considerably slower reflexes,
in time to see a brief flash of movement on the roof before
a gust of wind brought a light waft of the dispersing cloud
his way. He closed his eyes and stepped back, the recess
of the doorway preventing all but a smattering from
blowing in.

The gathering in front of the barrier had not been so
lucky. The Coat must have turned his head at an opportune moment, or simply withdrawn, tortoise-like, because
he got off considerably lighter than the rest. The ARU guys,
however, looked oven-ready, their faces coated and their
hair thick with powder, the effects of which were making
themselves swiftly and decisively manifest. The poor
bastards were consumed, effectively decommissioned as
surely as if someone had taken them prisoner. They were
coughing, they were rubbing their streaming eyes, they

were vigorously brushing and slapping at themselves, but most of all they were scratching. It was as though they had been swarmed by a million fleas, each one of the armed officers clawing compulsively at any exposed skin, and gymnastically attempting to get hands inside their clothes to the places this spreading plague had penetrated. One of them chucked his gun to the ground and began pulling off his armour where he stood, while unsullied colleagues made feeble (and visibly reluctant) gestures of assistance.

Soon enough, people in the crowd were scratching too, but in a far less extreme manner, and in sufficiently separate instances as to suggest a psychosomatic response. It did get them backing off even further though, as was the case on all three sides of the cordon. Shiftit and Liftit, with no option to similarly retreat, looked marginally but nonetheless satisfyingly afflicted.

# two tribes

Michelle's deduction that the robbers were in it for the long haul was proving to be arse-numbingly accurate. After all of the initial tension, confusion, fear and excitement, there was now a whole lot of nothing going on, apart from the occasional and persistently unheeded loud-hailer address from the cops outside. Inside, fear was turning to boredom, confusion into frustration; excitement was long gone, but tension was an ever-present.

The last major development had been Dali's foray 'upstairs', which she had naturally assumed to mean the previously ignored management offices, but turned out to be the roof. Chagall, monitoring Buchanan Street through his spy-holes, had reported the arrival of armed police; the arrival of all previous varieties audibly heralded by sirens. Following shouts, screams and a general rise in the overall rubbernecker hubbub volume, the lookout clown announced happily that the armed cops had been 'dusted', a term Michelle recognised as one of the seemingly countless euphemisms Americans had for killing people. With her fellow hostages clearly sharing this concern, and contemplating its ramifications for their own plight, Chagall was moved to assure them that it was 'not what you think', but irritatingly offered no further information.

Since then, there had been nothing to do but worry and, in Michelle's case, suffer. Her hangover symptoms had temporarily abated amidst the distractions of the robbery's more frantic early stages, but now her mind was free to concentrate on how rough she was feeling and how long it had been since her last dose of painkillers. The Grant Kelly issue had altered a little, however. Now, every time she remembered him, instead of worrying about him blabbing what happened last night, she was worrying about him getting himself or everybody else killed, Jarry's remarks about 'nasty surprises' and 'accidents' lingering ominously in her mind.

Untroubled by any such knowledge or fear, certain of the customer-hostages were increasingly disinhibited about vocalising their own primary concerns.

'Haw, Jimmy, whit's the score here at aw?' one of The People demanded of Athena, who continued pacing without any visible inclination to respond. 'This is a bit ay a liberty, like. I mean, how long are yous plannin' tae keep us here?'

'As long as it takes,' Athena stated flatly. He hadn't said enough for Michelle to get a handle on his accent, but what she heard sounded American yet again.

'We're meant tae be at the Rangers gemme,' The People's spokesman persisted. 'I'm just askin, pal, d'you reckon we'll at least manage for the second hauf?'

'You'd have to ask Mr Ionesco that question,' Athena replied testily. 'But I hope you've set your video for *Sportscene*, that's all I can say.' This time the accent was readily identifiable: unconvincing attempted American with conspicuously raw Glaswegian edges.

What was also identifiable was that Athena didn't believe things were quite going to plan, a suspicion Michelle was already entertaining. Tom Peat had returned from his soul-destroying act of betrayal only minutes after being led away, and since then there had been no sign of

Jarry or Ionesco, suggesting that the safe hadn't just popped open at their smugly confident prompting. Maybe it was the early symptoms of Stockholm Syndrome, but she couldn't help but hope for their imminent success, reckoning what was good news for the robbers was good news for the hostages. The converse was also chillingly true. If you had to be robbed by somebody, you'd want to be robbed by confident, competent, smooth-talking criminals, rather than nervous, twitchy, desperate men, but all it would take to change the former to the latter was failure.

Once again, not everyone endured the rising tension silently.

'Can yous no' use your influence tae get us oota here?' The People's spokesman inquired of one of the Celtic-supporting Antarctic expedition.

'Whit?' came the reply, the look of contemptuous bafflement on the Tim's face enough to convey an aggressive incredulity that the Rangers fan should even be addressing him.

'Well this shower are bound to be Taigs, are they no'? Maist criminals in Scotland are. I thought you might be able to put a word in.'

'Aye, that's right, pal. An' there's nae Proddy crooks, is there?'

'I'm no' sayin' there's nane, just goin' by the law of averages. The percentage o' Taigs in Scottish prisons is umpteen times their percentage o' the population.'

'An' that wouldnae be anythin' tae dae wi' bigoted Orange bastarts discriminatin' against kaffliks when they go for a job?'

'Heh, we've got a joker here,' the spokesman told his mates. 'He's talkin' aboot Taigs tryin' tae get jobs. Why would a Taig work when he can scrounge aff the state in

99

a country he despises? There's an irony for yous: it's us taxpayin' Brits that's effectively subsidisin' the season-tickets tae a fitba club that actively promotes terrorism against oor country.'

'We're an Irish fitba club that just happens tae be playin' in a Scottish league. An' wan man's terrorist is another man's freedom fighter. If you want tae talk aboot a club promotin' sectarianism, it wisnae us that wouldnae sign a kafflik for a hunner years. And don't gie's that shite boot Don Kitchenbrand, 'cause we know yous only signed him 'cause you hadnae done your homework an' never knew he was a kafflick.'

'I'm no' listenin' tae any moral lectures fae a supporter ay a fitba club that covered up systematic child abuse for thirty years . . .'

And so on.

There was a certain breed of Old Firm fan for whom hatred of 'the other lot' was so all-consuming that it over-rode not only their (seemingly incidental) interest in foot-ball, but also their awareness of current circumstances, to the extent that they would probably pick a fight against the backdrop of a nearby nuclear explosion. Armed robbers were therefore a minor consideration.

'And at least we never had our European trophy presented tae us in a fuckin' cupboard because oor fans were riotin' ootside. Yous are the only team in Europe tae be banned fae defendin' your ain trophy.'

'Says wan o' the coin-chuckers, the "Greatest Fans in the World", who pan the ref's windaes in when they get beat an' splits refs heids open when he gi'es decisions against them.'

Athena continued to pace up and down nearby as the argument raged on, giving a far less convincing impression of ignoring the combatants than they were of ignoring him. Inevitably, however, something had to give.

'. . . cheek tae talk aboot a sectarian signing policy when your shower went mair than a hunner years withoot ever havin' a Protestant on their board of directors. Wouldnae even offer Jock Stein – your greatest ever manager – a seat on the board 'cause he wasnae a Tarrier. Still, he wasnae bitter aboot it – otherwise he might have came clean wi' whit he knew aboot Jim Torbett an' the Boys Club scandal.'

Michelle had consistently no idea what the hell any of them were gibbering about, but this last remark had evidently crossed a line. The Celtic fan got to his feet and aimed a kick at The People's Ambassador, but the Ambassador sprang up also, with a speed that belied his girth, and retaliated with a swing of his own boot that just missed the head of the cowering Kathy Claremont. Before any of their mates could join in the absurd fray, Athena stepped forward and slammed the butt of his gun into the Ambassador's face. He collapsed, bleeding heavily from his nose, at which juncture the minimally dressed Tim lunged forward with the intention of taking full advantage. Instead he found his face in close proximity with the other end of Athena's weapon. He stopped in his tracks with a visible shudder and began backing away, but apparently not fast enough. Athena changed his grip on the gun and drove the butt into the man's stomach.

'Mister Athena!' called out a loud voice. Michelle turned her head to see Jarry standing in front of the security door, his own weapon slung around his back. Athena stepped away and Jarry began walking towards the hostage huddle. 'Can you tell me where the spare hostages are?' he asked Athena, loudly enough to be intended for all ears.

'What spare hostages?'

'My point exactly. So please don't damage the ones we've got.'

'They were—'

'I know. But cool off. Take five.'

'Yes, *sir*,' he responded with obvious sarcasm.

Jarry bent over the Old Firm contingent as they assisted their injured. 'My apologies. What can I say? Goddamn Partick Thistle supporters, huh?'

The Ambassador looked up, holding a hanky to his nose. 'It's as well he jumped in. I could take that Taig prick wi' baith hauns tied behind my back.'

'Well, let's not try and prove it again, or we'll maybe have to tie your feet up, too.'

Jarry stood up straight. 'My apologies also to the rest of you. It seems we'll have to detain you good people a little longer while Mr Ionesco sweet-talks the computer into opening the safe. She's been giving him the come-on, but is so far turning out to be a bit of a tease.'

'How long?' asked Athena grumpily.

'To paraphrase Oscar Wilde, Mr Athena, great theft, like great art, takes time. But while we're waiting, Mr Chagall, perhaps you could provide our guests with a little distraction?'

'Oh, I'm sure they wouldn't be interested, Mr Jarry,' Chagall replied, exaggeratedly bashful. 'I'd hate to take advantage of a captive audience.'

'Too modest, Mr C. Go on, I implore you.'

'Oh, okay then. But if I start to bore anyone, please, just raise your hand.'

## witness accounts:
## angelique de xavia (don't even think about it)

There was, as she had been promised on the phone, a blue Rover waiting for Angelique outside the main stand, the car easy to spot even when she turned the corner as it was the only one the uniforms on traffic duty weren't summarily telling to bugger off. She felt another tiny little part of herself wither and die at the sight of it, partly in response to the prospect of where the car would take her, but more so at its confirmation that they *did* know where she could be found on her free Saturdays. The car had already been dispatched to Ibrox before the buggers even made the call; probably waited till three so that there would be no crowds to wade through outside.

Wading through the crowd inside had been bad enough.

'Haw hen, gie them a chance, it's no' that bad already surely,' one Bear had called out as she made her conspicuous way towards the exit tunnel less than two minutes after kick-off.

'The Subway Loyal are gettin' earlier every week,' joked another.

'Will ye come back if Big Eck promises tae take Konterman aff?'

She wanted to call out a reply, show them a wink and a smile, even thought of a rejoinder about not watching another shitey 3–4–3 formation, but just didn't have the heart. Instead she kept her head meekly bowed and walked briskly down the stairs, past the scurrying, breathless late-comers and the Cholesterol Loyal still loading up with Bluenose Burgers in case malnutrition set in over the next forty-five minutes.

She walked up to the Rover and waved cursorily at the driver, who leaned over and opened the passenger side door for her. She recognised him: Bailey, new kid on the CID block, young, diligent, deferential and enthusiastically eager to please. A couple of years and one Dubh Ardrain ago she'd have found it refreshing, even endearing. These days she saw instead a careerist kiss-arse on the make and another 'one of the boys' in the making.

'Hi,' she said curtly, climbing in.

'Afternoon, Inspector,' he greeted her with a smile. 'Sorry to have to drag you away. I didn't know you were a—'

'Let's not go there, okay?' she interrupted tersely, determined to terminate this entire avenue of discussion. It didn't work, however, DC Pollyanna still imperviously unable to recognise 'fuck off' when he heard it.

'No, no, I'm not on the wind-up. I'm a blue—'

'—bottle who's still getting used to his plain-clothes suit and tie. So just drive the car.'

'Yes, ma'am,' he muttered, chastised and noticeably crestfallen. Petted lip coming up.

They whipped along Paisley Road West towards Tradeston, siren on, weaving through traffic as Bailey transferred both his huff and his unflagging desire to impress into his driving.

'What's the score, then?' she asked him, details having been scarce during the phone call. 'Why can't another armed unit handle this? I'm Special Branch and it's my fucking day off. We must have more than eight bloody ARU guys in the whole city, surely.'

104

'There's more coming in,' Bailey replied. 'But McMaster asked for you specifically.'

Angelique allowed herself a bitter sniff by way of a laugh, shaking her head as she did so.

'What?' asked Bailey.

'Nothing,' she muttered, but her sour smile remained.

McMaster. One of the all-knowing Star Chamber wanks who had stuck it to her at the inquiry. 'Reckless' had been his favoured censorious epithet, issued frequently from a mouth like an arsehole in a snowstorm. 'Accountability' was another hard-ridden hobby horse from the McMaster stable, alongside 'command lines'.

She had a couple for him now: 'hypocrisy' for one, closely followed by 'brass neck'. Angelique didn't know whether to feel vindicated or even more pissed off, but either way it was confirmation of what she'd suspected all along. They knew they were screwing her, knew what she was worth, knew what she could do, but they were fucked if they were going to admit it until circumstances made it absolutely necessary.

*McMaster asked for you specifically.*

Reckless. Unaccountable. Impetuously autonomous. Oh yeah, and when the shit hits the fan, who ya gonna call?

Bailey drove her along Gordon Street, slowing down as they approached the junction with West Nile Street, where a crowd was blocking the road. She could see the tops of police vans ahead, but she wasn't going to get much nearer by car. Bailey reached to put the siren on again, but she told him to pull over instead. 'I'll be quicker on foot.'

'Before you go,' he said, blurting it out as she reached for the handle like it was his last chance to ask for a date. 'I know we're unlikely to cross paths much, so I just wanted to say . . . what you did, you know, at Dubh

Ardrain . . . That took all the balls in the world. I know it's naff, but I wanted to . . .' He offered a hand for her to shake, too bashful or perhaps timidly reluctant to actually say it.

Angelique gave it a firm squeeze. 'Still two balls short of enhancing my career prospects around here,' she said. 'But thanks.'

She made her way less than briskly through the crowd, her progress slowed less by the throng than by an unshakable sense of ambivalence about reporting in to this numpty. Any notion of enjoying his discomfiture at having to turn to her in his hour of need was strongly countered by the prospect of whatever he might require her to do. As far as she was aware, this was an armed siege that was in progress, and she hadn't been 'asked for specifically' because she was known for her diplomacy or negotiating skills.

Even with so many bodies milling about and a loud-hailer obscuring his coupon, McMaster was not difficult to spot, engulfed as he was in that ridiculous coat. He looked like one of the Anthill Mob from the *Wacky Races* cartoons, though today his favoured attire was looking unusually piebald, nae bovine.

'I repeat,' he screeched through the bullhorn, 'we have the building surrounded.'

Christ, did he really just say that?

'You are in a no-win situation, but we are ready to negotiate to protect the hostages.'

Course we are. We're holding all the cards. That's why we're calling in reckless and negligent Special Branch officers on their day off.

Angelique approached the coterie gathered behind their makeshift roadblock and held up her warrant card in practiced anticipation of the nearest bluebottle reckoning she looked too wee to be a cop and telling her she couldn't pass. Instead he immediately turned and tapped McMaster on the shoulder, the words 'DI de Xavia, sir,' readable on his lips. All of the group turned around, each of them quicker than the sartorially encumbered main man. She recognised the faces: Dave Keogh, Graeme Hardie, Judith Newman, Bob Hogg. Big hitters all. The line-up was top-heavy with experience, authority, intelligence and expertise, while lined up all around the periphery was an abundance of muscle. What they needed Angelique for was therefore not immediately apparent, but she was starting to suspect that the word 'mug' might turn out to be an appropriate description of the role. Or 'fall guy', sex notwithstanding.

McMaster's eyes were horribly bloodshot and ringed with a pink-tinged swelling. Upon a second glance around the gathering Angelique noticed similar if less pronounced symptoms on several others.

'Angelique,' McMaster said with a nod and, golly, was that a glimmer of a smile? 'Thanks for coming, and sorry to pull you away on your day off.' Politeness, too! Mug was definitely it. 'I hope you weren't in the middle of anything vital.'

'No, sir,' she dutifully assured, by which time Bob Hogg had started whistling the tune to *Follow, follow, we will follow Rangers*, earning him a stern glance that he just laughed at. 'So what's the script?'

'In short, we've got five masked gunmen in the bank, armed with automatic weapons, holding an unconfirmed number of hostages, possibly twelve, maybe as many as fifteen.'

'Unconfirmed?'

'We're going by the estimates of the ones they let go.'

107

'They let some hostages go? Why?'

'They didn't make the grade,' Hogg chimed in. 'They released OAPs, a mother and child, a pregnant woman, bloke with a dicky ticker, even asthmatics.'

'Is this a robbery or an aerobics class we're talkin' about?'

'This wasn't any smash and grab that's gone wrong,' McMaster resumed. 'We believe they're planning a long game and they needed hostages who could stay the distance.'

'So what are they holding out for? What are their demands.'

McMaster visibly seethed at this question. Judith Newman answered it for him.

'They haven't made any. They're refusing to respond. They don't seem interested in entering into any kind of dialogue.'

'*Yet*,' McMaster added archly, sounding like he was trying to convince himself.

'They've also painted over the doors and windows, as well as the bank's CCTV cameras.'

'Can we access playbacks of when they walked in?'

'Way ahead of you,' said Judith. 'But they were already masked when they entered the building.'

'Stockings over the heads as they walked up the steps, then. What about exterior CCTV?'

'They were masked outside, too.'

'Surely you're not telling me they walked along Buchanan Street and up to a bank on a busy Saturday, wearing stockings over their heads, without anybody noticing anything suspicious?'

At this point, McMaster looked like he could have strangled several small furry animals and still had glowering tension to spare.

'They were dressed as clowns, DI de Xavia,' he said, barely controlling the rage in his voice. 'They posed as street performers before entering the bank.'

'They did a dance to an old Madness number. Drew quite a crowd according to—'

'Yes, thank you, Inspector Newman. I think we can dispense with certain of the less pertinent details.'

'Certainly, sir.'

'And what happened to the ARU?' Angelique asked.

McMaster began blinking at the mere mention of these words, then started rubbing his eyes. A couple of his colleagues followed suit in psychosomatic sympathy.

'We were subjected to an attack using some form of powdered skin irritant, fired from the roof,' McMaster said.

'Pump-action shotgun/grenade launcher, we reckon,' added Hogg. 'A SPAS or a LAW, something like that. Quality kit.'

'Our armed officers appear to have been targeted specifically, so they took the brunt of it,' McMaster resumed.

'Skin irritant?' Angelique enquired, failing to keep a degree of ridicule from her expression.

'Well, if you need both hands to scratch, and you can't see a bloody thing because your eyes are streaming, you're not going to be much of a shot, are you?'

'I guess not, sir.'

'The poor bastards are all away for saline baths up at the Royal Infirmary. It was nasty stuff, I can assure you.'

'It sounds like they've a sense of humour anyway.'

'Forgive me if I don't find anything funny about it myself, Detective Inspector.'

'No, I mean they were making a statement. They fired this stuff at the ARU. People accuse armed polis of having "itchy trigger fingers". That's always the phrase, isn't it?

Maybe it was their way of saying they didn't want this to end in a shooting match.'

'Well it's a good job you're here to interpret these semiotics, DI de Xavia, seeing as that's the only communication we seem likely to receive.'

'Anything to assist. But I can't imagine that's why you've asked me here, is it, sir?'

'No,' he said, handing the loud-hailer to Hogg. 'Come with me.'

McMaster led her back towards West Nile Street, away from the roadblock.

'You're here because of Grant Kelly,' he told her.

'And who might he be?'

'At the moment, our man on the inside.'

'On the job?'

'No,' he said, irritated. 'Staff. Fucking Financial Advisor. We rang his boss to make sure the name was legit.'

'I don't follow.'

'He was out of sight when these eejits took the bank. Upstairs in the office suite, where nobody's meant to be on a Saturday. Anyway, he called us on his mobile to say he was stuck there, and that the gunmen don't know about him. That's what I mean by checking he was legit, as opposed to some joker in an office round here taking the piss.'

'Got you.'

'He's been able to sneak a few quick peeks at what's going on, because some of the offices have windows looking down into the main hall. Only problem is, he's understandably shittin' himself in case they find him, so he's been communicating by text messages since the initial call. The girl that took it thought he was the world's stupidest pervert at first, heavy breathing to the police

110

switchboard, but it was just that he was whispering. He's also got the ringer turned off, so we can send replies without attracting attention.'

McMaster turned into a lane leading back towards Buchanan Street north of the West Regent Street roadblock. As Angelique rounded the corner she saw a large black van parked halfway along, hidden from sight of the bank. Outside it stood six unpowdered ARU personnel in Kevlar body armour and, this time around, visored riot helmets.

'The texts are coming through to this phone. Not much doing of late, but he's sending one every so often to let us know he's still on the loose.'

'Where do I come in?'

McMaster opened the rear doors of the van. The interior looked like the polis had just raided PC World, possibly confiscating the gear as evidence in a consumer rights crackdown on shops who cynically fleece the gullible and under-informed. There were rows of monitors down either side, being scanned, operated and generally tended to by two female uniformed officers, who must each have climbed over the corpses of a hundred slaveringly technophile male colleagues to get the gig. Most of the screens displayed live-feed windows from CCTV cameras in the area, manipulable via joysticks and keyboards in front of each. On a shelf by the left-hand door there sat, ominously, a spare Kevlar vest and an elaborate headset with integrated video camera, earpiece and microphone. Next to these were two further compact video cameras and two small parabolic microphones with plastic stands.

'Let me guess. You're having trouble with one of these tellys and you heard I was a whizz with a screwdriver and a soldering iron.'

'There's a hatch on the roof of the bank, accessible from

111

the second floor of the office suite. That's how their sniper got up there. According to Kelly, nobody's been back up the stairs since, and he'll keep us posted in case that changes.'

'That's why you haven't put another ARU out front: to prevent any further sorties upstairs.'

'Exactly. We want them to think we're in a holding pattern.'

'We *are* in a holding pattern.'

'For now, yes.'

'I don't like where this is going, sir.'

'Simmer down, de Xavia. We're not planning any reckless assaults.' That fucking word again. 'I've no intention of charging in there and causing a bloodbath. But we're sitting here blind and deaf at the moment, so we need some eyes and ears.'

His own eyes alighted on the headset and assorted snoopware. Angelique took another lingering look at it too, then back at McMaster.

'Why me?' she asked, her tone so confrontational it all but barged him in the chest.

He sighed loudly.

'I mean, is this hatch on the roof so small that I'm the only one who can squeeze through it? Or is the headset maybe too wee to fit anybody else?'

'What do you want, Angelique? Do you need me to eat some humble pie? Do you want me to stroke your ego for a while? Because there's people over in that bank with more important things to worry about. We need to give them the best we've got to offer, and in this kind of situation, that means you. You know it and I know it. There, I've said it. Are you happy now?'

'I'd have settled for please.'

'Then I'll throw that in as well. Please.'

'The magic word will get you everything.'

McMaster stepped outside while the two surveillance officers briefed Angelique on the operation and desired positioning of their equipment. They wanted two fields of vision, which meant the cameras had to be placed at either end of the offices overlooking the banking hall. The parabolic microphones were remotely operable, rotating on their stands so that they could be directed towards wherever their targets stood. These therefore had to be set up on an elevated flat surface close to the centre of the mezzanine windows.

Angelique pulled on her body armour and stepped out of the van, gadgets in a foam-padded nylon satchel slung round her left shoulder, headset dangling from her right hand.

'Just got an update from our man,' McMaster told her. 'Coast is still clear.'

'I need a gun.'

'Wilson,' McMaster commanded. The nearest of the armed officers unslung his MP5.

'Not one of those clumsy efforts. I'll be clanging off the walls. Gimme a hand gun, and as many spare clips as you've got.'

Another member of the ARU stepped forward and dutifully surrendered his Walther P990. 'It's forty calibre in the clip, as opposed to nine millimetre,' he began explaining, 'so there's only twelve—'

A higher calibre glare cut him short.

'Officer de Xavia won't be requiring any weapons instruction,' McMaster clarified politely.

Angelique checked the piece, ejecting the magazine and checking the action on the top slide before slamming the clip home again and chambering a round. She then took the spare clips and thrust them into the padded bag.

'Ready?' McMaster asked.

'Not yet. I'm still missing one crucial item of equipment. Has anybody got an elastic band?'

'Eh?'

While the ARU looked at each other helplessly, one of the surveillance officers reached into a wall-mounted pocket and produced a selection.

'Cheers,' Angelique said, picking one and using it to secure her hair in a tight pony-tail before pulling on the headset.

'*Now* I'm ready.'

# the gentleman thief

Further to her previous ruminations, while Michelle was under no doubt that a greater danger was posed by incompetent bank robbers, she was thoroughly ignorant as to whatever the received wisdom might be on insane ones. The description 'mad' was one of the most over-used and seldom appropriate epithets in modern parlance, right up there with 'nightmare' and 'ironic'. 'You must meet my pal Mandy, she's mad.' 'They're all mad down our pub, so they are.' 'You should've been at Eileen's party, it was mad.' The most ordinary and dull people were awarded this status as a kind of personality compliment, usually on the basis of a truly minor quirkiness or in testament to some occasion of (usually drunken) shared hilarity. Everybody was 'mad'. Friends were mad, family were mad, colleagues were mad, TV presenters were mad. Except that they weren't. They were just people you found even slightly interesting.

The people robbing Michelle's bank, however, were utterly, utterly fucking nuts.

She had become more and more convinced of this with each passing development, but what put the tin lid on it was what she had witnessed over the past half-hour. With Ionesco still busy trying to get the safe open, Chagall had been charged with the less-than-orthodox hijacker duty of keeping the hostages entertained, which he had done by recreating famous works of art on the whited-out windows and doors, all the time inviting contributions from the assembled 'audience'.

First he had drawn an anguished figure on a bridge, head in hands, with two further individuals lurking in the background. Michelle recognised the image, but couldn't have told anyone it was called *The Scream* before Chagall solicited this from one of the customers. He then amended the image so that one of the lurking figures was shouldering an enormous ghetto-blaster, and asked for suggestions as to what song it might be playing. *My Heart Will Go On* was deemed the winning entry, rewarded by its title being scrawled for posterity amid a rising flock of musical notes.

After that he drew on one of the double doors an incongruously serene man, riddled with arrows as he slumped against a tree. It was *The Martyrdom of Saint Sebastian*, according to the same apparently art-loving client, and became the subject of a caption competition. 'Missed!' proved the most popular, amid what Michelle guessed to be a lot more laughter than was generally normal for an armed siege.

On the second double door he drew 'with apologies to Van Eyck' a heavily pregnant woman standing before a man in medieval garb, making this the subject of further, predominantly lewd, captions. ('That's the last time I'm letting the Mediaeval Baebes tour with Oasis' got the nod on this occasion.)

Then finally, on the right-hand window, he recreated another painting Michelle recognised, of a number of wretches dead and dying as they clung to a storm-tossed raft. The People's Ambassador took it as evidence to back up his previous argument. 'I tell't you they were fuckin' Taigs. He's drawin' thon album cover fae that Republican, terrorist-loving Provo scum, The Pogues.' Or *The Raft of the*

*Medusa*, as one of the (presumably Pogue-loving rather than art-loving) said Taigs was able to inform them.

Whatever Chagall's plans were to adulterate this particular masterpiece, Michelle did not get to witness, as Jarry made one of his periodic reappearances and was called to by a strain-faced male customer who was, in his own words, 'touching cloth'. It was perhaps indicative of the paradoxical level of trust he had engendered that the bloke should wait to ask the leader rather than just tell one of the others that he was bursting.

Jarry ascertained who else required use of the staff facilities and instructed Athena to escort them there in pairs. Michelle, still thoroughly dehydrated, had no such need, but she indicated otherwise because she felt she could use the chance to at least stretch her legs. That chance came, but not in the way she intended.

As he reached the security door, Athena, who had not yet been through it, asked the nearest hostage what the code was. Disastrously, the nearest hostage happened to be Grant Kelly's client. When he responded, apologetically, that he didn't know, Athena merely looked to someone else to answer, but Jarry zeroed in on the significance right away. The next thing he zeroed in on was Michelle.

She felt her cheeks burn as his gaze fixed upon her, wanting to stare at the floor but feeling compelled to look up, fearful of offering anything else that might be construed as defiance. Jarry stepped closer and gestured for her to stand, cupping his hand and beckoning her with four fingers. Michelle climbed to her feet, her innards now in non-alcohol-related turmoil.

'You're a cool customer,' Jarry said. 'I'd sure want you in *my* corner if I was hiding out.'

A couple of the other clowns looked over, curious.

117

'We're missing a member of staff, guys. But don't sweat it.' He looked at her name badge. 'Michelle here is gonna help me clear this up, aren't you?'

She said nothing, just concentrated on not falling over, all of her bones threatening to turn into the same gooey mush that was churning in her guts.

Jarry followed her through the security door and told her to head for the entrance to the mezzanine. 'Ionesco swept down here and, let's face it, there's not a lot of hidey-holes. Your upstairs offices don't open on a Saturday, but I guess somebody had a key, huh? Who are we lookin' for?'

They both stopped at the door.

'Financial Services Advisor,' she mumbled.

'Oh that's good to know. Maybe he or she can help me out with how to spend what's in the safe. But actually, I was looking for a name. Look, you're not betraying anybody. You did a pretty good job of covering up for this long.'

Betrayal couldn't be said to be the primary source of Michelle's reticence. It was a little more to do with being content to have remained out of Grant's sight for the duration of events so far; to say nothing of her continuing embarrassment rendering her almost incapable of speaking his name. *Almost*. It's amazing what the sight of a machine-gun can do for your sense of priorities.

'Grant Kelly,' she whispered, the words threatening to break up in her throat.

'You guys close or something?' Jarry asked, noting the emotion in her voice. Michelle felt her face flush once more. 'Actually, that's none of my business,' he added, which in a way was worse than further prying, to which she could at least offer denials. 'So, what do you figure? He shows his client to the staff bathroom, presumably at the end of his meeting, and then sneaks off upstairs, where, strictly speaking, he shouldn't be, naughty boy. Why?'

'Better bathroom,' she said with a shrug.

'That works. Chagall found an *FHM* shrink-wrap but no *FHM*. And you guys were quarter of an hour from closing, so why not wait it out where nobody can bother you? I admire that. You can't say slackers lack initiative.'

Jarry unlocked the door and led her quietly upstairs, stopping in the corridor.

'Call his name,' he whispered. 'And tell him it's you.'

'Oh God,' she croaked, entirely involuntarily. Jarry wiggled the machine-gun. Michelle swallowed, took a breath and then finally spoke, trying forlornly to banish the image of what she had been doing the last time she spoke to him. 'Grant, it's Michelle.'

Jarry nodded and gestured with his gun. She took it to mean 'again'.

'Grant. Can you hear me? It's Michelle. Where are you?'

There was only silence. She looked along the corridor, where doors lined both walls, mostly ajar and some wide open.

'Mr Kelly,' Jarry called, loud and stern. 'I know you can hear me and I know you can hear Michelle. You have ten seconds to give yourself up or I'm gonna splatter her fucking brains all over this carpet right in front of me.'

Michelle turned around to look at Jarry in sheer horror. He shook his head and waved a hand dismissively, but began counting aloud. When he reached five he pulled a lever on the edge of his weapon. It made a noisy ratcheting sound that bounced threateningly off the corridor's walls.

'Four, three, oh and after Michelle here, please bear in mind who I'm most likely to kill next.'

At this, the words 'Okay, I'm in here,' issued hurriedly from the doorway of Bob McEwan's office, from which a hand tentatively waved.

'Stay right there,' Jarry ordered him, indicating to Michelle to head to the doorway first.

She'd rather have been facing more gunmen. Grant, however, was standing there looking like last night was a long, long way from his mind. He was physically shaking, his pallor deathly pale and his eyes filling up. Not having witnessed the ongoing cabaret downstairs, he had nothing but a terrified imagination for company.

Or so she thought. Jarry spotted differently.

'Would that be a cellular in your pocket or are you just pleased to see Michelle?'

'Oh God,' she and Grant said at the same time, for very different reasons. Grant surrendered the mobile in response to Jarry's gesticulation.

'Take a seat,' Jarry told him, then nodded to Michelle, too. They backed into the regional assistant manager's office, from where she could see the front of the banking hall. The Raft of the Medusa was now being attacked by The Lady of Shallot, whose coracle was packing a cannon not normally seen in reproductions.

'Nice view,' Jarry said. He held up the mobile. 'Who you been talking to?'

'N-nobody,' Grant spluttered. Michelle tutted and sighed. It would make last night a whole lot easier if he could appear just a *little* masterful and impressive.

'Shit, what a waste,' Jarry said. 'Me? I'd have been on to the cops in nothin' flat.' He began pressing buttons, his eyes intent on the phone. 'Course I'd have to keep my voice down, what with the bank robbers coming and going. Maybe even send a text message.'

120

Grant said nothing.

'Look, what do you know? 15:56 "Stl ok. gmen stl dstrs. good 2 go". Good 2 go. Now, whatever could that mean? And let's see, before that. 15:47 "gman paintng on windw. 1 out/sight". 15:39 "stil ok". 15: 29 "stil ok". 15:22. "hstgs fightng selfs. gmen hittng hstgs now". 15:17 "stil ok". And all the way back, yadda yadda yadda.'

Jarry's thumb continued to work the keypad as he scrolled through Grant's messages. 'Quite a little running commentary you've been filing. Don't think much of your prose style, by the way, but shit, you're under pressure. Woah.'

He stopped pressing and stared hard at Grant, anger visible in his eyes, even if his painted-on expression still suggested a more benign countenance.

'They're sending someone in,' Grant blurted out. 'Please don't shoot me. I'll tell you everything I know, everything I've told them.'

Jarry waved the phone in his hand. 'There's nothing you can tell me that I can't read from here. I know they're sending someone in. But that's not why I'm pissed.'

Grant looked confused, to add to his wretched terror. Michelle was thinking she ought to be less judgmental, as she'd been just as pathetically compliant a few minutes ago when she feared she'd been the one to bring down the wrath of an armed robber upon herself. Poor bastard. What he'd done had taken a lot of bottle.

'11:48 "Donny old bean! What a nite. Michelle J gave me a gobble. Details later".'

Jarry glanced again at Michelle's badge to check her surname, but the look of mortification on her face made it unnecessary; nor would he need to ask whether it was true.

'You complete prick,' she screeched.

121

Grant bowed his head, colour rapidly returning to his cheeks, mainly red.

'Who's Donny?' Jarry asked.

'My mate,' mumbled Grant, unable to look at either of them.

'This isn't the kind of detail gentlemen should really confide, in their mates or indeed anyone else. Is Donny's number on here? Oh yes, here we are.'

Jarry began thumbing the keypad again, keeping a finger of his other hand over the trigger-guard of his gun.

'I'm sorry, I'm sooo sorry,' Grant said, sounding like he might be about to burst into tears.

'Bit late for that,' Jarry said. 'But reparations *can* still be made. Here we go. "Donny old bean! Bet that had you going. Michelle J? In my dreams. G".'

Jarry pocketed the phone and gripped the weapon with both hands, stepping forward and sticking the muzzle right under Grant's chin. 'Now, here's the deal. You learn to keep a lady's secrets secret, and nobody has to find out about you jerkin' off to magazines in the upstairs bathroom. Cool?'

Grant's eyes bulged again as he wondered whether anything of his own was secret any more. Michelle might have felt sorry for him if she didn't at that moment hate him with every hungover molecule in her body.

He nodded, as much as the gun-barrel allowed. 'Yeah, yeah. Absolutely. Whatever you say.'

'Good. Now if you don't mind, it seems I've got visitors to prepare for, so let's get your asses back downstairs.'

Jarry nudged Grant to take the lead, giving him a dig in the back with the machine-gun. It was as though he'd been jabbed with a cattle-prod, yelping and shuddering at the sudden touch of metal.

Suffer ya bastard, Michelle thought.

122

It wasn't Stockholm Syndrome that was making her feel closer to the gunman than to her fellow hostage. Only one of them had treated her like a lady. Admittedly there could be some jaw-dropping personal hang-up behind it, or some psychotic rage that might be triggered by the wrong confluence of events, but right then it didn't seem very likely. That said, neither was she likely to start fantasising about the man behind the mask. She'd had her act of sexual desperation for this year, thank you, and by the least probable combination of events, it looked like she was ultimately going to get away with it.

They returned to the downstairs admin area, where Ionesco was staring with consternation at a computer monitor. Jarry looked at his watch.

'How's it going?' he asked.

'Slowly,' said Ionesco.

'Slowly but surely?'

'Surely as day becomes night, but I couldn't say what's gonna happen first.'

'What's up?'

'It's this fucking 256-bit encryption.'

'But I thought you tested the compiler on 256-bit.'

'The compiler's fine. Trouble is I wrote it and tested it on a 2.2 G Athlon.'

'And these are?'

'Fastest CPU in here is a Celeron 400.'

'Fuck. So . . . prognosis?'

'I've tweaked the set-up as much as I can . . . stripped down the OS to bare bones. It's making a difference, but I still can't say how long. There's nothing else I can do but wait.'

'No point in you sitting here, then. Come on, I'm gonna need you out front.'

'You got it.'

The four of them walked out into the banking hall, where the other clowns immediately looked to Jarry for an update. Ionesco fitted Grant with the standard plastic restraint and told him to take a seat on the floor. Michelle, meanwhile, walked around the group to take a spot as far from Grant as space allowed.

'Gentlemen, we've got a few issues to deal with,' Jarry announced. 'First of all, we've got a visitor coming. Cops are sending someone in to plant a few bugs. Bless 'em, they've gotta try. We've got a few minutes, though. I've told them to hold off for now.'

'*You*'ve told 'em?' asked Dali.

'I'll explain later. Mr Chagall, if you're all out of canvas space, I think you'd better get busy warming up Plan B.'

'Aw shit,' Dali said.

'Bollocks,' agreed Athena, adding further unnecessary confirmation that he was about as American as Mom's sausage supper.

'It's just as a back-up. Mr Athena, I need your particular talents upstairs. Dali and Ionesco, the hostages are in your charge.'

'You got it.'

'Cool.'

Plan B, Michelle thought. No matter what reassurances Jarry was offering his comrades, there was no question their operation was running into trouble. This was precisely the kind of development she knew to fear most, but instead a calm detachment was beginning to envelope her. Her hangover had substantially subsided since Jarry sent that text message, which made her wonder just what processes of transference had been going on in her head up until then. Despite the guns, the siege and the insanity, Jarry and his men were not the thing she'd been most afraid of. That having been lifted, she felt confident she could deal with everything else.

It was undoubtedly six degrees of inappropriate to feel gratitude towards a gun-wielding thief, but she wanted to express it nonetheless; and besides, it wouldn't hurt to remind Grant who she had in her corner.

'Mr Jarry,' she called as he was about to disappear through the security door. He stopped and walked over, crouching down beside her.

'I just wanted to say . . . thanks. I don't get it, though. I don't get it at all, but . . . thanks.'

'Hey. Just because I'm a bank robber doesn't mean I'm the bad guy.'

And with that he walked away.

# when it all goes wrong again

'Al clr. gmen chckd u/strs – bck dn now. gmen w8tng 4 smthng? gd 2 go'.

A curse on text messages, Angelique thought. She hadn't seen so many heartless crimes against the English language since she'd worked a paedophile sting and had to spend hideous hours in internet relay chatrooms, longing for the sight of a vowel. gmen w8tng 4 smthng. Thanks for the scoop.

She was walking briskly through the Princes Square mall, accompanied by two of the ARU numpties, the very sight of their group scattering shoppers from their path. The most depressing aspect was that she was the one drawing most of the looks, and not just because she was female. All three of them were wearing Kevlar around the chest, but only one of them was sporting light blue phat pants below the waist, or headgear that made her look like a recently assimilated Borg. Well, at least it distinguished her from the Double-Y chromosome escort, kidding themselves they had a protective role when they were about to simply wave her off and wish her good luck for when she went in on her jack.

Even worse than the physical accompaniment was that she had McMaster's disembodied voice in her ear. Now she knew how a schizophrenic must feel, though in the schizophrenic's case at least the voices might seem to make sense now and then, if only at the time. The thought that

126

he could see what she was looking at and hear what she was hearing was truly uncomfortable. It was one remove from knowing what she was thinking, and just as well that he couldn't, as it would have been less than reassuring. For one thing, she remained suspicious to the point of paranoia about why she had been brought in on this farce, with the most plausible explanation being that she would make a handy scapegoat if it all fucked up and a civilian got shot. 'Ah yes, DI de Xavia, past record of reckless and impetuous conduct. Tendency to go it alone outwith the chain of command.' Blame it on one gung-ho cop rather than tactical mismanagement.

Arguably even more disturbing for a telepathic eavesdropper was her current lack of confidence in her abilities, and greater lack of conviction about implementing them. Not only was she pondering how this morning's lacklustre performance at the dojo didn't constitute ideal preparation for the task ahead, but she was also finding it difficult to focus on the imminent reality of it. Normally at this point she'd be well in the zone, but despite being mere minutes from harm's way, she found her eye (and therefore her camera) distracted by a purple top in the Whistles window, and by thoughts of what trousers might best go with it.

She was about to mutter 'I'm too old for this shit,' when she remembered that the listening audience was greater than the usual quorate.

With the assistance of a security guard, they made their way on to the roof of the shopping complex, from where Angelique had to abseil two storeys to reach the bank. She pulled on her harness then had a look over the edge while her escorts assembled the pulley and found something sturdy enough to attach it to.

The hatch was not only visible, but still open, presumably

for rapid access if the police were daft enough to send another ARU out front. Even with forewarning, they wouldn't have much to aim at if the bad guys were firing from an elevated position, and if the cops wanted to get nasty, it might not be skin irritant that came raining down on them next time. The thought was enough to belatedly bring Angelique some of the sharp focus she'd been missing thus far. A pump-action grenade launcher, such as a SPAS or a LAW, would be more normally employed in its principal fire mode, which was as a fully automatic shotgun. The pump was only required for projectiles that weren't gas-ejected. When it came to regular shells, those babies could take eleven in the breach and one in the pipe, and blast out all twelve in a matter of seconds. Angelique knew what a shotgun blow to her Kevlar-protected chest felt like, and that was just the best-case scenario.

The ARU goons finished setting up the rig and took positions overlooking the bank's roof, levelling their HKs at the hatch. Angelique resisted asking what the hell they were going to shoot, other than her. Oh well, whatever made them feel useful.

She made another check with the phone upon McMaster's aural prompting, hitting the shortcode to send a prepared message: 'Going in now. Still clear?'

Thirty seconds, maybe a minute passed, enough to worry/hope the bloke had been rumbled, before the phone vibrated silently in Angelique's hand.

Gmen stil w8tng. Good 2 go.

She tucked it into a pocket in her trousers and clipped herself on to the cord.

'You bastards seriously owe me,' she said for McMaster's benefit, then kicked off down the wall.

She landed softly, bending her knees to absorb the

impact, then swiftly unclipped the harness and stalked towards the hatch, gun drawn. From a crouching position she could see one wall of the room beneath, shelved untidily with stationery supplies. It was a storeroom, the suits understandably not wanting tackety boots on their desks any time workmen needed access to the roof. She crouched close to the gap, not yet peering directly in, listening for the sound of movement. A breath of wind carried the chatter of the crowd from below, and if she looked up she could see all the way to Central Station, taxis queuing outside, pedestrians swarming up and down Renfield Street. The rest of the world had a coldly blithe way of just getting on with itself at times like this, oblivious of the drama and danger unfolding mere streets away.

There was an air vent less than a foot from the hatch. Angelique tested its temperature and then hooked one knee around it, pulling her calf tight to her thigh. Gripping the Walther in both hands, she took a breath and swung herself forward into the gap, tensing her stomach muscles to pull her head almost level with the ceiling inside. She scanned as wide an arc as her balance allowed, then relaxed her stomach and leaned further forward, checking behind by dangling upside down. There was no-one to be seen, just more shelves, cupboards and spare office furniture: desks and chairs either still in bubble wrap or at the other end of their service life. The bad news was that the ladder was out of reach, resting against a wall five or six feet away, so she had no option but to 'dreep', as the technique was known locally.

She needed two hands for this, so she had to tuck the gun into her waistband. This was not something she normally regarded as advisable, but in the case of a P990 it was okay to make an exception. The Walthers had three separate safety mechanisms including the catch, so it was nigh impossible for the things to go off by accident; to actually fire them you all but needed to sign a disclaimer.

Angelique climbed into the hatch and lowered herself nimbly and silently until her arms were at full stretch. This done, her feet were still a metre from the floor, which wasn't a long way to fall, but was liable to make a bit of a thump. There was a desk a few feet to her left, so she manoeuvred herself around ninety degrees and began swinging back and forth to build up sufficient momentum to reach it. On the fourth swing, she let go and leapt forward, landing off-balance but upright on the hardwood, much of the impact absorbed by the frame.

Upon her feet hitting the desk, Angelique had to quickly compensate for her rear-leaning stance, lest she topple backward with a louder (and more painful) thump than the one she'd been trying to avoid. She managed this via that classically elegant technique (though not to her knowledge pioneered by Nadia Comaneci) of bending forward while flapping her arms like a particularly uncoordinated fledgling heron. This did achieve the desired result, but with the practical drawback of her hands being uselessly extended either side of her when two clown-faced bank robbers stepped from the shadows and levelled their full-autos.

'Fuck.'

The taller of the two delicately plucked the P990 from her waistband and placed it in his own, while McMaster uselessly muttered, 'Oh Jesus' in her ear.

'Headset too, please, and the bag,' the taller clown added, his American accent confirming the accounts of the released hostages.

'Be my guest,' she told him, handing over the headset first with no regrets.

'These things expensive?' he asked, dangling the gadget in his hand as Angelique lowered the padded bag on to the desktop.

'I forgot to look at the receipt.'

'Well, my apologies to the taxpayer in any case,' he told her, before dropping the rig to the floor and crushing it under his heel. He then took hold of the bag by the strap and stepped away.

'Mr Athena, if you wouldn't mind furnishing our guest with the standard party tags?'

Angelique climbed slowly down from the desk to face 'Mr Athena', whose eyes were burning with an unchecked animosity that his latex expression failed to hide.

'Turn round,' he ordered gruffly, filling the comple-mentary 'bad robber' role with a passion she suspected owed little to the Stanislavsky Method. Confirmation of this came after she obeyed, when he struck her in the back of the neck with his rifle-butt, shouting, 'On your fuckin' knees, bitch.' Anger betrayed his albeit pitiful pretence of an American accent. This was 100 percent pure Glaswegian bampot, proven by his instinctive resort to violence at the very sight of a police officer.

The blow was more surprising than powerful, and Angelique dropped to her knees out of deliberate compliance rather than the force of its impact. He then pushed her, roughly, into a prostrate position and knelt on her back, tying her hands with a white plastic restraint. That done he gripped her painfully by the nose, still kneeling on her spine, and pulled her head up by the pony-tail so that her ear was closer to his mouth. Before he could speak, however, his companion loudly cleared his throat.

'Mr Athena, just a small question . . . Ehm, *what* the fuck are you doing?' He spoke calmly and softly, as though it was a casual inquiry.

'I'm just makin' sure this pig knows the score,' Athena said, growling it into her ear.

'I'd imagine the police officer, if indeed that's who you're referring to, has firmly appraised the current situation *vis a vis* us having all the guns. They're trained to be observant, you know.'

'That's not all they're trained for, IS IT?' Athena replied, pulling harder on Angelique's nostrils. 'See, you forget how it works, *Mr Jarry*. If you give these cunts a glimpse . . .'

'Well let me put my argument another way. You take your hands off the lady or I shoot you where you stand. You die and the rest of us get a bigger share of the money. How does that work for you?'

Athena got off Angelique's back but kept hold of her nose, pulling her up to a kneeling position. 'You don't have the balls,' he said. 'And it would mess up your clever masterplan.'

'Mr Athena, I'd call you an asshole if it wasn't that an asshole is something I can't do without. You on the other hand . . .'

Athena eyed the weapon levelled at him and finally let go of Angelique's nose, but only so that he could take hold of his own machine-gun in both hands and point it at Jarry the second his guard dropped. Angelique didn't recognise the models, but they looked state of the art. In any case, from that range, an eighteenth-century duelling pistol would be adequate.

She fought the urge to close her eyes. All it would take was Jarry to grab his weapon again and the storeroom would be turned into a giant Moulinex. Jarry, however, remained impassive.

'Mr Athena, we're in the process of stealing a large sum of money. Could you try to stay focused. Once we've got the cash, you can pay a shrink and work on your ego problems *that* way.'

'Take your hands off the gun,' Athena commanded.

Jarry obeyed with a sigh, letting it hang from the shoulder strap. To her considerable surprise, Jarry then looked away from Athena and down at Angelique, still as calm as though it was a bunch of flowers being pointed at his chest. 'My apologies, officer. It's a teamster thing. Every bank robbery crew must employ one psychotic shithead. You don't mess with the unions.'

'Yeah, I'm a psychotic shithead and you're the genius. But how about I blow *you* away, blame it on the pig, kill her, and then *I* get a bigger share of the money? Never thought of that, did you, prick?'

Jarry addressed his fellow robber once again, the small note of exasperation in his voice like that of a patient but weary father. 'Dude, I thought I'd made this pretty clear, but let me outline it one more time. This is my show, and you are still one entire brain short of being able to fuck with me. So how about you put the gun down and let's get on with what we came here to do.'

Athena looked from Jarry, to the weapon in his hands, to Angelique and then back at his adversary. 'Actually, I prefer my plan,' he said, and pulled the trigger.

Angelique dived forward on to her face, turning her shoulder to cushion her impact. Above her, Athena stood holding his machine-gun, staring with uncomprehending eyes at the flag that had appeared from the barrel when he'd attempted to fire it. It said, in bright red capitals and blue lowercase:

133

# A
# Trigger
# Happy
# Empty-headed
# No-brain
# Asswipe

'What the fuck is this?' he asked incredulously.

'Proof that you're predictable as well as everything else the flag says.'

'I checked and loaded this gun myself.'

'You checked and loaded *a* gun, but not that one. And now, thanks to you, the police officer is in on a little secret.'

'Are any of the guns real?' Angelique asked him.

'Yeah, this one,' he replied, taking the P990 from his waistband. 'So the situation is as you were. Mr Athena, fortunately for you, I'm a forgiving kind of guy, so if you get your ass back downstairs and be a good little shithead for the rest of the day, nobody else needs to know what just happened here.'

'And just what does everybody else know?' he asked, pushing the spring-loaded flag back down the muzzle of his gun.

'What do you think?'

'Fucking pricks,' he grunted, and made his exit.

'I'll be down in a minute,' Jarry called after him. 'Meantime think of the money.'

'What fuckin' money?'

Jarry waited for Athena to stomp huffily down the corridor then went over and helped Angelique to her feet. She thought briefly about kneeing him in the balls, but with her hands tied behind her back and him holding the only confirmed functioning firearm, it would have been no more than a foolish and possibly suicidal gesture.

'You have a shotgun somewhere too,' she remembered.

'Oh yeah. No ammo, though. Just those powder bombs. Have a seat,' he said, gesturing towards a bubble-wrapped swivel-chair. He leaned against the desk she'd landed on, rather idly poking about inside the padded bag. 'More expensive gizmos. I guess you weren't meant to be the cavalry.'

'Not exactly, no.'

He took a couple of steps closer and looked her up and down. 'Where's your badge?' he asked. Angelique lifted one thigh to indicate a velcro-fastened pocket. Jarry flipped it open and removed her warrant card, examining it carefully.

'Cool name,' he said.

'Thanks. Don't suppose you fancy telling me yours?'

'Not today.'

'Then you have the advantage of me,' she said, instantly regretting it. Oh yeah, flirt with him Angelique, he'll be putty in your hands. Idiot.

'Wouldn't that be my lucky day,' he said, distractedly enough for him somehow not to sound like an arse. 'But right now I'll settle for robbing the bank.'

'Boom boom,' she replied dismissively. 'So what do you want to talk to me about?'

'Ehm,' he mumbled, as though either suddenly bashful or improbably forgetful of the otherwise conspicuously heightened circumstances. 'Oh yeah. Responsibilities, I guess.'

I *guess*?

'A bank robber wants to talk to *me* about responsibilities?'

'Yeah. Where there is power, there has to be responsibility. Right now, you're the one with power.'

135

'That's not what it looks like from where I'm sitting.'

'No. I said right now. I meant . . . We're gonna go downstairs in a minute, where as you now know we've got sixteen people being held hostage by unarmed men. As things stand, those hostages aren't going to get hurt.'

'As long as your pal Athena doesn't start whacking them again.'

'Again? Oh. You got a text message about that, huh? It wasn't what it seemed. Well, it was what it seemed, but he was breaking up a fight between the hostages.'

'The hostages were fighting amongst themselves? With gunmen standing around? Aye, right. You expect me to swallow that?'

'Well . . . I ain't from round here, so you're in a better position to judge. Some of them were wearing blue and some of them were wearing green. How's my credibility hangin' now?'

Angelique sighed. 'Pretty good,' she conceded.

'The point is, the situation is under control, so the people downstairs are safe right now, and they're your responsibility, right? Unless you got a lot of stock in the Royal Scottish/Great Northern Bank.'

'Not last time I checked my portfolio.'

'So the most *ir*responsible thing you could do would be to tell those people the guns ain't real, because then we might have a situation that was out of control. That's when bad things can happen.'

'Only if you fire the Walther,' she reminded him, bouncing the moral onus right back.

'*If* I fire the Walther, but not only if. Your Armed Response Unit buddies don't have the best reputation for care and discretion in the heat of the moment. I'm told a chair leg in a plastic bag is good enough for them to drop you. And it's not just the hostages' lives that are valuable, as far as I'm concerned.'

'You're very humanitarian for an armed robber.'

'Recently armed. Robber, yes. But I'm not the bad guy.' There was laughter in his voice, like he didn't expect her to agree but didn't need her to either.

'Why don't you just leave me up here, then?' she asked, though she'd have been disappointed in him if he'd been daft enough to do so.

'Sure, if you'd prefer. But I'd have to keep you in a real uncomfortable position in case you did something completely unexpected, like try to escape. These plastic ties: they're good enough for gunpoint hostages you've got your eye on, but they don't take much to wear down. I could always gag you, I guess, but it would be insulting your professionalism.'

'How so?'

'Because it'd show I didn't trust you to be responsible like we just discussed.' Again the laughter: gentle, friendly and distractingly incongruous. 'And I figure the first person the cops sent in would have to be someone *they* trusted not to jeopardise the hostages.'

It was Angelique's turn to laugh, but hers was scornful to the point of bitter. 'Yeah, *that*'s why they picked me.'

'Huh?'

'Chances are it was more to do with . . . Never mind,' she said, trying not to contemplate what it suggested about her current state of mind that she had just come embarrassingly close to opening her heart to an armed bank robber in a clown mask. His remarks also reminded her that she couldn't have it both ways: either they were cynically using her as a potential scapegoat, or Jarry was right and it was further confirmation that the bastards knew she had been anything but reckless at Dubh Ardrain.

'More to do with what? Am I not givin' you your due? They sent you in because you're the number-one bad-ass or somethin'?'

He was taking the piss. Not derisively, but the bastard was amused at her, not something Angelique had ever been particularly tolerant of.

'Haven't you got a bank to rob?'

'Oh, shit, yeah, *that*. Let's get downstairs. You can see what the gmen and hstgs are w8tng for.'

Angelique rolled her eyes towards the ceiling. That explained the two-man welcoming committee; at least it meant she hadn't given herself away by being too clumsily noisy. Jarry had been sending the text messages; or at least the more recent of them.

'Was it you all along? Did you want a police hostage?'

'We found the guy. I could have put you off after that, but yeah, I figured a cop would be a valuable addition to our collection below.'

Jarry stepped aside and bowed beside the door, mock-ceremonially inviting her to go first. Angelique sent him a glare, but she wasn't feeling quite as much animosity as someone in his profession would ordinarily generate.

'So how's it going?' she asked, getting up from the chair.

'Huh?'

'The *robbery*.'

'Oh. *Comme çi comme ça*, you know. Hostage handling/ police control aspects all got big ticks against them. Large-scale cash withdrawal part still kind of greyed out.'

'Bummer.'

'Yeah. Computer problems, but we do have a Plan B. Appreciate your solicitude, by the way.'

'I'm a cop: we care, we can't help ourselves. Feel the love.'

'I'm feelin' it. Nine-millimetre love, here in my hand.'

'Forty calibre, actually. There's a lot more outside, too. Us Brits get nervous when you point guns at civilians. What do you need all these hostages for anyway?'

'Well, right now they're the only things stopping your buddies from stormin' in here and makin' us do some of that Warren Beatty/Faye Dunaway breakdance action.'

'You know what I mean. They're your bargaining chips as well as your human shield. What are your demands?'

'What are you sellin'?'

'Me? I'm not a negotiator.'

'No point in me demanding anything from you, then, is there?'

'Give me a break here.'

'Golden rule of bank robbery, Officer de Xavia. Don't negotiate until you've got the money. What use is a helicopter ride and safe passage to a non-extradition country if you're broke?'

'Better than a cell, a trauma theatre or a mortuary.'

'You don't negotiate until you're out of options.'

'I take it you've done this a lot?'

'What do you think?'

'So what options do you have?'

Jarry overtook her in order to open a door at the foot of the stairs. There seemed a keen politeness to it until she remembered that with her hands tied behind her back, she wouldn't have been able to open it for herself anyway.

'Quit diggin',' he said, holding the door open to reveal the bank's back office. 'There ain't anything much you can do now, so why don't you consider yourself off-duty?'

'I *was* off-duty until you . . . eejits showed up.' She was about to say clowns, but couldn't bring herself.

'My apologies. If there's anything we can do, you know,

short of calling off this little work in progress . . .'

'Don't suppose you happen to know how the Rangers are getting on?' she replied, figuring that as he wouldn't even know what 'the Rangers' were, it was as good as a polite fuck off.

'Just a second,' he said, and reached into his overalls for a mobile phone. He pressed a few buttons and looked at the LCD window. 'Sixty-six minutes. Three nil. Arveladze, two, and an OG. Guntveit. Cool?'

Angelique was flabbergasted. Was this bastard telepathic? She couldn't see the LCD window herself, so it was possible he was just making it up, but then how would he know what names to give, or that Cato Guntveit was a plausible candidate for blootering it past his own keeper?

'Is there anything going on here today that you *don't* have complete control of?'

'Yeah, that,' he said, pointing to a computer monitor sitting on a nearby desk. There was a progress bar on display in a window in the centre of the screen, the blue line having made it less than halfway across.

'What is it?'

'The software that's supposed to be opening the safe for us. We thought, what with being a billion-dollar international concern and all, that the bank might have a decent PC for us to run our hacking routine on.'

'How inconsiderate of them.'

'I guess they're just trying to save their customers money. Banks care.'

'Sounds like having cheap computers might be saving their customers a *lot* of money.'

'Hey, I'm the one in the clown mask. I'll do the jokes. And I'll be laughing last. The software's running slow, but

140

I didn't say it ain't working. And time we got. Let me illustrate.'

'So what's this Plan B about?'

'Still diggin'?' he asked, leading her to another door.

'You can always gag me,' Angelique reminded him, though she had no idea why she should be doing so, or more poignantly why she felt certain he wouldn't. Something about their entire on-going exchange was just . . . disarming. Wrong, even; but wrong as in it didn't add up, not wrong as in bad. It should have been bad. She should have been seething with resentment and dripping with contempt, whereas talking to this guy was starting to feel like the easiest thing she'd done in an otherwise markedly difficult day. Perhaps it was merely resignation kicking in: as Jarry had pointed out, the hostages were safe as long as she did nothing, so maybe this was some wiser, buried part of her sub-conscious telling her she might as well kick back, for the time being at least.

Experience told her the sight of sixteen terrified hostages would rapidly alter that mindset and her attitude to their captor.

Jarry opened the door and ushered her quietly through into the rear of the banking hall. The hostages were arrayed with their backs to her, all of them seated either on chairs or desks as they faced the front of the building. There were plastic cups of water dotted liberally about the floor, a couple of puddles marking spillages. She could see spoof artworks etched vividly on the painted-out doors and windows, captions and speech-bubbles supplying punchlines or merely added irreverence. Standing in front of the restrained gathering were two gunmen, one of them the midget mentioned by witnesses. A third, undoubtedly Athena, was standing off to the side. Despite their identical latex faces and uniform dress, the gang's requisite 'psychotic shithead' was not difficult to distinguish, as it was impossible to imagine him engaged in his two colleagues' present activity. They were talking to each other in a heightened register, their exchanges too absurd and inconsequential to be anything other than dialogue, by which much of the forcibly assembled audience were nonetheless intrigued.

'What do we do now?' the little one asked.

'Wait.'

'But while we're waiting?'

'What about hanging ourselves?'

'Gets my vote,' shouted one of the hostages, prompting a few giggles.

'We'd get a boner out of it,' resumed the little one, to greater laughter.

Angelique looked round at Jarry, who was closing the security door gently, as though to avoid disturbing the performance. Similarly affected, Angelique spoke to him in a whisper.

'What the fuck is this?'

'I told you they were waiting.'

'What for?'

'You're a detective, you work it out.'

Angelique watched in silence for a few more disbelieving moments.

'Am I heavier than you?' the midget asked his strappingly built companion.

'You tell me. I dunno. There's an even chance. Kinda.'

'So what do we do?'

'Nothin'. Safer that way.'

'Wise words,' Jarry reminded her.

'Let's wait and see what he says,' suggested the little one.

'Who?'

'Godot,' whispered Angelique in tandem with the midget, the penny belatedly dropping. 'You absolute arsehole,' she hissed at Jarry, but was unable to prevent a brief giggle as she spoke.

Jarry's shoulders were shaking with silent laughter.

'Are you hoping to plead insanity? Have you heard Carstairs is nicer than the Bar-L?'

Jarry reopened the security door and beckoned her back inside. A member of the 'audience' turned around at this point, noticing the movement behind her. She looked briefly at Angelique, enough to take in the significance of her body armour and the greater significance of her restraints, then back at the performance, evidently the larger draw upon her attention. Having satisfied herself that the intrusion was not about to precipitate a full-scale rescue, Angelique was half expecting the woman to say 'shhh!'

Not everybody was watching the show, it had to be said. There was a group of men squatting on the floor behind the seated hostages, mostly wearing football colours: some Rangers, some Celtic. They were talking, but quietly so as not to disturb the performance. She made out a few words here and there, beneath the declamations from the 'stage', enough to suss that their rivalries had been temporarily put asunder as they discussed the one thing that bonded and unified them: how much they hated those sheep-shagging bastards from Aberdeen.

Angelique paused in the doorway, reluctant to take her eyes off the spectacle. Her statement was going to read like it had been written on Mescaline.

Jarry waited patiently for her, holding the door.

'What does it say under Spike, there?' she asked him.

'Spike?'

143

'Yeah. Saint Seb.'

'Oh, him. "Missed".'

Angelique drew on years of training and hard-learnt professional discipline in her attempt to keep a straight face, but failed utterly.

'Yeah, I liked that one too,' he agreed. 'Can't give Chagall the credit – that was one of the hostages' suggestions.'

'Chagall?'

'Yeah. You ain't seen him yet. He's workin' on Plan B.'

'I can imagine what he looks like. Roughly.'

Jarry leaned against the desk bearing the remarkably sluggish PC, and gestured to Angelique to take a seat. She opted instead for leaning against another desk, not wishing to concede the psychological advantage of being physically spoken down to.

'Who are Vladimir and Estragon?' she asked.

'*Still* diggin'. For the record, Ionesco and Dali, respectively. Dali is the taller of the two. You're familiar with the play?'

'I know it better in French. They're taking some liberties with the translation.'

'Oh sure, *that*'ll be why you didn't recognise it straight off. Excuses, excuses. You speak French?'

'I speak French, Spanish . . .' Angelique stopped herself mid-sentence, some remnant of practical awareness enough to derail her inexplicably casual train of thought. 'What's going on here?' she asked. 'I mean, is this all . . .' She fumbled for words, unsure of even what her questions should be.

'I guess at this point you're thinkin' it would be easier to get your head around if we'd cracked open a few skulls and everybody out there was pissin' their pants.'

'Sounds messy. But you're right: I was off the day my

cadet class did Situationist Robbery Counteraction Techniques. Care to give me a few pointers?'

'You're doin' okay so far. Strictly speaking I wouldn't say Situationist. Situationism is by definition an end in itself. What we're doing is merely a means. Though whether skull-cracking or Situationist, your priority is the same: hostage safety.'

'I think what's got me off-balance is how much of a priority it seems to be for you.'

'I told you: I'm not the bad guy.'

'No offence, but given what you're doing here, you're not quite coming off as the good guy either.'

'You're telling me this isn't a face you can trust?'

Angelique smiled, having decided it was pointless to resist. In light of the unfolding events, she was feeling decreasingly motivated to play the police's 'number one bad ass', as he put it, and guessed it wouldn't make much of an impact anyway. She was also under the unavoidable impression that he liked her, and felt strongly drawn to preserve this status. This was for three reasons, only two of which – self-preservation and professional expedience – could be classed as rationally justified under the circumstances. The third was that Jarry was being as solicitous, respectful and pleasantly attentive as anyone had been to her for a long time, and she wasn't in any great hurry for it to stop.

'I'm not the good guy,' he continued, Angelique's smile encouraging him to open up. '*You*'re the good guy. Girl. Woman.'

'Thank you.'

'But I do find it practical to be a *nice* guy. Hostage psychology. They know you're in control as long as you're the one pointing the gun, so you don't need to scare the shit out of them the whole time. Those people out there know we ain't about to let them go if they just ask nicely, but they ain't worried we're about to blow their brains out either. So they sit there, doing what they're told, waiting, patiently.'

'For Godot.'

'Boredom adds to the stress factor. Nothing else to think about but fear. Fear leads to desperation. So we help them pass the time.'

'It would have passed anyway.'

'Touché. You *do* know the play.'

'And what if they decide to stop taking you seriously?'

'Do I look like a guy who wants to be taken seriously?'

'Yes: as long as you're carrying a gun, it doesn't matter how you're dressed.'

'Correct. But if you mean am I worried about someone tryin' to be a hero . . . Again, that's why you gotta be nice. The vigilante impulse rises to the surface because guys feel threatened and resentful of the power you've got over them. Minimise the animosity – let them see you're stickin' it to the bank, not to them. Hey, maybe the *bank* is stickin' it to them. Before you know it, they're even rootin' for you.'

'You've done this a lot?'

'What do you think?'

'Not round these parts. We'd have noticed, even the polis. Can I ask a less stupid question?'

'Still diggin'. Do you need the overtime? If you want, I'll sign an affidavit confirming that you pestered me for information throughout the entire duration of your detention, save us both a lot of trouble.'

Angelique took this as a No, but asked anyway: 'How are you planning to get out of here?'

'Richer,' he replied.

She threw her head back and sighed in exaggerated exasperation. What was the use? Like the hostages out front, she ought to just sit back and enjoy the rest of the show. When you find yourself in a hole, you should know when to . . . ah, shit.

'About this affidavit,' she said.

Jarry clapped his latex-sheathed hands. 'She's learning.'

'I finally sussed why you've been telling me to quit digging. It wasn't a reference to information, was it?'

Jarry shook his head. 'Friendly advice.'

'I wish you'd been there to offer that advice when I made the mistake of getting out of bed this morning.'

There followed a pause, brief but long enough for both of them to uncomfortably contemplate the involuntary indiscretion of Angelique's last remark.

'There are a *thousand* ways you don't want me to reply to that, Officer de Xavia, so let me pay you the compliment of saying, simply and sincerely, that I wish the same thing.'

Angelique felt her cheeks burn, partly in embarrassment at those thousand other possible replies, and partly out of anger at having dropped herself into yet another hole. Jarry had enough advantages without her gifting him the opportunity to be patronising and lecherous towards his captive. The fact that he chose not to take it seemed neither here nor there. The cumulative emotional impact of the day so far was suddenly threatening to catch up with her, and for one extremely horrible moment, she feared she might actually cry, after which she'd have no option but to hurl herself at him in the hope that he'd blow her brains out.

Get it together, girl. She proffered another smile by way of camouflage. 'I'm still digging and I can't help it.'

Jarry saw through it, Angelique's mask not being as

substantial as his. He looked at her silently for a second or so, his blue eyes penetrating and inscrutable as they peered from behind the latex. Angelique's reflex was to avert her own gaze, but she fought it, out of a mixture of defiance and curiosity. Those eyes were all she could see, all she'd have to identify him if their paths ever crossed again, but somehow she knew it would be enough.

The seconds stretched, the silence grew, muffled Beckett dialogue somewhere in the background.

'I get the impression it hasn't been your day so far,' he said, his voice suddenly softer.

'You got that right,' she said, sniffing back a drop of liquid that she would affirm and swear in the highest court in the land to be mucous.

'Who knows, maybe there's still time for it to work out.'

'There's a very big deficit to recover, believe me.'

'How big?'

'You mean besides getting yanked into work on my day off, to go abseiling into a besieged bank, being taken prisoner by Situationist bank robbers, getting pistol-whipped by your union-statutory psycho and having the piss taken by a smart-arse in a clown mask armed with the police-issue handgun *I* brought here?'

'Yeah,' he said, laughing. 'That's penny-ante stuff. What else you got?'

You asked for it.

'I turned thirty today.'

'Shit. Now *that's* gotta hurt.'

'Still think it could all work out?'

'Anything's possible.' He took hold of his mobile again and thumbed some keys. 'At least your team's doin' their part. Four nil. Hughes, ninetieth minute. There you go, things are lookin' up already.'

148

'I'm supposed to be going to my parents' house for dinner.'

'Okay, I'm starting to see what you mean about a deficit. On the plus side, you could still be a hostage at that point.'

'Is that a promise?'

Before Jarry could answer, they were interrupted by the emergence of another clown from a security door at the rear of the admin area, next to the staff toilets. By a process of elimination, Angelique deduced that this was the one Jarry had referred to as Chagall, who was 'working on Plan B'.

'Mr J,' he said, his voice naturally booming but slightly breathless, as though he had been running upstairs.

'Mr Chagall. Meet Officer de Xavia, who's dropped in for a while. It's her birthday, you know.'

'Hi there,' he said uncertainly. 'And happy birthday.'

Angelique sent Jarry an admonitory glare, but he was looking at Chagall.

'Are we ready to rumble?'

'Well, yes and no,' Chagall said anxiously.

'Huh?'

'I mean, we're definitely gonna rumble, but I ain't sure we're ready. You better take a look.'

'Shit.'

Jarry hopped off the desk and nodded for Angelique to do likewise. 'Where I go, you go,' he told her.

They followed Chagall hurriedly through the door and downstairs into a basement corridor, at the near end of which loomed the entrance to the safe. The glinting steel door looked like the portal to an air-lock: it was cylindrical, jutting out from the frame like a blister, hung on two enormous four-pronged hinges that tapered almost organically into the front panel. The safe was opened using a huge circular dial that looked as though it ought to be servo-assisted, and in the grip bisecting the dial's centre was a keypad with a numerical LED display, currently reading nine zeros.

Ionesco's electronic safe-cracking having become bogged down by a superannuated CPU, Chagall had been busy working on a more traditional method. There was plastic explosive - *a lot* of plastic explosive – moulded around each of the hinges, and an even larger third charge had been shaped, like a crescent moon, around the other half of the outer circumference. A network of wires connected the three moulds, traversing the door from the topmost hinge like a spare pleat from Rapunzel's tower.

Angelique was no expert, but it looked a highly professional arrangement, and she had little doubt it would be enough to take the door off of the safe. What seemed less certain was whether the building would still be standing afterwards.

'Looks good to me,' Jarry observed calmly. 'What's the problem?'

Chagall nodded towards a gadget on the floor, into which all of the wires ultimately led. Like the dial on the door, it bore a numerical LED display. Unlike the dial on the door, its numbers were changing; as in counting down in minutes, seconds and blurred decimals thereof. There were less than eight minutes remaining.

'The timer's on a ten-minute default setting,' Chagall said.

'I know,' Jarry replied, impatience creeping into his tone. Everyone present could guess what was coming, but they all still needed Chagall to hurry up and admit it before they could move on.

'So when I pressed the reset to clear it, it started counting down instead.'

'You pressed the wrong button? But there's a "confirm" option when you—'

'No,' Chagall interrupted. 'I'm telling you I pressed the reset button and the fucking thing over-rode me and started the timer.'

'But we're not ready. We're still waiting for . . . Jesus Christ, man, what the fuck?' Jarry's air of unflappable calm was evaporating rapidly. 'How could it over— I mean, how many times have you run-tested these things?'

'A thousand.'

'I've *seen* you run-test these things.'

'That's the point. I did what I've always done, but it's malfunctioned. I dunno, probably got damp in the circuits from all the fucking rain in this goddamn city.'

Jarry sighed restlessly, the tension visibly starting to exercise his limbs. 'Should have used a remote,' he said, almost under his breath.

'We went over this. There's too much stone. Banks back home are all rebar and gypsum. This place is like a goddamn cathedral. That's the only reason we could even attempt to blow a safe like this. This much charge would level most places.'

'How do you know it won't level this one?' Angelique felt compelled to inquire.

'Can't you defuse it? Just disconnect the fucking thing?' Jarry asked, both of them ignoring Angelique's question.

'Best I can do is try and run a bypass with an auxiliary circuit.'

'What will that do?'

'Given that the box is already malfunctioning, I can't honestly say. Theoretically it'll take the timer out of the loop, but it's also possible it'll just trigger the charges.'

Jarry grunted in frustration, anger rippling through him. It appeared to have passed, but then he grabbed his fake machine-gun with both hands and battered it off the wall.

151

'All that planning, all that waiting, rehearsing. We're this close and it all comes down because of one fucking short-circuit.'

'I'm sorry, man. But we have to decide what we're gonna do.'

'I need a second here,' Jarry said defensively, turning away from the two of them. 'I gotta think.'

Angelique looked again at the timer, now reading less than six minutes.

'You don't have a second,' she told him. 'You've got sixteen civilian hostages upstairs, and frankly I'm less convinced of how this building's liable to cope with what you've got wired-up down here.'

Jarry put a hand on the wall as though he needed support to stand up. He looked at Angelique but said nothing. His eyes were filled with understandable anxiety and less affordable indecision.

'Thinking about it, I'm pretty sure the auxiliary circuit should be okay,' Chagall said, less than convincingly. 'I'll give it a shot.'

'No!' Angelique demanded, stepping between Chagall and the timer. 'The circuit's screwed up.' She was trying not to shout but was unable to keep the anger from her voice. 'You can't chance it, you could bring the whole place down.'

Jarry pulled the P990 from his waistband and pointed it at Angelique to ward her away.

'You didn't risk anyone's lives before, why start now?' she pleaded. 'You're not the bad guy, remember?'

Jarry looked at her, then at the safe, at Chagall and finally back at Angelique.

'You're right,' he said, lifting a pair of pliers from among Chagall's tools. 'Turn around.'

Angelique complied. Jarry kept hold of the gun in his

152

left hand and snapped off the plastic fastener with his right.

'Thanks,' she told him, relief enhancing her sincerity. 'You're doing the right thing.'

'Come on,' he said, putting a hand on her forearm and leading her back up the stairs. 'Dunno what you're thanking me for – you're gonna make dinner at Mom's now.'

'Yeah, but at least I'll be alive to eat it.'

Jarry stopped before the security door that led to the main banking hall, holding up the Walther in his right hand. He ejected the magazine into his left and handed Angelique the empty weapon.

'Happy birthday.'

'You shouldn't have.'

'You got that right. Okay, now when we go through that door, I'm gonna call off the dogs and you're gonna lead out the hostages. Dali'll open the doors for you, I'll make sure of that. You just make sure nobody gets shot, okay?'

'Consider it done,' she said, reaching into a pocket for the mobile McMaster gave her. 'What about you?'

'Once the hostages are clear, I'll give Chagall the okay to run the bypass. If it works, then we'll have ourselves a little leverage again. No hostages, but we'll still have a bomb.'

'And if it doesn't work?'

'Let's not think about that right now, huh?'

'Fair enough.'

He reached for the doorhandle.

'Jarry?' Angelique said.

Jarry paused and turned around. 'Yeah?'

'Take care of yourself.'

'You too, Officer de Xavia.'

# exit strategies (i)

Andy was thinking about calling it a day. Darkness had
fallen and the cold was starting to take its toll on his chords,
but more significantly, the crowds had been noticeably
dwindling due to the lateness of the hour and the on-going
lack of spectacle. Since that woman with the pony-tail had
abseiled from the roof next door and disappeared into the
bank, there had been a whole lot of nothing to look at, the
front of a building being no more interesting than usual,
even if you knew there were armed robbers inside.
Nonetheless, this being Glasgow, there had been a steady
procession of shoppers gathering behind the cordons just
to verify for themselves that there was, as the police liked
to put it, 'nothing to see here', and Andy had done very
well out of the passing trade.

Even the cops – well, one of the cops – had flashed him
a smile when he gave voice to Neil Young's plea for deliv-
erance from 'the powder and the finger', though most of
them were looking less than impressed with the same
artist's reminder that there was 'still crime in the city'.

He had just closed the clasps on his guitar-case when
the cops all burst into life simultaneously, as though they'd
suddenly had their batteries changed. Radios were held to
ears, arms were pointed, heads were turned and a sense
of near-panicked urgency was palpable. Naturally, all of
this ultimately manifested itself in shouting at the public
and telling them to back off. Unlike before, the public were

enthusiastically cooperative this time, the use of the word 'bomb' proving far more efficacious than the earlier 'please'.

Andy looked back at the bank as he retreated. The double doors had opened and he could see the cop with the pony-tail leading people down the stairs, all of them moving with as much haste as their tied hands would allow. They were met by cops who escorted them away from the building at speed, putting arms around their shoulders to assist their balance as they ran.

The polis forcing the crowd back stopped at the corner of West Nile Street, but few onlookers seemed inclined to stay anyway, Andy among them. Armed sieges were one thing, but exploding buildings, like motor racing, were a spectacle best witnessed on television. You got the benefit of replays, multiple camera angles, running commentary and, most importantly, a far, far reduced risk of being disembowelled by airborne blazing debris.

He decided to head for Buchanan Street Underground Station, which was the other side of West Regent Street from where the cops had closed the pedestrian precinct. The place would be teeming with huns on their way back from the game, but as he needed the line heading towards Ibrox, his platform would be comparatively quiet.

All in all, it had turned out to be an unexpectedly successful day, almost making up the deficit inflicted by the Reverend Mumbles over recent weeks. The only down-side had been when a woman he vaguely recognised reached out and threatened to help herself to some of his takings as 'a refund'. As she rather heatedly explained, she had asked him several weeks back where she could find a recording of a tuneful little number he'd been singing about a broken relationship, having found the song personally

poignant and even a little touching. It subsequently tran-
spired that she had been disappointed, to say the least, to
discover that in Blink-182's original version of *What Went
Wrong*, Tom deLonge was not mourning the fact that his
ex had *mucked* up his life; and she didn't go a bundle on
the one about shagging household pets, either.

# exit strategies (ii)

McMaster was in his element, able to do some quality ordering about now that the tables had been turned and the bank robbers were no longer richly taking the piss out of him in front of dozens of polis and hundreds of civilians. Not even the hostages were being spared the ostentatious 'I'm in charge' performance, as he ordered them to be detained en masse in a recently commandeered bar in Mitchell Lane, off Buchanan Street.

Angelique's plea to cut them some slack after their ordeal was met with a full payload of dick-compensating authority.

'They're no longer hostages, DI de Xavia, they're now witnesses, and I want them held until they've all been logged and accounted for.'

Angelique reckoned if he got any more puffed-up, he'd be in serious danger of actually filling that coat. His smugness would have grated her nerves at the best of times, but standing there, still slightly breathless from escaping the besieged – and imminently exploding – bank, she was finding it particularly difficult to take.

'I'm leaving no loose ends,' he told her. 'These guys are going down. If you pull a stunt like this on my patch, then you pay the piper.'

Yeah, right. *His* patch. His collar. She didn't remember McMaster climbing into any buildings or facing down any gunmen, and the implication that the end of the siege was down to anything he had done was frankly embarrassing.

Up until the timer malfunction, Jarry had cut McMaster out of the entire equation.

She looked at her watch. There were less than three minutes left, unless Chagall got a result. She had only been out of the bank a matter of moments but it already felt a world away; and explosives aside, right then it seemed a preferable world to the one she'd escaped to. The company was better, for a start. There had been something about Jarry and his orchestrated insanity that at least challenged her expectations, which was a lot more than could be said for what the boys in blue had offered her lately. She'd even have to admit that part of her had been disappointed in the collapse of Jarry's scheme, if only because she'd never get to know how he had planned to escape. And while she could hardly condone Jarry's actions, it nonetheless stuck in her craw to hear McMaster talk about 'taking him down'. It was like some colonial smout in a pith-helmet shooting a snared lion. Head to head, it had been a no-contest until dumb luck intervened. Given Jarry's ingenuity, adaptability and resourcefulness, it seemed an ironic and undeserving fate that he should be collared by such a by-the-numbers dunderheid. He had anticipated so many pitfalls and improvised contingencies against other unforeseen developments, such as Angelique's own incursion, it was incredible that he should be brought down by something so trivial as a damp circuit.

Utterly incredible.

'Bastard.'

'What?' asked McMaster, outraged and misinterpreting.

The guy had the balls to mount a major robbery with fake guns, so what would he be doing with real explosives?

'It's a decoy,' she said. 'The fucking charges are fake, same as the guns. This is how he gets away, sneaky bastard.

We all run away from the building and he fucks off.'

'You're right: why would they be messing about with computers and hostages if they could just blow the door off the safe?'

Angelique drew the Walther. 'Somebody give me another clip for this. I'm going back in.'

'You're going nowhere, de Xavia, and neither are they. I've deployed armed units at all possible escape routes. Did you not think I'd anticipated this? They won't be sneaking out of any back doors or fire escapes, believe me. Clown masks and itching powder, eh? Well we're about to see who gets the last laugh.'

Which was when the explosives went off.

The sound was loud but slightly muffled; contained might even be the word. There was no flying debris and the ground didn't shake any more noticeably than whenever an underground train passed beneath the street. Angelique's first thought was to concede that they had been right about what the grand old building could withstand. Her second, upon looking at her watch and seeing that there should still have been almost a minute to go, was to hope Jarry was all right. Chagall, rather – he had been the one planning to tamper with the circuits. All of them, in fact. She hoped all of them were all right.

McMaster stepped out from behind the cordon and summoned a group of four armed officers towards him. 'Time to mop up,' he said.

'Can I come too, sir, or do I only go in when the bad guys are packin' heat?'

'Don't be huffy, de Xavia. You are required, yes, and I want you to bring the duty manager. We'll need him to reset the systems.'

The ARU went in first, in standard two-by-two cover

formation, Angelique shaking her head at the sight. McMaster looked disapprovingly at her.

'They're unarmed, sir, remember? Their guns were fake.'

'The guns were fake?' asked the duty manager, a drink of water in a suit by the name of Thomas Peat.

'You saw *one* gun that was a fake,' McMaster chided. 'The rest we don't know about.'

'I figure the one Jarry was smashing off the wall won't be up to much now, either.'

'Then you've got nothing to worry about.'

Having made their storming entrance into the building, the ARU then had to wait for Peat to open the security door so that they could access the staff-only areas. It was like seeing Rambo at a bus-stop. Once inside, they split into two groups to scour the premises, one heading upstairs to the office suite, the other more cautiously approaching the vaults below. Ignoring McMaster's orders to wait, Angelique followed the pair bound for the basement, impatiently brushing past them on the stairs as they persisted with their slow, silent stalk.

'Jarry?' she called. 'Chagall?'

The lighting in the lower corridor had failed, and visibility was further hampered by the smoke and dust that was hanging in the air. However, there was enough light from the stairwell to reveal not only that the safe was still intact, but that so were the explosives attached to it. Angelique stood staring at it in bafflement as the two armed officers ventured slowly past her, torchbeams barely penetrating the corridor's smoky darkness. McMaster and Peat followed behind them, The Coat's own curiosity for once over-riding procedural prudence, but not enough for him to go further than the foot of the stairs.

'These didn't go off,' McMaster noted, showcasing the

detective skills that had propelled him so far up the ranks.

Peat, however, made the more significant observation. 'The safe is open,' he said.

'What are you talking about?' McMaster asked. 'Look at it.'

'I'm looking at the dial. The LED is all zeroes. That's what it reads when it's unlocked. It's only this crap round the rim that's holding it shut, in fact. The door's weight makes it swing out as soon as the bolt retracts.'

Peat reached towards the moulding gripping the door's outside edge, but was grabbed by McMaster.

'Don't touch it. It's still wired up.'

'If whatever else blew up down here didn't set it off, then I don't think moving it a wee bit's likely to,' Angelique reasoned, and yanked the 'explosives' away before McMaster could issue a further eminently sensible note of caution. As Peat predicted, the door swung open to reveal a glaringly empty chamber.

'Jesus,' said the suit. 'They've cleaned us out.'

'How much?'

Peat swallowed. 'Neighbourhood of eight hundred K.'

'Upmarket neighbourhood,' Angelique remarked.

McMaster looked like he was about to retreat into the coat.

'Sir?' called a voice from the blackness. 'You better get down here. They've blown a hole through the wall.'

McMaster spun on his heel and looked down the corridor, but there was still nothing to see but a faint glow of torchlight dancing in the dust.

'Through to where?'

'Looks like a tunnel. There's tracks.' Even amid the smoke, Angelique could see McMaster's Adam's apple bobbing involuntarily in his throat. 'It's blocked at the near end. I think it's a siding for the underground. I'm not quite sure of my bearings, but I think it's heading north.'

'Buchanan Street Station,' Angelique said.

'Oh, *fuck*,' was The Coat's reaction, from which she assumed he concurred.

McMaster was issuing frantic orders into his radio as he waddled hurriedly back through the bank and into the street. One look at her watch told Angelique his efforts would be futile, and not just because Jarry's men had several minutes' start.

She walked behind him through the double doors and stood at the top of the stairs, from where she was able to attain visual confirmation. Beyond the cordons, a couple of hundred yards up the hill, there were approximately a dozen officers running flat-out towards the entrance to Buchanan Street Underground Station, where they would have absolutely no chance of getting down the stairs, because there were several hundred Rangers supporters currently swarming up them.

Angelique turned around again to face into the bank, the much-punctured Saint Sebastian staring at her from the inside of the wedged-open door. The solitary word 'missed' seemed more apposite than ever.

'You fly devil,' she said, to a man who was no longer there, and who had indeed got out richer.

'De Xavia,' McMaster growled angrily from the street. 'Get your arse down here. What are you looking at?'

But in truth Angelique wasn't looking at anything. She was just facing the other way so that he couldn't see the size of her grin.

## the lyre of orpheus plays *Follow Follow* then segues into . . .

'There's not a team like the Glasgow Rangers, no not one and there never shall be one.'

The cramped carriage was vibrating even before it pulled away, the raucous singing and stamping creating a sense of energy almost as powerful as that running through the third rail. Zal, standing next to the doors, knew he looked like the happiest guy on a train full of happy guys. His unmovable grin might not have been conducive to his disguise had Rangers lost, but as he'd known they were playing Aberdeen it hardly constituted a lucky break.

Merkland, on the other hand, was looking conspicuously pissed off, but was fortunately facing the doors, his back to his fellow passengers.

'You don't have to sing along,' Zal told him quietly, hand cupped to his ear, their conversation engulfed by the noise. 'But if you don't crack a smile soon you're gonna blow your cover.'

'What's there to fuckin' smile about?'

'Your "team" just got a result. Four-nil. Look happy. Or are you playing the never-satisfied purist?'

'Aye, that's me. See, *my* team didnae exactly get the result they were lookin' for, did they? Call me a purist if you like, but I prefer games to end with me gettin' a win bonus, in cash, know what I mean?'

'You don't think we'd all have preferred that? But we've

still gotta be professional. We always knew we had to leave the field at the final whistle regardless of the scoreline, and unless you want to be pulled aside for a very long post-match interview, you'll get into character fast.'

Merkland flashed a brief sarcastic smile, then glared at Zal again and bowed his head, at least keeping his seethingly miserable mug out of sight. What could you say? Some people simply weren't cut out for acting; perhaps if he was he'd have been better equipped to see through the performances of the four guys who were at that moment stiffing him. From the second they took off their masks until the second they stepped on to the busy platform, they'd all been faking grave disappointment at having to bail out 'empty-handed', as well as sniping bitterly at Karl for the 'failure' of his software. Jerome and Leo in particular deserved accolades, as surely even Olivier would have found despondency difficult to affect with four hundred grand strapped to his body. However, once they were in public sight, all dressed in vibrantly colourful Rangers regalia, they were able to make their true feelings manifest as part of effectively blending in.

No-one noticed five more Bluenoses slip from a door at the rear of a platform already mobbed with fans who had just disembarked and were anyway all facing the stairs. Nor did anyone on board pay any heed to the fact that they were getting *on* the train at Buchanan Street, where dozens of those en route from Ibrox were getting off. When it was as crowded as that, the guys nearest the door had to step on to the platform to allow the others to exit, so every carriage at every stop would witness a few Bears hopping aboard.

Jerome, Leo and, crucially, the money got on to a different carriage from Merkland, Zal and Karl, with all of them due to get off again at separate, pre-designated stops. Merkland was to exit first, at Cowcaddens, which meant Zal only had a couple more minutes to endure his resentful scowls. Endure? Enjoy was more like it. Zal could watch an asshole like that suffer all night. It was the only downside of using latex masks that Zal hadn't been able to see Merkland's expression when the idiot tried to shoot him. Still, priceless as it would no doubt have been, it was nonetheless nothing compared to how he was likely to react when he turned on the news and found out that close to a million pounds had walked off the train at St George's Cross and Kelvinbridge respectively.

Merkland was supposed to get into a third carriage on his own, but had predictably tagged on to Zal, still doing that 'I've got my eye on you' thing. It would have been annoying if it wasn't just plain laughable. Really, was there anything more pitiful than a would-be hard-ass who just couldn't accept that you didn't find him intimidating?

'You know, the only reason you're still alive is that you're useful to us,' Merkland growled. 'I think you should bear that in mind in light of today's grand-scale balls-up.'

'I'll meditate on it, dude. But shit, man, if usefulness was the principal criterion for survival, your ass would have been Darwinned way back.'

Zal heard Karl snigger, which warned him to keep his voice a little lower.

'Aye, very good,' Merkland sneered. 'I'm just sayin', you're bein' tolerated, for now. But when the time comes to let the dogs loose on you, I'm gaunny be there.'

'Well, that should boost my chances, shouldn't it, considering you're eternally bound to fuck up.'

'You're kiddin' yourself if you think my gun won't be loaded next time, pal.'

Zal gazed cheerfully out of the window at the station

signs as the train pulled into Cowcaddens, demonstrably ignoring Merkland's attempted threatening stare. There had been a time when guys like that could frighten him, but it was three years, seventy stitches and two bodies ago. He met Merkland's eyes again just before the doors slid open.

'And you're kidding yourself if you think it'll make a difference. Now fuck off back to Hannigan. It's your stop.'

Zal watched him walk away, but waited until the train had plunged into the darkness of the next tunnel before nudging Karl. Karl had a Rangers baseball cap pulled down to cover his face, so that to all witnesses he appeared to be a kid coming back from the game with his father. He didn't look up, but Zal could picture his grin anyway. Instead he held his palm up for Zal to slap, their fingers tightly inter-linking afterwards for a very precious couple of celebratory seconds.

It was time to breathe out. The song was starting up again, that irresistible force of volume and energy filling the air and ringing out even above the rumble of the wheels and the occasional screams of protesting metal. Zal felt as though he was channelling all of it, an exhilarated swell expanding inside him like a chain reaction as he clenched a fist and joined in. Giving it voice was an exquisite release, but only in that release could he glimpse the magnitude of the euphoria welling within.

'*Follow we will, follow we will.*'

His system had been charged with adrenalin for more than five hours, throughout which his mind had been processing, suppressing and controlling more numerous and intense emotions than anyone would normally be required to cope with over five months, maybe years. This wasn't to say he hadn't enjoyed it, every goddamn second, but like a victorious footballer, it was only once the game was over that he could let all of those stored feelings course through him.

'*Though the straits be broad or narrow . . .*'

The release, the euphoria, the catharsis would have come anyway, but that it should be in the throes of this song caused it to disturb something stored far deeper, and thus Zal found himself singing with tears in his eyes and a treasured sadness in his smile.

'*If they go to Dublin, we will follow on.*'

His dad used to sing him that song, though in its original form, without that shitty '*Dundee, Hamilton, even to the Vatican*' adulteration. He'd learned it and sung it as a kid before he even knew what it was about, before he really understood that this place his dad came from and missed so much wasn't just another town in Nevada. But he now realised that, apart from on TV, he had never heard anyone else sing it, so to hear it up close, in that accent he'd once associated with only one person in the world, made him feel suddenly very vulnerable and more than a little alone.

Maybe it was just as well, as he needed something to rein in his jubilation. It was one thing to blend in with the guys coming back from the match, but nobody else had been looking quite so delirious. After all, it was only Aberdeen, and only four-nothing.

He watched Jerome and then Leo drift away along platforms, among more departing Bears, then it was his and Karl's turn at Hillhead. They said nothing to each other, keeping their accents to themselves, Karl's head bowed and the peak of his cap still tipped low over his face. Byres Road was dark, busy and very wet. The rain must have started recently, as all the Bears on the underground had been bone dry and nobody in the street seemed to have an umbrella. People were walking close to the buildings, dashing between awnings and hovering hesitantly in shop doorways. Zal and Karl just had to hit the sidewalk and head towards Great Western Road. They made it as far as Hillhead Library when they saw Leo's car approach, identified to them in the dark and rain by a flash of the headlights and the fact that it was indicating to pull in.

Karl opened the rear passenger-side door and climbed in, pulling off the baseball cap once he was out of sight. Zal leaned inside. Nobody said anything, they just all smiled and laughed then joined in a brief three-way grip.

He closed the door and watched the car pull away. There was still important business to be concluded in Glasgow, but given the rarity of American-accented adults under four feet in the city, it was vital that Karl laid low until he was next needed. They were heading south, to Newcastle, where they had a restaurant table booked for 8:30 as well as a pocketful of forged on-course betting slips from that afternoon's race meeting at Gosforth. Even now, Karl would be downloading the results to his WAP phone then filling in the final odds and discarding any winners, bookies having a better memory for people they paid out to.

Jerome was still in town, but Zal didn't feel a desire for celebration, even if it was private and discreet. He stepped back and took temporary cover outside the library's front entrance. With the rain still running down his face and the world busily rushing past, he felt much as he might if he'd spent the afternoon in the cinema: once he was back outside in a cold, wet reality, what had just unfolded, however dramatic, was nonetheless already closed off and filed under Memory.

He could still feel a buzz running through him, but it was hard to connect it to specific moments, merely a residual impression. The euphoria was fading, as were the tension and the fear. They would be replaced in time by satisfaction and relief, followed a little later by exhaustion. However, for now, something else remained; something he hadn't quite noticed until more immediate concerns were out of the way, but which had been there for a while nonetheless, occasionally glimpsed amid larger but temporary distractions.

It wasn't to be trusted. It was like an email attachment from an unknown sender: he didn't know where it was coming from, and that meant it was potentially disastrous to do anything other than ignore it.

There were a number of plausible sources, any one or any combination of which could be responsible for a fragility that might be causing him to obsess. He was suffering an inevitable come-down after the robbery, a natural reaction to running on nervous energy for five, maybe six hours. There was an unavoidable anxiety bound to be preying on his insecurities considering he had just stolen almost a million notes and was about to have every cop in the country looking for him. Then there was that song, and all the little emotional cluster-bombs it had scattered. He was missing his father, loving him again, hating himself for hating him before, all that shit. To say nothing of those Rangers fans on the train and the bond among total strangers as they joined in the singing; united by something that made them feel they belonged together, made them feel they belonged period.

And maybe it was none of that. Maybe it was just something that had snuck in through his defences while his mind was busy dealing with everything else. But the bottom line was that he couldn't get the girl out of his head. While every other aspect of the robbery was fading to the point of feeling like it had happened to someone else, she remained vivid, tangible, real; and without question she had happened to him. He didn't know how, he didn't know why, but then again who ever does? She was striking to look at, that was a no-brainer. Admittedly, not having been laid in four years kind of lowered the threshold on what it took for a female to grab his attention, but that considered, none of late had held his eye quite so demandingly, even after she'd been disarmed. Zal didn't have a Kevlar fetish or anything, but it was difficult not to be taken by the sight of a woman so apparently petite and unquestionably pretty, yet kitted for action and dressed literally to kill.

However, none of that would have been more than jerk-off material if it wasn't that *some*thing had been going on back there. Needs had dictated that he be at his most rationally analytical throughout the afternoon's proceedings, so it wasn't merely his imagination that she had seemed on the verge of opening up to him a couple of times. She was trained to remain cool in that kind of situation, granted. Despite what she'd told him, she was probably also an adept negotiator. These things offered a plausible explanation for the fact that they had shared a civil conversation under circumstances in which basic politeness might ordinarily have been a lot to expect. But goddamn it, Zal knew when he was being 'managed', and that didn't include sniffing back tears or confiding that you turned thirty that morning and weren't handling it too good. This while he's standing there with a clown mask and a gun?

No. Something had definitely been going on. She had all the reason in the world to be pissed at him, even if that asshole Merkland had just tied her up *without* taking a few easy digs. To give himself some credit, after that Zal must have seemed surprisingly civilised, not just by comparison, but by expectation. He'd been on the receiving end from plenty of asshole cops in his time, as had anybody engaged in trying to earn a dishonest living, so he understood why the average dick didn't get many Christmas cards from D-Block. However, the one thing he couldn't understand was how sore some cons were on all cops, as a rule, like they were offended by the very idea of these guys attempting to catch them. They were fucking criminals, for Christ's sakes. What did they want? Understanding? A greater tolerance of their alternative lifestyle, and in particular the aspect involving unauthorised removal of other people's property?

It had briefly crossed Zal's mind to tie up Merkland and let de Xavia loose on him, but they at least needed the fucker to be able to walk, and bloodied faces didn't blend inconspicuously with football crowds, except maybe after Old Firm games.

He wasn't sure she'd have taken him up anyway. Whatever she said, if she was the one the cops sent in first, then it meant she could be trusted not to lose it, especially in the face of provocation. Chances were it also meant she could seriously take care of herself and she wouldn't need Merkland tied up to kick him six ways from Sunday. She'd barely given Merkland a thought, in fact, once the phoney gun had been revealed and the threat lifted. All she cared about were the hostages. Zal had known cops who would leave the victim bleeding on the sidewalk while they chased down a mugger, because to them it was a war, with bagging bad guys counting more than collateral damage. De Xavia was no such zealot, and it didn't sound like she was exactly at one with her colleagues, either. She had attitude. Nah, that was a stupid word, over-used to make some kind of cheap virtue out of being an arrogant loud-mouth. Thus devalued it didn't describe her at all, and it certainly didn't do her justice. She had *character*.

He liked her accent, the sound of her voice, especially when she was being casually deprecatory and yet somehow polite. It was, it was . . .

It was nuts. This was nuts. Having just done, well, what he had just done, he should have been basking in the after-glow, reflecting on what it all meant, whatever. Instead, he was standing in the rain and trying to picture her face, wondering where she was right now. Picking through the evidence, taking witness statements and generally making preliminaries towards nailing his ass, was the answer to that.

Forget her. Get the girl out of your kitchen, man.

The rain was getting heavier, and a wind was picking up, whipping the downpour under the awnings and into the doorways to deny any real shelter to those not behind bricks and glass. He could hail a cab, but he could already hear the hack giving his statement: 'Aye, I picked up a bloke with a Yank accent on Byres Road around the time you're talkin' aboot. He stuck in my mind because he'd a Rangers scarf on, but he didnae seem tae know much aboot what happened at the gemme.'

There was a bus-stop across the street. Any bus heading across Great Western Road would do, as long as he had change. He put a hand in his trouser pocket and was surprised to encounter a piece of plastic, which he pulled out and examined. It was de Xavia's ID card.

'Angelique,' he spoke quietly to himself, staring at her picture. Insane thoughts were filling his head. He was already calculating probabilities, exposure, contingencies, cover. If he could rob a bank of over a million bucks and walk out under the noses (okay, twenty feet under the noses) of at least fifty cops, surely he could find a way to . . .

Don't be nuts.

No, it was insane. Possible, but insane.

Possible.

No.

No.

No.

And that's final. Closed. Over. *Punto.*

Good. There was too much at stake, too much already worked for, too much still to be done. This was no more than a dangerous distraction, and he was glad to have torpedoed it before it did any damage. But with that resolved, what would it hurt to . . .

# stolen property

Angelique advanced quietly on the balls of her feet and stopped a few yards short in the corridor, holding her breath. She hadn't been seen, she was sure, otherwise there would have been a reception committee already in wait. There had been a look-out posted, visible from a distance to the trained eye, but her practised stealth in the approach ensured they wouldn't have the drop on her. Mind you, she'd thought the same thing on the roof of the bank, and look how that had worked out.

The door was in sight, but she needed to be psyched before she made her move. She felt a low, sinking dread, dull and heavy in her stomach like a regretted haggis supper. Why the hell was she doing this? she asked herself for the dozenth time. The answer remained the same, inflexible and unfeeling: duty. It covered a multitude of endurances and sacrifices, didn't it? None of which ever really had to be explained or justified while they hid behind that word.

Duty. Aye, right. This, under any other circumstances, constituted self-harm, and she didn't remember signing up for it.

But bugger it, what else was she going to do at this stage? Walk away? Tempting in theory, but experience told her the required explaining would be a worse ordeal still. There was no going back, so she might as well just accept it and concentrate her efforts on survival.

She took a deep breath, bit her lip and rang the door-bell.

'Angelique, *mon cher*, *mon petite*, happy birthday!' her mother yelled, her voice booming around the close as she pulled her into a warm embrace, reminding Angelique as always why she really 'put herself through this'. Here was one person who would never let her down or take her for granted. Of course, within ten minutes she'd be climbing the walls to escape, but it wouldn't be family otherwise.

'Dad didn't see your car, we were looking out for you. Come in, come in, birthday girl. It's great to see you.'

'You too, Mum.'

She stepped into the hallway, bracing herself and wondering how long it would be before her mum brought up those horizon-dwelling males. The current average was approximately five minutes, roughly as long as it took to boil the kettle, dish out some biscuits and sit her daughter near-forcibly on the new settee. However, this being some-thing of a milestone occasion, a new record might be set at either end of the scale: all-time quickest to cut desper-ately to the chase, or all-time latest if it was kept for a more profound – and prolonged – contemplation later.

Her dad emerged from the kitchen and gave her a hug and a kiss. It felt the same now at thirty as it had when she was three. Comforting, safe, home. The ten-minute rule, however, still stood.

'There's something for you in here,' Mum said, causing Dad to roll his eyes with an indulgent but slightly arch smile. 'We're dying for you to see it.' Mum wore a strangely conspiratorial grin as she led the way, beckoningly impa-tient, towards the living room. To Angelique, it felt like an ambush, and she should know.

She walked towards her usual spot on the settee, but her

mum was pointing towards the fireplace, doing a good impression of an over-excited toddler about to wet herself. Angelique turned around, ready to be blindsided for the second time that day. At least this time nobody would be pulling at her nose.

In front of the fireplace was the most elaborate and beautiful bouquet of flowers Angelique could imagine outside of Graham Norton's dressing room.

'They arrived earlier this evening,' Mum said, barely able to contain herself. 'And there's a little card. Are you going to open it?'

The temptation to say no was enormous, but Angelique's own curiosity was probably close to rivalling her mother's. Who the hell would send her flowers? If she had a secret admirer, then he had certainly lived up to the name, covert enough to be in MI5. Probably from someone at HQ to say thanks, having remembered that rescuing the hostages was quite important, even if the RSGN did lose close to a mill.

She bent down to examine the envelope, sitting in the heart of the arrangement. It said simply 'Angelique', no rank, no surname. So much for 'thank you' then, realising as she read it how absurdly implausible her first theory had been. She pulled the envelope delicately away from the flowers and gently tore it open with her thumbnail. Her forefinger slid out a white card, which appeared to be blank until she turned it over to reveal only the words 'Happy Birthday', hand-written in ornately calligraphic script. Secret admirer right enough, so anonymous as to be taking the piss.

'Who's it from? Or aren't you going to tell us?' Mum said with exaggerated coyness.

'It doesn't say,' Angelique replied. She squeezed her hand to scrunch the envelope, which was when she felt that there was something else inside, smaller than the card, but flat and stiff. 'Hang on.'

'What?'

Angelique flattened the envelope and reached inside it, pulling out her own laminated warrant card.

'You've got to be kidding,' she said, swiftly pocketing the ID before her mum had time to see what it was.

'What is it? Who's it from? Do you know?'

'Oh, I know,' Angelique said, unable to keep a sly grin of her own off her face.

Mum clapped her hands, still the excited wee lassie. 'I knew it! You've been keeping secrets. Who is he?'

'I can't say,' she replied truthfully.

'Oh come on, tell us. Is it someone you know through work?'

'Eh, yes, actually.'

'A lawyer? Please not another policeman.'

'He's neither, he's . . . kind of in an associated profession.'

'Why didn't you tell me? Has this been going on long? Have you had many dates?'

'No. Just the one, to be honest.'

'But it must have gone well, eh?'

'Mum, please.'

'Look at her, Joseph, she's going all bashful. I bet he's handsome. Is he rich?'

'He has just come into some money, as it happens.'

'Oh, I knew it, I knew it. Now, you've got to tell us more.'

'It's very early days. We barely know each other.'

'But you *are* going to see each other again, right?'

Angelique looked again at the bouquet and nodded.

'Believe me, I'll be doing everything in my power to make that happen.'

177

# II

# for my next trick
# i'll need a volunteer

It is as pleasant to be cheated as to cheat.

**Edwin Sachs,** *Sleight of Hand: A Practical Manual of Legerdemain*

# the american ambassador

Fuckin' great.

Another fuckin' city, another fuckin' hotel, but oh my, thank you sweet Jesus, another fuckin' blow-job.

Wasn't that just the cure-all? Jet-lag? Hangover? Lower-back pain? Stress? You fuckin' name it, a retail blow-job could make it all go away. It was the only thing that honest-to-God, guaranteed, truly worked, and that was probably why it hadn't been patented, processed and packaged by Astra-Zeneca or SmithKline Beecham. Drug companies weren't interested in *cures*, because where's the fuckin' money in that? They cure you and you fuck off, go do somethin' else, make *money* for somebody else. They were only interested in shit that they could sell you to make you feel just a little bit better, so you'd keep coming back for more. That was why there were no TV spots or celebrity endorsements for retail blow-jobs. 'Here's Don Simpson, for 1-800 SUCK-YOU . . .' Or 'Hi, my name is Hugh Grant. Whenever I'm feeling under the weather, I reach for . . .' Seriously, who the fuck would want Demerol after seeing that?

'Course, one of the major contributors to stress in your life can be wondering where your next blow-job is coming from, and that's no fuckin' joke. Prior to this little gift from the gods dropping into his lap within the past hour, this had been shaping up to be one bum trip.

Glasgow for Christ's sakes. Who the fuck even knew where the place was? He'd never heard of it six months

181

ago, and up until Saturday night he'd never have thought he'd be learning more about it than its name. But that was before Innez fucked the Scottish guys, the Scottish guys phoned Alessandro, Alessandro shit a brick and called Miguel, and Miguel told Harry to get on a fuckin' plane and straighten things out. What was there to straighten out? Nothing that he could see. The main event was unaffected – not even Innez would mess with them over that. But feathers were ruffled, egos were bruised and everybody was suddenly a whole lot more jumpy.

'We need an envoy,' Miguel had said.

'We already got Rico and Gomez goin' over for the exchange. Why can't we just bring their trip forward?' Harry protested.

'Rico and Gomez are just bagmen, and let's face it, they look like fuckin' bagmen. Innez has got the Escoceses thinking either we're gonna fuck them or that we don't take them seriously. We can't send over those two hotrods. We need to send someone of weight, smooth them down, show them some respect.'

'So I gotta go over there and kiss ass, too?'

'No, entirely the opposite. You're goin' over there to show we mean business. You're goin' over there to show we don't take shit from nobody.'

'I can't spank Innez's ass for bein' a bad boy, Mickey. Especially not at the request of some piss-ant third party. He knows there's only one threat that matters while we still need him to get what we want.'

'We all know that, Harry. So your job is to tell them that if we ain't worried about Innez, they shouldn't be neither.'

'Can't we do that over the fuckin' phone? To my mind, sendin' someone out there on the overnight makes it look like we *are* worried.'

'There's a difference between lookin' unworried and lookin' like we don't give a fuck. Your job is also to show them we do care that Innez pissed them off, as well as providing a little on-site management for us. You're gonna be our ambassador, Harry.'

'Yeah, sounds like a fuckin' honour.'

'It is. Haven't you ever wanted to visit Europe?'

'Scotland's in Europe?'

'Of course. Where the fuck you think it was?'

'I dunno. I guess I never thought about it before.'

'You better start thinkin' about it now. You leave LAX at six-thirty this evening.'

'Fuckin' great.'

Mickey had made it sound like they'd be lining up around the block for this job, just because it was overseas. Europe, yeah right. Fuckin' A. Did Mickey think Amerigo sailed because he *liked* fuckin' Europe? Hell no. It was the First World, and that had to be better than the Third World, but if you already had the New World, what the fuck would you want with the old one? And Scotland? What the fuck was in Scotland? Men in skirts? If he wanted to see that, he could go down to West Hollywood or up to San Fran. Jesus, did they even have TV in a country like that?

But boom, here he was. One minute he's making plans to hit Vegas for a few days, maybe bet on the play-offs, the next he's barely got time to pack his bags before catching the Saturday night flight, connecting in London and checking into the Glasgow Hilton by dinner time Sunday. Local dinner time, leastways. He didn't know *what* fuckin' hour it was back in civilisation, and his body was still running its LA schedule. As a result he felt constantly hungry but nauseous as soon as he ate anything; drop-dead tired but wide awake whenever he closed his eyes.

The hotel was, fortunately, your regular standard Hilton: same shit as every other fuckin' Hilton he'd ever been in, but that was a comfort when he was feeling disoriented and a long way from home. It turned out they did have TV too, though a shitload of good it was. The play-offs were on back home – the fuckin' play-offs – and not one fuckin' channel here was showing them. Click: soccer. Click: soccer. Nothing but fuckin' soccer. It was a disappointment if not a surprise. As far as Harry was concerned, it just proved a long-held belief that the further you got from civilisation, the less American sport was on the goddamn TV. If the immigration department wanted to smoke out the illegals in East LA, they just had to look in a few windows and the wetbacks would be the ones watching soccer. You want to blend in properly in your new, adopted home, you watch fuckin' football or baseball or basketball or hockey. The only way you'd blend in watching soccer is if you're an eleven-year-old, middle-class white girl in La Jolla. Outside of the Burbs, soccer denoted a lack of true Americanisation, and the further from the USA you got, the more pronounced the problem. Christ, at least in Mexico you still got some wrestling, but it stood to reason that if you went all the way back to Europe, to the fuckin' source, if you like, you'd find no trace of New World sport whatsoever. No use clicking your heels together, Dorothy. You and Toto won't be watching any fuckin' play-offs, even if you are bored, alone and completely incapable of sleep.

Within three hours of arriving in this alien environment, he'd therefore decided he needed the reassurance of a blow-job like never before. Sure, he was soothed a little by the comforting familiarities that the hotel had to offer, but as head wasn't on the room service menu, Hilton weren't going to be able to meet quite all of his business-travel needs.

The bad news, as it turned out, was that neither were the local purveyors he encountered during his brief nocturnal drive. A few discreet enquiries got him directed towards the Blythswood area, just a few blocks away, but when he slowed down to get a look at what was on offer, he suddenly understood that there was a more than semantic difference between saying you were desperate for a blow-job and *being* desperate for a blow-job. Jeez, what a fuckin' sorry sight. Heroin skank after heroin skank. No way he was leading one of those through the hotel lobby, never mind letting her near his dick. He'd left LA in such a hurry, he didn't have time to find out what shots he needed to visit Scotland, but he was sure there were no inoculations against what these bitches might give him. Yuck.

So instead he decided to hit the hotel bar, figuring as sleep was proving difficult, he should attempt to anaesthetise himself. In the event, sleep continued to elude him for another few hours, but the local anaesthetic was still pretty fuckin' good. Scotch, he discovered, was made in Scotland. Can you fuckin' believe that? Who knew? He'd just assumed the term denoted one of two types of whisky, the other being Bourbon, and if anyone had asked where each was made, he'd have guessed Bourbon in the South and Scotch north of the Mason-Dixon. Just goes to show: travel does broaden the mind, even if it also flattened the brain cells. It sure broadened his palate: there were dozens of different 'malts' as they called them, and he found himself taking a miniature guided tour of the Highlands and Islands via Water of Life Travel. The bartender was only too happy to tell him about the background of each and every shot that he lined up, and Harry was happy to listen, not least because it shut the guy up from talking about how Scotland invented every fuckin' thing of use on the goddamn planet.

Harry woke up at two in the afternoon, feeling better than he had any right to given how much whisky he had consumed. It was probably just the relief of having gotten any sleep at all, after reaching that stage in jet-lag where it feels like you've lost the basic ability. That didn't mean he felt good, understand, just not quite as bad as he had the same time yesterday, or maybe just as bad but for different reasons. You knew where you stood with a hang-over, at least; knew how to deal with it and how it was going to deal with you.

He took a shower and phoned Hannigan, offering him lunch at the hotel. Hannigan was having none of it, however, and insisted on entertaining Harry at some uptown restaurant where he was noted and quoted.

'You're in my town,' he said. 'Let me show you some Glaswegian hospitality.'

It was a nice touch. Nothing confrontational, nothing sulky or impatient, either. It showed respect. Subtle, too. No home court advantage bullshit like if he'd insisted Harry come to his office, with piss-ant goons hanging around trying to flex their muscles. Just the two of them over what was lunch for Hannigan and breakfast for Harry. The guy even had the grace to wait until the meal was over before broaching any shop-talk. It was little things like that that were the mark of a real boss, things that Alessandro showed no hint of understanding. Patience, for instance, wasn't a sign that you were tolerant of being dicked around: it translated into an expression of confidence that you would in time get what you wanted, because you were used to getting what you wanted. Showing deference to a guest illustrated that you recognised the criteria for respect in someone. How could you ever obtain true respect yourself if you didn't give the impression that you even knew what it was?

But the greatest evidence that the guy was a true player was that he could see the bigger picture; specifically that Innez giving them the finger wasn't worth getting too upset about when there was a deal this size to be concluded. Hats off to Miguel: it didn't take Harry flying all the way over here to make Hannigan understand this; he understood it fine, but Harry flying all the way over here *anyway* sent out all the right messages.

'I appreciate you making this trip, Mr Arthur, especially at such short notice.' Hannigan had been politely spoken throughout their prandial small-talk, but nonetheless Harry could tell the careful articulacy was a courtesy to him. He appreciated it, but it wasn't entirely necessary. The local accent was sure unusual, but back home you could hear folks talk differently if you drove over the county line. Having travelled extensively for his work, he had discovered that you can understand just about any dialect of the English language if you look the speaker in the face and actually listen to what they're fuckin' telling you. You might miss the occasional finer nuance here and there, but you seldom missed the headlines, especially in this line of work, where subtlety in communication was rare to the point of extinction.

'Please, call me Harry.'

'Sure. I didn't mean for someone to be despatched forthwith, you know? It's not that we were panicking this end, just . . . concerned, and thought you fellas would want to know the latest.'

'We appreciate that, Mr Hannigan.'

'Bud.'

'Huh?'

'You can call me Bud.'

'Oh yeah. You got it. Sorry, just sounds kinda informal where I come from, you know? Like pal.'

'Long as we're doing business, I am your pal. But it's just what people call me.'

'Bud. Cool. So, how much did he take you for, Bud?'

Hannigan sighed and took a sip of espresso. He didn't particularly like the question, which admittedly Harry could have phrased better if his brain could only catch up with the clock.

'The amount itself is not relevant, and let's be honest, it was never my money for him to take. It's certainly not significant in comparison to what we're doing business over.'

'I heard eight hundred large, sterling. What was your end?'

'Twenty percent.'

'Not exactly chump change, but yeah, it pales in the grand scheme. Plus it's twenty percent of, as you say, somethin' that was never yours. Gotta sting, though.'

'A little, yes. Kind of hard to miss the "fuck you" implied by the whole affair, which has pretty substantial ramifications for our relationship with Mr Innez, wouldn't you say? A man in my position, a man with my responsibilities, would be negligent in the extreme if he didn't interpret this as a very vivid warning about what this man is capable of.'

'Innez is not gonna waltz off with the prize this time. He's got no way of moving it, so it's worthless to him.'

'And what consolation would that be to us if we were

left empty-handed after he pulled another flanker?'

'He won't fuck us on this. Delivering it is the only way he's gonna get Alessandro off his back, and believe me, that's what Innez wants most of all.'

'Yes, I was given the impression that he is working under some duress. I'm not sure I'm entirely comfortable about that. People who don't have a vested interest in the bottom line aren't the most valuable employees, in my experience.'

Harry nodded. 'Between you, me and the sugar-tongs here, I'm not entirely comfortable with it myself, but it's what we're stuck with.'

'So is it plausible that Innez would be looking for some way of throwing a spanner in the works?'

'Innez? You bet your life he'll be lookin' for it. But as long as we've got our leverage, he won't actually do it. He ain't cut in on the bottom line, but he does have a vested interest in the success of the operation, and that's what counts.'

'You trust him, then?'

'Fuck no. But I'd say we can rely on him. He'll do what he's told.'

'Hmmm. He'll do what he's told. That was what Alessandro said. You'll forgive me if Saturday's wee pantomime tends me towards the sceptical.'

'No, I'm saying he'll do what he's told over this.'

'Alessandro gave the impression Innez was under his control.'

Harry just about managed not to laugh, but was unable to prevent a smile crossing his lips.

'I guess you didn't need what happened on Saturday to tell you otherwise,' Hannigan observed.

'Alessandro is . . . used to having people under his control,' Harry said, trying to dig himself out of dissing the kid in front of a guy they were doing business with. 'He knows that ultimately he has Innez by the balls, but he maybe didn't anticipate all the vagaries of a situation where—'

'He said Innez was on a leash. Those were his exact words.'

Oh Christ. The guy wouldn't be lying, either. Fuckin' Alessandro. Fuckin' asshole.

'He said he'd be obedient and cooperative, and he'd be effectively under my control until the big job was done.'

It was Harry's turn to sigh. No point bullshitting the guy any further; Alessandro had done that enough.

'I'll level with you, Bud, just between you and me. Alessandro doesn't know Innez, okay? I do, as much as anyone outside that freakshow can, which admittedly is not a fuckin' lot. Alessandro does have Innez by the balls right now, and yes, he will deliver. I ain't got a doubt about that. But that doesn't mean he's gonna do it with a fuckin' smile on his face and wrap up the merchandise with a big silk bow. You ask me, the bank thing was Innez markin' his territory, carvin' out a bit of pride. It was his way of sayin' yeah, he's here to do what we want, but that don't mean we own him, that don't mean Alessandro can loan him out like a fuckin' lawn-mower.'

'You reckon he robbed a bank just to prove a point?'

'Well I reckon the eight hundred K sterling was probably why he robbed the bank, but knowing Innez, yeah, provin' a point was probably on the agenda.'

'And now that he's proven his point, what's the chances of me seeing my twenty percent?'

'Zero. Nada. Stiffin' you was his way of remindin' us that we can't hurt him while we still need him to do the job. You can chase him for it later, but I would give long

190

odds on you ever seeing the guy again, never mind the money. He'll be puttin' as much effort into planning his out as into stealing the cookies. Feel free to try and second guess him.'

'Not after Saturday.'

'That's what I figured.'

'Who is he? I mean, what's his story?'

Harry held his palms up in a don't-go-there gesture, though he couldn't rightly say whether it was advice or a plea.

'I don't know much, and nothin' I *could* tell you would make you feel any more at ease. Let's just say I'll be a relieved man when this is done, and if Innez wants to disappear after that, I reckon two hundred large is cheap insurance against him coming back.'

'I hear you, pal. Do you know where he is now?'

'I can contact him, yeah. He has to stay in touch as part of the arrangement. I'll be lookin' him up pretty soon. Want me to say hi?'

'Aye, sure,' Hannigan said, returning Harry's smile.

Hannigan disappeared the check and escorted Harry to his car. Harry scanned the landscape for Hannigan's own ride. There was a Mercedes across the street with a guy in a suit behind the wheel, waiting observantly for a nod.

'Anything I can do for you while you're in town, just ask,' Hannigan said as Harry climbed into his hire car. 'Seriously. I'd be offended if you didn't. Food, drinks, theatre, tickets for the game.'

'Still recovering from the flight right now, but I'll let you know. Appreciate it.'

Harry closed the door and was about to drive off when he remembered. He rolled down the window, causing Hannigan to turn around again.

'Say, you wouldn't happen to know where I can get me a decent blow-job, would you?'

Hannigan said nothing, acting like Harry had just made a big fuckin' joke. In fact, he walked away from the car, laughing and making a 'get outta here' wave with his left hand, leaving Harry to drive back and contemplate his austerely lonely options for the evening. These pretty much amounted to watching soccer on the TV, getting shitfaced to the accompaniment of Scottish Inventions and Achievements Volume II, or forsaking his dignity and venereal well-being for the ministrations of a zombie hooker. Problem was, both of the first two had enormous potential to precipitate the third, out of, respectively, sheer desperation and gross disinhibition, though it came to much the same thing in the end. The embarrassment of letting an undead heroin skank near his dick would seem less important after a dozen shots of Glen Whatever, just like genital herpes would start to look like an acceptable risk after two hours of fucking Scottish television.

But blow the fuckin' bagpipes if this little five-foot hottie didn't just show up at his bedroom door in a tartan miniskirt, chewing gum behind an exquisitely bored smile. 'Hiya, my name's Morag,' she said, looking him up and down but hiding the results of her appraisal with practised professionalism. 'Mr Hannigan told me you might appreciate some genuine Scottish hospitality.'

'Not today, thank you.'

Yeah, right.

'Step right in, Morag. You're a sight for jet-lagged eyes, believe me.'

'Jet-lag, is it? I know just the thing.'

Aw yeah.

# fables of the reconstruction

Less than two hours into her shift on Monday morning, Angelique was starting to wonder whether she had obliviously slept for forty-eight hours and was now trying to catch up with the week. Investigations could progress rapidly in the Glesca Polis, but change normally happened at a geological pace, so the differences since she'd left on Sunday afternoon were proving a lot to take in.

She had been generously allowed to clock off after submitting her report, though it had remained dubiously hazy whether this was in acknowledgement of her contribution the day before or a cheap way of buying back the day off they had peremptorily nabbed. Either way, she was glad to leave early for a change, even if it was only to spend an evening alone in her flat, 'drinking supermarket Merlot and listening to that depressing Mogwai garbage', as her brother James had accurately predicted over dinner on Saturday night.

When she'd left, McMaster was throwing tantrums as his CID underlings set up their incident room. Angelique had enjoyed the luxury of being amused by it, figuring Special Branch's connection to the case had begun and ended with her being briefly roped into the rescue mission.

Come Monday morning, it seemed the scenery painters had been confusingly busy overnight. As she passed on the stairs she could see that McMaster's incident room had been struck, barely a drawing pin left, while further down

193

the corridor there was a lot of purposeful lifting and carrying going on. When she got to her desk, there was a message waiting for her, requesting that she 'nip down and have a word with DCS Shaw as a courtesy'. A brief toddle downstairs not only revealed the full extent of the upheaval, but also happily confirmed that 'nipping down' would not entail a flight to London, where Jock Shaw had been working for at least the past three years.

Angelique got a heads-up from Pollyanna Bailey, whom she had encountered as she stood staring at the ferment of unaccustomed enthusiasm surrounding the assembly of a new, larger hub for the inquiry. In short, McMaster had been binned, or rather was 'taking leave due to stress', though there were unconfirmed reports that his coat had turned up for duty on its own. The gen was that as he had had the piss taken out of him so comprehensively by the robbers already, the brass weren't backing him to make up the short-fall in the second leg. Thus, Jock Shaw, the one-time star player who'd since moved on to bigger things, was being brought back on loan to try and turn the tie around.

She had never worked with Shaw, but had sure heard plenty about him in the years since he had gone to the Big Smoke. The impression she'd been given was preposter-ously larger than life, as people only become when the real thing isn't around to temper exaggeration. He was 'old school', she heard guys remark with embarrassingly boyish reverence. By this she assumed they meant he was a thug with a badge, with only marginally more regard for the law than the neds he put away but a robust sense of self-justification best expressed through clichés about doing a dirty job and not being able to make an omelette without breaking a few noses. In fact, as she quickly realised within minutes of meeting him, these guys were talking about some bedtime story *übercop*, 'the kind they don't make any more', that they wished Shaw had been, rather than the reality, which was a wily but pragmatic thief-taker who'd never have got where he was if a fraction of the myths about him were true.

He was directing the placement of a series of blown-up photographs of the bank's interior around the walls of the incident room when Angelique politely introduced herself. Shaw turned around and greeted her with an unsettlingly knowing smile, then ushered her out towards his temporary office.

'I read the report on Dubh Ardrain,' he said, leading her along the corridor. 'Pile o' shite. They were just coverin' up the fact that you bailed them oot. They've written it up so it looks like everything that was touch-and-go was doon to you bein' aff the leash, rather than doon to them no' havin' a scoob what was happenin'. Bawbags, the lot o' them. You're the wan keepin' them in a job, Detective, and don't forget it.'

It was going to be hard to dislike him after that.

The 'courtesy' turned out to be at least a little on his part too, in as much as he was politely asking for her input even though he had already cleared it with her superiors for Angelique to be informally assigned to his investigation. There was a time when she would have thrown a quality strop about falling behind on her own on-going cases, but right now she just couldn't be arsed. Maybe it was all that Merlot and Mogwai inducing an existential listlessness, or maybe it just didn't seem to make much difference whether she was being fucked about by CID or fucked about by Special Branch.

'You were there, you spoke to the guy,' Shaw explained. 'That doesnae mean you could spot him in a crowd,

195

obviously, but I reckon you'll at least be able to tell us when we're barkin' up the wrong tree. I just want you to sit in on briefings and let me sound you out when I need to. That fair enough?'

'Sure.'

There were worse ways to spend a Monday morning, and it was instructive to watch the proceedings from the comfort of an 'informally attached' perspective, particularly when it gave her a ringside view of how Shaw operated.

Angelique didn't know whether the exact statistics backed it up, but it was an enduringly valuable truism that most murders were solved within twenty-four hours. Thereafter, the chances of a solution diminished at an exponential rate, with the seven-day point demarking the steepest drop-off. This was usually explained in the media as being due to the 'trail going cold' or 'the chain of evidence breaking down', or some other such melodramatic keech. In practice, the reason for the tapering success rate was quite simply that most murder cases were laughably obvious, and if an arrest hadn't been made within twenty-four hours, it was because it had turned out to be a bit less straightforward than husband/boyfriend stabs wife/girlfriend or jakey lowlife bludgeons fellow jakey lowlife after three-day drinking binge. When you found a strangled corpse in the kitchen, you didn't have to round up Professor Plum or Colonel Mustard if the kitchen also contained two used syringes, half a dozen tea candles, twenty-odd screwed-up scraps of aluminium foil and one incoherent but weepingly contrite smack-head.

With a robbery, the investigative odds followed a similar curve, but Shaw, despite a degree of private candour towards Angelique, wasn't acknowledging that in front of the troops. It was easy to see how he earned his popularity and commanded so much enthusiasm. He was working the room energetically, part showman on stage and part manager in the dressing room, drawing contributions from all voices in the gathering. Some were significant, some banal, but the important thing was that everyone felt involved.

At this stage, an exciting sense of momentum always built up as the available information was collated, giving the impression that pieces of the puzzle were already starting to fall into place. But sitting on the outside for a change, Angelique could see that they were really only recapping or confirming what was already known, and as any child could tell you, the first pieces of a jigsaw to match up were the straight bits around the outside, which seldom gave any clue as to what was at the centre of the picture. Shaw's talent was in making his charges believe they would find it anyway.

'All right, as you all know, I just got here at pretty short notice and therefore I've not had time to wade through forty-odd witness statements, fascinating as I'm sure they all are. So I'm gaunny outline what I think I know so far and I want you lot to fill in the blanks.

'At approximately 11:45 on Saturday morning, five men dressed in overalls and clown masks exit – and it would be fair to say abandon – a van in a lane off South Hanover Street. What do we know about the van?'

'Total rustbucket stolen a fortnight ago from a builder's yard in Maryhill, sir,' came a reply. 'Owner very disappointed about it being found, as an insurance write-off would have been a better deal than trying to offload it or even scrap it. All prints exterior and interior matching owner or employees, consistent with accounts that the perpetrators were wearing latex gloves.'

'So they steal a heap of shit with wheels that nobody's likely to be keeping an eye on – or an eye out for later. It doesn't matter that it's not a reliable getaway vehicle because they only need it to get them there. After that, they wander casually round to Royal Exchange Square, attracting plenty of attention but crucially no suspicion because, well, let's face it, it's broad daylight on a busy Saturday morning and if you're up to something naughty you don't dress like Ronald McDonald. To compound this and indeed maximise their visibility, they make the short trip round to Buchanan Street, dancing to the accompaniment of music on a portable hi-fi, and proceed to perform for the passing . . . What is it?' Shaw asked, in response to a raised hand.

'It's who they were dressed like, sir. It wasn't Ronald McDonald. We interviewed this busker, and for what it's worth he said they were all supposed to look like somebody called Zal Clermiston. He was pretty strong on the point, said not just the masks, but the colour pattern on the overalls were a match too. Clermiston was—'

'An Edinburgh suburb,' Shaw interrupted. 'Zal *Cleminson* was, if I can remember the Seventies through the haze, the guitarist with the Sensational Alex Harvey Band, late of this parish. Described once as a cross between Jimmy Page and Marcel Marceau. An unmistakable sight in his time and one that these blokes must have known would be recognised by at least somebody.'

'Sorry, sir. Cleminson. The busker also said they were playing an Alex Harvey song on their stereo as they entered the bank.'

'Which one?'

The officer consulted his notes. '*Faith Healer*.'

'Very dramatic. Now, it's a wee while since I've been in

Tam Shepherd's, but I don't imagine five latex Zal Cleminson masks would be available over the counter. Somebody get on to where they came from: if they were made to order, who by?'

'Yes, sir.'

'Now, still dancing, they enter the bank, where everybody, including the staff, thinks it's a stunt up until the point that guns are drawn and orders are given. They speak in American accents of varying authenticity. I'd say this could be an attempt to put us off the trail and disguise the fact that they're local, if it wasn't that nobody round here has ever given the impression of being remotely capable of pulling off something like this. If they were, they'd have done it before now. That said, we now know they chose to dress up as a Seventies Glaswegian rock guitarist, the significance of which I have no time to dwell upon.'

Another hand went up.

'A similar anomaly, sir: several witnesses report that the leader, "Jarry", commenced the robbery with the words "Alakazammy, stairheid rammy". Two witnesses and in fact a few officers have remarked that the phrase is familiar, though they're all buggered if they can remember where from.'

Shaw nodded thoughtfully. 'Rings a bell with me, too. The stairheid rammy part is familiar to anybody who's ever witnessed an argument up a close, obviously, but the first bit sounds like a magic word. Abracadabra, Open Sesame, that kinna thing. Another smart-arsed joke, perhaps, of which we know these guys are fond, and very possibly another red-herring that it would amuse them to know we were fishing for.'

Shaw walked a few feet towards one of the interior blow-ups.

'So far, it's a lot of show and clever distraction, but no matter how good your element of surprise, you're still not gaunny stop somebody hitting the panic button and locking down the vault. At that point, you can maybe pull a couple of grand from loose cash behind the till and then hopefully walk back out into a crowd who already think you're harmless. No, *here*'s where they really start to distinguish themselves. They're after the big prize and they're in it for the duration, so they need to get themselves dug in. They take hostages, but not everybody who happened to be there at the time. They release the very young, the very old, the pregnant and the infirm, eradicating liabilities and rogue elements, such as a heart attack or a woman going into labour. It also goes down pretty well with the remaining captives because it suggests they're not being held by merciless psychopaths. In fact, on the whole they are polite, calm and even respectful, with one exception, of whom more anon.

'With several folk being allowed to walk out the front door and the silent alarms triggered, they know the cavalry will be along soon, so the next thing they do is blank out all views into the bank, meaning we can't see what's going on and definitely can't start taking pot-shots when the ARU arrive. Moving this one stage further, they effectively take out our ARU using non-lethal means and causing no lasting damage. It's a message, telling us that they don't want anybody getting shot and that everybody should just cool their jets.'

Shaw then paced across to another photo, this time showing the improvised gallery that had been exhibited on the bank's doors and windows.

'Meanwhile, inside, their crowd control is . . . ostensibly mental but practically superb. They paint pictures, invite audience bloody participation and even put on a play. Every apparently insane thing they did was actually for a very good reason. In this case, they reduce the tension and with it the risk of desperate action on the part of their hostages, who stop worrying about getting their heads blown off and instead concentrate on wondering how long they're gaunny be stuck there. But this in itself is part of the ruse. They get the duty manager to submit his pass-code and tell everybody what their plan is: hacking the computer system to open the safe, which is gaunny take a wee while so everybody might as well get comfy. All the time, however, they know they're leaving at the back of five. Why is that, Officer Ford?'

Ford grinned bashfully, happy that his techie obsessive-ness had earned him a rare moment in the limelight, but in true geek fashion not entirely comfortable about addressing more than three people outside of IRC.

'Because they had actually hacked the computer system twenty-four hours previously, sir, and may in fact have had full remote access privileges for days, even weeks before that.'

There were many sighs and much wry head-shaking around the incident room.

'They had complete control of the local intranet and shut down all exterior connections a few minutes before the robbery commenced,' Ford went on. 'One staff member says she remembers her internet browser hung up just before the five men entered the bank.'

'So they had a sixth member on the outside?'

'Possibly, but the sub-routine could easily have been set on a timer. The main purpose, though, was so that no-one at the bank's HQ could access their system once they knew they were being robbed.'

'To circumvent the dual code system.'

'No, sir. The dual code system didn't need to be circumvented, because the security sub-routines had all been disabled anyway. The automatic call to the police still went out, but the vault shut-down command did not. To any of the staff who happened to look at a monitor, the system would have appeared to be reacting as it should, but in fact the computer had no idea the panic button had been pressed. The exterior connections were terminated so that HQ couldn't attempt to regain control of their own system. Meanwhile, the robbers had the power to open the safe at any moment they chose.'

'Any moment they chose,' Shaw repeated, once again addressing the whole room. 'And yet they *chose* to string it out, giving everybody, including our own DI de Xavia, the impression that the ball was on the slates. This is because no-one would be expecting them to make a break for it until they got what they came for, unless something untoward was to intervene. Something duly does, in the shape of our wee bomb-scare, which gets everybody, including the polis, running *away* from the building while they make their escape. Then, by the time the smoke has literally cleared and we figure out what's happened, not only are they gone via the Underground, but we cannae get near the place because it's teaming with Teddy Berrs on the way back from Ibrox.

'They walk away with around eight hundred grand in cash and leave us with bugger all but a communal riddy. No fingerprints, no physical descriptions (apart from the unmissable fact that one was a midget), merely a final punchline in the shape of a canvas bag containing five fake machine-guns to let us polis know precisely how badly we've been hung oot.'

Shaw paused to let them feel the sting of this slap to their collective pride, like Alex Ferguson tapping into that siege-mentality resentment reservoir for motivation. It should have doubled Angelique's own determination, but something was keeping her in a state of comparative ambivalence; possibly her 'informally attached' status.

'So,' Shaw resumed, 'who were they? What *do* we know about them? These names they used, what were they again?'

'Jarry, Athena, Chagall, Dali and Ionesco, sir.'

'I'm assuming the names didn't register on any database of known aliases – these guys are too smart for that – but they're not Mr Blue, Mr Pink and Mr Brown, either, so what's the score?'

'They were surrealists and absurdists, sir,' ventured Pollyanna Bailey with quite the least-expected contribution of the morning.

'Eh?'

'Dali and Chagall – both surrealist painters. Jarry and Ionesco were absurdist playwrights. I believe two of the robbers performed *Waiting for Godot* by Samuel Beckett, which could also be classed as absurdist, though to my knowledge it has more than two parts.'

'They used hand puppets,' someone informed him. 'Well, I mean, no' puppets, but they made their hands talk, according to the hostages.'

'How do you know this stuff?' Shaw asked Bailey, with a look of distaste bordering on outright disapproval.

'PC Internet, sir. The officer with all the answers.'

Shaw looked relieved, having been previously appalled to think that someone who knew about drama had been admitted to the Glesca Polis in the time since he left. Angelique was relieved too: up until then she'd been revising too many preconceptions for comfort, so it was good to see some hard evidence of where this 'old school' tag had come from.

'So what about Athena? He was the bampot of the bunch, Mr Guess-who-doesn't-belong. What did PC Internet have to say about him?'

'Her, as it turns out, sir. Greek goddess of wisdom. Makes him the odd one out, in more ways than one.'

'Wisdom. They really were taking the piss.'

Angelique laughed, having suddenly worked out what the name really meant. Prior to Bailey's contribution, she had only heard of Dali, but now she got the gag.

'They were taking the piss in more ways than one,' she said, her laughter having attracted Shaw's attention. 'Dali and Chagall were great artists, and in a broader sense, you could say Jarry and Ionesco were great artists too, yeah? Athena, on the other hand, was that chainstore where you went to buy cheesy posters, like the one of the female tennis player scratching her bare arse.'

'Are you sure? Do they have those stores across the pond?'

'No idea, but they seemed pretty clued up on other aspects of our domestic culture. Seems too much of a coincidence, given their overall attitude to the guy.'

'And yet,' Shaw mused, 'he was the one their leader chose to back him up when they went upstairs to intercept you. Reliable for muscle, perhaps.'

'No, sir, he was the guy Jarry least minded getting shot if anything went wrong when the polis came through the roof.'

'Fair point.'

'According to the hostage statement I took,' offered another officer, 'he was the one they placed in front of the doors prior to painting over the glass. If anyone was going to take a bullet, they were making sure it was him.'

Shaw was nodding thoughtfully. 'This guy could be our best route in. He doesn't fit with the others and it's obvious they neither like him nor trust him, so what's he doing there at all? They're like nothing we've ever encountered and he's just your common or garden ned, so what did he bring to the table? Local knowledge? Whatever connects them to him strikes me as their weak point, if only we can suss what it is. He also strikes me as the one most likely to screw up after the fact, maybe by flashing his cash now that he's minted. Let's put out feelers to our friends in low places, see what they know. If we find Athena, I can't imagine there's any way he wouldn't squeal on the others.

'Also, these fake guns – I want to know where they came from. Ironically, these days replicas are more easily traceable than the real thing, so let's get on it. The face masks and this skin irritant, too. What actually was it? Is it freely available or could the purchase be traced? And I want somebody on to Interpol to see if these heidthebaws have hit anywhere else. I cannae imagine the precise MO will have been repeated, or we'd have seen it on the tail end of the TV news, but there's no way this was a debut.'

Around the incident room, notes were keenly taken and determined heads were nodded. They were raring to go; probably would have been even without Shaw's pep rally. Angelique could tell when cops were having fun, and a case like this sure beat the usual depressing bread-and-butter stuff. They had already taken a gubbing from these guys, so there was a professional score to settle, but while there were no corpses to clear up it would feel like light duty.

Shaw clapped his hands together to silence the growing

mutterings. 'Just before you all go off and get busy, is there anything I've missed?'

'Yes, sir. There is the small matter of Mr Jarry sending flowers to a police officer following some weird meeting-of-the-minds, mutual-flirtation encounter that went down during the robbery,' Angelique didn't say. Instead she watched the briefing wind down and disperse before making her way back upstairs. It marked her first, albeit minor, betrayal of her loyalties to the force. She'd known it was coming, known all along she would be keeping it to herself, but it was only once the opportunity to volunteer the information had come about that it felt like any kind of deed had been committed. As acts of disloyalty went, it hardly compared to some of the duplicity people frequently justified to themselves in this line of work, but she still felt a tug of conflict, like picking up winnings after secretly betting on her team to lose. A line had unquestionably been crossed.

However, it wasn't like she was on the start of a slippery slope. Quite simply, owning up just wasn't worth the grief, not for what it would contribute. She had done her own trace on the flowers, naturally. They had been delivered to her parents' place by a Via-Flora courier. She called the despatching branch, but found that the order had been placed through the company's centralised website, paid at premium rate for delivery 'within the hour'. She then contacted Via-Flora's main offices in Walsall as an overture to tracing the payment card, but was told the order had been paid for using internet credits. These, it turned out, could be purchased using cash at any Post Office, and most crucially, were data-protected to the nth degree so that the credit-holder's identity could not be faked online. Finding out who had held the credits that bought the bouquet would take a lot more than a warrant, and even then it struck her as unlikely that the 'identity' behind them would be Jarry's real one. The (inevitable) hotmail account used to confirm the order was prefixed jarry@.

If she did tell Shaw about the flowers, the only practical impact on the investigation would be to put her in the spotlight for having been the recipient, subjecting her to no end of unwanted official scrutiny – surveillance, wire-taps, who knows? – to say nothing of the juvenile innuendo that would go along with it all. Fuck that.

The flowers were now sitting in a jar on her mantelpiece, and had fairly brightened up the room, but due to their source had proven a bigger distraction than a blaring TV. The Mogwai and the Merlot were always conducive to a bit of Sunday-night soul-searching, but the bouquet had diverted her ruminations into some strange and dangerous places. Many questions, few answers and but one conclusion: she was keeping this to herself, long after the flowers were wilted and binned. No-one needed to know, no-one was going to know and no-one *could* know.

Threatening to instantly disprove this was the sight of Shaw waiting for her at her desk when she got back upstairs. Reminding herself that 'old school' did not mean telepathic, she remained calm and waited to be told what he did want.

'Sir?'

'This Athena bloke,' he said. 'I'm trying to get a handle on the dynamic here, if you like, between him and the rest. You had this wee rammy with him just before he tried to shoot whatsisface.'

'Jarry.'

'Aye. What's the score there? How do *you* reckon he fits into the set-up?'

'All I can say is not very well. The animosity was well fermented. Jarry gave the impression he had been forced to slap him down before, but Athena struck me as too stupid to learn the lesson. Jarry told Athena he was a brain short of being able to fuck with him.'

'I don't doubt it. And yet they still have him along for the big job. There's something just doesnae add up about this. They were so cute and calculated about everything else, so why bring along this liability?'

'Maybe they calculated that too, sir. When I first went in I thought it might be a bit of good-robber/bad-robber psychology, but nah. The more I look back, the more I think he was being used.'

'Used?'

'They used me, didn't they? I was the one they got to come down to the vault to see their supposedly malfunctioning explosives. I doubt I was part of the original plan – probably one of the hostages would have done – but a cop falls into your lap, who better?'

'So how were they using Athena?'

'I'm not sure, but I reckon they were relying on him to be himself. Jarry's as smart as they come and clearly has Athena's number, so he could definitely have handled it cooler when they got into a stand-off – if he'd wanted to. He *provoked* Athena into firing that gun – what came out of it proves they were expecting him to do it at some point – and Jarry made sure it happened in front of a witness but away from the hostages.'

'What if he'd fired it downstairs? Bit of a risk, no?'

'The hostages would have no way of knowing about the other four guns, would they, especially if he was being obviously ostracised. But this was a safer way of getting it over with, letting Athena know he was snookered.'

'So that's why Jarry took him upstairs. That and, as you suggested, to be a human shield.'

'Hmm,' Angelique said, her logic circuits making another belated connection.

'What?'

'Well, it's starting to dawn on me that there could have been still another reason: to keep him out of the way while they got on with something downstairs that they didn't want him to see.'

'Like what?'

'Like stashing the money. Neither myself nor any of the hostages thought the safe had been opened, so who's to say he did either? In fact, there's no way he was in on the real plan. I couldn't see his face, but there was no mistaking that he was pissed off because he thought the whole thing was going sour. He remarked upon it several times, and I find it implausible that out of the five, he was the one with a real acting talent.'

'But they got a convincing performance out of him nonetheless.'

'Out of me, too. I was actually begging *them* to let the hostages go and clear the building, in complete accordance with their plans. They played me, they played everybody, so why not a tube like him?'

'Especially if it meant twenty percent more to share out. Fuck, well there goes the chances of him makin' any ostentatious purchases, eh?'

'Yes, but if we do find him, he'll be even less conflicted about grassing them up.'

'Except that he probably knows close to fuck-all about them. If they knew they were gaunny screw him, they'd cover their arses against the consequences.'

'He'll have seen their faces. That's more than anyone else.'

209

Shaw sighed, sounding weary in a very non-old-school kind of way.

'True,' he conceded, 'but just between you and me, de Xavia, I think we've got close to hee-haw chance of catchin' these guys, whether we know what they look like or not. No prints, no descriptions, probably some clever alibis, too. Short of a confession, we could be struggling even if we did have somebody to arrest.'

'With respect, sir, that's not exactly the up-and-at-'em attitude I was led to expect of you by the keepers of your flame.'

Shaw grinned at this last remark, and in that moment a few things were silently understood between them.

'Oh, I'm all that and a puddin' supper,' he said after a moment, 'but you need to be realistic aboot what you're up against. I brought down a lot of bad bastards round here, aye, and quite a few in London as well. But you know what they all had in common?'

'They all loved their mothers?'

'They were fuckin' eejits. You don't go intae crime if you've got much of a brain, let's be honest. I don't mean tae get sociological aboot it, but if you've the faculties tae make a decent living . . . you know what I'm sayin'. Look at that job in the papers last month. Bunch of arseholes in Cambuslang stole a bulldozer fae a buildin' site and tried a ram-raid on a cash machine. Brought half the fuckin' bank doon on themselves, all got read their rights in hospital. That's what we're normally dealing with: numpties wi' tights over their face haudin' up the local buildin' society wi' a sawn-off shotgun. Not this. Poor Drew McMaster'll be laid up for a month, gettin' his cerebral cortex unravelled.'

'So why even bother?'

'I like a challenge,' he said, again sporting that sharp grin in acknowledgment of the vacuous cliché. 'Naw, here's why. Perfect crime, down in the Smoke a few years back. Two blokes kill a guy to order: no witnesses, no motives, no connection. Then comes the clever part. They bury the body in a recently filled-in grave in a cemetery. Nick in during the night, the earth's still loose, wheech oot the coffin and put the corpse *under* it, in case the plot gets used again. Cover it over and it looks same as it did the day before. No motive, no corpse, no crime. Smart, eh?'

'Very.'

'So how do I know this happened? Why are they baith servin' life in Parkhurst? Because their idea was so fuckin' clever they told everybody in the pub aboot it. These guys, our guys, are probably too sharp for that, but the point is, if they do find a way of screwin' up, I'll be waiting.'

Angelique's phone started ringing as she watched Shaw walk away. *If they find a way of screwing up.* In the wise words of Harry Hill, what were the chances of that happening?

She lifted the receiver.

'De Xavia speaking.'

'Hi.'

He didn't say anything else for a moment, and neither did Angelique, though she wasn't sure she'd have been capable even if she'd wanted to. There was just no precedent, no known means for responding to something like this, and yet there was no question in her mind about precisely who she was failing to respond to. Can you recognise someone's voice from just 'Hi'? Can you recognise even an accent? Either something inside her instinctively knew who she was talking to, or else she was merely projecting on the basis of who she *hoped* she was talking to, and both options said more than she cared to hear about her current state of mind.

'You know who this is?' he asked, utterly misinterpreting the growing silence.

'Mm-hmm,' she mumbled, suddenly and irrationally afraid of being eavesdropped upon, presumably by colleagues who were also telepathic and possibly omniscient, given the brevity of their exchange so far.

'Okay,' he confirmed, preceding another pause, during which Angelique's nervousness seemed to become contagious. She heard a swallow at the other end, then he resumed, less hesitant if no more certain. 'This is gonna sound a little obsessive,' he said. 'I realise under the circumstances I probably don't seem the sanest person, but . . .' Another sigh, another swallow. 'I got the feeling, and maybe I'm just going nuts, but I . . . I got the feeling you and I ought to talk. And I don't mean about . . . well, if you know what I'm talking about, you'll know . . . what I'm talking about, I guess.'

'And what we're not talking about.'

'Yeah. Otherwise, I'll put down this phone and walk away, right now.'

The next silence had a timer on it, an ultimatum: every second it grew carried an increased danger that the line would go dead, and she very much didn't want that to happen. What was he talking about? Angelique couldn't articulate it any better than he had, but she still felt she knew; at least knew enough.

'Presumably you know that it's now professionally incumbent upon me to do anything in my power and say anything I can think of in order to keep you *on* this telephone,' she said, part stalling, part thinking aloud.

'And that anything you do say is interpretable according to that consideration, yes.'

'So if I answer yes, why would you believe I'm telling the truth when you know it's not an option for me to answer no?'

'Because you wouldn't be asking me that if you were lying.'

Angelique found herself looking around the office, this ridiculous paranoia remanifesting itself. No-one was paying her any attention – why would they? And yet she feared scrutiny, like a wean following an unauthorised withdrawal from the biscuit barrel.

'Okay, say we did have something to talk about. What then?'

'We meet. I buy you a drink. We talk.'

'And I do this without informing any of my colleagues, in abject dereliction of duty.'

'That's your call, but right now I'm just a voice on a telephone. Do you inform your colleagues every time you meet someone for a drink?'

'You're not just anyone, though, are you?'

'What are you afraid of? I'm the one taking a chance.'

'Afraid? I'm not afraid.'

'Then why are you whispering?'

'I'm not whispering,' she whispered, lowering her voice even further than it had already involuntarily slipped.

He laughed. 'So what do you say?'

'Let me get this straight. You want to meet in a pub, face to face, you and me. How would you know half the customers weren't plain-clothes cops waiting to nail you?'

He laughed again, harder this time. 'I'd know,' he said. 'Cops don't need to be wearing uniform for you to see

213

blue. That colour never washes off. It sometimes fades, though,' he added pointedly.

'If I do this, I'd advise you never to lose sight of what I am,' she warned, rebutting what he was hinting at but aware she might be protesting too much. 'You've no rational reason to trust me, and as you've already played me once, I owe you, remember?

'I'm very much aware of the stakes. But I've got a pretty good hand right now. I walk in there and I think it's a trap, I can walk back out again. Until I introduce myself, you don't know what I look like.'

'But once you do, it's the point of no return.'

'It's not a date with destiny, it's a drink. At the end of the night we can both walk away.'

'Return to our trenches after the kickabout?'

'The war is over, believe me. You guys lost.'

'So why are you still here?'

'Maybe that's one of the things we're not going to talk about.'

'Maybe. Fair enough. At least you didn't say it was because of me.'

'Would you have bought that?'

'You played me once, pal. I'm on the lookout from here on in.'

'So does this mean we're on?'

What was that about not being on the start of a slippery slope?

'What have we got to lose?'

'Just off the top of my head, everything.'

Angelique smiled, though she knew he wasn't entirely kidding.

'My kind of stakes,' she told him.

## just a little drink/just a little pregnant

It was way past time for a bit of quality soul-searching –
harsh, unflinching, look-yourself-in-the-mirror stuff. Item
one on the agenda: what the fuck do you think you're
doing? Alternatively, he could just phone Karl in Newcastle
and tell him what he was planning. The guy would go
straight into Jiminy Cricket mode and the effect would be
roughly the same.

'What, is everything going too smoothly, you feel you
need to put the whole operation on a knife-edge to keep
you sharp?' he'd ask. Something like that. Or maybe,
'We've gotta cross this river of burning lava, but you figure
it would be better if we all did it on a tightrope?' Yeah,
that sounded more like him.

'You could end up horsing this for all of us because of
a girl you don't even know.'

Closer still, to Karl and to the truth.

What the fuck *was* he doing?

It didn't feel like he was selling anybody out. Not yet,
anyway. He hadn't walked into that bar, he'd only made
a phone call. Even if she turned on him, the cops still had
no physical evidence that it was his face under that mask.
If it actually made it to court, which was improbable, he'd
walk, same as he could walk from the bar if it didn't feel
right.

He hadn't done anything he couldn't back out of – so
far. But what he was contemplating was unquestionably a

risk, to himself and, inescapably, to his friends also. At this stage he could still merely think of it as a conflict of interest, but the second he placed a drink in front of that woman, he was making himself a double-agent in that conflict. Even if nothing came of it, he was still putting their safety down as part of his stake, without their say, without even their knowledge, and that part just didn't sit easily with him.

It didn't matter that he thought he could handle it, thought he could make it work. The point was that this risk wasn't merely his to take. They were in this together – Karl, Leo and Jerome – risking their asses to back him up because of a debt that only they felt they owed him.

So what was he going to do, have a poll? Besides, that wasn't the only reason they were in this, was it? There was the matter of another, larger debt that they all quite definitely owed someone, and in the grander scheme, Zal was fully authorised to speculate on their behalf when it came to ensuring they could pay it in full.

Chill. He wasn't betraying anybody. If it all went fugazzi, it would have been because he'd been negligent, and that wasn't a charge anyone had ever made stick so far.

Too much emotion, that was the problem, with its Alpine molehills and white-squall tea-cups. It was also the upside. They had never been closer and never worked better, not since New York anyway. This, however, was far more intense, for any number of reasons. Those New York days had been a kind of adrenaline-addicted, hedonistic existentialism, transparently symptomatic of an attempt to extend their adolescence and its intoxicating delusions of invincibility. There was no shortage of adrenaline in Glasgow, but here it was merely fuel for the engine, and they weren't doing anything simply for its own sake. Here there were no delusions, most certainly not of invincibility. Here was where they, the defeated, divided and scattered, had regrouped: older, stronger, smarter and wiser, grateful for what they had together and singularly determined to make up for what had gone wrong.

In Zal's case, to that potent concoction you also had to add the unsettlingly giddy effect of just being in this city, which could at times feel like a giant theme-park based around his father's memory.

Since his dad's death, Zal had known he would come here some day, just like he knew he would see his friends again, just like he knew they would eventually have to deal with Alessandro. Blind fate, prompted by Cream-T's serendipitous career move, had dictated that all of these things should happen at once. There were ways in which he understandably felt this put him at an advantage, but it sure was a lot for his heart to take in. After Folsom, just a few drinks with his buddies would have been emotion enough to last him a month or two. Instead they were working on (and so far pulling off) the riskiest jobs of their lives, in this place that had been his childhood's Neverland, and in which he kept finding scattered fragments of the mould that shaped the man who, for better or worse, had shaped himself.

He did get that reunion drink with his buddies; it just got eclipsed in the hot competition for sweetest moment since he was paroled. Violating said parole within hours of release by leaving not only the state but the country and in fact the continent was a pretty good start.

They were all waiting for him at Glasgow Airport. There were no high-fives, no grand gestures, just confident smiles that demonstrated how intently everybody understood what they were all there for. They'd been there the best part of a month before Zal got out of Walla Walla, scoping, researching, confirming and preparing. As Zal's dad had taught him, you have to make sure everything you're going to need is already in place before you even make your entrance.

He'd seen all of them at some point during his time inside, but geography meant visits had been understandably far from frequent, with only Karl showing up more than once due to living in California. Jerome had gone back to his family in Vermont after his release, Leo to live with his sister in New York, and it was more than two years since he'd seen either of them in the flesh.

They were all looking damn good, or maybe they were just looking damn good to him. People never look their best when you're peering at them through steel bars or reinforced Plexiglas, no matter which side of it they're on. Karl's last visit to Folsom had been only two months back, but even he looked different now that they were all breathing free air. It was difficult to pinpoint: not any specific physical feature, more an aura, a sense, something in the way they stood, walked, laughed. Nobody had that haunted air about them, that look of fucking apology, shared guilt, regret and repression.

This was their time, and they knew it. Everybody understood what stakes were on the table, but everybody was equally happy to be in the game. Zal couldn't say it was like old times, because what defined every second was a common awareness that those times were gone and they were different people now, but every second was valued all the more for that.

Leo and Jerome were still bitching mercilessly at each other the way they always had, but it was like a self-conscious parody of the animosity they once took so much perverse mutual pleasure in generating; like Spock and Bones in the *Star Trek* movies compared to Spock and Bones in the original series. Way back when, their games of verbal brinkmanship skirted recklessly close to very dangerous territory, there being no such thing as agreed limits between them. Now, however, there was no risk of real escalation because no-one was letting himself become distracted from the task in hand. There was also the matter of everybody having a vivid appreciation of each other's fragilities these days. In the past, they attacked each other as a form of play, like tiger-cubs, because they didn't know what it was to be truly hurt.

That said, anyone who didn't know their history might sometimes find it difficult to believe that these people considered each other friends. A sample exchange, stemming from Jerome's objection to Leo's less than crucial choice of which Beckett play he and Karl should perform to entertain and distract their hostages:

'That's it. That is fuckin' it. Tonight, I'm gonna find me a girl who takes it in the ass, I'm gonna dress her up like a spoiled white-boy preppy fag, all cravats 'n' shit, an' I'm gonna call her Jerome. Then maybe when I'm fuckin' her, like I said, up the ass, I can ask her what's goin' through her vacant little mind an' begin to understand just a bit about what it must be like to be you.'

'You know, the more time I'm forced to spend with you, Leo, the more I'm happy my ancestors were slave owners.'

Zal wasn't sure whether it would help an uninformed observer to learn that the hammily effete (but strictly heterosexual) Jerome hailed from Vermont blue-blood Unionist stock, any more than it would to know that Leo was gay. He'd long ago given up his attempts to make sense of what went on between them, and knew only to

219

stand well back if you wanted to watch the fireworks.

Sweet moments, so many sweet moments. However, if he had to pick just one to savour, it would have to be an incident during 'rehearsals' for the bank gig.

They had presented themselves to Hannigan and his people shortly after Zal hit town. Quite a shower. So far from home, it was comforting to observe that while gangsters' sartorial predilections differed across the continents, they were at least united in their belief that paying out serious green for anything with a label on it was more than a substitute for taste, elegance or even practicality. Zal could picture these guys wearing their Armanis in the swimming pool and still thinking they looked the cat's ass.

Alessandro had predictably given the impression that Zal and company were entirely at Hannigan's disposal, maybe just short of pulling on aprons and cleaning out his sunken-style jacuzzi (actually, he had no idea what Hannigan had in his house, but there was just no way in this universe that the guy *didn't* have a sunken jacuzzi). Zal chose to reinforce this by stubbornly disputing the arrangement and struggling against Hannigan's attempts at control, figuring that by tugging on the leash it would emphasise to everybody that the leash was there. A demonstration of compliant obedience struck him as being interpretable as potentially devious, and while the guy might look like an asshole, he wouldn't be where he was if he was stupid.

The RSGN robbery was never part of the agreement, far less what Alessandro had sent them there to do, so Zal had to make sure Hannigan got wind of what they were planning. Otherwise, the first he'd have known about it was when he heard it on the news, put two and two together and come up with the only four guys in town who could have carried it out. Bringing him in this way fitted the enforced compliance angle.

Zal 'reluctantly' acceded to Hannigan's insistence that he put a man on their team for the bank, and that a one-fifth split should kick back to him for 'allowing them to work on his turf' (yeah, right). The guy, one Barry Merkland, would have to shadow them every step of the way (stop laughing at the back), become integrated into their plan (I mean it, you'll be sick) and be given a pivotal role in the robbery itself (oh look, you've even got me started now).

Perhaps the funniest part was that Merkland thought they were taking the piss when they *were* telling him what was going on. It was fair to assume his recreational tastes didn't veer towards the fine arts, nor that he understood that the practice of theft could be executed in subtler ways than pointing a gun at someone and yelling 'gimme all your money'. Consequently, his patience with Zal's methods wore swiftly thin, while his resentment at having to comply with Zal's orders grew more simmeringly transparent by the day.

Karl was running a book on exactly when Merkland would lose it, with an impartiality agreement that no-one should provoke him in an attempt to win the bet. Jerome scooped the pool the day they broke it to the guy that he'd have to learn not one, but two synchronised dance routines.

'This is fuckin' bollocks,' he decided. 'I'm fucked if I'm daein' any o' this shite. Nae chance, man. Yous can fuckin' whistle.'

'Cool with us,' Zal told him. 'We can live without a passenger, though I'm sure Hannigan will kit out a replacement for you just as soon as the Versace shop opens.'

'Or maybe he'll decide we're gaunny take this whole

thing over an' show yous cunts how we dae things roon here.'

'Oh, that I'd love to see. Thinking about it, why would you need us when you've already got such genius at your disposal?'

'I'll fuckin' show you whit we've got at oor disposal, son, if you're no fuckin' careful.'

'Are you really dumb enough to believe your capacity for violence gives you some kind of edge here? We're robbing a bank, not mugging a senior citizen.'

'It gies me enough of an edge that I shouldnae have tae staun here an' take shite fae fuckin' poofs like you.'

'Well I can't see how you work that out, considering you *are* standing here and taking shit from me, and will continue to do so as long as your boss commands it.'

It might have been ruled a technical provocation if Zal hadn't already lost his stake by that point, having backed Merkland to freak a day earlier when they told him about the itching powder.

'Is that right?' Merkland asked, which was as close as he came to subtlety, a hand-written warning that he was about to attack Zal being considered marginally too obvious even for him.

Zal couldn't say he entirely enjoyed what happened next. He couldn't say he didn't enjoy it just a little, either, but he had his regrets. None of these were for what Merkland suffered, but instead over the means by which that suffering was inflicted and the reasons they were at his disposal. There had been a time when a seasoned hardcase like Merkland could have knocked Zal down with his spit, six feet tall or not, but that was the guy who walked *in* to Folsom. The guy who walked out dropped Merkland bleeding to the deck in about six seconds. Still, there was

222

no doubt in Zal's mind as to which one he'd rather be, given the choice.

So that wasn't the sweet part. The sweet part was when Merkland got back up and pulled a gun.

'No, wait, don't do it,' Zal implored.

'Aye, you're no' so fuckin' smart noo, are ye?'

'I was talking to Karl, asshole.'

Keeping the gun pointed at Zal, Merkland stepped around ninety degrees so that he could get Karl in his line of vision. He was standing on a box near the door of the warehouse, holding a knife in his right hand.

'How, whit's he gaunny dae?'

'Okay, Karl, show him.'

In a twinkling, the gun was in Leo's grip, via the floor, while Merkland clutched his injured hand in his fist, squeezing and yelping.

'Oh, put a sock in it, it was just the handle. Next time he'll hit you with the blade, and that'll really give you something to howl about.'

'You fuckin' bastards.'

'Yeah, yeah. Word of advice, dude. We all have to work together, and it seems there ain't nothing we can do about that, but it would be a whole lot easier if you just accepted that you are one brain short of being able to fuck with me. Now let Jerome stick a couple of band-aids on you and then you better get yourself ready to shake your thang.'

'I'm not sticking anything on him,' Jerome objected.

'Why the fuck not?' asked Leo. 'You're the expert when it comes to layin' hands on pricks.'

'I think it's too bad for Merkland your sister isn't here, Leo. I don't know whether she's much of a nurse, but I'm sure it would make him feel better to be in the company of someone who goes down quicker than he just did.'

And so on.

Not everyone was as dependably stupid as Merkland, but they had nonetheless played things pretty much faultlessly so far, usually because they accurately identified what they *could* depend on in individuals, organisations or institutions. They could depend on bank security protocols to turn a robbery into a siege; they could depend on the cops to turn a siege into a circus, and they could depend on everybody at the circus to run away from what they thought was a bomb.

Angelique de Xavia, on the other hand, was an unknown and therefore unpredictable quantity. Zal had no idea what he could or couldn't depend on from her, and it was this, rather than merely the fact she was a cop, that made what he had in mind such a risky proposition. However, it was also the reason no will on earth was going to be able to stop him walking into that bar.

Angelique couldn't remember ever feeling so nervous, not even going into Dubh Ardrain. Leading a two-person assault against a dozen terrorists holding thirty-odd hostages in an underground fortress really ought to have held more fears than nursing a G&T in a city-centre pub, but the difference was that during the former, she'd known what she was doing and what she was up against. She had also enjoyed the advantages of stealth, secrecy and the resultant element of surprise. Here, she felt like nothing more than a sitting duck, having voluntarily walked into a situation that was entirely someone else's to control.

But that wasn't the sole source of the butterflies, now was it, girl?

Oh, gimme a break, she argued with herself. What other source could there be? What other source did she need?

She was exposed, vulnerable and isolated, going out on a limb for reasons that had admittedly seemed easier to rationalise before she walked into this place. But for God's sake, she didn't even know what he looked like, so it wasn't like she fancied him or anything. She was just . . . curious, and who wouldn't be under the circumstances?

Curious, sure. That was why she went through three changes of outfit before finally making it out the front door, not to mention half an hour wrestling with the hair-drier and her first resort to make-up since the late Nineties. Curiosity.

Jesus, what the hell was she doing?

She was sitting in a booth opposite the bar in a newish place called The Institution, the venue chosen by Jarry. She'd never been in it before, indeed hadn't heard of it prior to his phone-call, and figured that he must have opted for it because it was central and, like most large, modern pubs, conveniently anonymous. These places did have regulars, but they were nobody's local, and the bar-staff turnover was too frequent for them to remember many faces. However, it was only when she arrived that she understood his reasons to be less cautiously tactical: the joint was a converted bank.

Angelique sipped at her drink, caught between the need for the alcohol's disinhibiting properties and the desire not to finish it too quickly. Sitting on her own felt sad enough, but sitting on her own with a second drink said 'stood up' in very big letters. She was practising that invaluable self-kidding psychology: until she reached the bottom of the glass, there was no need to look at her watch, because hey, she hadn't even finished her drink yet, so the guy couldn't be *that* late.

He could be here already, in fact, which was just one of

the things she was finding very uncomfortable to deal with. The place was busy, from the bar to the overlooking gallery level upstairs, and as in any crowded pub, there were many eyes scanning around the gathering – looking for pals, looking for talent, or just people-watching. She'd caught a few eyes glancing at her, and didn't know whether she was attracting looks because she was a woman on her own, or simply that being on her own, with no-one else to look at, meant she was more alert to looks that would have come her way anyway. Either way, the attention felt intrusive when there was the possibility that any pair of male eyes could be his, sizing up the situation or maybe even sizing up her ('Oh dear, you looked so much better in Kevlar'), before deciding whether to just walk away.

There was relief on offer in that eventuality, but only from her own wretched insecurities. This inexplicable sense of guilt was still lingering, making her feel like she'd been caught dogging school. It was crazy. She hadn't done anything to be guilty about yet. That mythical line hadn't so much been crossed as snagged on her belt and stretched. Who was to say she couldn't yet use this situation to bring the guy and his accomplices to justice? No-one, no*thing* had been betrayed. She was following up a lead that was only open to her if she acted on her own.

Aye, right.

'Impetuously autonomous,' anyone? 'Going it alone outside the chain of command'? No, she wasn't betraying anybody as long as she was engaged in precisely the kind of conduct the Star Chamber had wrongly accused her of in the past.

This thing had disaster written all over it; the only uncertainty would be over the scale of the damage. Nonetheless, she knew that if he didn't show, by far her strongest emotion would be disappointment. That was why her G&T was likely to evaporate faster than she was drinking it.

She stared into the glass, toying with the plastic stick, toying also with necking the whole drink and hitting the road. But she knew she wouldn't. If the bastard didn't show, she could be here until closing.

*This is gonna sound a little obsessive . . .*

No kidding.

She hadn't been able to get those words out of her head, not just because of what they had heralded, or even the fact that they were an appropriate commentary on most of her actions and thought processes since. There was something else: they were naggingly familiar, even the way he'd spoken them. He was quoting, she decided, some American movie she must have seen a dozen times, but she was buggered if she could remember which one. Further confusing her, she was sure it was a woman's voice that she could hear speaking when she tried to recall. It would come to her eventually, she reckoned; it was unlikely to be of any great import, but neither would it stop repeating until she'd nailed it.

'Hi,' said a voice, sounding yards away as it stirred her from the absorption of contemplating both her drink and the unidentified movie quote. She looked up to see a figure looming over her table. He was wearing a grey business suit with the tie loosened, holding a pint of lager which he was clearly summoning the courage to place masterfully on her table. He wasn't there yet. 'Please understand, I'm not in the habit of bothering women when they're on their own,' he said. Such an apologetically considerate gambit could only be the work of a true shark. It sounded well rehearsed and well used to the point of stale.

Angelique glanced over his shoulder. There were three

other suits staring her way, carefully observing how their pal was getting on. They'd be on hand to back him up verbally if he was getting anywhere, just as readily as they were preparing their merciless demolition in advance of his failure. Ripping the guy was a temptation, but these types had thick skin, and the chorus loved a reaction.

'And I'm not in the habit of humiliating polite but unsolicited suitors. Let's neither of us make any exceptions tonight, eh?'

'Can't shoot a man for trying,' he said, offering what he thought was a boyishly cheeky smile.

'Operation Flavius would suggest otherwise,' she told him.

'What?'

'SAS in Gibraltar. Quit while you're ahead, son. Your pals are waitin' on you.'

The shark held his hands up in jokey surrender and maintained the magnanimous expression for the benefit of observers, but 'Eat shit, dyke' was emanating sincerely from his eyes. He pirouetted on one heel and began walking away, to the accompaniment of eager laughter from his buddies.

Angelique sighed and looked back at the empty seat across from her, then drained the drink, bringing it down on the table with a frustrated thump. Screw you for putting me through this, she thought. She knew at the same time that she wouldn't yet be able to leave, but the sense of compulsion was starting to diminish.

She stared at the empty glass, almost but not quite ready to look at her watch. A second drink on her own wasn't necessarily 'stood up', was it? Anybody could be late, and until she looked at her watch, she wouldn't know how late. Anything less than half an hour was a missed bus, a tailback or some other transport problem. Beyond that, the chances of him actually putting in an appearance began to tumble.

Bollocks. There was only so much self-kidding her dignity could endure. She pulled back her sleeve and took a look at her watch, sighing with incredulity at what it revealed. It felt like she'd been there long enough for the Blue Nile to release a new album, and yet the dial told her it was quarter past eight, meaning she'd only been there twenty minutes. He was quarter of an hour late, so allowing for a standard five-minute error margin between their respective watches, to his mind he could be running as little as ten minutes behind. Nothing to worry about.

Self-kidding rocks. Dignity? That's what gin was for.

She decided to get up and head for the bar, which was when she saw him, standing a few feet inside the door, appraising his surroundings with a casualness that surely belied the degree of analysis going on behind his sharply scanning eyes. It was him, had to be. Even allowing for the skewing effects of wishful thinking, Angelique had little doubt that the man who had just walked in was the same person she'd been held by on Saturday afternoon. There was an ease about the way he stood there that was definitely familiar: an unaffected sense of being undaunted by whatever was going on around him, and yet within it an undistracted sense of purpose that was focused without seeming intent. He looked as though a mass brawl could break out around him and he'd still be calmly taking in his surroundings, maybe holding up a powerful arm to deflect a flying body here and there.

He had shoulder-length hair, peroxide blond, more than a hint of Californian surf punk about it, a look somewhat at odds with the blue chinos and crisp white shirt visible

229

beneath a flowing overcoat: Californian surf punk scrubbed up to impress and wrapped warm for the Glaswegian winter. She pictured him in overalls, replaced his face with that of a clown.

Definitely.

Angelique, having been taken for a mug on Saturday, decided to let him know she wasn't daft. She waited until his attention came roughly her way and met it with a very small wave, barely a ripple of the fingers on her only slightly raised right hand. Self-discipline hid her smile as his eyes caught the movement, homed in on it and then locked there as he deduced that he'd just given himself away.

Made.

She did him the courtesy of looking elsewhere again, allowing him to approach without any sustained scrutiny. Or maybe she just wasn't ready to fully face down his gaze quite yet. She stared into her empty glass as he slid into the seat opposite, then looked up to finally confront him.

He didn't say anything at first, which seemed improbable given his performance on Saturday and his antics since. Instead they just looked at each other for a few seconds, Angelique fronting an intense expression of impassive scrutiny to disguise two things: the dawning appreciation that she had little chance of sussing out what was going on behind this guy's eyes, and the fact that she nonetheless felt compelled to try. For his part, he simply stared back with these two penetrating pools of deep blue chaos, which hinted at a thousand things but betrayed not one, not even whether he was about to smile or scowl.

'You're late,' Angelique said, unable to take much more of the silence and attempting to put him even slightly on the back foot.

'You're dry. Me too. What can I get you?'

'Eight hundred grand and five convictions. But right now I'd settle for a gin and tonic.'

'You got it.'

He turned and began looking around the pub, scanning this time with considerably less care to be inconspicuous. Angelique failed to either suppress or disguise a smile.

'What?'

'This is Glasgow, pal. You'll be a long time looking for a waitress.'

Without looking back at her, he bit his bottom lip, closed his eyes and briefly shook his head, then turned to face her with a genuinely tickled smile.

'See me? See cool? I'll be right back.'

Angelique felt a grin spread across her face as she watched him walk to the bar. He returned with her gin and a pint of something dark for himself, placed the drinks down and took off his coat before sidling into the booth once again.

'Let's start over,' he said, offering a hand across the table.

'I'm Angelique,' she said, shaking it. 'And you are?'

'You can call me Zal.'

'The guitar-playing clown. Very good. Do I not even get your real first name to be going on with?'

'That is my real first name. Well, strictly speaking it's Sal, but I preferred it with a Z, so that's what it became.'

'Sal?'

'After Sal Mineo. My mom was a big fan of *Rebel Without A Cause*.'

'So the Zal Cleminson look – that was kind of your way of putting a signature on Saturday's events?'

He took a sip of his beer and gently shook his head. For a moment she thought he was about to elaborate, until she deduced that it merely meant he was not going to answer the question.

'Was that a double bluff?' he asked.

'What?'

'The abject lack of subtlety. Make me think you can't be wearing a wire because if you were you'd be more cute about asking loaded questions?'

Angelique thought about it, not having anticipated that he'd have this concern. Now that he'd brought it up, however, there was no way of making it go away, short of taking her top off, so she thought she might as well play along.

'What answer would you believe?' she asked, offering a coy smile.

'That's good,' he replied, nodding. 'That's very good.'

'I suppose for the purposes of this conversation, you're going to assume that I am wearing a wire.'

'Kinda. Except that if I really believed you were, we wouldn't be having this conversation.'

'And yet you're going with the assumption. *Kinda*.'

'Let's just say I wouldn't consider the irony to be poignantly poetic if it turned out my instincts were wrong. It would be a little discourteous, too.'

'Discourteous?'

'You were the one who warned me never to forget what you are. I didn't interpret that to only mean being a cop.'

'What else does it mean?'

'That if I lose sight of the things that attracted me to you, I'll be in a lot of trouble.'

Angelique sensed a surge in her bloodstream at the sound of the word 'attracted'. It felt like a momentary burst of static in her head, fading out her surroundings until there were just the two of them in the booth, and no room, no bar, no people beyond. Couldn't he have said 'interested'? Couldn't he have said 'intrigued'? Attracted had connotations of . . . of . . . all the things that made this meeting so dangerous, ill-advised and yet impossible to resist. Now that she had seen his face, she could tell that matters weren't about to get any less complicated. Part of her – that big, cowardly part of her that was there to protect the fragile bits – had been hoping he'd look like he'd been cobbled together from the pieces Michael Jackson's plastic surgeon threw away. Physically, there was nothing of this guy that she'd want discarded. Even the hair looked acceptable, if only on him. And he was 'attracted' to her. Yes, sir, he went on the record with that. However, no matter what he looked like, she couldn't lose sight of what he was, any more than he could of her.

'You're saying you consider me . . . a threat,' she clarified, dampening those connotations and cursing herself for it. 'Or a match for you might be putting it better? I must say, I find it hard to believe you would think so highly of me after the ease with which you hung me out to dry.'

He opened his mouth to respond, but remained silent and took another gulp of his pint instead. 'Now that was cute,' he told her. 'I was almost leaping in to defend you. A far more subtle way of getting me to stray on to matters I can't talk about.'

'So what matters can you talk about? Because if we don't find some pretty soon, then what's the point in us being here?'

'I guess that depends on whether you're interested in more than what I was doing on Saturday afternoon; and even if you're not, I figure you're smart enough to know that not all of the answers you seek lie there anyway.'

233

Angelique considered his words carefully, taking a sip of her own drink as he spoke. She put the glass down and looked again into his eyes. His gaze was forbidding yet compelling; like his evasively enigmatic statements, the more he sought to conceal, the greater grew her determination to find out what he was hiding.

'Okay, here's one. Why *are* we here? I mean, why did you invite me?'

'Why did you accept?'

'Are you going to answer all my questions with questions of your own?'

'I watched a lot of *Jeopardy* in . . . recent years. But I figure if you answer my question, you'll answer your own.'

Which put them squarely in the territory of matters *she* didn't want to talk about. Why did he ask? Why did she accept? And which, if either, was the crazier for doing so?

'I had nothing to lose,' she said, which was untrue but plausible. 'And I'd have to confess to being more than a wee bit intrigued. Who wouldn't be.'

'By me personally or by the circumstances?'

'I consider both to be inextricable.'

'I guess that's your job.'

'Actually, in my book it's *your* job that makes the man difficult to separate from his deeds.'

'You're saying I wouldn't have got a date if I was a bank clerk?'

'Bank clerk? As opposed to bank . . . ? Impossible to know now, isn't it. If you were a bank clerk I'd have at least known in advance what you looked like. Anyway, who says this is a date? All it would take is for me to read you a caution and it would be a formal interview.'

'Figure of speech,' he said, smiling. 'It's kind of like a date, though, isn't it? Boy meets girl, we have drinks in a

234

bar, we ask each other questions and try and get to know a little more about ourselves.'

'Boy holds girl hostage, boy plays girl like a cheap fiddle while boy robs bank, then later, yes, boy buys girl drink, but boy speak with forked tongue and boy evades all of girl's questions. The only thing I know about you now that I didn't half an hour ago is your first name.'

'So ask me something else.'

'Okay. Where are you from? Assuming the accent is genuine.'

'Lots of different places,' he replied, grinning in acknowledgment of her exasperation. 'But originally Vegas.'

'Appropriate. A place that's made artifice a way of life, and where everybody's looking for fast money they didn't earn.'

'Ouch. Back in the knife drawer, Officer Sharp. Maybe I'll offer you up a few harsh generalisations about your town.'

'Fire away. They'll probably be true.'

'No, it wouldn't be polite. I'm a guest here.'

'And you don't consider it impolite to rob your hosts?'

'Morality and decorum are different issues.'

'But not entirely separate ones.'

'Not always, no,' he conceded. 'Hypothetically, shall we say, pointing a gun at an unarmed bank customer is not a very pleasant – or morally upstanding – thing to do. But it doesn't mean there has to be a suspension of common decency.'

'Common decency. You're talking about something more than politeness there.'

'I guess I am.'

'And morality is definitely bound up with that one.'

'All gets pretty fuzzy, don't it?'

'The law isn't.'

He laughed. 'Law and morality. Now there's two issues that are definitely unrelated.'

'I'd say they were hand in hand when it comes to taking things that belong to other people.'

'Theoretically, yeah. But while the law remains black and white, morality has more of a greyscale spectrum.'

'A greyscale spectrum?' Angelique asked, laughing. 'You thought that one up yourself?'

'Sure,' he replied, just a hint of the bashful about his smile. 'The white end we know about. But there's a difference between mugging some old grandmother for the savings she needs to live on and stiffing a major financial institution for a few Gs that they're barely gonna miss.'

'A few hundred Gs. And they are going to miss them, believe me. There's an old phrase round here that goes "every mickle maks a muckle". It's a philosophy that lies at the heart of every financial institution, major or minor.'

'It's not gonna break them, though, is it? Or weaken their stock, or make them vulnerable to a hostile takeover.'

'I wouldn't know. But I know that ultimately, it'll be the ordinary punter who takes the hit. The fat cats arenae gaunny make up the shortfall out of their annual bonuses, are they? So if the books don't balance, the charges go up and maybe a few staff will get laid off. That old grandmother you mentioned banks at RSGN, so maybe now her savings won't be earning as much interest, and her bank-teller granddaughter who helps out with the rent is now skint because she got laid off.'

'You speak the truth, if served with a heavy ladling of melodrama.'

'You reckon I overdid it?'

'A little, but I played the frail grandmother card first, so fair enough. But what you described . . . the same shit happens if a flood takes a bite from the insurance arm; Jesus, RSGN could lose the same amount if one of its stock traders had one beer too many over lunch. There are worse crimes than what happened on Saturday. Worse thefts. I ain't saying it's right, but I'm morally at peace with it.'

'Morally at peace? What does that mean?'

'It means that it isn't keeping me awake nights, but that doesn't preclude wishing it didn't have to be this way. Do you know what I'm saying?'

'I think so, but let's imagine I don't, and then maybe you'll say something that doesn't sound like the whines of a thousand previous losers seeking to justify their actions to themselves.'

'It wasn't my fault. I've had it bad, you don't know what it's like. Society made me do it. Or do I have to come up with something better than that?'

'Glaswegians make a tough audience.'

'Legendarily so. Under threat from rotten tomatoes, I guess what I'm saying is that certain events can seriously alter your perspective from that crisp black and white divide you start off looking at. And even though you remember how it looked from there, and you wish it could still be that way, with you standing safe on the white side of the line . . . I dunno. The places you find yourself, the things you need to do to survive mean you can't afford to worry about keeping the division so neat.'

'So you surf back and forth along that greyscale spectrum?'

'I'm not selling you this, am I? I'd like to, though. I'd like to explain and I think you'd listen.'

'You think I'd listen as a cop or just listen as myself.'

'You are a cop. I don't believe there's some other you that's entirely detached from that.'

Angelique had to stifle a sigh. He was depressingly right:

there was no way to deactivate it, no place to retreat from it and no way of cordoning off the rest of herself. That was why so many polis ended up in relationships with colleagues: they were under no illusions about what they would each be sharing their partner with. Up until now, she'd have said fellow cops were the only people who could understand. She'd forgotten the crooks might have a handle on it, too.

'I am what I am,' she said. 'To quote Gloria Gaynor. Or was it Popeye? Either way, I'm listening.'

'Problem is, I can't tell you anything without telling you everything, and I just can't do that right now. But believe me when I say this whole thing isn't just about a chunk of change.'

This whole thing. So it definitely wasn't over, and what-ever *it* was, was weighing heavily on the guy. He wanted to talk, and something had made him reckon she was the right person to listen. Angelique was appalled to feel an unworthy pang of disappointment that this might be the real reason he had called her.

'So how did we get from Vegas to this anyway?' he said, breaking the growing silence, inviting her to collude in changing and forgetting the previous subject.

'How did you get from Vegas to here might be more pertinent,' she said, obliging for now. 'In fact, I didn't think anybody was actually *from* Vegas, other than Andre Agassi. I thought people just ended up there.'

'Gamblers who got jobs to pay the tab and ageing crooners who can't get arrested anywhere else? Oh yeah, we got 'em. But it's also the fastest-growing city in the US. People do get born there. I was.'

'Your daddy was a gambler and your momma was a showgirl?'

'I'd tell you off for taking the mickey, except you're not a million miles off.'

'Your mum was the gambler and your dad was a croupier?'

'No. My mom was a showgirl. Latterly, anyways. Just a plain ole stripper when my dad met her. Well, not that plain, and not that old, but a stripper for sure.'

'That might explain a thing or two.'

'Like what?' he asked. He remained calm, but she sensed a fairly spiky defensiveness was being suppressed.

'I'm sorry, I didn't mean any disrespect. Just thinking aloud.'

'Well it's out here now. What did you mean?'

'Your mother being a stripper. I thought it might have had certain consequences for your attitude towards women. Or rather your conduct regards other men's attitudes towards women.'

'You'd be right, though I have to concede I'm at a loss as to how you got there.'

'About time I had the advantage of you, I'd say. And I'd tell you, but it's in that domain we can't talk about.'

'You can talk about it. I just can't respond.'

'Okay. I read through all the witness statements and noticed one in particular was very reluctant to say anything negative about you, despite being held captive for five hours. She almost seemed afraid to say anything that could be used against you. I went to see her, got her chatting off the record. You know what I'm talking about yet?'

He nodded.

'Please say yes or no for the benefit of the tape.'

He smiled and took another gulp of heavy.

'You asked me earlier why I accepted your invitation to come here tonight. What that girl said played a part.'

'Glad to hear it. My old man was never gonna make the hall of fame for fatherhood or husbandry, but he did pass on a few strong values. How you treat women was one of them. 'Course, ideals and practice ain't always the same thing. When you're walkin' out on somebody, bein' courteous ain't gonna be an awful big consolation.'

'Sounds like we're getting back to the difference between morality and decorum again.'

'Just as long as you didn't think we were back to clichéd explanations for being a loser.'

'I mentioned previous losers. I never said you were one. Not while you're sitting on a quarter share in eight hundred K.'

'I thought you guys were looking for five robbers?'

'We are. But we also figure one of them is desperately looking for the other four.'

'Did I say you were good before? I take it back. You're real good.'

Angelique couldn't help but smile. It was a fun game they were playing, and it felt good to score a point, even when it struck her that he had learned something about the cops from it without her learning any more about the robbers. Nevertheless, he was tending towards the expansive when it came to family, which constituted a major area of development.

'So if your mum was a stripper, what was your dad's line in Vegas?'

He turned those blue headlights on her again, full beam. Reading what was in them was much like her attempts to pick out and describe the flavours in a good bottle of wine: there were notes and nuances she felt sure she could discern, but all the time there remained the possibility that she was just imagining it all and consequently talking out

240

of her arse. Her guess at this current vintage was a touch of appellant sincerity, a hitherto undetected hint of vulnerability and a sizeable dollop of calculated risk.

'You're a detective,' he told her. 'I'm gonna leave that to you to work out.'

'Do I get any clues?'

'All the evidence is already out there, but you only get one guess, so take your time.'

'Fair enough. I'll work on it. I've sussed who the gambler in the family is, though.'

'No shit.'

'What I can't suss is what could be worth the stake you're putting down by being here tonight. But then maybe it's about playing the game. They say the serious gambler doesn't get the buzz from what he might win, but from what he has to lose. Is that you?'

'I'm not in this for thrills. Once upon a time, maybe, but . . . these days I've got a pretty firm grasp of what I value. You said Vegas was the world capital of artifice, and you might be right, though LA's got it run pretty close on that score. And you said it was where people went in search of fast money they didn't earn. That's true too, but you gotta understand that what Vegas is really all about is entertainment. People go there to have a good time, whether it's to see the bright lights, watch the fancy show or play the slots and tables. To have fun doing those last two, you spend what you've got going spare. You win, great; you lose, you had fun anyway. But you never gamble with what you truly value, because there's no odds can make it worth the bet.'

'Which brings us back to my original question. Given everything you've just said, why are we both sitting here?'

He finished his drink, put it aside on the table and leaned

forward, looking at her now with an intensity that would have made her recoil if it wasn't simultaneously so imploring. Having shifted his position, his shirt hung open around his neck, revealing the snaking black coil of a tattoo across the top of his chest.

'Do you really want to talk? And I don't mean any more of this cat and mouse, cops and robbers bullshit. Just you and me, saying whatever we've got to say to each other and dealing with the consequences *after* we've found out where the truth takes us?'

There was no glib 'yes' to this question. Angelique didn't know what he had in mind, but she knew it was balls-to-the-wall for real. They'd had their games over whether she could be wearing a wire, but she was sure this was something he'd never suggest if he thought for a second that her interest was purely professional.

'I won't know anything until I know everything,' she stated.

'You got that right.'

'So let's talk.'

'Not here.'

'Where, then?'

'The question is more of when.'

'When?'

'When can you get a couple days off?'

'I'm off next Thursday and Friday. Time in lieu. Your call.'

'Thursday morning, then. The airport.'

'So you can do a runner if you think I'm about to huckle you?'

'Neutral ground.'

'What's neutral about the airport? It's just Paisley, it's still in our jurisdiction.'

'Yeah, but Paris isn't.'

# interlude: scotland's most intrepid reporter (no, not that one)

Want to get ahead in the brave new Scotland? Simple. Go and stick your penis up another man's backside and you will be, in the vulgar modish parlance, sorted. Alternatively, you could get yourself a bright, bushy tail and call yourself Basil. Foxes and sodomites had it good in the post-devolution apocalypse. Feel like buggering a cherubic sixteen-year-old? Fine by us. Wouldn't want to impinge upon your human rights while you're violating a confused and vulnerable schoolboy, would we? And what's that? You want to adopt? Marvellous. Please don't let anyone suggest your predilection for anally penetrating the barely pubescent should be considered an obstacle. It's obvious you love children. That's why we've abolished all legal impediments to you proselytising in our schools.

What's that? Education system in tatters? Standards dropping faster than a single mother's lacy panties when the rent man comes a-calling? Crime on the rise? All-out surrender in the war on drugs? There, there, don't make such a fuss. This is a caring, liberal society, hadn't you heard? We love those little foxy-woxies. Couldn't countenance a hair being ruffled on their fluffy and cute little carnivorous, snarling heads. It's because we care. We care so much it hurts. It makes our little hearts bleed to think of all the suffering in our harsh, nasty society. That's why we have to protect the rights of criminals, because how else can we take away the sadness in their souls that makes them do such beastly things? That's also why we have to defend the rights of homosexuals to nail each other's gonads to planks of wood if that's what floats their boat. And shame on you for calling them perverts, you horrid bigot. There's no such thing as perversion any more, didn't you know? No such thing as pornography, either. It's all *free expression*, you see. Whether it be buggery in a public toilet or hard-core sex videos in a municipal art gallery, it's simply a vibrant celebration of the human condition.

We mustn't prevent people from expressing themselves, must we, not in the new, liberal, forward-looking Scotland. Oh, unless of course they happen to be white Christian heterosexuals with a concern for the innocence of our youth and an at least rudimentary understanding of what the word morality once meant. Those scum are a plague on our society, and are to be silenced at all costs.

Walter Thorn was under no illusions about it: he was effectively an outlaw. Guilty of thought-crimes, and defiant in the face of the charge. Persecuted for his beliefs under a regime whose favourite buzzwords, with no hint of irony, were 'tolerance' and 'inclusiveness'. Oh yes, we're tolerant, but we don't tolerate just *anybody*. Thugs, junkies, scroungers, pederasts, murderers, blasphemers, pornographers and deviants – we tolerate all of them, but we have to draw the line somewhere, and you 'dinosaurs' with your 'obsessions' are on the wrong side of it.

Great God, when did decency, when did morality, when did *values* become obsessions? Difficult to say. It had started a long way back, and had been a slow, putrid and decaying process, but unquestionably its official ratification was stamped 1 May 1997.

He'd been on the thought-police's hitlist ever since. There

were no round-ups, no mass executions in football stadiums (not yet, anyway), but as a known dissident, he'd been marked down for disappearance nonetheless. Instead of a knock at the door in the middle of the night, it had come over time, excruciatingly by degrees. In the past, he had been chief speech-writer to two different Scottish secretaries: Howard Clark and the tragic and much-misunderstood Alastair Dalgliesh. He was prized and lauded for his wit, his clarity and his passion; whether they needed to put fire in the bellies of the faithful, or fear in the hearts of the enemy, he was the man they trusted to deliver. There was no thorn in the flesh of the left like Walter Thorn. But those enemies did not forget, and would never forgive; nor could they afford to let a dangerous subversive remain loose armed with such a powerful weapon as the truth.

After the British electorate's Gadarene mass-suicide of '97, like-minded veterans gathered to one another in pockets of resistance. He returned to the vocation where he'd made his name, accepting offers from two friends to write columns for their newspapers, albeit only in the regionalised editions. (Bloody everything had to be regionalised, like bloody everything had to be divided, distinguished and compartmentalised in case you gave offence to a one-legged Welsh-speaking Pakistani lesbian.) So for a while, he had still been able to strike back, shaming the hypocrisy, ridiculing the absurdities and generally sending out a clarion-call to the silent majority, reassuring them that they weren't alone in their anger and disgust. But the resistance was being slowly crushed, and in such times there will always be traitors, turncoats and capitulators selling out their comrades to save themselves. His column was dropped from the *Sunday Tribune* when its editor-in-chief shamelessly abandoned his principles in order to preserve

245

his own job following the stable's sale. The craven quisling did everything but wear a pink frock and decorate his office with Judy Garland posters in order to appear ideologically on-message to the new 'gay-friendly' proprietor. The *Tribune* papers were 'reinventing themselves as a centre-ground alternative', which was marketing speak for watering themselves down for the politically correct palate and waving a white flag from the parapet. White flag? Pink flag, surely.

At *The Post* his jettison was less blatant. He'd had a relationship with the paper going back to the Sixties, having started off there as a campaigning reporter before going on to work as a columnist and leader-writer. All of that would have stood him in fine stead if it wasn't that his old friend, Michael Dunn, had recently retired and been replaced as Scottish editor by some upstart female who short-sightedly regarded the longevity of Walter's association with the paper as a burden rather than a pedigree.

'It's the way forward for the right. IDS is big on this. We need to be seen to be trying to shape the future, rather than always harking back to the past. From now on this paper is going to be about making people think that Conservative doesn't mean old-fashioned, or disapproving of every-thing. This doesn't mean our core values have changed, but in expressing them we need to come across as pro-active forward-thinkers, rather than moral spoilsports.'

Moral spoilsports. An editor (editrix?) of the *Daily Post*, albeit in a regional bureau, had actually said that.

Of course, she didn't have the gall to just summarily ditch him from the paper (and she was aware he still had friends up the chain who knew he'd been penning editor-ials when she was reading the *Bunty*). Instead, she was trying to make things uncomfortable for him in the hope that he'd fall on his sword. His column was axed first, then he was edged off the leader team and finally the politics desk, but he was not laid off and he was damned if he was surrendering and giving the bint what she wanted. She even gave him the letters page to edit, which she must have been sure would finish him off, but she under-estimated both his professionalism and his certainty that if he bided his time, he'd still be around to see her get her jotters. He'd seen plenty of deluded mediocrities knocked from their perches in his time, and she'd be no different. Eventually, she was forced to change her tactics, giving him an assign-ment she surely thought he'd make a sackable mess of.

'You made your name in this game by being in touch with the values and feelings of the silent majority,' she told him, in an act of utterly transparent flattery. 'Now more than ever we need to show the discrepancy between what the man in the street really believes, and the politically correct mumbo-jumbo he's being force-fed.' If the flattery wasn't enough, the fact that this sounded like music to his ears tipped him off that he was being set up, even before she told him what she had in mind.

'I want you to go under-cover.'

'Eh?'

'Have you heard of FANY?' she asked.

'Fanny who?'

'Family and Natural Youth. It's a new pressure group, kind of rising from the ashes of Families for Innocence and all that lot.'

He remembered Families for Innocence all right, having applauded them in print as 'the first wave of a rising tide', ordinary people fighting back against the Executive's dogmatism. They had come to prominence a couple of years back, when they organised a Scotland-wide picket of the Greencross chemist chain. Greencross was in cahoots with Holyrood to set up 'advice' clinics for teenagers at its major branches, the advice of course being that they should have lots of sex and buy plenty of contraceptives from the scheme's selfless patron. The group was disbanded amid the hysterical media backlash after a couple of Greencross staff were allegedly assaulted during the pickets, one claiming to have had acid thrown in her face. It was unquestionably down to the work of infiltrators, out to discredit both the pressure group and the position it represented. Why no-one else was able to see through this was a matter of 'none so blind'.

'Liam McGhee was the driving force behind FFI, and he's been involved in a few things since, under various banners. Those Marie Stopes protests last year, and that big stushie over links with Operation Rescue.'

'I know who you mean.'

'Well, he started up FANY a few months back, with a far wider agenda than in the past. It's not just another anti-abortion or contraception pressure group. He says they're about "putting the moral reality in front of the politicians' ivory tower", something like that. They've not made much of an impact so far; in fact a lot of folk thought McGhee had just about chucked it after the reception they got at their launch, but it turns out he might just have been keeping his powder dry. The whisper is that they're planning some really high-profile stunts.'

'And where do I fit in?'

'I want you to sign up. Get involved. Be there for the exclusive, and have the in-depth inside track afterwards. This sort of thing is precisely what we need – a marriage of old-style values with a modern dynamic. It shows that being conservative can be, you know, a bit rock 'n' roll, a

248

bit kick-ass. Taking a moral stance doesn't only mean Disgusted of Tunbridge Wells firing off an angry letter before going out to the bowling club. This is passionate, it's pro-active, it's *sexy*.'

Sexy. Indeed. How very him.

Walter thought about it long into the night, eventually going downstairs when his tossing and turning became enough to irritate his wife, Mary, even across the gap between their beds. Getting through almost a whole bottle of barley water (it was just one of those nights), he sat in his study and mulled it over until close to dawn.

He came very near to just chucking it. Going undercover at this stage in his career, for goodness' sake. That sort of thing was a task for the young and keen, greenhorns with plenty to prove and little option to say no if they wanted a career in this game. Walter Thorn had nothing to prove to anybody, least of all some mini-skirted flash-in-the-pan who didn't have the sense to realise she'd only been hired as window dressing because the publishers wanted to look more 'woman-friendly' in this sorry age of 'positive discrimination'.

She probably expected him to balk, he realised, not even get as far as messing up the job. Then she could fire him without any substantial recourse from the powers that be. He was supposed to just go quietly into the night, make way for the new generation, in which case pity help us all. When even the *Daily Post*'s moral spine was buckling, it was a sign of grim times indeed, to say nothing of the declining standards of reporting evident throughout the press in general. Take the nonsense the papers had been full of lately, this bank robbery fiasco in Buchanan Street.

'SURREAL GONE QUIDS – ARTFUL DODGERS MAKE OFF WITH A MILL'

'ART ATTACK – CLASSY ROBBERS PAINT COPS INTO A CORNER'
'CROOKED CLOWNS LAUGH ALL THE WAY FROM THE BANK'
'TRICKY SITUATIONISTS – THIEVES STEAL £1M FROM UNDER COPS' NOSES'

Unbelievable. They were treating crime as if it was entertainment, practically applauding these villains simply because their methods were a trifle more colourful than any other bunch of shotgun-wielding thugs. They weren't just thieves, you see, they were artistic thieves, so that made it all right. Did that mean, then, that it would be all right to anally rape a schoolboy as long as you sketched a faux Picasso on the wall above the scene of your crime? None of Walter's supposed journalistic peers seemed to be asking that. Instead they were proving as distracted by the criminals' frippery as the police had sadly been on the day. What was worse was that they didn't appear to have a clue what they were writing about. From page to page they couldn't decide whether they were dealing with surrealists, absurdists, situationists or even Dadaists, when it should have been signally obvious that they were merely dealing with crooks. Dadaists, indeed. That particular hack had only used the term in order to show off that he was familiar with it; a pity, then, that he didn't also know what it actually meant.

The details of their allegedly artistic antics were appallingly contradictory too, where they weren't exaggerated beyond any plausible belief. Depending on which paper you read, they had, in the midst of their misdeeds, staged a full performance of *Waiting for Godot*, *Hamlet* or *The Pirates of Penzance*, and had apparently daubed the walls with recreations of half the Musée D'Orsay.

What the police were thinking, God only knew. It would never have happened under Thatcher, that was for damned sure: no pussyfooting around outside, minding your step in case you happened to cause a crook emotional upset by loitering with intent to arrest. In those days, the police knew that the government had their backs. They'd have gone straight in and mopped it up in no time, and nobody would have asked any questions later about a few dead scum or even a few hostage casualties. Back then, people knew the blame lay squarely with the bad guys, not the forces of law and order. Instead they'd been run rings around while they worked out how best to politely request the robbers to desist without infringing any human rights they could sue over later. That was the real tragedy of the situation, as much as the missing money, but the press were too busy congratulating the crooks on their ingenuity to notice.

Amid such reflections, Walter realised that he had a duty to hang on, however grimly, even if it was only to remind these idiots of the standards the newspaper had lost. He wasn't going to be elbowed out just to make room for more half-wits who wouldn't have lasted a morning back in the old days. And thus resigned, the more he thought about the assignment, the more it began to appeal. If he was a decorated veteran of the old campaigns, then this might well constitute the new breed of resistance. The left had had the Sixties, their activism, their radicalism, their 'counter-culture'. Maybe now was the time for the right to get militant, for what was conservatism these days if it wasn't counter-culture?

By the end of the night, he felt sure he'd made the right decision, and by the end of the week he'd have said it was inspired.

Family and Natural Youth was, as the editrix told him, the latest venture of Liam McGhee, who had become an ardent moral activist after rediscovering his faith while serving a prison sentence for aggravated burglary. McGhee had fallen into a life of petty crime after being expelled from a seminary for selling its silver communion chalice, though he claimed to have been framed for this crime by 'a bent Marist Brother' whom he alleged had spent the proceeds on rent boys. Upon seeing the light and renouncing the sins of his past, McGhee was seized with a burning religious energy, which he channelled initially into pro-life activism before broadening his scope to include a wider spectrum of family and moral issues. His media profile rose spectacularly in those early days, as he represented a new, grass-roots voice in an arena previously dominated by the more polished presentation and methods of clerics and their spokesmen. Then, just as suddenly, his star was forced to fade again in the aftermath of the Greencross incidents, amid mock-outraged accusations that his rhetoric and 'in-your-face' tactics had somehow incited campaigners to violence.

Family and Natural Youth was supposed to relaunch him into the public eye and remind the powers-that-be that he hadn't gone away, any more than the issues he was bringing to their door. Unfortunately, the media's reaction following the group's initial press conference suggested that they were more than reluctant to allow him a second bite at the cherry. There were a number of highly unflattering reports, dismissing him as, in one callous phrase, 'an attention-seeking ned', and accusing him of mounting moral crusades to avoid confronting the shames of his own past.

However, what had really buried him was the name. He had chosen it to reflect the concerns and values the group sought to represent, with the term 'natural youth' in particular drawing attention to matters such as the Executive's highly corrupting sex education policies, which when they weren't trying to turn children queer, were aimed at sexualising them before they were out of primary school. At the launch, assistants freely handed out car stickers reading 'F&NY', as McGhee sat in front of a banner bearing the same legend. The ampersand was picked out in red, the idea being that the logo resembled those I ♥ NY stickers that tourists brought back from America. Unfortunately, as the editrix's shorthand would attest, the liberal reptile element seized upon an alternative acronym, referring to the group collectively as 'Fanny', and its members individually by an equally predictable term.

McGhee confessed to Walter that he had been thoroughly depressed by this response and was not by any means 'keeping his powder dry', instead seriously contemplating disbandment and a move to America, where there were people who would harness – and better appreciate – his efforts. So it was perhaps appropriate that the group's recent renewed impetus should come in the form of a new arrival from those very transatlantic shores.

His name was Monty, short for Montague Masterton: a tall, burly and well-presented New Englander, who spoke in a drawling accent that drew out every vowel sound but took a refreshing pride in pronouncing every consonant. He had introduced himself to McGhee two or three weeks back during F&NY's picket of the Dalriada Gallery, in protest at its forthcoming 'History of Allegory' exhibition. They got talking and, well, a few minutes talking to Monty Masterton and you'd understand how things must have developed from there. He was truly a breath of fresh air, capable of blowing away the cobwebs and invigorating the most jaded mind or embattled conscience. Whether he was addressing a meeting or just chatting over coffee, he made one feel the moral war was not in the cataclysmic endgame it often seemed, but merely beginning, if only we had the courage to fight it.

'I have one very important thing to say to you,' he had addressed the room on the first night Walter encountered him. 'One thing that may seem simple, but only because our enemies have clouded the facts, confused the issues and made us afraid of ourselves. And it is this: It's okay to hate fags. I'll say it again: it's okay to hate fags. Pretty simple, isn't it? Again, with me: it's okay to hate fags. And you know why? Because GOD hates fags. Don't ever forget that. Never. When they're whining about equal rights or they're complaining about discrimination, you just keep that in sight. You're being discriminated against because you're a fag? Well, buster, that's because YOU'RE NOT SUPPOSED TO BE A FAG. God wants you discriminated against, and who can argue against that? You don't have equal rights? Oh boo-hoo. You don't get rights – you're a fag. You signed a waiver on all those rights when you took the decision to put your dick in another man's ass. Got it? God hates fags, you hate fags, I hate fags. It's okay. It's how it's meant to be. This, as my coloured brethren would say, is called keeping it real.'

It seemed revelatory, though it was obvious stuff, plain as the nose on your face. But that was his talent, making people see how obvious and simple things were when you got rid of all the distractions that had been put there to confuse you. It reminded Walter of himself once upon a time, when he had an equally uncompromising way of cutting through the camouflage to expose the truth.

'And don't be under the misapprehension that a fag is merely a queer. All homosexuals are fags, but to be a fag, you don't need to be homosexual. The apologists, the fellow-travellers, the politicians who are helping them proselytise, the do-gooders who want to put drugs and pornography in classrooms: these are all fags. I have seen how they operate, seen the damage they have done back in my own country, and believe me, it is up to you to act now before it's too late.

'Fags are resourceful, fags are inventive, fags are insidious. And the worst kind, I would say, are the art-fags, without doubt the most insidious of the lot. They are the propaganda wing of the fag war machine, every one a little faggy Goebbels. If you have any doubt about this, then ask yourself how *your* tax dollars have come to be funding the display of pornographic materials in a place innocent children have free access to. Danger: fags at work. You are already aware that the Dalriada Museum's forthcoming exhibition will feature hard-core – *hard-core* – porno videos as part of a so-called "installation". But did you also know that the museum's trustees have paid more than twenty thousand pounds for a statue of a man sucking his own Johnson? You couldn't make this stuff up. This city's schools are struggling for books, but hey, that's okay, because if the kids are at a loose end, they can go to the municipal gallery and look at twenty grand's worth of fag-propaganda.'

This, incredibly, was no exaggeration. The Canadian cretin in charge of the Dalriada, one Thomas White, had indeed seen fit to splash out the mentioned sum for what was supposed to be a pertinent example of twenty-first century allegory. This came in the form of a statue entitled *West Coast (,) Man* (the comma in parentheses apparently never to be omitted from the name). In a vulgarly unsubtle attempt at social satire, this gratuitously offensive metal monstrosity depicted a man bent into a grotesque contortion in order to perform oral sex on himself, while at the same time sniffing a line of (supposedly real) cocaine from the shaft of his penis. A snaking tongue apparently protruded from the mouth and led, with tiresome predictability, up his own anus, as two of his four arms held mobile phones to each of his ears. His remaining hands were reportedly engaged in obscene gesticulations, but Walter had not bothered to disturb himself with further details when he read the art correspondent's description.

Now, there would always be those who objected to public money being spent on the arts, and Walter did not normally count himself among them. In this day and age, there would be no opera without it, for instance. There had recently been an almighty fuss over what it was going to cost the Kelvingrove Museum to upgrade its security arrangements in order to temporarily host the Treasures of the Aztecs exhibition 'when it could be spent on schools and hospitals etc etc', and Walter had sided with the council over that one. If you wanted the chance to see several million pounds worth of ancient gold and jewels, you had to cough up to make sure none of the local scruff decided to melt it down and flog it off. But great God, who wouldn't draw the line at funding unadulterated filth?

It was too late now, of course: the money was spent, and F&NY's efforts to publicise the threat to children had been largely ignored by the media. But that was before Montague Masterton got involved.

'Family and Natural Youth is a public voice and a public face for beliefs that ordinary people have been intimidated from expressing, and it must continue in those roles. But as you know to your cost, faces and voices can be ignored. Action cannot.

'I am looking for volunteers tonight, volunteers to form an offshoot, the elite unit that will take the fight back to the fags and the hypocrites. That offshoot will be known as Positive Action Direct. Who's with me?'

The editrix, even if she had been genuinely interested in what the rejuvenated pressure group might be planning, could have had no idea of just how big a story this was going to be. What Monty had up his sleeve was not merely more audacious than any publicity stunt, it was proof that the battle for hearts and minds was about to become a guerrilla war. And he, Walter Thorn, would be seeing active service as well as filing from the front line.

He had not chosen to be an outlaw, that had been thrust upon him. But when the law itself was unjust, it was the duty of just men to break it. It was time for the good guys to show they could fight dirty.

'This may not strike you as the biggest issue in this world right now, or even in this city right now,' Monty told them. 'And it may not strike you as the greatest threat we face. But the fight has to start somewhere, people, and the battle against propaganda is one of the most important in any war. We have to warn them that they can't ignore the will of decent people and they can't hide behind the barricades of political correctness anymore. F&NY-PAD are here now, and it's gonna get bloody.'

# be my downfall

'All this villain-catching stuff boring you, de Xavia?'

Angelique looked up from the statement she was reading to see Shaw standing a few feet from her desk. The remark sounded like a polite way of announcing his presence in an open-plan office sadly bereft of doors to be knocked. However, she wasn't aware of having yawned, which was what usually provoked such a comment.

'Sir?'

'I've just learned that you're buggering off on me. Time in lieu, starting Thursday.'

'Yup,' she said, offering no further elaboration, her way of communicating that it was non-negotiable. Angelique had a long record of voluntary cooperation when it came to cancelling her own time off, something she used to tell herself was a form of investment in her career. Latterly, with the returns on that investment making Eurotunnel shares look like blue-chips, she had been forced to consider the possibility that the truth behind her uncomplaining flexibility was instead that she was a sad mug with no life. Nothing was going to stop her getting on that plane with the mysterious Zal, especially not any laboured sense of duty towards her job when the best available means of doing her job was to get on the bloody plane.

'Well, look, it's inconvenient, but given the informality of the arrangement, it's not worth me bein' a prick over.'

'And yet you're here,' Angelique said pointedly. 'No offence.'

Shaw laughed. 'I'm here, aye. I'm just wondering whether your plans are a reflection on how you rate our chances of success. I cannae imagine someone of your reputation wanting to miss out if things started to get . . . interesting.'

'They've been interesting since the bank, but I'd put down half my pension you're no' gaunny catch this guy before I get back.'

'You're off somewhere, then?'

'Paris. You'll still be able to get me on my mobile if you just need to pick my brains.'

'Paris, eh. Very romantic.'

Bloody polis, always prying. Even small-talk constitutes a line of inquiry.

'I'm going with a friend,' she said. And an enemy, it could be argued, but did she lie?

'Bit of Christmas shopping? Very nice. And I do have your mobile number, but I don't imagine you'll be giving much thought to whoever robbed the RSGN while you're gaddin' aboot in gay Paris.'

'I'm sure he won't be too far from my mind.'

'He? And you said "this guy" before, too.'

Angelique felt a shudder of panic.

'Sorry, it's just he was the only one I spoke to, so I was kind of focusing, you know. When I think about what happened, I tend to think first about him, and . . .'

She was babbling, trying to cover up something that would have been hopelessly obvious to anyone who actually knew to be looking for it. Fortunately, that did not include Shaw.

'Keep the heid. I wasnae makin' oot you fancy him. Just

259

wondering if you concur that Jarry's the one to concentrate on. Cut off the head and all that. Well, the brain anyway.'

Thus reprieved, Angelique recovered well. 'He's not the only brain among them, that's for sure, but that level of orchestration doesn't happen in a democracy.'

'Doesn't happen without a tight crew, either. Skills, loyalty, mutual respect for what each other brings to the table. But the man with the plan's got to be a bit special.'

'He's just a thief to me, sir.'

'I meant to them.'

'Oh, absolutely.'

'So, half your pension, eh?'

'Well, I've never worked with you before, sir. I wouldn't want to risk serious money in case you surprised me.'

'And what would I have to stake against that?'

Angelique saw the story behind the banter.

'You've got something, haven't you? What is it?'

Shaw smiled coyly and shrugged. 'Maybe. Nothing dramatic, but there is something I'd like you to take a look at. That's if you're not too busy packing your suitcase.'

'Oh, I've got servants to do that, sir. Have to find some way of spending the salary, and the south wing's been painted already this year.'

Shaw took her downstairs to the incident room, where he had a TV and a VCR set up on a desk. The blinds were turned to prevent theoretical glare on the monitor, a highly optimistic gesture for the time of year. Shaw pressed play on a remote and the screen filled with a black-and-white, closed-circuit image of Buchanan Street, swarms of shoppers jump-cutting their way back and forth between staccato refreshes.

'Is this the day of the robbery?' Angelique asked.

'Saturday before,' Shaw replied. 'Notice anything?'

She stared for a few seconds. Nothing struck her as remarkable or out of the ordinary.

'Gap's got a sale on?'

'Very good. There's a dug has a shite in this corner at one point as well. Anything else catch your eye?'

'Sorry, sir. Just looks like Buchanan Street on a Saturday to me.'

'And to everybody else, except one person. You see this area here, against the wall? Empty. Know why? There's usually a busker stands there, the bloke that ID'd the clowns as Zal Cleminson look-alikes.'

'Where is he?'

'At this point, still at hame, because of this guy.' Shaw pointed to close to the centre of the screen, where a figure was standing in the middle of the concourse, holding a book and a microphone. 'Bible-thumper was queering his pitch. Naebody could hear his singin' for this guy's blethers; blethers, I should add, that were in an American accent.'

Angelique looked closely at the al-fresco evangelist, tiny in the centre of the cluttered image. Detail was low at that range, nor was it helping that he was facing away from the camera, so only when he turned could she see even enough of his head to note a bushy black beard and equally bushy black hair. However, it was what he was facing toward that significantly dominated the picture: the Royal Scottish/Great Northern bank. Angelique noted the time-code. 'Saturday morning, 11:38.'

'Aye. According to our busker, this guy started showing up three weeks back, every Saturday morning.'

'Why did the busker not find a new pitch?'

'These guys are awfy territorial. Plus, he knew the Bible-basher never stayed after lunchtime. Knocked off around the back of twelve every week.'

'When the bank closed. He was casing the joint in broad daylight.'

'Perfect disguise. Naebody hassles a man doing the Good Lord's work, and naebody pays a blind bit of notice to him, either. Just goes to show you should never trust these God-bothering bastards.'

'I'd lift them on-sight if it was up to me.'

'Needless to say, there's no sign of him on the tape for the day of the job.'

'Not without a more colourful costume anyway. Can we get a better picture than this?'

'These recordings are time-lapsed to save tape, so the quality is generally shite, but we've had some enhancements done.'

Shaw produced an envelope and upended it, allowing two laser proofs to drop on to the desk. 'We've no current plans to put them on posters, as I'm sure you'll appreciate. The hair's probably a wig and the beard'll be long gone if it was ever real to begin with. But the eyes are pretty clear in one of them, and seeing as that was all you'd have seen, I thought you should have a wee swatch.'

Angelique looked. One of the proofs was little more than a profile, the contours of the face deliberately obscured by the excessive hirsuteness. The other offered little more by way of shape, and though the eyes were visible, the detail was poor and the image pixelated to the point of blurry. Nonetheless, there was no mistaking who they belonged to.

'Zal,' she said.

'Zal?'

'I mean Jarry. So many bloody aliases, it's very confusing. But that's him.'

'You sure?'

'Well it's not the dwarf, and another of them was black,

so it's fifty-fifty, but I'd bet the other half of my pension it's him.'

'Fifty-fifty's better than most of our leads have worked out lately, so I reckon your first half's safe.'

'How come?'

'Ach, it was tuppence-hapenny stuff anyway. The guns, for a start. They're not replicas. They're not real either, but they're not reproductions of any fire-arm known to man, or at least known to Ballistics. Total originals, and therefore effectively untraceable. No joy on the face-masks either, but safe to say, if they've the means to design and construct their own fake weaponry, the Halloween outfits would be a dawdle.'

'Especially for blokes with a proven talent for the visual arts.'

'Aye. Mind you, here's a thing. Everybody's talkin' aboot these guys being artists, what with the names and the costumes an' aw the rest of it. I don't know, though. I think this Jarry character's somethin' else. He's a showman, all right, and he can act when he needs to, but that's all part of the greater performance, if you ask me. The paintings, the play, the lot – it's all part of his show, but it's not an art show and it's not a drama show. It's a magic show. Distraction, sleight of hand, misdirection. Spectacle to keep your eyes off where the real work is being done. A volunteer from the audience to become an unwitting accomplice in the deceit. And for his last trick he makes five people and the best part of a million sheets disappear. Alakazammy, stairheid rammy!'

'A magician,' Angelique agreed, looking again at the laser proof.

Like his father before him.

*　*　*

Sometimes you have to let your conscience have its say, even when you know you're going to do what you intended anyway. Maybe it's on the off-chance that it'll tell you you're actually doing the right thing, or maybe it's so you can pretend to yourself that you balanced up all the arguments before taking an informed decision. Either way, Zal was pretty sure he wasn't the only one who did it. However, for most people it was a matter of internal dialogue, rather than a confessional phone call to an obsessive midget with an over-developed sense of responsibility.

'You don't change, Zal, do you? I mean through the years, prison, everything.'

'What's that supposed to mean? I'm assuming it's not a compliment.'

'You know exactly what it means, same as you know the parts that are a compliment and the parts that are a warning to save you from yourself.'

'I know what I'm doing, Karl. You know I can make this work.'

'I know what you can do, buddy. I've known you longer than anybody, and there's two other guys under no illusions about how far you're prepared to go. But I'm not sure we'd all agree on what constitutes "making it work". This girl is a cop, a cop we took hostage, and you know little more about her than her name. And yet, despite all of that, you're sending her flowers, buying her drinks and flying her to fucking Paris. I don't think you have any idea of what you're dealing with.'

'I am entirely aware, I am on high-alert aware, of what I'm dealing with. It's the very fact that she's a cop that makes—'

'Zal, I'm not talking about her. I'm talking about you. There's things loose in your kitchen that you don't know how to handle, man. The fact that she's a cop isn't the only thing you gotta worry about – it's just the only thing you *know* to worry about.'

'After Folsom, I can handle a lot, believe me.'

'Surviving is not the same as evolving.'

'New flesh still grows beneath scar tissue, Karl. I have to let her in close for this to work, but if it doesn't, we can still revert to Plan A. I always have an out, you know that.'

'Okay, I take it back. You have changed, but you've changed in ways you're not even aware of, and that's where the danger's coming from. You think this is just another girl you can walk away from, same old Zal, like you walked away from a dozen before.'

'I didn't walk away from anybody. Relationships break up, Karl. Just because you and I are practically married—'

'Bullshit. You always have an out, just like you said. An exit strategy, to make sure you don't get hurt. You always walk away. You walk away before they can walk away from you. And now you probably figure this one's the ultimate: she's a girl you'll have no choice but to run from in the end. Well, maybe that won't be as easy as you think.'

'How can you say that? You don't know her, you barely even saw her.'

'Like I said before, Zal, I'm not talking about the girl.'

Damn it.

Okay, so there was another reason for letting Karl loose in Jiminy Cricket mode, which was that he was a highly accurate sounding board for the legitimacy of whatever happened to be worrying Zal about himself. If Karl didn't mention it, then it could be written off against general nonspecific anxiety, self-doubt, hormones, biorhythms, the alignment of the planets, bad burritos – the usual shit. On this occasion, though, Karl had zeroed in with digitally calibrated, on-board laser-guidance towards exactly what was making Zal apprehensive about what he was getting into.

*This girl is a cop. You know little more about her than her name. And yet . . .*

And yet.

Karl wasn't worried about what Angelique de Xavia did for a living. He was worried about what she was doing to Zal, which made two of them. However, there are certain mistakes that you know you just have to make, know you're *going* to make, no matter what conscience, logic or fear are telling you.

It's a simple truth of human existence. Across thousands of years of civilisation, throughout the rise and fall of empires and our stumbling ascent from the forests to the stars, greater men than Zal had contemplated the wisdom of their intentions before coming to exactly the same conclusion.

And there was usually a girl involved, yeah.

# paris v achilles

It was a cold and clear December Thursday, around noon, and Detective Inspector Angelique de Xavia was walking briskly through Montmartre in the direction of the Seine, trying to keep up with the tall, athletic, charming and highly untrustworthy American male who had flown her there at his, or more likely the RSGN bank's expense. All of the previously documented conflicts and doubts persisted, and she remained as wary of his long-term intentions as she was of her own unaccustomed vulnerabilities, but one thing was indubitably sure: it beat the hell out of working.

They had flown out of Glasgow at seven-thirty, Angelique keeping her head down much of the time to avoid confirmatory eye contact with any security staff or cops on duty who might recognise her.

Zal had been waiting for her in the Departures hall, greeting her with a slightly surprised (and not a little nervy) 'You came.'

'You don't sound sure that's a good thing. You getting cold feet?'

'I'm from Nevada and this is Glasgow in December. I've always got cold feet.'

They were surprisingly comfortable in their chatter on the flight and in the cab, trading banter and small-talk like they had known each other for years, probably due to each trying very hard to disguise their own apprehension. Angelique certainly was, and she knew that deceptive impressions were something of a forte of her travelling companion. However, there was to be no cutting to the chase, something Zal made obvious with his now familiarly irritating ability to not only bodyswerve the subject, but to refuse to even acknowledge it.

The hotel was like nothing Angelique had experienced or expected, though this might have been different had she concentrated on her expectations of Zal rather than her expectations of Paris. It seemed to have made a stylistic and architectural virtue out of being neat and horizontally compact, by basing its entire design around boxes and rectangles. Even the minimalist reception desk was a neolithically simple structure, one horizontal block on top of an only slightly narrower vertical one.

'It's the world's first Cubist hotel,' Zal informed her as she took in her surroundings. 'The aesthetic of geometry even extends to the fittings in the rooms.'

'You've been before, then?'

'No. I read about it in . . .' He paused, long enough for Angelique to interject.

'Stir?'

'I was actually trying to remember the name of the magazine, but yes, that is where I was at the time. Very good. How'd you guess?'

'Well, a crook doing some jail-time is hardly a million-to-one shot, but you gave it away the other day, said you "watched a lot of *Jeopardy* in—", then censored yourself.'

'Bound to slip out, I guess. When that's where you've spent the past three years, it tends to dominate the conversational motifs unless you stay on top of it.'

'Three years? What for?'

'Getting caught. What else?'

Angelique was relieved not to have to negotiate any

awkwardness over rooms, the receptionist handing her her own keycard and a separate details form when Zal quoted his reservation code (naturally in lieu of a surname). She dumped her overnight bag in her regimentedly geometric double room, ruffling the duvet as a statement of aesthetic dissent, then met Zal back in the lobby, where he announced their destination as the Louvre.

Despite the cold, neither of them suggested a preference for the convenience or warmth of a cab. This was Paris, after all, and on a school day. In fact Zal's walking pace would have almost seemed philistinistic if it wasn't helping raise their body temperatures, but as he spoke, Angelique realised the real reason for his haste was that he simply couldn't wait to get there.

'It was Diderot's suggestion that they make the place open to more than just the elite. Dunno what he'd have made of the Belaggio, I have to say, but definitely a man after my own heart. There's an egalitarianism about what the Louvre represents that, to me, is the quintessence of art's relationship with society.'

He was talking, with some knowledge and no little articulacy, about the history of the world's largest museum, but the unabashed enthusiasm and restless anticipation was that of an excited wee boy going to Disneyland.

'After the Revolution, they displayed works that had been pilfered from the clergy. I love that. Napoleon added a shitload of stuff that he'd plundered from his campaigns, though most of it got plundered straight back after the fall of the empire.'

'A shitload? Is that the collective noun for accumulated art treasures?'

'In my neighbourhood, sure. And do you know the Richelieu wing was claimed back from the bureaucrats by order of Mitterand in the early Nineties? It housed the Ministry of Finance, and now it houses the truly invaluable.'

And so on, until they were outside the glass pyramid, where Zal turned slowly to look at the palace enclosing them on three sides.

'Okay, tell me,' Angelique said. 'Are we just two more interested tourists here today, or are you casing the joint? *Reverend.*'

Zal laughed, slightly taken aback, blindsided by the last jibe as he prepared to respond to the first. 'I guess you now know I'm not a natural blond,' he said.

'Yeah, like it took seeing a beard to tell me that.'

'I'm not casing the place, rest assured. There's six hundred and fifty guards in there, and besides, it goes against my principles.'

'To steal art?'

'Oh, shit no. But publicly owned art, that's sacred, and this is a temple. Come on.'

She followed Zal down an escalator into the subterranean entrance hall, where he paid for their admission while she bought herself a bottle of water.

'So why *have* you brought me here?' Angelique asked, wiping her mouth and accepting the fold-out museum map he was proffering. She offered him the bottle, which he drained and binned before starting off towards the Denon wing.

'Who needs a reason to come to the Louvre?'

'Nobody. Nobody with a soul, anyway. But a thief needs a reason to bring a detective here, even if she didn't have a better offer for her day off.'

'We can talk here, that's why.'

'I can talk anywhere. Art makes you garrulous, is that it?'

'Loosens my tongue more than the finest wine,' he said,

before skipping ahead of her through the arch of a metal-detector. He turned around and smiled, taking a small bow, at which point Angelique got it: she couldn't pass through if she was wearing a wire. She made a sarcastic gesture of applause and followed him through the machine.

'Did you really believe I'd set you up?'

'It's moot now, that's the point.'

'But if you didn't trust me . . .'

'I'm still paying you your due respects, remember? Making you walk through that arch doesn't mean I didn't trust you before you did it. And just because we're on the other side of it doesn't mean I trust you now. But if a wire was what I was concerned about, we could have talked at the airport. Come on, I want to show you something.'

'Show me something? You mean there's something to see here?'

'Yeah, I heard they got a coupla paintings, you know? Probably shit.'

Making occasional reference to his floorplan, Zal led her to the Denon wing's humbling hall of large-scale French paintings. The seeming endlessness of riches made her feel like she was Alice and someone had spent a few billion doing up Wonderland's ever-stretching corridor. Zal clearly had a specific destination in mind, and her curiosity made her keen to reach this place where he might finally talk, but despite this, she couldn't help stopping before several of these imposing masterpieces.

Her companion was in no hurry himself, and appeared at times to be spellbound before gods. Awestruck or not, Angelique's flippant suggestion that art made him loquacious proved to be right on the money, as he blabbered sometimes breathlessly about David, Lorrain, Delacroix and others. He did, nonetheless, restrict himself to a mere smirk as they passed Gericault's *Raft of the Medusa*.

Eventually they reached their destination, their progress latterly slowed not merely by the distractions on the walls, but by the rope-cordoned queue they had joined. Angelique guessed correctly at the source of the hold-up, but had to confess a little surprise at it being what Zal specifically wished her to see.

'The *Mona Lisa*?'

'*La Gioconda*,' he confirmed, the pair of them taking a couple of steps back to allow the next group of gawping initiants their turn at the altar. 'There she is, staring out at five million people a year from behind six millimetres of bulletproof glass. The real thing, all present and correct: the mouth, the hands, the eyes, and Mordor there in the background. The name means joyful, but the smile is ambiguous, huh? The mystery of that curious smile, is that what brings thousands of people filing past here every day?'

'I don't know. She looks kind of smug to me.'

'Well, you see the path there, and the bridge? Those are the only evidence of human industry or artifice in the landscape, representing man's limitations because they lead off where she's looking: a dream world beyond. Is it contemplation of that message that's led to a hundred yards of rope down that hallway at our backs?'

Angelique didn't see what he was driving at, and feared he might, under the influence of too much intoxicating art, be seriously wigging.

'Who can say?' she muttered patiently.

'I can say. And the answer is no. There's five million people a year standing in the spot where we are now simply because this is the most famous painting in the world and therefore you just *have* to go and see it. Doesn't matter if you're more naturally drawn to landscapes, battle scenes,

272

religious paintings, whatever: you *have* to go see the *Mona Lisa*, so it remains the most famous and popular painting in the world by virtue of *being* the most famous and popular painting in the world.'

'So what, you think it's shite?'

'I think it's magnificent, but that's not the issue.'

'Where are we going with this?'

'Café Richelieu is where we're going with it, first of all.'

'Hark, I hear the sound of procrastination.'

'Oh, I'm talking, girl, but I need a seat and an espresso.'

'You'll get them. But start talking now.'

'Okay,' he agreed, picking up the pace towards a massive staircase. 'I'm talking about values. Who's to say what makes the *Mona Lisa* greater than any one of the works we saw on the way here? Nobody, right?'

'I think Leonardo's mum would probably be quite strong on the subject.'

'Exactly. Bias, taste, personal preference. But what makes one guy's work worth a million bucks and the other not worth the canvas and oil?'

'Talent.'

'In an ideal world, absolutely, but it's not the only thing, not in this world. I guess I should have phrased it differently: what makes one guy *get* a million bucks for a painting while the artist next door can't raise the price of his canvas? Could be dumb luck, could be connections, could be the right gallery, the right agent, the right work at the right time. In New York, probably the same in London, if a certain dealer decides you're the dopest trip this month, bang, you're made. Yesterday you were this close to eating out of a dumpster, today this dealer is selling your work for six figures to a wealthy client who *needs to be told* what is good and what he likes. Suddenly you're a hundred

273

grand richer than the guy working in the next studio, but what makes you worth it?'

'What makes an actor worth twenty million a picture?'

'Box-office receipts. The thing about remuneration in the art world is that it requires no proof of popularity. You don't have to appeal to a lot of people, just the right people. Sure, it's arbitrary in Hollywood: a pretty face and a few breaks and you're on percentage points for phoning in a performance any number of actors could match. Tom Cruise gets twenty mill for a cute smile and, oh yeah, he can shake his fist if you need him to do angry, but Tom Cruise can turn around and say fuck you, my picture opened to *seventy* million bucks in its first weekend.'

They had reached the entrance to the café in the Richelieu wing, and joined a queue for a table only marginally shorter than the one preceding *La Jocunde*.

'Is this the part where you tell me you're an undiscovered genius with a grudge against an indifferent society?' Angelique asked.

'No, I'm an undiscovered mediocrity. A non-entity, in fact. Mediocrity makes it sound like I'm mid-table in the same division as talent. I'm a failed artist, yeah, justly and correctly undiscovered. We all are, except Karl.'

'The Cleminson Collective, you mean?'

'The Failed Artists Collective, to be precise. That's what we called ourselves back in the day.'

'But you were an artist.'

'I studied art, I wouldn't call myself an artist. Karl is an artist.'

'Which one's Karl?'

'The Failed Artist formerly known as Ionesco. He's the one with talent.'

'Talent as in whizz-kid computer hacker?'

Zal laughed. 'Oh man, he'd love that. He knows his code, yeah, but he wouldn't call himself a hacker, and definitely not a whizz-kid. And why is it anyone who's any good with computers is a whizz-kid? The guy's in his thirties.'

'Whatever you call him, hacking a bank's security system is more than just knowing your code.'

'True, but not as much more as you clearly imagine.'

'You up for telling me how he did it then?'

'Long as we remain in no danger of getting a table, why not? Karl just dropped a sub-seven trojan into the manager's hard drive.'

'In English.'

'A sub-seven trojan, as in Trojan Horse, though sub-seven Greek would be more accurate if you know your Classics. They hide out in the system and can do things ranging from reporting back with information to allowing you full remote access. The one Karl used was pretty basic. It wouldn't give you full access just by being there, because of passwords protecting different levels of the system.'

'So how did he manage it?'

'His trojan recorded keystrokes, pretty common hacking tool. That got him all the manager's passwords and ultimately full control of the system.'

'But how did he get it into the system in the first place? Didn't they have virus scanners?'

'You only have to be one day's modification ahead of the scanning software. He put it on a website and sent a link to the manager, but changed the account details so that the mail appeared to have come from a colleague elsewhere in RSGN. The guy clicks on the link and the first thing his PC downloads from the page is the trojan.'

'What was on the page?'

'404. File not found.'

'What, the poor bastard didn't even get a peek at some porn out of it?'

'He didn't need any more, from what Karl said about the dude's temp cache.'

'So if this kind of thing is all in a day's work, where does his real talent lie?'

'Someplace in the space between art and code, software and hard copy. Since he got his first Commodore, he was always doing amazing things with artwork programmes – 2D, 3D, animation – but he was eternally frustrated that it could only exist on a monitor. The computers got more powerful and the software more advanced, but that part never changed, not in time anyway. If you can imagine someone who starts off painting and finds two dimensions a limitation, then he can move on to sculpture or installation, whereas Karl couldn't. He could sculpt in three dimensions, but the only way of rendering it was still restricted to two.'

'And that's why he's a "failed artist"?'

'Yeah, pretty much. Snobbery attached to computers didn't help, especially back in those days. But in the main, his difficulty was his own frustration. He became fascinated with this gap, this barrier that as he saw it imprisoned his creations. He was just ahead of his time, that was the problem. Five years down the line he could have worked with holographic projectors and all sorts, but by then it was too late.'

'Why can't he do that kind of project now?'

'Things have been . . . complicated in recent years. Plus, time goes by, the impetus alters, ambitions and enthusiasms change. He's still obsessed with bridging that gap, though. He's been developing technology for creating computer-generated moulds, using a grid of thousands of tiny, length-adjustable pins. You know, you sculpt on-screen, this gizmo mimics – or inverts – the shape in three-dimensions, then you pour on your working material – cement, clay . . .'

'Latex, perhaps.'

'Indeed. Latex works pretty good. As I'm sure you can appreciate, the gizmo's got huge potential, but these things always need development money.'

'I do hope he finds a benefactor. And does the gizmo work with metal, may I ask?'

Zal laughed. 'You're talking about our guns? Nah. One day, maybe.'

'So who made them?'

'They were hand-crafted,' he said, grinning rather coyly. 'Not the artist's best work, but they did the job.'

'The SPAS-12 wasn't hand-crafted.'

'Spaz what?'

'The shotgun cum grenade launcher.'

'Oh, that. Borrowed. Wiped clean. Returned. Forget about it.'

At last they were shown to a table, where the sight of the menu transformed Zal's need for espresso into a desire for beer to wash down the platter he ordered. Angelique was going to opt for more mineral water, but the opulence of the surroundings and the lingering awareness that this was her time off won out in favour of a second Kronenbourg.

'Cheers,' Zal said, raising his glass. Angelique chinked hers against it, but wasn't for letting him get off track.

'If you're a sculptor, how come you know so much about paintings?'

'I'm not a sculptor and I'm not an artist, but I did study art.'

'Where? Vegas?'

'No need to be facetious. LA.'

'Is that where you guys met?'

'No, I've known Karl since we were kids. We lived in the same street, grew up together. His father worked at Circus Circus. He was a knife-thrower and an acrobat, and more reluctantly a clown, too.'

'Reluctantly?'

'He didn't like the idea of being considered a figure of fun just because he was short. I think it kind of weighed heavily that people saw him as a novelty even when he was doing his other stuff, no matter whether he was the best knife-thrower they'd ever seen. Which he undoubtedly would have been. You don't notice this so much when you're a kid, but in retrospect I reckon he wasn't entirely comfortable with what he did, period. He taught Karl a lot of stuff – every kid wants to copy dad – but he was determined Karl wasn't going to follow in his footsteps.'

'He was encouraging of his artistic ambitions, then?'

'No, not entirely. He knew Karl had a head for numbers and a facility with computers, so he'd have been happy to see him go into IT or accounting or something. Even Karl being a graphic artist, as opposed to a performer, was still too close for comfort, still the chance, as he saw it, of Karl being a novelty. "I don't want you being made an exhibition of," he used to say. It was the usual parental psycho-bullshit – transference of guilt, surrogation of your own regrets – you know the deal. Ironically, he pretty much got his wish. No exhibitions for Karl.'

'And that's why you're sore on the *Mona Lisa*?'

'Hey, I'm not taking it out on her. Shit, everybody knows somebody like Karl, somebody who's way more talented than a dozen, a thousand more successful others, but never got the right break. I knew talented guys who did get the breaks, too. Karl and I had a friend at art school in LA, a sculptor who just *had* it, and we knew he'd make a name for himself. It probably helped that his family had money, but you couldn't take that away from his talent. You don't get angry at the successful geniuses, you get angry at the successful mediocrities, and at the people who can't tell the fucking difference.'

'Forgive my obsessive professional angle on this, but I'm curious as to how your anger is given cathartic expression through robbing banks.'

Zal helped himself to another forkful of quiche before answering the question, unfazed by but unavoiding of Angelique's directness. There was something arguably more surreal about his current candour than about any of the methods he had employed to rip off the RSGN, and she couldn't help but wonder where was the catch, or the sting. In her more paranoid moments she found herself thinking of Kevin Spacey spinning his web of lies in *The Usual Suspects*.

'Karl and I moved to New York after college, back when he was still undeterred by his inability to fully express his gifts and I was still deluded about my lack of having any. Possibly the dumbest move of either of our lives. We were on the periphery of the art crowd there, you could say, kind of like Pluto is on the periphery of the solar system. Two guys from Vegas were never gonna be welcomed into the heart of the most bitchy, elitist and cliquey scene on the face of the earth, but we hung in there. Meantime, back in LA, where we had contacts and *did* know some people, our art school buddies were getting hired as critics, assistant curators, putting on shows together. But we'd decided New York was where it's at, and we are two stubborn sons of bitches. We took jobs in galleries, real dogsbody stuff a lot of the time, just to keep ourselves in the frame – pun intended – figuring if we held out long enough, we'd eventually get noticed. That's where we met Leo and Jerome.'

'Being Dali and Chagall.'

'Now you got the full set, yes. They met at art school and had hung out ever since. I'd say they hit it off together, but if you ever saw how they behave towards . . . never mind. We kind of found each other. They were fellow failures, and they didn't fit in too good, either. So we had our own little clique of outcasts, misfits and failures, trying to make each other feel better about all of the above.'

Zal smiled in reminiscence of something and took a drink of his beer as he savoured the moment.

'There was this guy, called himself Mercurio, but his real name was something like Brant Hetherington the Third. Rich-kid asshole. Jerome knew him from prep school, but being a preppy wasn't very cool, so Brant had reinvented himself as Mercurio. Jerome couldn't reinvent himself if he was on the Witness Protection Programme, so he was stuck being what he was. Mercurio, meanwhile, was an utter hack, but he had money to throw around on clothes and parties, plus he was very good at kissing all the right asses. So before you know it, there's an influential dealer exhibiting his crap and these over-remunerated yuppie assholes buying it for upwards of fifty grand a canvas.'

He let this sink in while he finished off what was on his plate.

'We decided these people needed to be taught a lesson in value,' he continued.

'What did this entail?'

'We got the names and addresses of everyone who

bought one of Mercurio's paintings and we stole them. Well, replaced them.'

'What with?'

'A framed message. It read – now let me get this right – "Anyone who can afford to spend $50,000 on a piece of shit can afford to lose $50,000 worth of shit. This message has been brought to you by the Failed Artists Collective." We thought we'd get that in before everybody else pointed out our petty and transparent motives.'

'How did you steal them?'

'We researched the owners' schedules and went in when only the help was home. Walked right in the front door of their apartments in broad daylight and took the paintings off the walls, telling the help we were taking them away for insurance valuation. The replacements we mailed later. We hit all four in the same day so that we could use the same MO. All you need is some paperwork, a couple of dudes in overalls and one friendly guy in a suit who speaks Spanish like his Mexican mother.'

'You. But they could ID you later.'

'Leo could work with latex and make-up a long time before Karl's gizmo came along. Not much we could do about Karl's distinguishing feature, though, so he drove the van.'

'What did you do with the paintings?'

'Jerome wanted to burn them, but Karl and I were kinda squeamish about that. Even if it's shit, it's still someone's work. We put them in a lock-up in Newark. To my knowledge, they're still there, along with a few others.'

'You did it again?'

'There was a lot of over-valued shit out there, and a lot of idiots with money to burn.'

'Weren't they on their guard by this time?'

'Oh yeah, eventually, but we varied the technique. They told the help not to let anybody lift their paintings, no matter how official they looked or whatever documentation they presented. We countered this at first by claiming to be from the IRS, there to confiscate the painting because there was tax due on it. Believe me, nobody is gonna tell the IRS to fuck off, and definitely not some illegal on five bucks an hour. Of course, we couldn't use that one forever either, so later we'd just use distraction: I'd keep the help busy in another room while Leo and Jerome lifted the shit. We were a photographer and his assistants, there to shoot the apartment for a magazine, scams like that.'

'Again, forgive the predictable angle, but what were the NYPD doing while all this was going on?'

'Worrying about real crimes, where people get hurt. The cops didn't need a framed message. To them, someone who can spend that kinda money on any painting, never mind a shitty one, ain't gonna be on food stamps any time soon.'

'Still, money talks.'

'You would have thought so, wouldn't you. But you gotta understand, this is New York we're talkin' about, and the art crowd at that: the most self-conscious, faddish, style-obsessed people in the world. It became cool to get robbed by us.'

'You have got to be kidding.'

'I shit you not. All of a sudden, you're nobody unless you've been ripped off by the FAC. Most of them didn't *call* the goddamn cops. I'm saying they told the help to look out for us, but really we just assumed that. A lot of these assholes probably did nothing of the kind in case we came calling and *didn't* get away with their stuff. I even heard about one sad sack who bought a Mercurio, hid it and then faked one of our message frames.

'Ultimately it got counter-productive. That's why we

stopped. There were people buying crap in the hope that we'd steal it, and we raised the profiles – to say nothing of the bank balances – of losers like Mercurio.'

'While making nothing for yourselves.'

'Well, we did get some kudos out of it. I mean, people knew it was us. Nobody could prove anything, but they knew, so we were cool for a while; a nanosecond or so. Plus I finally discovered that I did have some kind of artistic talent.'

'A hereditary talent,' Angelique stated softly. 'For making things disappear.'

Zal nodded, smiling at her deduction, but there was undisguised sadness there too: regret, missing.

'We used to tell ourselves the FAC was a form of performance art, and maybe that was true in its context, but in practice it was . . .' He tailed off, his eyes looking away from her, retreating, but not far enough for him to be able to hide the beginnings of tears.

'Come on,' he said, standing up and giving a small laugh as though to disperse the moment just passed. 'It's time I showed you a painting I hold in greater esteem than Ms Jolly back there.'

After a brief consultation of his guide, Zal led her downstairs to the lower basement entrance of the Sully wing. There they followed the pathway around the vast moat, stone columns and buttresses forming the foundations of the medieval fortress that first stood on the site.

'I had no idea all this was down here,' Angelique remarked. 'It's incredible.'

'Pretty cool, yeah. I mean, we've got better shit in Vegas, and what's more, our castle at Excalibur is *new*, but you gotta give these Frenchies some credit.'

Angelique watched him as he walked. The jokes would

fool nobody: the guy was enthralled, an awe-struck innocence about those erstwhile cynical and calculating eyes.

'You've never been here before, have you?' she asked
sincerely, trying not to make it sound like a jibe or another
showy deduction.

He shook his head. 'Never been to Europe before. This
is my first time out of the US. Rumbled again.'

'You look . . . very happy. I take it it's everything you
expected.'

'And then some.'

'You were going to come here anyway, weren't you?
Nothing to do with me.'

'Yes to the first part, but no to the second. I always
wanted to come here, long-term dream, if you like. But it
was also a long-term dream that I'd come here with a girl.
Pathetic teenage romantic ideal stuff, I know, but it stuck.
Once we got talking the other night, I started thinking, why
not?'

'I could think of a few obvious reasons.'

'I could think of a shitload, too.'

'I'm glad you didn't.'

'I'm glad you didn't, either.'

Angelique had spoken before she could censor herself,
but was surprised to find that she didn't regret it once it
was out. It didn't feel quite as unguarded as she might
have feared, nor did it even feel silly; it just felt easy, and
that was arguably even more scary.

'In this fantasy, were you always going to take the girl
to see the *Mona Lisa*?'

'I think when I conceived of the fantasy I probably didn't
know the *Mona Lisa* was here. I used to think it was in the
Vatican because it was Italian.'

'As this is your first time, then its kind of ironic that it was the first thing you made for, given everything you've said.'

'I made for the Denon. We saw a lot of cool shit before we got to Ms Jolly.'

'Cool shit? Is that another technical term?'

'I told you I went to art school.'

'And where are we making for now?'

He checked the guide. 'Sully, *deuxieme etage, salon vingt-huit*. Almost there.'

'Do you speak French?'

'Nah. Just Spanish and American. You?'

'*Oui*. Spanish too, plus Dutch. Once I get around to Italian, I reckon I'll have all the main criminal tongues under my belt, apart from Cockney.'

'A valuable gift. You can hear people lying to you in four languages.'

'Aye. Then you come along: someone who doesn't even need words in order to deceive. *That*'s a gift.'

'I'm not the first, as Monsieur La Tour would attest. Get a load of this.'

They stopped in front of a painting of four people around a table, two men and a woman playing cards, a second female in attendance, pouring wine.

'*The Cheat Holding the Ace of Diamonds*,' Zal said. 'This is one that really speaks to me. Check it out. The poor sucker on the right is being taken in for the second time that day, the first being by whoever sold him that stupid hat with the feather. As well as the ace of diamonds, Rob Lowe over there on the left also has the ace of spades tucked into his cummerbund, probably the card Foghorn Leghorn's holdin' out for. And everybody's in on the con: the woman's looking for a signal from the servant girl, who's got her eyes on the sucker's cards; dumb fop probably doesn't even think the hired help understands the game.

'But here's the killer: Rob Lowe looks bored, like he's lost interest in playing. That's the true panache in this con, that's what lays the kid wide open. You worry about an intent opponent, not one who looks like he's about to jack it in and hit the bar. The card up the sleeve is mere technique, like Karl and his sub-seven. The real art is in selling the illusion.'

'Like fooling some sap into thinking you're a bumbling amateur who's about to level a bank because his explosives have malfunctioned?'

'It's about letting people see what they want to see and believe what they want to believe. You know the phrase, "the hand is quicker than the eye"?'

'Gie's a wank while naebody's lookin'.'

'Huh?'

'Old chestnut. Yes, I'm familiar with the phrase.'

'It's bullshit. Light travels at three hundred thousand kilometres per second, so there is no hand in this universe that can be quicker than the eye. It was coined and put into usage by magicians to suit their own devious purposes. The audience is always on the look-out for actions that aren't even gonna be attempted, which means they don't notice what the magician is really up to. Sleight of hand is an invaluable part of it, but misdirection is the name of the game. The hand doesn't need to be quicker than the eye if the eye is looking in the wrong place. Everything the magician does is about misleading the audience, everything: how he stands, where he looks, where he points and especially what he says. He will never be doing what he says he is doing, and if he tells you what he's *about* to do, he's lying.'

'I'll consider myself warned.'

'You'll never be warned, because he's like a chess-player: he's always thinking several moves ahead. Allow me to demonstrate.'

Zal produced a pack of cards from his jacket pocket and sprung them expertly from one hand to the other before shuffling them and fanning them out in front of Angelique. The flicking sound attracted a few interested glances from elsewhere in the room, not least the nearest security guard.

'This kind of thing is normally restricted to around the pyramid outside,' she chided, but he was not to be put off.

'Then you better hurry up and pick a card, get it over with.'

Angelique took one and examined it. It was the seven of diamonds. She was about to put it back into the proffered pack, then withdrew it again.

'How about *I* put it back in the pack and *I* shuffle it?'

'What you worried about? That I'm gonna use a pass, surreptitiously put your card somewhere convenient near the top or bottom of the pack? Or a Hindu shuffle, maybe?'

'All of the above. Gimme the cards.'

He handed them over with a resigned sigh. Angelique had another look at the security guard, who was now giving them a grin. 'He likes my style,' she said, looking Zal in the eye. He glanced over to see what she was talking about, at which point Angelique slipped the card randomly into the pack and began shuffling.

'Okay, find my card now, Mr Chess Player.'

Zal accepted the pack and shook his head with a small laugh, smiling bashfully. 'I can't.'

'Why not?' she asked, allowing herself a triumphant grin.

'Because Rob Lowe's got it,' he told her, and walked away.

She looked again at the painting. The eponymous cheat

at the end of the table, as well as concealing two aces behind his back, was holding the seven of diamonds in his right hand.

'Bastard.'

Angelique followed him into the corridor, where he was waiting for her, chuckling.

'Okay, how the hell did you do that?'

'First rule of any trick: make sure all the pieces are in place, where you need them, before you begin. I'm very familiar with the painting so I knew what all the players were holding.'

'But how did you get me to pick the seven of diamonds?'

'Trade secret. It's called a "force". There are many techniques but one intention: get the subject to choose the card you want them to.'

'What if they don't?'

'You have a contingency. A lot of times, you'd just abandon the intended trick and do a new one that doesn't rely on a force. My dad used to have a good way round it, though. He'd ask someone else to pick a card too, giving him a second chance to force it, then he'd get a third member of the audience to "choose which card to throw away", announcing very dramatically that this was to prove he *couldn't* be forcing a card. If the third person picked the right one, he'd say "You want me to use this card? Very good." And if they picked the wrong one: "You want me to throw *this* card away?"'

'What were you going to do if I didn't pick the forced card?'

Zal fanned the pack again, this time face-up. Every card was a seven of diamonds.

'Like I said, before you begin, you make sure everything you need is in place.'

'I need some air,' Angelique said. 'My brain's over-heating.'

'The sculpture courtyard is—'

'I think I'm gaunny need more air than that.'

Angelique was aware that Zal could have happily wandered around the Louvre until they physically chucked him out, so she considered it solicitous that he acquiesced without complaint when she suggested they leave. They took a walk along the banks of the Seine. The cold air was blowing away plenty of cobwebs, but her brain still felt like it had been tied in knots.

'Getting me to take the hostages and clear the bank, that was a force too, wasn't it?'

'You can find new ways of applying them, but the principles of illusion are always the same.'

'Principles every magician's son learns.'

'Yeah, whether he wants to or not.'

'You didn't want to follow in your father's footsteps?'

'Not exactly, no. I mean, when I was a kid, a young kid, I thought he was the greatest, and I loved it when he taught me stuff. I could do the Hindu shuffle before I could read. At that age, every kid in the world wants to be his dad. But nobody wants to be their dad when their dad starts bein' an asshole. A lot of guys end up turning into him anyway, but that's probably because they're still trying to be the guy he used to be.'

'What did he do, to be an arsehole, I mean?'

'Disappearing acts. Appropriate, huh? His greatest work, only performed for a select audience of his wife and son. Now you see him, now you don't.'

'Drink?'

'I could use one if we're getting into this, yeah.'

'I meant—'

'I know. And yeah, he did. Came and went all the time, you never knew what state he'd be in when he did show up. I hated it when he wasn't there, because I worried he'd never be coming back. Then when he did come back, he and my mom just fought so much I wanted him to go away again. I got my wish long-term. He got fired from one gig too many, pretty soon no-one in Vegas would hire him, so he went on the road looking for work. Said he'd send money home, which he did once in a blue moon. Every second blue moon he'd show up in person, usually because he was broke.'

'How long did this go on?'

'Until I was thirteen.'

'What happened then? Did they divorce?'

Zal stopped walking and looked away, out over the river. 'My mom's car got hit by a drunk driver on Las Vegas Boulevard. She didn't make it.'

'I'm sorry.'

He nodded, then turned around and looked at her with years of sorrow in his face. Amid her sympathy, Angelique felt strangely grateful for what he was sharing. Often when you thought people were opening up to you, they could tread into this kind of painful territory and suddenly clam up tighter than before, shutting you back out with a slam.

'I could use a seat,' he said, and they made their way to a nearby bench.

'What happened to you after that?'

'Weird. My dad cleaned up his act, literally overnight. Moment of clarity, sudden kick to the head, all that shit. Saw, once it was all gone, what he had been wasting. It was too late to make it up to my mom, so he was gonna make it up to me; or make it up *through* me. I went where he went. Reno for a while, a few smaller casino towns, then further afield. He'd get bookings at hotel lounges all over. I musta changed schools every six months. Probably why I stayed so close with Karl: he was the only real friend I had, only one who I knew would always be there; Vegas the only place I knew we'd always come back to.

'My dad worked evenings, mainly, and I helped out backstage a lot of the time. I think my inner nine-year-old was still really pissed at him, because I decided I didn't want to be what he was, but I learned it all the same.'

'Did your dad want you to don the white gloves after him?'

'Oh, you better believe it. Nothing would have made him happier than seeing me on a stage waving a wand. He wanted the opposite of Karl's dad, and there you go: Karl and I did the same thing but managed to make both of them unhappy. My dad said I was far better than he could ever be. Said I had better hands, better technique, a greater feel for the psychology of an audience. But I had made my mind up a long time back that I wasn't gonna be like him. Soon as I graduated high school, I was out of there.'

'He give you a hard time?'

'Nah, he knew he'd already done enough of that. He didn't make any secret of his regrets, but he gave me his blessing. Money too, what he had. He tried, he really tried after Mom was gone. I don't think there was anything he wouldn't have given to have her back.'

Zal looked away again, but no amount of misdirection could hide his pain.

'He's dead too, isn't he?' Angelique asked.

Zal nodded, gazing at the fast-flowing Seine, tourboats battling the current as they returned to Ile de la Cité.

'Died while I was in prison, nearly three years ago now. I never got to say goodbye. Or "I forgive you", which was what he really needed to hear.'

She reached down and grasped his hand. He didn't react, other than to squeeze hers by way of acknowledgement, or possibly thanks.

'That's why you came to Glasgow, isn't it? To say goodbye and I forgive you in his old home town?'

Zal looked back at her. 'How did you work that out?' There was no surprise or accusation in his face, just an inquiring sincerity.

'Alakazammy, stairheid rammy. You said it at the bank. That was his Abracadabra, wasn't it?'

'No. He used it, sure, but he didn't coin it. It was the Abracadabra of the guy who taught him, a stalwart of the Glasgow music halls.'

'Who was that?'

'Uh-uh, that's a whole different story. Maybe another time. But yeah, when I was inside, I resolved to visit where he came from. Kinda to say goodbye, but as much just to know him a little better. I grew up on tales of this far-off city that formed a big part of my childhood and yet I'd never seen it. But that's not the only reason I came. Or rather, I'm saying, I'd have come one day anyway, but . . .'

'What?'

He stood up.

'I'm startin' to freeze my ass off out here, how about you?'

'I'm not from Nevada.'

'Well I'm only half-Glaswegian. I need shelter. How about I buy you dinner?'

'Ooyah, stop twisting my arm. Okay, okay, but only if I can go back and get changed. Put on my glad rags.'

'And your wire.'

'That too.'

Angelique stood under the warm cascade, enjoying the feel
of the water, but enjoying her surroundings more. She
looked up at the square steel head, wondering blithely
whether a Cubist shower got you any cleaner than a normal
one. Regardless, it felt good; *she* felt good. She thought back
to the morning of the robbery, and a shower she didn't
want to get out of because it felt like sanctuary. This one
was embracing her, and Zal had told her to take as long
as she needed, but she knew she wouldn't stay under for
long. She was anxious to learn more and, no point denying
it, impatient to be back in his company, particularly when
it entailed dining out in Montmartre. There was still a voice
in there asking if she knew what she was getting herself
into, but there was no chance of her heeding it. Taking on
terrorists was filed in her memory and her conscience
under Doing the Right Thing. If this was a mistake, then
may all her mistakes be just as inviting.

They ate close to the hotel, the temperature having plum-
meted beyond even Angelique's tolerance, and certainly
beyond the lower threshold of the outfit she'd brought. Zal
also looked like his choice of attire had bent closer to the
needs of looking good in a warm interior than the consideration of getting there on a December night.

A waiter took their jackets as they reached their table,
revealing Zal's shirt to be of the short-sleeved variety, ordinarily something of a fashion crime in Angelique's eyes,
but exceptions could be made when they exposed arms
like his. What they also exposed were the lower parts of
more tattoos, coiling black designs, like vines growing
around his biceps.

293

'Hell of a birth mark,' Angelique remarked, making light of being caught staring.

'Prison,' he replied. 'It's funny, I never even thought of having one before. Wasn't exactly peer pressure, more a matter of ready availability and time on my hands. I got pretty good at it.'

'You did them yourself?'

'Some of 'em. Not at first, but the guy who did me, we got talkin'. He found out I could draw better than him and had a steady hand, so we kinda got in business together there for a while. It's kinda like . . . controlled damage, a way of wearing your mental scars. You remind yourself of the ways you've changed and the permanent ink means you can never change back. Lessons you've learned, things you've survived.'

'What was the first one?'

He pulled the sleeve up on his right arm, displaying four words inside a frame that had too much of the Charles Rennie Mackintosh about it to be entirely coincidental. The words read: 'This too will pass'.

'The story goes, William Wallace once asked his men to come up with a thought that would cheer him when he was feeling low, but spell caution when he thought he had it good. Thus: this too will pass. You need something like that in jail. Good cheer and caution, only way to survive.'

'Am I allowed to ask what you were in for now?'

'It goes back to New York. You remember I said we were cool for a nanosecond? Well, it was the wrong nanosecond.'

'How so?'

'There was another spoiled little rich kid putting himself around, but not like all the others rebelling against their parents until they rejoined them for summer in the Hamptons. This guy was trash with cash, kind of a walking exaggeration of every cliché about the nouveau riche. Lot of money to throw around, but zero class, zero taste, and talent? Jeez, he made Mercurio look like Francis Bacon. He just kinda showed up. I don't think he was even at art school, he had just *decided* that he was artistic, that he knew about art, and I think he was pretty much used to getting whatever he wanted up to that point in his life, so he expected . . . Actually, I don't know what he expected; whether he'd make a name for himself with his paint-by-numbers efforts or just be welcomed into the heart of the art crowd and get invited to all the right openings and parties. Neither happened, needless to say. Unlike Mercurio, he didn't know how to spend his money to make an impression, and he definitely didn't know how to kiss *any*body's ass, let alone the right ass. He was far more used to people kissing his.'

'Why? Who was he?'

'His name was Alessandro. That was all we knew at the time. We nicknamed him Sandy. He thought we were cool – like I said, it was *that* nanosecond – and he wanted to hang out with us, get in on the action. No, it being Sandy, he wanted us to hang out with *him*, be his latest playthings or accessories, I don't know what. Maybe he thought being tight with us would make him look better to the people he wanted to impress. Anyway, we told him to take a hike. That was before we knew who he was. It probably wouldn't have made a difference, but we might have been a little more circumspect about our choice of words in dealing with him.'

'Gangster?'

'Nephew of Hector Estobal, head of a major crime syndicate straddling the border in southern California.'

'Shit.'

'Uh-huh. Alessandro was Hector's little golden boy too, as he didn't have a son of his own. So he was used to getting everything he wanted. Colossal ego, nil self-awareness, probably just convinced himself he was "artistic" on an adolescent whim because he liked a few pretty pictures. That was it, off to New York where everyone would indulge him the way he was accustomed to. I think I must have been one of the first people he ever heard say the word "no" to him. Definitely the first to tell him to go fuck himself.'

'So did he send the boys round?'

'He was still a kid, maybe nineteen, twenty. He had money, but he didn't have people on the East Coast. The syndicate did, but not at the command of some hot-head adolescent. When he didn't get what he wanted, he blew, back home to LA where they'd make him feel like a big-shot again. A very big shot, as it turned out. A few years down the line, old man Estobal dies, and guess who gets promoted to head of the family?'

'But he was just a kid.'

'He was the anointed. Hector couldn't see past him; definitely had a blind spot for his limitations. Family's all; no meritocracy in that world. Suddenly he's the big boss and those guys on the East Coast *are* at his command.'

Their wine arrived. Zal deferred to Angelique to check it, which she did with a brief sniff.

'What did he have them do?'

'It was what he had us do. He came out to New York and had a couple of guys bring me to meet him. I was expecting a warehouse and a beating in a chair, but we met in a fancy restaurant. It was so that he could show off his status, while I'm sitting there in the clothes I slept in. The restaurant's across the street from the Gigliotti

Museum – it's a big municipal gallery. He shows me post-cards of two paintings: a Poussin and a Lorrain. They're both on loan to the Gigliotti, the Poussin from a movie mogul and the Lorrain from a museum in France.'

Zal took a gulp of his wine, swallowing it with little relish, but the bad taste wasn't coming from the glass.

'Next he shows me a photograph of my dad. He says they're going to kill him unless me and my FAC buddies steal both of these paintings for him. I start saying it's impossible and he says that's my problem. So I changed tack, pointed out that these paintings might be worth a lot of money, but you couldn't possibly sell them.'

'Because everyone knows they're stolen.'

'Exactly. So the sonofabitch says he has no intention of selling them. It's like corporate relations, he tells me. You walk into the HQ of a big company and they've got major artworks in the lobby. This would be the same deal: when people came to his house they'd see that he had things that were meant to be unobtainable, work that you were supposed to only be able to see in a museum. The whole world knows it's stolen, and here it is on your wall. That was his line, anyway.'

'What do you mean?'

'I don't believe he really expected us to pull it off, no matter how smart he thought we were. I think he just wanted me to be his bitch. Jerk me around on his chain and make the four of us do something that would get us jailed or shot. But what was for sure was that he was serious. When I got back from our little dinner, I found out Karl was in the hospital. Three of Alessandro's guys had picked him up around the same time as they apprehended me. I got dinner; he was the one who got the warehouse and the chair. They beat the crap out of him. Almost lost an eye. The surgeons saved it, but it was touch and go for a while. Motherfuckers.'

Zal winced at the memory, taking another gulp of wine to help swallow back the lump in his throat.

'Real tough guys, going after Karl,' Angelique observed.

'It was to demonstrate their ruthlessness. Go after the most vulnerable, show no mercy, let us know they were happy to hurt us through hurting people we cared about. It was a message to demonstrate that we were out of options. I gave Alessandro his wish.'

'How?'

'I went ahead, devised a plan. We acquired the building schematics, bought or built the equipment we needed, constructed disguises, wrote software, rehearsed, prepared and practiced, until everybody believed it would work: the guys, Alessandro, everybody.'

'But it didn't.'

'We'll never know. The way I saw it, we couldn't afford for it to work. If we got him those paintings, he wasn't going to just let us walk away afterwards. He'd be after something else next, we'd never be free of him. We couldn't refuse, obviously, or they'd have killed my old man, no question. So I figured we had to fuck it up and get ourselves caught. That way, Alessandro gets his revenge and forgets about trying to use us, because we're just a bunch of losers, nothing like what he imagined.'

'But you'd go to jail.'

'That was always gonna happen. If not at this job, then maybe the next thing he blackmailed us into. This way, at least, it would be on my terms.'

'What did you do?'

'I didn't tell anyone things had changed, and we went ahead as planned. I drove the van, with the rest of the guys and some of the equipment in back. But when we got there, I locked the doors on them and went into the museum alone. I figured it was the only way to minimise the damage. We all got busted, but I was the only one to get caught on the spot committing overt acts, breaking and entering. The rest were arraigned on conspiracy charges. I got three to five, they all got twelve months max.'

'Greater love hath no man.'

'They didn't see it that way at first, as I'm sure you can understand, but they sure came around when the lawyers started explaining things.'

'I've heard of honour among thieves, but that was . . . selfless to the point of noble.'

'It would only have been selfless if I had been giving up another option. Like I said, I was going to jail at some point. I just chose when, and I saw a way of doing it without taking the rest of them down with me. Well, not for as long, anyway.'

'Don't kid yourself. You found a way to save the three of them and your dad from Alessandro. I'd put it down to more than just taking one for the team.'

Zal looked up from his barely touched starter plate. He seemed welcoming of her solicitude, but unconvinced of her sentiments.

'Who did I save? We all went to prison. Some longer than others, but six months in there is enough to fuck you up for a long time after, believe me. Alessandro got his pound of flesh. We carried out his orders, we fucked up, we went inside.' Zal glanced away for a second, as though he was about to reach again for his wine, then looked back at Angelique. 'And then he killed my father anyway.'

There were no tears, just a calm, quietly burning anger.

'Christ. I don't know what to say.'

'I under-estimated him. I thought if we looked like losers, if we cooperated but were incompetent, he'd forget about my old man. I was wrong.'

'You can't blame yourself, for Christ's sake.'

'I don't. Not for a second. I blame Alessandro, and I blame him every day I'm still drawing breath. I blame him for my father's murder, I blame him for fucking up the lives of my friends, and I blame him for all the things that happened to me inside; as well as all the things I did in there to survive, many of which were not pretty. But I blame myself for not saying certain things to my dad back when I had the chance.'

Again, Angelique reached for Zal's hand, this time on top of the table. 'You're not the first to think you had more time to put it right with someone.'

'Yeah, but who's to say I would have? Maybe it's only when it's too late that you can forget about all the bullshit and see what was really valuable. Jesus, I threw away his name – that's how much I hated him. I took my mom's surname instead. Well, sorta. My mom was Mexican and her name was Innez, but she changed it to Innes because it sounded less Spanish. I changed it back. I wanted to be more my mom's son than my dad's; more Mexican than Scottish.'

'Innes sounds Scottish, actually.'

Zal smiled, the first time in a while. He had a forkful of salad, using his right hand so that he didn't have to let go of hers with the left.

'That's what my dad said when he was hitting on her.'

'When did Sal become Zal?'

'When I was nine and saw the Sensational Alex Harvey Band on TV. I bought a few albums, posters for the wall.

If I'd known they were from Glasgow, it might have tempered my enthusiasm at that period, but by the time I found out I was way too hooked.'

'So let's recap: you ditched your dad's surname, took your mum's but reverted it, and altered your first name. Do you have a middle name, and if so, is it still intact?'

'Oh yeah. Unadulterated. McMillan.'

'After the prime minister?'

'Yeah, but not the one you're thinking of.'

'I don't think I'm thinking of the one you think I'm thinking of.'

'Try saying that with a mouthful of linguine. Which one are you thinking of?'

'The wee one.'

'Ian. Correct. But I forgot – I pulled you away from the game on Saturday, didn't I?'

'I forgive you. Ian McMillan was a wee bit before my time, obviously, but I've heard the tales.'

'Jim Baxter stealing the ball for him at the end of the '63 cup final. Yeah, I've heard 'em all. I was raised on those stories. I remember – probably one of my earliest memories, in fact – my dad throwing a party outside the house in 1972 when they won the European Cup Winners Cup. The neighbours didn't have a clue, but hey, there was beer and a barbecue. He had to call a bookie at Caesar's to find out what was happening; they took bets on games all round the world, so they had contacts on the news wires. I remember my dad pacing up and down the carpet that afternoon, calling this poor guy every ten minutes. Eventually he just dropped to his knees, then got up and started running around, hugging me and my mom. Fortunately it was a couple of days until he found out about the riot afterwards. That cut him up.'

'Two sides to every story. The Spanish police grossly over-reacted.'

'Is that your opinion as a police officer or a Rangers supporter?'

'My professional opinion,' Angelique assured him, smiling. 'They went in heavy against guys just trying to celebrate, which was stupid enough, but nobody had told them that Glaswegians don't react well to being baton-charged by fascists.'

'The cops got their asses kicked?'

'Oh yeah. The Catalonians don't remember it as a riot, they remember it as the night Franco's polis got a right good leathering.'

'Still, better to be remembered just for who won the game.'

'True. I get defensive about these things, go into automatic debating mode. Too many arguments with my brother. He's a Celtic supporter, sees them as an ideological paragon of liberal virtue. Aye, right. We get on okay otherwise, but when it comes to football, together we're like a microcosm of all that's self-defeating about Old Firm fans: definitely an *un*healthy rivalry. Each side is always finding ways to denigrate the achievements or history of the other until both end up looking shoddy. The saddest thing is that to most people, if you mention Rangers or Celtic, the first thing they think of isn't football.'

'Yeah, my dad explained . . . well, nobody could *explain* it. He told me about it. He said it was a shame because Scotland should be able to be proud of these two great clubs, and that was pretty hard while they had all this crap attached to them. Okay, I'll admit he had to be in a pretty good mood before he'd say *two* great clubs, but you know what I'm saying.'

'Better than most. You're talking to someone who started

going to Ibrox in the early Eighties as a Catholic schoolgirl.'

'Jeez. How'd that come about?'

'Racism, mainly. Let's just say I didn't get made to feel much like I belonged at school, so I thought I might belong among the *other* people my classmates hated.'

'And did you?'

'Well, nobody called me a black bastard, which was a start. I'm not saying they wouldn't have if I'd been on the other side of the segregating fence, but for a change I got to feel I was being categorised by the colour of my scarf, not the colour of my skin. But as for belonging, I'm not sure that one's ever been resolved. Ask me when we're singing *Follow Follow* after scoring in a European tie and you'll get a different answer from when I'm sitting on a wet Saturday listening to yet another song about fucking Ulster. And yes, the club's got a lot of fans from over there and blah blah blah, but God, between that and Celtic fans going to a football match to sing about a potato famine . . .

'I suppose what it taught me is that football stadiums are full of people searching for a sense of belonging. Each person who falls in love with a team would like it to represent to everybody what it represents to them. So I'm sitting there getting pissed off because nobody's singing about Rangers. Couple of rows back there's some eejit who thinks you're not a true fan unless you subscribe to his anachronistic ragbag of ideological and pseudo-ethnic bollocks; what he doesn't realise is that the guy in the next seat thinks *he's* not a true fan because his anachronistic ragbag isn't hardline enough. And all around are folk who think the pair of them are an embarrassment to the club.'

'But you all feel *you* belong, so fuck anyone who thinks you don't.'

'You got it. It was a valuable philosophy to learn,

growing up in Renfrewshire with the wrong colour of face.'

'Oh, I'd say the colour suits you,' Zal said. 'Don't change it, you know, unless you see a jacket that just calls out for pale skin.'

'Why, thank you. Do you like me in purple?' she asked, indicating her blouse.

'Sure. But after Saturday I'll always picture you in black.'

'You think Kevlar suits me?'

'I think you *know* it suits you. But you're not as sure as you once were about how much you suit blue.'

Angelique nodded. 'You're very perceptive.'

'Nah. You told me as much on Saturday. You didn't say a lot, but what you did say was pretty candid to be sharing with a thief during a bank robbery, so it had to be weighing pretty heavy.'

'It was my birthday too, so it was weighing even heavier under the circumstances, but not so heavy as I'd have shared it with anybody. I found you dangerously easy to talk to.'

'Feeling's mutual. That's why I had to take a few precautions. But I can't be that dangerously easy. I'm the one spilling his guts today.'

'Between cop and thief, that's how it ought to be.'

Zal squeezed her hand gently. 'I'm not the only one who needs to talk to somebody, Angelique.'

He was right. So over the rest of dinner she told him the whole sorry tale of the Black Spirit, Ray Ash, Dubh Ardrain and the aftermath.

It felt good, like a concentrated dose of the counselling she never got, neither professionally nor from her times with Ray. Zal was more than just a good listener; he was an audience, rooting for the heroine, unashamedly partisan when appropriate, objective (or at least pretending to be) when required. It was cathartically vindicating to hear his gasps of astonishment, see him reel at the horror, and most importantly, share the understanding that just because the heroine killed all the bad guys didn't mean she lived happily ever after.

'Which is why you're in Paris having dinner with a wanted criminal.'

'Yes, but let's be clear: just because I'm in Paris having dinner with a wanted criminal doesn't mean I'm about to jack it all in. That philosophy I learnt at Ibrox still applies. I don't compromise in order to fit in, and I'm not giving in to any arsehole who wants to make me feel I don't belong wherever I put myself.'

'We're alike in a lot of ways,' Zal said. 'It's not that we don't belong, it's that we've learned we don't need to.'

'Amen to that.'

They were holding hands again as they walked back to the hotel. There was no eye contact to mark the moment; in fact, Angelique didn't even notice where and when it had happened – as they left the restaurant? The street outside? That first road they'd run across? Neither of them seemed to acknowledge that it was happening, but neither seemed much for letting go either. She couldn't remember the last time she'd walked down a street holding hands with anybody. Relationships in recent years had been terribly adult (ie dull, functional and ultimately doomed), where it seemed, absurdly, that just because you were having sex with someone was no excuse for engaging in such juvenile frivolity, or even petty affection.

She didn't have to try not to think about what it might mean or where it might be going. The moment was enough for now.

They had late-night armagnacs in the hotel bar, served by the only member of staff still on duty, who cheerfully and indulgently doled out the measures in between washing down the coffee machine and filling out paper-work at the front desk.

The brandy glasses were, of course, Cubist.

'This time last Thursday, I was freezing my arse off on a surveillance gig in Partick, waiting for a suspected coun-terfeiter to empty his bin. If someone had told me then what I'd be doing right now, I'd have lifted them for class A possession. I feel like I'm dreaming.'

'I definitely am. Have been for a while. I'll need to be careful, that was my dad's downfall.'

'How?'

'He went from Garnethill to Vegas; music halls to five-star casinos. Met a beautiful Mexican stripper nearly twenty years younger than him, and married her. Raintown to desert heat, and a place where the Sixties really swung. It must have been like he stepped into a movie. He was living a dream come true, no question. But maybe when you're living your dreams, it never quite seems like reality, and for that, in his case I don't think it ever felt like home. He missed Glasgow, no matter how good he had it in Vegas, and I think he felt lonely, kind of isolated. That was why he drank.'

'Why did he leave? Did he get "discovered" and made an offer he couldn't refuse?'

'He never told me. Not that I didn't ask; he wouldn't tell me. I think there was a serendipitous combination of trouble at one end and an opportunity at the other, but I never found out the details. I only saw the result: a man who never quite connected with his new life, quite possibly because it felt too good to be true. That was why I got steeped in the culture he'd left behind. He loved talking about it to me, would probably have liked nothing more than the two of us visiting the place together some day. The weird thing about it is that Glasgow now feels like my dream. I see things that were practically mythologised in my childhood, and for that they seem less real than the artifice I grew up with in Vegas. Sometimes it feels like a theme park, or a movie set.'

'Glasgow as Disneyland. Doesnae sound too probable to me, but I'm sure the city council would love to have you in the tourism department. Just don't let on you're not a Catholic.'

'I'm not kidding. I feel I can do anything there because it isn't real. You think I'd have the balls to rob a bank back home? Forget it.'

'You're not telling me that was your first time.'

'That is what I'm telling you.'

'I don't believe it. No way. You seemed like seasoned experts.'

'Oh we are, at a lot of things. As for the rest, faking it is my gift, remember.'

'But the scale, the elaboration . . .'

'Over-egged the pudding here and there, didn't we? But we needed all that stuff – the painting, the play – to keep everybody's mind off the hostage situation.'

'I don't think the hostages could forget the situation they were in even if you—'

'Not their minds – ours.'

Angelique laughed, though she knew he wasn't joking. She just wished she could see McMaster's face if he ever learned any of this.

'I'd never have attempted anything so audacious in the real world. But in Glasgow it feels like the usual rules don't apply, including the law.'

'Maybe us cops just aren't good enough at applying it.'

'Oh, I'm sure you're plenty good enough. That's why I have to remind myself it's not a dream.' He glanced around at their bizarrely designed surroundings, then back at Angelique. 'Being here with you isn't helping,' he said softly.

Angelique slipped her shoes off and pulled her feet up on to the leather sofa they were sharing. She snuggled back into a corner, cradling her Cubist glass in both hands and extending one leg towards him. He placed a hand on her instep and just left it there: warm, human, mildly electrifying.

'When you called me up, the first thing you said . . . You were quoting, weren't you?'

'This is gonna sound a little obsessive,' he confirmed, rather bashfully.

'I thought it was from a movie and I thought it was a woman's voice. It drove me nuts but I eventually worked it out. Well, I didn't work it out, I just happened to put on the right album. It was Everclear, that song *Unemployed Boyfriend*. The girl leaves a message on her pal's answering machine at the start.'

'Yeah, sorry, I wasn't trying to be cryptic. I just didn't know what to say and I guess my sub-conscious just threw that one out there. I certainly didn't mean for you to pick up on it.'

'I love that song.'

'Me too. So does my sub-conscious, apparently.'

'I'm not exactly the last of the great romantics, but I like the idea of a man fantasising about being the right guy, about all the things he'd like to do for a girl, rather than about what he wants *from* her or putting her on a pedestal like in most songs.'

'What are you talking about? That song is about a *girl*'s

fantasy of the right guy just walking into her life. She's sitting bored in the unemployment office, for Christ's sake, and this guy comes along and actually thinks her blonde streaks look good. Get out of here.'

Angelique gave him a gentle kick.

'It is *so* a male fantasy. He's seen this girl around a few times, he fancies her and he's daydreaming about making her happy.'

'Oh and how,' Zal replied, sitting up straight and putting his glass down. 'This guy's gonna go to chick-flicks with her, *voluntarily*, and says he's gonna make her the mother of his kids. Yeah, right.'

'Well how about saying he'll always make her come,' Angelique countered. 'If that's not a male fantasy, nothing is.'

'There you go. I'd have said that lyric was the clincher for *my* argument. Not only is he gonna do all these other things, but he's gonna be a great lay, too.'

Angelique sat up and put her glass down also, laughing at his mock vehemence. 'Your Honour, I think you'll find the clincher is that at the end she says he's actually quite attractive, and she's obviously planning to call him. He's gaunny get what he wanted: it's a dream come true.'

'Garbage,' Zal insisted, laughing. 'At the end she asks her friend whether this can be for real? And on the music track Alexakis sings NOOO! at the top of his voice: the voice of reality. It was just a fantasy, just a dream.'

'It was both their dreams,' Angelique stated softly, offering a truce.

Zal met her gaze and nodded. 'Just like this is ours,' he said. 'Being here, the thief and the detective, taking a vacation from reality.' The humour had gone from his tone, replaced by a gentle regret. 'Vacations can't last. We both have to go back, where I gotta do my job and you gotta do yours.'

'But not yet,' Angelique said.

She leaned forward and kissed him, delicate and tentative at first, then deep, engulfing, abandoned. 'Not yet.'

Angelique never considered herself to have had much luck with sex up to that point in her life, and if she was being honest, she'd have to say much of that was her own fault. She had gone into so many liaisons with low expectations (unavoidable when the men were cops) or one eye on the door (inevitable when they weren't), and if there really were people out there who could have amazing sex but lousy relationships, then she certainly hadn't slept with any of them. People talked about 'physical compatibility' as if there were technical obstacles that couldn't be overcome between mismatched couples, but she thought it sounded like an excuse to cover the fact that other more important things were missing. Angelique had had unspectacular sex with men she found highly desirable and who had assured her that the reciprocal was true: physical compatibility was definitely not the problem, but neither was it enough. She wouldn't dispute that there was such a thing as sheer, instinctive physical attraction, but sexual attraction was a more intricate process, and the greater part of it happened in the head. Good sex needed commitment, and by that she didn't mean honourable intentions or proven longevity. Commitment was about how much you were prepared to let go. If you were with someone long enough, that came through trust. Otherwise, it had to come through abandon.

Nobody in their right mind would trust Zal Innez. Fortunately, abandon was something he had inspired in her from almost the moment they met.

She had never felt so comfortable naked with someone before, nor so relaxed about what they were doing; so much so that she felt no anxiety, only a little surprise, when he came almost instantaneously the second she put her hand around his penis.

'Jeez, I'm so sorry,' he said, looking appalled. 'It's been a long time.'

'Don't worry. We've *got* a long time. Not three years, but tonight at least.'

'Just gimme a few minutes,' he assured her.

'There's no hurry. You'll just have to find some way of keeping me amused in the meantime.'

He did.

A perennial disappointment about Angelique's previous lovers was that because she was renowned for being 'able to look after herself', they seemed to assume sex with her should take the form of unarmed combat. Perhaps they were a little intimidated and thought they had to be physically masterful in order to prove themselves, or maybe they reckoned that as she spent a lot of time rolling around on floormats, then wrestling with her on a mattress was the way to turn her on. Either way, she didn't appreciate it, and they'd be a long time looking for a female who did. Like every other woman on this earth, whether they nursed babies or wrestled alligators, in bed she wanted to be treated like she was precious.

Zal had hands that had mastered uncommon subtlety of touch, fingers that could manipulate with imperceptible delicacy. He touched her with a softness and gentility she had never known, until she didn't want him to be gentle any more.

When at last he came again, tears came too. Not the silent weeping that had manifested throughout the day, but

311

great purging sobs. Afterwards he lay holding her for a long time without saying anything, just stroking her hair or occasionally kissing her forehead. Angelique said nothing either, not wishing to break the silence. She knew he would speak when he was ready, and eventually, he did.

'It's only when you reach a place so high that you can truly see how far down you were when you bottomed out.'

'Jail?'

'Oh yeah. All these assholes – Republicans, Conservatives you'd call them . . .'

'Assholes works for me.'

'. . . who say jail should be tougher, I'd sure like to hear their ideas for what could be tougher than some of the shit that goes on inside.'

'You'd be surprised at their imagination. Have you ever read a *Daily Post* editorial?'

'A so-called family newspaper wouldn't even be able to mention this stuff. All the stories you've heard are true, and most of them happened to me. I wasn't cut out for that shit, I wasn't a tough-guy. I was just fresh meat. You'll get guys beatin' up on you . . . they don't know you, they ain't even got anything against you, but the law of the jungle says predator or prey. If you ain't beatin' up on somebody, then you're the vulnerable one. You gotta look like a bad motherfucker, or at least make it obvious that there's easier meat than you on the block.

'I had it bad. After I heard about my dad, I came pretty close to the edge. Somebody pulled me back: an older guy, name of Parnell.'

'Why? If I'm not being too cynical.'

'He'd been there too, way back. The guy was nearly sixty, made a lot of mistakes, lot of regrets, you know? He taught

312

me how to survive. Got me workin' out, physically and mentally.'

'Mentally?'

'Yeah. Your body has to be ready for the fights but your mind has to be ready for the headgames. In prison, guys are constantly probing for any weakness they can exploit, even in what ostensibly appears to be a civil conversation. It also involved what I might term a disciplining of the conscience, by which—'

'Don't worry, that needs no further explanation.'

'That was the hardest part to master, but I got some help with that too. Not in quite such an obliging way, though. When I said how low . . .'

Zal swallowed, a bitter expression on his lips, like the memory had caused bile to rise in his throat.

'Parnell made sure I knew how to look after myself, but nobody can be your guardian angel. Everybody's gotta watch their own back first, and there's some fights that nobody else can win for you.'

He paused again, his reluctance feeding the grimmer aspects of Angelique's imagination.

'Whatever you think I'm talkin' about here,' he said, 'you're right. The guy's name was Marsh, real bad-ass, lot of clout, and tight with one of the guards, Creedie. They were both . . . involved. Tuesday afternoon, always Tuesday afternoon.'

'Was there a reason for . . .'

'Yeah. They had more than me to play with: different guy every day, practically. You see, Creedie had responsibility for the role on the metalshop's work roster. That was how he covered himself in case anyone was ever stupid enough to make an accusation. He and Marsh could have their fun, and if anyone tried to tell tales, he could say it

313

was impossible, 'cause he had it in black and white that you were in the shop the whole time. There were other guards in on it too. Not *in* on it, but they knew Creedie'd scratch their backs on other scams.'

Zal shook his head. 'I thought they'd get bored, move on to somebody else. I didn't understand: prison is full of routine, even things like that almost get sucked into the mundanity of it. So I had to make it stop.'

'How?'

'I killed them both.'

He stared into space for a second, almost incredulous at his own words, proving that this was not an oft- or fondly revisited memory.

'It was the same routine all the time. Creedie took me to this laundry store-room, then Marsh would show up a little while later. Creedie liked getting his dick sucked. He used to point his gun at my head, but that was only at the start, until I became reliably cooperative. Stupid fuck just left it in his holster.'

'You shot him? What about the noise?'

'I didn't. I beat him to death with his riot stick. Then when Marsh showed up, I shot *him*. Put the gun in Creedie's hand, slipped back to the workshop while the guards were coming to investigate. And according to the role, I was there the whole time.'

'But the other guards . . .'

'I left a scene that looked plausibly self-explanatory, and nobody was in a hurry to investigate otherwise. Maybe they suspected, but they couldn't say anything without admitting a whole lotta shit that they didn't want the authorities knowing about.'

'Jesus.'

'The thing about prison: everybody knows everything,

314

nobody says shit. It was never spoken, but it was received wisdom that I killed Marsh and Creedie. There wasn't a big queue to fuck with me after that.'

'What about Marsh's friends?'

'Yeah, I was worried for a while, but Parnell told me – guys like Marsh don't have friends, they have hangers-on and sycophants, flies on shit. You take the shit away, they'll just move to a new one. He was dead-on.'

'Had he done a lot of time?'

'Oh yeah. This was his fourth stretch.'

'What for?'

Zal smiled. 'Can't you guess?'

She could now. 'Life inside wasn't the only thing he taught you about.'

'Hell no. Anybody can commit a crime, but if you want to learn to be a real criminal, you can't beat jail. Months and years of nothing to do but compare notes on what you did, how you did it, what you wish you'd done when you had the chance, what you're gonna do when you get out . . . I don't believe there is a university on this earth where the students are so committed and intensely dedicated to their chosen subject.'

'And you had one-on-one tuition.'

'Oh, Parnell knew it all. Security systems, staff protocols, individual institutions' policies and procedures, police response times and tactics, you name it. He had a dozen ways to avoid hostage situations, mainly because they were usually the ones in which he got caught, but when it was unavoidable, he wrote the book on making sure nobody lost their head.'

'Was there a chapter on surrealist painting or absurdist drama in this book?'

'Different practice, same principle. Parnell had a few

party pieces, sure, but the main thing was just to treat them with as much politeness and dignity as the situation allows.

'The most important lesson he taught me, though, was that you plan a heist backwards. Any punk with a piece can walk into a bank and get them to hand over the money. It's getting out again, free of handcuffs and gunshot wounds, that's the entire focus of your operation. That's the first thing you should look at when you're planning a job. If you don't know how you're getting out, don't even think about going in. With the RSGN, I was looking at plans of the underground, a map showing all the parts that people don't know about: disused tunnels that weren't upgraded in the revamp, sidings, access passages. The main thing was to get out unseen. Before I saw this map, I was originally planning to hit a bank in Saint Rollox: it's next to a warehouse conversion apartment block, and the warehouse used to be a whisky bond. The basement extends beyond the building's outer wall into foundations of a previous building on the site. Backs right up against the vault. I hope you're taking notes.'

'Where do you get this stuff?'

'Mitchell Library. A vast, untapped criminal resource, if you ask me.'

'What about the explosives? Did Parnell teach you that too?'

'No, that was Jerome's specialist subject. He did less than a year, but he shared a cell with a guy who ran a demolition business. He was in for fraud, but talking about explosives made him sound a lot cooler on the cell-block. Parnell would never have touched a fire cracker, never mind a stick of dynamite. He didn't even like using guns, though it was usually unavoidable.' Zal smiled affectionately. 'He'd have been pretty proud of us last Saturday.'

'Is he still inside?'

Zal nodded, his expression more sincere.

'What?' Angelique asked.

Zal sat up, pulling his knees towards him under the covers.

'Parnell's why I'm here. I mean, not here.'

'Glasgow. How?'

'Alessandro. Fucking asshole. Same shit all over again. There's something he wants me to steal for him, except this time there's no question over whether he really wants me to succeed. He wants this . . . *stuff* real bad, and he figures I'm the guy who can get it.'

'But at the Gigliotti—'

'I failed, yeah, but Alessandro's not stupid. Well, actually, he is stupid, but even he must have worked out that I screwed up deliberately – that's why he killed my father. At the time he didn't know he was gonna need me later, so now that he does, Parnell is the only person left he can threaten. Maybe not the only one, but the easiest to get hold of, and someone I owe a debt to.

'Son of a bitch came to see me in prison, laid it all down. This time, I can't screw up, deliberately or otherwise. No excuses, no alternatives: I deliver or Parnell dies, and it won't be by painless lethal injection.'

'And then what if you do deliver? It'll be exactly what you made your sacrifice to avoid. He'll order you to steal something else and you'll never be rid of him.'

Zal closed his eyes and shook his head. When he opened them again, he looked sorrowfully apologetic.

'Parnell's first rule: plan your exit before you plan anything else. We deliver and we disappear. That's what the RSGN was for: our escape fund. Alessandro will get what he wants, then he won't see any of us ever again.'

317

Angelique felt a tightening in her chest as the harshest solitary consequence struck home. 'And nor will I.'

He took hold of her right hand and gave it a squeeze.

'Unless you catch me.'

'Don't even joke about that. Knowing what you've just told me won't make it any easier, but I can't stand back and turn a blind eye.'

'Angelique, I didn't tell you this so that I could ask you not to do your job. I told you so you'd understand why I have to do mine.'

'And doing yours could put you right back in jail. You're not up against the same idiot you took the piss out of at the bank. The guy in charge of this case now is as sharp as they come, Zal. He thinks you're long gone, but if you give him a chance, he'll take you down, believe me. You caught everybody with their pants down before, but this time we'll be ready.'

'Ready, sure. Except you don't know what, you don't know where and you don't know when.'

'And I'll be trying my hardest from here on in to work all of that out. It's gaunny do my head in, knowing the consequences, but I can't stop myself, either. This is what I do, Zal, it's who I am.'

Zal ran a hand through her hair. 'I wouldn't have it any other way,' he said.

Angelique looked across the bed at him. He was smiling again, but those blue eyes were once more sparkling with inscrutable intent.

'Once we get back to Glasgow, it's game on, and I'd be disappointed if you didn't try your absolute best to answer those questions and catch me in the act. But the thing that's really gonna mess with your head is, how do you know I'm not counting on that?'

# III

## the sacred art of leaving

I only had to be cut once to know how to bleed
I know why we tend to love most those who know
how to leave

Take my hand and let me tell you
All but my love will soon be gone
And the exit wound will be quick and clean
So the sacred art of leaving passes on.

**Billy Franks**

# hunted

Within moments of Angelique walking into the station, she had sensed there was something wrong, and that whatever it was, it was wrong with her. Averted eyes, sudden silences, furtively traded looks. It could be that way any time you came back from leave, the natural guilt and insecurity of having lost some ground on your colleagues, swanning off to live it up while they were still busy at the coalface. Normally this effect required an absence of at least a week rather than a fly couple of days, but the identity of her travelling companion accelerated the process and amplified her paranoia.

That said, it could be imprudent to let paranoia account for all of your perceptions, and Angelique knew she was detecting an authentic whiff of mischief, even malice in the air. In the dank, unhealthy, badly ventilated atmosphere of the station, gossip travelled like a disease. If one person walks in with it, pretty soon everyone's got it, and this wasn't the hushed discomfort of a group of colleagues who've already learned some bad news and know you'll be the last to find out. She hadn't exactly gone out of her way to become the most popular person in the place, so there was definitely a smug satisfaction about a few faces as she walked through the cramped and stuffy building, among the crappy aluminium and chipboard partitions, past the open doors of offices. Clearly she was getting some sort of comeuppance, and she didn't even know it yet.

By the time she had made it upstairs and reached her desk, she was in need of a friendly face, or even just someone who had the balls to come out and say what was on their mind. Fortunately, McIntosh met both remits, though the friendly face didn't quite extend to being a happy one.

'Robertson wants to see you soon as. He's in his office, waiting.'

'Cheers,' Angelique told him, putting her bag down next to her desk. 'I'll just dump this and go right in.'

She had begun walking towards the DCI's office when McIntosh spoke again.

'I should warn you, he knows what you were doing in Paris.'

Angelique felt her breakfast turn instantly to lead in her stomach, her eyes widening in response to McIntosh's information. She was scrabbling to choose between a dozen questions when his phone rang, and he grabbed it like it was a lifebelt in a sea of embarrassment.

It was only a few yards to Robertson's door, but it felt like a long walk. It reminded her of the time she'd been sent to the heidie's office at school for lamping some racist bitch with a hockey stick, except this time she wasn't quite so focused regarding her own moral indignation.

She knocked on the door and walked in. Robertson was standing with his back to her, looking out of the window in a posture that just had to have been deliberately composed for effect. He wasn't a habitually pompous individual, and in fact Angelique had a lot of time and respect for him, professionally, but there was something about the wielding of authority in chastisement that brought out the Terry-Thomas in every superior officer.

'Have a seat, Detective Inspector.'

Angelique would have preferred to stand, but she complied, not feeling particularly defiant under the circumstances.

'I have to say, I'm most disappointed to have to do this, though I'd have to admit there's a strong whiff of the inevitable about it. The signs were all there, and I suppose certain of us really ought to look at ourselves, given the way you were treated after Dubh Ardrain, but none of that makes a difference now, does it?'

'Sir?'

'Paris, DI de Xavia. Care to do me the courtesy of coming clean about what you were doing there?'

Shite. How did he . . . how *could* he . . . ?

She regrouped, tactical defensive reflexes kicking in. Robertson was a good boss, and she didn't like to treat him this way, but right now he was acting as the instrument of Them, the Star Chamber, the enemy that had ultimately put her in this position. She was fucked if she was going to make it easy.

'I was on leave, sir. That means it was my business alone what I was doing there and you've no right to ask.'

'Well that's a tacit admission if ever I've heard one. Jesus, Angelique, we've been colleagues a long time. You know and I know what you've been up to behind everybody's backs, so there's no point in carrying on the pretence.'

'I don't believe I know what you're alluding to, sir,' she stated, stone-faced.

'It strikes me as a hell of a coincidence, then, that I should get a phone call *yesterday* from Gilles Dougnac in Paris.'

Christ. Everyone said it was a small world. What they didn't tell you was that it had a cop on every fucking corner. It had gone up the chain to Dougnac and then directly back to Glasgow.

323

'It leaves a bad taste the way it's come about, but there's no avoiding the bottom line. You're out of here.'

'You're firing me, sir?'

'No, I'm not firing you, but I'll certainly be expecting your resignation on my desk very shortly.'

So that was that? No formal inquiry, no procedure, not even the nerve to address the issue at hand and the can of worms it would open. Instead she was being handed the revolver and told to get on with it, spare everybody a lot of paperwork, embarrassment and inconvenience.

'I must say, I'm rather disappointed in Gilles, too,' Robertson added. 'He had to inform me, obviously, but he had the bloody cheek to play as dumb as you are.'

'About what?'

'Oh for fuck's sake, de Xavia, how far are you willing to take this?'

'To the point where you stop tip-toeing around the subject, sir. Let's talk like adults.'

'I'm not the one who's . . .' Robertson stopped, took a breath, closed his eyes and opened them again. 'You're saying you didn't meet Dougnac in Paris?'

'Yes, sir. I mean no, sir. I mean . . . I was there with a friend, and no, I didn't meet Gilles Dougnac. What the hell is going on?'

'Fuck. Does that not make me all the pricks of the day, then.' He sat down, sighing heavily, then laughed with embarrassment. 'I must apologise, though you have to admit you can't blame me for how it looked.'

'Sir, with respect, any danger you could tell me what you're on about?'

He nodded and composed himself.

'Dougnac's putting together a pan-European counter-terrorist operation. Intelligence, tactical resources, rapid-response, pre-emptive action. Best of the best.' Robertson sighed again and looked her in the eye.

'He wants you.'

## it's beginning to look a lot like . . .

Bad sign: Harry wanted a drink and it was only ten o'clock in the morning. Jet-lag was no longer an excuse, as his sleeping and eating patterns had returned to pretty much normal; though his drinking patterns were turning into something of a sprawling miasma. He'd never been anywhere on Earth where there were so many bars, which wouldn't normally have been an issue because, hey, who wants to sit and drink alone like a loser? But in this town, it was almost impossible to drink alone, because the second you lined up a quick one at the bar, some uninvited asshole started yakking to you; then before you knew it, you'd heard his life story and lost count of what you'd drunk somewhere between his mother's heart operation and the Celtics winning the European Superbowl in nineteen-sixty-whatever.

He was running out of brain cells and beginning to worry whether he'd still have a liver to take back to LA with him by the time this whole stupid business was concluded. Yet here he was, pushing a spoon disinterestedly around his bowl of rapidly cooling porridge, thinking he could really use a shot before his breakfast 'guest' showed up.

His lack of appetite was ominously symptomatic, too. He'd started on this porridge stuff a few days back, kind of a 'When in Rome' deal, and since then he'd been unable to start the morning without it. The sugar and cream probably weren't doing him much good in the long term, but you needed internal insulation in this town, as well as something to absorb the deluge of alcohol that would inexorably follow throughout the day. This morning, however, he couldn't face more than a couple of spoons, and the reason was due in the door any minute.

Innez.

There was nothing made Harry more nervous about this operation than that crazy son-of-a-bitch's involvement, but that was okay, because right now it was Harry's job to be nervous about precisely that. Nervous meant cautious, nervous meant on-edge, sharp, vigilant, and he was all that and a bag of chips. However, it wasn't just nerves that were making Harry so apprehensive as to be playing with his breakfast like a huffy kid.

Innez made Harry uncomfortable on a whole number of levels. One was that when it came to being cautious, on-edge, sharp and vigilant, he knew he could never be nervous enough. If Innez figured 'screw Parnell' and decided to fuck them over, then there was no way Harry would be smart enough to out-manoeuvre the guy. Another level was that Innez had been shanghaied into this thing by the very people he had the most reason to *want* to fuck over: the people who had murdered his father. But the principal level had to be that it was Harry who'd carried out the hit.

When you killed people for a living, you kind of forfeited your right to describe yourself as a man of conscience, but you still knew what was and wasn't right. In this business, you didn't get many contracts to take out innocent, frail grandmothers or retards in wheelchairs. You took out enemies, people who put themselves in harm's way and knew what the fuck they were doing when they made that decision.

Killing Innez's father wasn't right. It wasn't like Innez

had called their bluff, and it certainly wasn't like Innez was the kind of guy Alessandro needed to make a point to. Alessandro should have had way, way bigger items on his agenda than settling scores against little piss-ant art-fags who posed him no threat. All ego and no character, that was the kid's problem.

Harry had spoken against the hit because he saw it as a waste of everybody's time and could see no upshot to making an enemy of someone who had very clearly got the message. The guy knew he was out of his depth, which was why he had put himself in jail rather than get in any deeper with Alessandro. But when you kill family, reason and fear take the train: you're making it this guy's purpose in life to get some payback, at whatever cost.

Alessandro didn't want to hear it, however. He threw a few toys out of his pram and started yelling about respect, the usual shit. Harry was given the assignment himself, as a punishment for his dissent and as an unspoken test of his loyalty to the new regime.

He passed.

Innez walked into the hotel restaurant, punctual to the minute. Harry hadn't seen him since he went inside. He appeared bigger, more muscular, and he had a serious blond dye-job on top, made him look like some punk-ass rock star. When he took off his jacket, there were jailhouse tatts visible around his neckline and upper arms. But the main difference Harry noticed was that he no longer looked scared.

'Innez,' Harry said, beckoning him to sit down and offering a menu.

'American Harry,' he replied flatly.

American Harry. That was Innez's way of letting him know that he was these days a lot more clued-in about the organisation he was dealing with, enough to know his nick-name and what it referred to.

Harry's real name wasn't Harry Arthur, but Javier Artero, and he took a lot of shit for his belief that roots were something best left buried. He was a born American – so fucking what if he wasn't obsessed with his ethnic background like the rest of these wetback assholes? He was sick of hearing guys like Miguel talk about embracing their native culture. Shit, if you want to embrace it that bad, why not move back across the fucking border, give up that nice house with the swimming pool in San Bernardino, your Mercedes convertible and your seats for the Laker games, huh? Harry *had* embraced his native culture, and it was the same culture all the rest of these jerks had bought into wholesale, no matter how much mariachi music they played on their goddamn Japanese CD players.

'How you doin'? This town's a piece of work, huh?' Harry said.

'I'm finding it more hospitable than the surroundings I've been recently accustomed to,' Innez replied.

'Oh yeah. Pretty fuckin' hospitable, I'm sure. The banks have certainly been generous towards you.'

'Well, you see, my employment prospects took a bit of a dent, what with having Walla Walla on my resume. Jimmy Hoffa used to hire ex-cons, but he ain't been seen around for a while, so I've had to find an alternative source of income.'

'You're not still pissed about a little thing like goin' to jail for three years, are ya?' Harry asked, trying to hide his discomfiture behind callously cynical humour.

'Life's too short for regrets, Harry. I wouldn't let some-thing so trivial weigh me down, any more than the fact that you motherfuckers killed my old man.'

Harry sighed, took a drink of coffee. Fortunately, his I-don't-give-a-fuck act was much-practiced and came easy to the point of reflex. Innez's anger was actually paradoxically reassuring. A pissed-sounding Innez was more predictable and less disconcerting than if he had shown up with a carefree smile and a spring in his step.

'Listen, pal,' Harry said. 'I don't wanna be here right now any more than you do, okay? I think it's a fucked-up situation and I'm not convinced it's all worth the risk, but you know and I know that my opinion counts for shit, same as yours. So how about we cut each other some slack and get the whole thing over with to our mutual satisfaction, huh?'

'To Alessandro's satisfaction.'

'Whatever. Look, do you want a cup of coffee? You should try this porridge shit, seriously.'

'I've already eaten. You called this meeting. Let's cut the support and get to the headline act. What do you want?'

'I just wanna know everything's going to plan.'

'Everything is just about in place, yes. Why wouldn't it be?'

'Well, you made a lot of people very nervous when you pulled that shit with the bank. Mr Hannigan took a lot of reassuring that he wasn't gonna get fucked over the main event, too. That's why I'm here: had to get on a fuckin' plane and come over here as a gesture of good faith.'

'Good faith? Pardon me if that sounds a little incongruous coming from someone of your pedigree. What is that, an honour-among-scumbags deal? Anyway, it wasn't me who gave Hannigan the impression I was at his disposal.'

'You know, I'm gonna let your attitude slide because I know you got reason to be angry, but don't fuckin' push it kid, okay? You could still pull off this job without your left nut, know what I'm sayin'?'

Innez stared back defiantly, but he said nothing, so Harry knew he'd made his point.

'Is the date set?'

'Yup. Same as ever.'

'Seems like a lot of lead time to me. You've been here how long?'

'I'm not knocking over a liquor store for the cash-register and a bottle of Mad Dog. Something like this takes preparation. Anyway, the lead time is irrelevant; it was the date that was crucial.'

'Christmas fuckin' Eve. Jesus. I'm gonna be stuck here on Christmas Day because of this shit.'

'It's the most opportune time. I've been through all this with you people.'

'Yeah, yeah. With us people. But not with the person who has to spend the fuckin' holidays here in fuckin' Glasgow.'

'You can go home if you like. I'm assuming Hannigan's been placated for now. Your part's done. It's Alessandro who has to come here for the hand-over.'

'Yeah, I . . . *what*? Alessandro? Yeah, right. No, kid, it's Rico Dominguez and Paco Gomez who're comin' over for that.'

Innez shook his head in a way Harry really didn't like. It didn't make him angry, just, well, nervous. Uncomfortable.

'What?'

'I'm handing the stuff over to Alessandro, and Alessandro alone.'

'Yeah, right. You think Alessandro's gonna haul his ass all the way over here for fuckin' Christmas, just because you say so?'

331

'He is if he wants the stuff.'

'No. *You* are gonna hand it over to Rico and Paco, or else your old jailbird Good Samaritan Parnell is gonna end his sentence slow but early.'

'You can only kill him once. Then what have you got? Oh no, wait, I fucked up, didn't I? Alessandro's gotta have at least a dozen guys lined up who could boost this shit out of a European museum, huh?'

'We could find somebody. Don't flatter yourself.'

'I'm not flattering myself. Alessandro's the one who rates my abilities, but you and I both know that's because Alessandro doesn't have anyone to compare me to. Given all the shit that's gone down between us, he wouldn't have come to me if he had any other options.'

Innez was right, and the fucker knew Harry knew it, too. Given the months they'd had to wait, they could probably have found someone else capable of doing the job in the meantime, but in Alessandro's limited mental process, it was: think museum, think Innez.

'Why do you want Alessandro to be there? Sounds like some kind of trap to me. It will to him, too.'

'No traps. I just want this to be over between us, face to face. I want to be able to hand this shit to him personally, not to some bagman. That way, if anything goes wrong, he can see I did my part, played it straight, gave him what he wanted. I don't want Parnell to die because one of *you* jerks screwed up.'

'If that's what you're worried about, forget it. We get the shit, Parnell's in the clear. It won't matter who you give it to.'

'It matters to me. That's the bottom line. Alessandro screwed up when he made it about Parnell. Maybe if he'd cut me in, he'd have more room to negotiate, but while

Parnell is all he's got and I'm his only option, those are my terms.'

'You're looking for a slice, is that what this is about?'

'No. I wouldn't accept a red cent from that piece of shit. I'm just pointing out the corner he's painted himself into: killing an old man in prison would be worth a lot less to Alessandro than what I can deliver. Especially with business the way it is . . .'

'What the fuck are you talking about?'

'You think the grapevine you guys tap in Walla Walla only runs one way? It's like the fucking *Wall Street Journal* of crime: whether you give a shit or not, you can't help but hear all about whose stocks are up and whose fortunes are down. It's no secret to anyone in that place that the SS Estobal is not a happy ship under Captain Alessandro. Hey, it's okay, you don't have to rush to defend him. I won't tell.'

Innez grinned, having rightly recognised that it hadn't occurred to Harry to defend him, not even for appearances' sake.

'Alessandro's young and inexperienced,' Harry said. 'But he's the head of the Estobals, and don't fucking forget it. We're a strong enough organisation to be able to withstand a few bumps and scrapes on the kid's learning curve.'

'Bullshit, Harry. Alessandro's head of the Estobal operation, yeah, but that operation doesn't exist in a vacuum. Other parties are looking on and taking note. Some of them are getting concerned, and others are rubbing their hands. He's got you all in some choppy waters, and the fastest identifiable route to calmer seas lies via Glasgow. Alessandro knows that, and so do you. If his ship went down with all hands, make no mistake, I'd be machine-gunning the life-boats and laughing as I watched all you fuckers go down. But if bailing him out is what I have to do to keep my friend alive, so be it. I know what I have to do, you know what you have to do, and he knows what he has to do.'

'Sounds like Christmas in Glasgow for all of us.'

'And a happy new year.'

# alchemy

Angelique waited alone in the glass-walled foyer of the Dalriada Museum, feeling sure about nothing save the knowledge that no-one else had any answers for her. It had been a long and discomfitingly empty few days. Some momentous events, once past, could very quickly fade or become distantly dream-like as you got on with life. That short time in Paris, however, echoed and resounded tangibly in her thoughts, her emotions and even her body. When she closed her eyes, she could still hear his voice, still see him standing by the *Mona Lisa*, still feel his hand clutched around hers.

The time since had felt hollow. She wasn't kidding herself about their situation: they had agreed at CDG that when they touched down in Glasgow they had to go their separate ways and do their separate, entirely conflicting jobs, but she felt like she was waiting for something nonetheless. Insecurities visited like old school friends: familiar, inevitable, and as welcome as a priest on a Pride march. To head them off, she made some inquiries, calling in a few favours at Interpol to get the gen from the US. It was all there in the files: the abortive raid on the Gigliotti, the deaths of prison officer Creedie and prisoner Marsh at Folsom, Innez's recent release and the on-going incarceration of one Dexter Parnell. Zal Innez might not be someone it was wise to trust, but he wasn't a liar, either.

In time what she was waiting for arrived, in the form of

a phone call, finally delivering what she had hoped for every time the thing had rung since she got home. He wanted to meet, and suggested the Dalriada as both a public and appropriate venue.

That was three days ago, so at least Dougnac's offer had given her something else to think about in the meantime. There was nothing quite like the possibility of uprooting yourself and leaving everything familiar behind to just peak that sense of being lost and alone.

She stood in the centre of the entrance hall, directly below the bust of John Milton Horsburgh, his marble countenance contentedly monitoring the flow of visitors to his vast bequest. It was a municipal museum, run by the city council, but Horsburgh had left a substantial trust fund to finance the exhibition and upkeep of his collection, not having envisaged palaces of the arts ever being considered public utilities. This meant the place drew far less from the council coffers than other attractions of comparable size, but evidently didn't stop some people whining about whatever public money *was* spent. She read recently that the usual religious halfwits had been bumping their gums in protest about the cost of the current History of Allegory exhibition. There was only one commissioned work and one purchase in the bloody thing, the rest being loaned works as it was a temporary display. However, as far as the God-botherers were concerned, the deposit off a crate of ginger bottles would be too much of an outlay if it was spent on something they disapproved of. As this included, at the last count, every non-religious work in history, that kind of narrowed the field.

John Milton Horsburgh. There was a man with no issues about his place in the world, or his sense of belonging in this city. The song said 'Glasgow belongs to me', and in his case a lot of it had, at one time or other. He was a ship-ping magnate, who made his considerable fortune through 'tobacco and cotton', according to the official blurb, which politely avoided reference to the darkest third side of the contemporary triangle trade between Glasgow, Africa and North America.

He wanted to be remembered by the place. Those were his exact words. Not by the people, but by the place, like he wanted his soul subsumed and absorbed by the city. Not a philanthropist, then, otherwise he might have thought to bequeath the odd penny to the poor of the city and be remembered for that. Instead he left his artworks and his trinkets, so that his taste, his personality, would forever leave its stamp. Thus: the Dalriada Museum, finally built by his executors after a good century of legally protracted arguing, and opened to the grateful city just too late for the Empire Exhibition of 1938. In accordance with Horsburgh's wishes, it belonged to Glasgow, whether Glasgow liked it or not.

But what about Angelique? Did she belong to Glasgow? Amin had booted her parents out of Uganda while she was in the womb, so she'd been born in the city and lived in it or its environs ever since. She'd been educated there, and apart from a few temporary secondments had always worked there too. She had the accent, the attitude, her flat in the south side. It felt like home, sure, but belonging, that was something else.

She had her season ticket to the 'Brox, but did she belong there? And, she found herself wondering, had she ever really wanted to? Was she drawn to places where she could feel isolated but defiant, because those were the places she had grown to most comfortably inhabit? Isolated but defiant: that's how she was in the Glesca Polis, that's how she'd been at school, and let's be honest, that's how she'd been at Ibrox, regardless of her passion for the game. It was a site of glories, a cathedral of sporting achievement, but it was also a place tainted by a history of exclusion. In some perverse way, maybe that was what she had sought. She was not a Catholic any more, but she knew that having gone to Sacred Heart, she was Catholic enough for some of the brain donors in the stands around her. She was a republican (small r) surrounded by hordes singing *God Save the Queen*, an anti-imperialist amid choruses of *Rule Britannia*. But she'd argue that Rangers were her team too – isolated but defiant.

'We are the people'. That was the fans' motto, far more than the club's official 'Aye Ready'. Her lefty-posturing, flexibly-atheist-but-Catholicism-defending Celtic fan of a brother took no end of exception to this simple little state-ment. It had sinister undertones, he argued, toeing some-thing of a rehearsed-sounding Tim party line. It had its roots in prejudice against Irish immigrants, those who were, by implication, *not* the people. It was a motto of Ulster Loyalist paramilitaries. It had connotations of racial supremacy. And it was an anagram of 'Hitler was right', nearly.

Angelique, who knew a lot more Bears than James, knew different. No matter who appropriated it, quoted it, used it or abused it, its origin was innocent, harmless and Glasgow through and through. We are the people meant we are the people. It was just a gallus affirmation of being happy with who you were, and good luck to anyone who felt that way.

Gallus. That was the only adjective that could truly describe it, a word whose meaning, usage and etymology were the quintessence of the place. It was coined at the hanging of a thief and murderer known as Gentleman Jim, who had remained his smiling, cocksure and witty self even on the gallows.

'We are the people,' and indeed they were. But the question remained, probing deeper in light of Dougnac's proposal: was Angelique?

She was stirred from her reflections by a snicking sound as something dropped at her feet. Looking down, she saw that it was a playing card: the seven of diamonds. She turned around to see Zal standing a few feet away.

'Howdy,' he said. Angelique wanted to hug him but restrained herself; then, reconsidering and concluding there to be no reason for restraint, did it anyway, her embrace quickly turning into a prolonged kiss.

'So you ain't here to arrest me, I guess.'

They took a walk through the museum, Zal noticeably guiding her towards the History of Allegory exhibition, Angelique making a mental note to check up on what he might specifically be guiding her away from. The exhibit was laid out in a V-shape, each work annotated by smaller prints or fragments of contemporary comparative pieces. Zal was less vocal than in the Louvre, possibly because he was less informed about what was on display, but he was drinking it all in again nonetheless. Less informed was still not *un*informed, however, so he insisted on standing Angelique a few feet to the left of *The Ambassadors*, a full-size print accompanied by a note acknowledging the location of the original at the National in London. From her deliberately skewed perspective, she was able to see the indistinct shape to the bottom left of the painting's eponymous subjects (and patrons) metamorphose into a skull, which Zal proudly announced was 'the most famous fuck-you in art history'. He was also able to inform her that *The Marriage Feast at Cana,* on loan from a museum in Toronto and attributed to 'the Unknown Master', was rumoured to be a fake, having 'resurfaced' in the conveniently tumultuous aftermath of the Second World War.

Whether Zal knew much about it or not, comment seemed superfluous regarding the controversial *West Coast (,) Man,* sitting shamelessly at the apex of the dog-legged hall. Angelique could muster no reaction more articulate than a fit of the giggles, and would go toe to toe with any critic who wanted to argue that its intention was anything more sophisticated than raising a laugh.

'These Christian protestors,' Zal observed, also giggling. 'I mean, if you can't laugh at a gigantic statue of a guy sucking his own dick, sitting here in the serenity of an art gallery, what the fuck can you laugh at?'

'Is it true the cocaine's real?'

'Dunno, though I could think of a quick way to find out.'

'I'm just surprised it's still there. Actually, in this town they probably have to replace it hourly.'

Their tour moved on to the equally prude-baiting *Voyeur.* It was a large, cube-like installation, inside of which was a bench facing a TV monitor built into one wall, showing a hard-core porn video. They went in and sat down for a couple of minutes, giggled a little more at what was on display, shrugged and walked out.

'What did you think?' Zal asked.

'Aesthetically speaking? I thought we did it better.'

'Yeah, we could give 'em some pointers. But look again.'

Angelique turned around to face the cube. On each of the four walls, what had appeared to be white panels revealed themselves to be video-projector screens, now showing the pair of them sitting on the bench watching the tape.

'Very droll, huh?' Zal observed.

'Oh aye. So does this kind of stuff rate above old Mona on your accolade-deservance scale? Or are you just here to case the joint?'

'Well, principally I'm here to see you, but admittedly I could be casing the joint. The problem you have is that you won't know whether I'm really casing the joint or whether I just want you to think I am.'

'Indeed, congratulations. You found a way of rendering just about anything you tell me effectively meaningless. But I take it from that remark that everything is as was. You're still going ahead with it, whatever it is?'

'You know I don't have a choice.'

'You have to do this, and then you have to disappear.'

'I have to disappear anyway, Angelique. I stole over a million bucks from a bank.'

'No. You got away clean on that score. We can't pronounce it officially, but believe me, as a cop I know when a case is dead.'

'What about your hotshot boss, Shaw?'

'He's already given it last rites. He'll be telling the bank otherwise, but he knows you left him nothing to go on.'

'Except for one of his detectives knowing exactly whodunnit.'

'I'm morally at peace with keeping that to myself.'

'Carefully chosen words,' Zal acknowledged.

'I'm less at peace with the thought of either never seeing you again, or only seeing you in the Bar-L visiting area. There must be a way around this, some means of taking Parnell out of the equation. What if we could get him protection, a move to another prison, a new identity, *something*.'

'With what? You've nothing to offer the US authorities

in return, and I've nothing to offer you. I don't think anybody's gonna buy it as a new incentive-based crime-prevention scheme. What would you tell your boss? Let's help this guy out so he won't rob someplace? He'd say: here's a better idea – let's lock the son-of-a-bitch up for robbing the last place.'

'But there's a crime being committed by Alessandro blackmailing you into doing this. The authorities on both sides of the Atlantic would surely be interested in that.'

'Not without proof. Angelique, believe me, I'm a guy who looks at every possible avenue, every contingency, remember? And there is no way of getting around what I have to do.'

He had finished speaking, but Angelique could definitely hear a 'but'. She looked at him and saw it confirmed in his face.

'But what?'

'There *is* another way of getting Alessandro off my back for good.'

Shaw had evidently lost the power of his lower jaw by the time Angelique finished speaking. If she had disclosed anything like the true extent of her relationship with Zal Innez, he might well have forgotten to breathe through his gaping mouth, but what she did reveal was enough to have him understandably aghast. Latterly, his silence had been due to being increasingly astonished at what she had to say, but she had warded off predictable early outrage by the calculated opening gambit of asking how he'd like Bud Hannigan served to him on a plate. She knew that was one hell of a hook-line for any Glasgow cop, but in Shaw's case the bait was extra tasty, having failed in his previous attempts to nail the slippery little bastard.

342

Hannigan was notoriously adept at both evading the attentions of the law and distancing himself from the activities that nonetheless paid for his mansion in Drymen and whatever his lady of the moment was driving. He had cemented his position as the major drugs player in the city following the death of his last serious rival, Frank Morris, victim of a quite untraceable hit. Morris had been found dead in his own back garden, having been shot through the eye, but though there was no exit wound, there was no bullet to be found, either. More curious still, less than a week later, the ned rumoured to have collected on the contract was found dead of a heroin overdose, a dashed unlucky break for someone not previously known to have a habit.

Shaw collected himself. It took a few moments, but he got there. He sighed, stood up, walked back and forth behind his desk, sat down, sighed again, stood up again, ran both hands through his hair, made to speak two or three times, then nodded decisively and returned to his chair.

'You didn't exactly play by the book, de Xavia, but then, what would you have got if you had done?'

'I think fuck-all would be the empirical measure, sir.'

'Quite. We've all got our snouts and we have to negotiate a few moral grey areas to accommodate them, but I think you now hold some kind of record. Nice to know I was right about the magician thing, by the way. Makes me feel not totally redundant to the process at hand. But bearing that specifically in mind, and without casting aspersions on your instincts or credulity, we can't lose sight of the possibility that he's forced another card on you.'

'Sir?'

'Well, he gives us his sob story and *you* suggest a deal,

not him, same as you insisted on evacuating the bank. He gets what he wants but he makes you think it was your idea, thus lowering your suspicions. He says okay, he can get us Hannigan and this Estobal punter, but he can't deliver either until *after* he's carried out his heist. So if you polis don't mind keeping oot the way for a wee minute . . . Then he nabs whatever he's after and fucks off, leaving us with no Hannigan, no Estobal and definitely no Innez. Christ, there might not even be a Parnell.'

'There is. I checked.'

'But even so, even if everything is true, including his motive, if he delivers for Estobal, he saves Parnell, and it would be easier if we're waiting around like mugs for something else to happen. He can get what he wants without giving us anything.'

'In which case why offer us a deal?'

'More misdirection.'

'I won't pretend I can second guess the guy; you'd go insane trying. But I know this much: he's not asking us to look the other way. He knows we can't do that.'

'Bloody right. If this guy is planning another robbery on my patch, you'd better believe I'm gaunny pull oot all the stops to prevent it. And I'll be expecting you to do the same, even if, as I suspect, you've a wee soft spot for him.'

'I'll be giving it everything I've got, sir. I don't know any other way. But if you'll forgive me, I feel I'm obliged to infect you with the little virus he dropped into my head.'

'And what's that?'

'I told him, Parnell or no Parnell, that we had no choice but to do our best. He asked how I'd know he wasn't relying on that.'

Shaw sighed again, blowing air through pursed lips in

344

a long, contemplative, pressure-cooker exhale. 'I'm not sure I will forgive you for sharing that one, de Xavia. That's a headfuck if ever I heard one.'

'It's also why I believe he's sincere about this deal.'

'Fair enough, but I think there's a gauntlet been thrown doon, regardless of whatever headgames he's trying to play. He's a smart bugger, but we didnae come doon wi' the rain, and this time he won't be catchin' us with our trousers down.'

'I told him that, sir. He said we should put on clean underwear just in case.'

Shaw laughed, but his smile was thin and there was a formidable determination in his eyes. 'Right. Now the gauntlet's *definitely* been thrown doon. What was it he said we didn't know? The where, the what and the when. Well, let's just see if us daft polis can possibly figure oot a thing or three.'

Angelique saw a near-gleeful enthusiasm grow in Shaw. He'd caught a taste of blood in the water, irresistible to a cop like him, with the added piquancy of a quite bare-faced element of challenge. She'd experienced the exhilaration, the energy of it herself a hundred times, and felt self-conscious that she did not share it today. She also, despite his confidence (or was it bravado), felt concern for Zal. Shaw would dearly love to bring down Bud Hannigan, but that counted as two in the bush, and he would not let even such a tantalising possibility distract him from the more immediate task in hand. In that way, he was immune to Zal's magic.

The same could not be said for Angelique. Up until now, it had all remained theoretical, but seeing Shaw with the scent in his nostrils rendered an unforgiving reality. It was her job to stop Zal from doing his, her job to prevent him from appeasing Alessandro, and her job to effectively ensure that Parnell would die. But Zal had known all of this, and had said only, with that infuriating glint in his eye, 'How do you know I'm not counting on that?' Maybe he hadn't just said it to mess with her head; maybe it was an absolution, a way of relieving her of responsibility because he knew there were things he could not rightly ask her to do. But equally, Zal was expert at getting you to do what he wanted while believing it was both your own idea and the right thing to do. Perhaps the words were paradoxically sincere, and that only by doing her job could she help him and, ultimately, his friend. Only by trying to stop him could she do the right thing.

She took a deep breath, bent down and reached into her bag. Then for Zal, for Parnell, for Shaw and for none of them, she got on with what she did best.

'Let's start with where,' she said, opening up the map and spreading it on Shaw's desk.

'What's this?'

'I got it from the Mitchell. It shows the old bits of the underground as well as the new, with the streetplan over-laid. Innez said he got the idea for the RSGN when he was looking at a map of these tunnels. I wondered whether this might have been while he was planning something else. Here's where he asked to meet me today.'

'The Dalriada Museum. Kinning Park. It runs practically underneath.'

'The tunnel's been bricked off for thirty years, but it's still down there, with potential exits close to Paisley Road West, the M77 and the M8.'

'They could be out of the city in minutes. But what with? You said yourself, fine art's valuable, but not sellable. It might tickle this Alessandro's ego to own a Rembrandt, but I cannae see Hannigan being too fussed. In fact, I cannae see where Hannigan fits in at all.'

'Allow me to illuminate. Innez took me to the History of Allegory exhibition, in the South Hall.'

'So what do you reckon he was looking at there?'

'It's what we weren't looking at. We didn't go into the North Hall, which houses the permanent Horsburgh Collection.'

'More unsellables.'

'Not quite. Upstairs, gallery level, you'll find the Horsburgh Hoard, as it's nicknamed. Trinkets, ornamentation, plates, cups, salvers, statuary, goblets, and even a very vulgar scale replica of the Horsburgh fleet's flagship; vulgar, but cast, like everything else I've mentioned, in solid gold.'

'Alakazammy, stairheid rammy.'

'There's silver too, plus precious stones, natch. Again, all of these pieces are identifiable, and unsellable once they're known to have been stolen, but not once you've melted them down. At that point the stuff would be worth far less, pound for pound, but it would also be untraceable.'

'Which is presumably where Hannigan comes in. But if this is the target, why wouldn't Hannigan just hit it himself? Even if it hadn't occurred to him, why not go it alone now that he knows?'

'Well, for one thing, Hannigan knows he's a big fish in a small pond, and the Estobals wouldn't be a very sensible bunch to start a war with. However, the main reason is he couldn't, or someone else in Glasgow would have tried by now. But Alessandro reckoned he knew a man who could. I'm guessing Alessandro identified the target and came to Hannigan with the proposal. Alessandro had the plan, and through Innez the means, but even recast, he wouldn't be

347

able to get the gold out of the country or into the US. So there had to be some localised arrangement with Hannigan, both to facilitate the smelting and to move the goods.'

'Reverse alchemy,' Shaw said with obvious satisfaction and approval. 'Turning gold into brass.'

'So that gives us a where and a what. We still need a when.'

'When matters less if you're monitoring the what and staking out the where. I'll get men undercover on the security staff, post officers in the tunnel.'

'Indefinitely?'

'Immediately, but indefinitely won't be very long. It's less than a week until Christmas. My guess would be that he'd hit when everybody's busy being festive. Christmas Day, Christmas Eve . . . Hogmanay would be a good one. Didn't someone hit the Ashmolean on Hogmanay?'

'Night of the Millennium, yes. Nobody could hear the alarm for fireworks, if there was anyone sober enough to do anything about it.'

'Well, we'll be sober this Christmas. And it'll be worth it to see the bastard's face when he walks in and finds us already waiting for him.'

'Hmmm,' Angelique said.

'What?'

'It's still just a theory, sir. I think we should keep a very open mind.'

'Absolutely, absolutely. But don't let Innez mess with your head either, make you think all your good ideas are wrong just because he might be expecting them. He's a magician, not a wizard. Magicians can't really read your mind, they just know ways of making you think they have.'

'Understood, sir. But I have to ask . . . if we're wrong, or if we're right and . . .' She shook her head. 'Whatever.

If we *do* fail to stop him, despite – or even somehow because of – our best efforts . . .'

'I'm a man of honour, de Xavia. If he delivers us that wee shite Hannigan, I'll move heaven and earth to make sure this Parnell punter's in the clear. It would be a small price to pay. We can make a recommendation to the judge too, get him a sympathetic hearing seeing he turned Queen's and all that. But if he's expecting immunity, for the Dalriada or for the bank job, he can whistle.'

'He didn't mention immunity sir. It wasn't on the agenda.'

'That's very noble of him. I suppose he's lain down his liberty for his friends before. An honourable, if inconvenient habit.'

'No, sir, I don't believe he thought it was an issue. Whatever he's got in mind for Hannigan and Alessandro, Innez doesn't expect to be caught.'

'My dear Angelique,' Shaw said, grinning. 'Name me one convict who ever did.'

# let us prey

'Ninety seconds,' Zal said, stopping his watch. 'Six slower than last time, but outstanding nonetheless. Even faster if this asshole Dominguez can handle a spanner. I'd say we're about ready for a job in the pit lanes.'

'No, man,' said Leo, 'I can't see Ferrari authorising that level of added weight.'

'Surely your adjustments don't add that much.'

'I wasn't talkin' about the adjustments, dude, I was talkin' about Jerome.'

'Shame on you when he ain't here to defend himself,' Zal chided.

'Oh, you sayin' you want me to play Queensberry Rules with that bitch-ass motherfucker?'

''Course,' said Karl. 'If you weren't here, I'm sure he wouldn't let a word be said about you. Not any nice words, anyway.'

'Well I'd sure hate to be around you guys when I ain't here,' Leo observed.

'Okay,' Zal announced, 'that's everything accounted for, double-checked, tested and in position. I'd say we're good to go. Let's go pick up our passenger.'

'Good to go,' Leo confirmed, 'soon as I'm through shakin' hands with the President. Or I guess it's Prime Minister round here.'

'First Minister,' Zal corrected. 'But they're all pricks.'

Leo headed for the bathroom.

'What about the girl?' Karl asked, clipping a newly charged battery pack into his laptop.

'The deal's confirmed. I double-checked that too.'

'That's not what I was talking about.'

Zal sighed.

'I know what you were talking about, Karl. Don't worry. We both understood what we were getting into, and we knew we'd have to get out of it too. Neither of us told the other any lies. That's gotta be a new phenomenon in one of my relationships. But she and I both know what has to happen.'

'Knowing won't make it any easier to leave.'

'Leaving's easy, Karl. I've been doing it regularly since I was a kid. Leaving's always easy. It's missing that's the real bitch.'


'As Neil Young once sang: tonight's the night.'

Shaw smoked a cigarette as he paced nervously in front of the squad car, a tall bundle of unused energy desperate for a focused outlet. 'I can feel it with every instinct I've got as a polisman.'

They were holding position in the carpark of a disused cash-and-carry, less than a quarter of a mile from the Dalriada Museum. There were two vans with them, one for the Armed Response Unit and the second accommodating six bluebottles, all as restlessly eager for action as you'd expect in men who knew they weren't getting off shift until this thing went down or dawn broke. At the museum itself, there were two armed undercover officers, as well as extra security staff, though the latter had been briefed against being over-vigilant. The last thing they needed was someone huckling the thieves before they actually tried to steal anything; or the guards over-reacting

351

to some minor incident and betraying that the place was under extra surveillance.

'Forgive me, sir,' said Angelique, 'but would it be considered insubordinate to remind you that you said the same thing last night, too. Right down to the Neil Young bit.'

'Aye, and I'll say it tomorrow night, ya cheeky bessom. It's the ranking officer's prerogative.'

'Yes, sir.'

Shaw had seriously stepped up the manpower the previous evening, after they learned from immigration that one Alessandro Estobal had entered the country at Heathrow earlier in the day, in the company of two known associates. The boss had necessarily prepared them for a major swoop that night, but to be fair to him he had always opined that Christmas Eve was the date his money was on. He had also reckoned on the robbery taking place when the museum was closed, rather than envisaging Zal risking a second hostage situation. They were ready for it nonetheless, but it seemed unlikely he'd back himself into a corner a second time, especially knowing that a surprise disappearing act couldn't work twice. An out-of-hours raid had the further advantage of there being only minimum security staff on duty, aside, that was, from the two armed cops who would be covering the Horsburgh Hoard until their relief showed up in the morning.

'He likes the cover of darkness,' Shaw had observed. 'He went into that bank in broad daylight because he needed it to be open, but he waited until it was pitch outside before making his exit. Unfortunately for us, at this time of year it's dark by four in the bloody afternoon.'

It was impossible to say that nothing had been overlooked, and Shaw wasn't arrogant enough to believe he could anticipate Zal's every move, but he was determined there would at least be no excuse for getting stung by the same method twice. Hence they had several poor bastards posted underground, as well as surveillance in place at several sites identified as potential entry/exit points to the tunnel system. An IT expert was brought in too, to install a new, state-of-the-art firewall and to monitor the museum's computer system for viruses and trojans. So far it remained inviolate.

Angelique hoped Zal's most perplexing remark really was just a form of absolution. She'd done her job, just as he'd told her she should, with the result that they now had the Dalriada locked up tight as a camel's arse in a sandstorm. If there was a way this giant rat-trap was going to help Parnell, then she sure as hell couldn't see it.

# wetwork

The first shots hadn't been fired yet, and the world didn't know it, but the good fight was well underway. To the untrained eye, Walter Thorn might look merely like a middle-aged man crouching on a toilet seat in a cramped and smelly lavatory cubicle, but in reality he was a highly trained secret operative engaged in a covert assignment that would take the moral battle right to the heart of the enemy.

He checked his pistol again, cradling its weight in his hand. It felt good, like it had felt good every time he'd picked it up to practice shooting until he could bullseye the target nine times out of ten from the required range. Everything about this felt good, so much so that he wished he'd gotten involved in something genuinely active years ago. He wouldn't say he'd wasted his time with what he had done – far from it, he'd performed an invaluable role – but let's be honest, that role had always been a matter of commenting from the sidelines. Now, however, he was in the thick of the action.

Even Mary had remarked that he seemed to have a spring in his step, and he'd have to admit that if this burgeoning sense of energy and vitality persisted, he might well have to insist on pushing their beds together some night soon.

His watch read 8:24. It was almost time. He'd thought the waiting would be tough, with boredom and the threat of doubt more a concern than comfort or cramp. However, the opposite had proven the case. With each hour that passed, his resolve only became stronger; while the sense of excitement and anticipation grew by the minute.

He was in the elite of the elite, the three operatives entrusted with the true 'wetwork' of the mission. The less exalted (but nonetheless invaluable, make no mistake) members of F&NY-PAD had completed their task and would by now have joined the rest of F&NY in holding an ecumenical vigil to pray for success. They had gone into the museum within an hour of closing time, six of them: Walter, Liam McGhee and Monty Masterton as the active service unit; the remainder as logistical support. With Walter and Liam both carrying concealed pistols, it was left to the others to smuggle in the hammers, chisels and hacksaws that were then deposited in the cisterns of the Male bathroom. After that, upon leaving the museum, it was the logistical support team's job to ensure that they each rotated the exit turnstile twice so that the numbers in and out appeared to tally. Then, right on closing time, the active service unit took up position in the cubicles, partially but not fully shutting them, and crouching on the seats to avoid the cursory check that was carried out before the front doors were locked.

It was a risky tactic, but it proved that Monty had more than symbolism in mind when he chose the date for their mission. As well as marking a night of Christian rebirth, it was also an evening when the staff would be keen to get closed up and out to the pub as swiftly as possible.

Vindication came after a thoroughly nerve-stretching twenty minutes, between the final PA announcement that the museum was closing and what turned out to be a negligently cursory check of the public conveniences. Whoever it was had barely entered the room, probably only far enough to see all five cubicle doors slightly ajar and the

355

urinals deserted. He'd called out 'Hello', and then, upon receiving no response, promptly retreated.

As Monty had assured them, such checks were only to make sure that no dopey visitors got locked in by mistake. The rest of the museum's security arrangements were considerably more stringent, but their weakness was that they were only intended to stop people getting out of the building with the so-called art work. There were no specific safeguards against them demolishing it.

The silence during the ensuing hours was oddly monastic. Walter could hear his companions breathing, but nobody spoke, as had been agreed. Instead, they remained aware of each other's presence, a reassurance that they were none of them alone and a reminder of what strength they had together.

The time ticked closer, less than a minute to go. Walter thought he might be dreading this point, but though he was trembling and almost nauseous with nerves, these were part of a greater exhilaration, an energy running right through him that would have to be drawn upon soon lest he explode.

'Gentlemen, it's time,' Monty finally announced, maybe fifteen seconds ahead of their synchronised watches. 'His judgement cometh, and that right soon.'

'Amen,' said Walter and Liam simultaneously.

It was time for F&NY-PAD to get stuck in.

They each pulled a plastic Halloween mask over their faces and exited the toilets. The corridor was in darkness, but the entrance to the exhibition hall glowed beckoningly ahead of them. The Fag Filth exhibition, as Monty called it, was in the new South Hall, which was largely walled with glass on one side, and thus partially illuminated at night by the building's pale green exterior lighting.

Walter had a pistol in his hands, a hammer in his belt, a chisel tucked into his sock, and, he was slightly discomfited to note, an erection in his underpants. Oh well, he thought, trying to put it out of mind. A few minutes ago he'd have said every fibre of his being was stimulated by this illicit activity, and now he knew it was no exaggeration.

'Remember,' Monty whispered. 'Once we cross this threshold, move swiftly and don't touch any paintings.'

They had gone over the procedure a thousand times, but Walter couldn't blame Monty for reiterating it now that it was for real: in the heat of such a moment, it would be easy to let the basics slip as one contemplated the principal task ahead. The paintings were secured by wires that would set off the alarms if they were even nudged off-balance, let alone pulled from the walls. However, as Monty had explained, their target, being such an outsize sculpture, required no such electronic tethering, as you'd need a charging bull to overbalance it and a forklift truck to remove it. Instead, it was monitored remotely by a CCTV camera; or rather it was surveyed by the camera, and monitored, like the ones they were currently dashing past, by a nightshift security guard reading the sports section of the *Daily Record*.

Nonetheless, the camera's output was recorded, and recordings could be awfully helpful to the boys in blue even if you were masked, which was why it was Walter's job to shoot the lens out with his air-pistol. Then they could get on to phase two. The black-out and the ensuing noise would bring the night watchman running to investigate, but that was what Liam's replica pistol was for. None of them liked the idea of threatening someone – it wasn't this poor chap's fault that the people he worked for saw fit to exhibit pornography to innocent children – but the fake gun would certainly make it a lot easier to

357

get him locked in a cupboard while they made their escape.

Monty and Liam stood close to the walls and made ready with their tools, waiting to move in once Walter had fired the first shot of this new holy war. He took aim with both hands, breathed in, narrowed his eyes, gave praise to Our Lord and pulled the trigger.

Bullseye.

Glass fragments flew from the camera and cascaded to the floor. Before the first shard hit the ground, however, several alarms began ringing all around them. Internally, Walter could hear bells, accompanied from outside the building by an electronic klaxon sound.

'Oh dear heavens.'

He looked disbelievingly at the pistol in his hands for a moment, too long a moment, then around the hall, where he could see his two companions running in opposite directions, neither having frozen like he had. At either end of the gallery, metal shutters were rapidly descending to lock them into the scene of a crime they hadn't even had time to commit.

Walter looked to his right, in time to see Liam roll under the descending barrier, disappearing through the narrowing gap just before it hit the floor. He turned to his left and observed that the other one was closed too, with Monty nowhere to be seen.

'Oh good Lord.'

Worse still, on top of the alarms, he was sure he could now also hear sirens.

He looked to the glass walls, then at the hammer in his belt. The moment of hope faded as quickly as it had shone. The walls inclined slightly from bottom to top, and each massive panel of glass was at least an inch thick. If he did manage to break it, he'd be showered with fragments.

Besides, if the police were on their way, he wasn't going to be able to outrun them.

However, in that doomed thought came a glimmer of reprieve. Nobody knew how many raiders there were, and ironically Walter's slower reflexes might yet prove his salvation. If Liam and Monty were caught – and given the speed of the police's response, surely they would be – then they might well be assumed to be the only perpetrators. Indeed, if they saw that Walter hadn't been caught, they certainly wouldn't betray him any more than he'd give out on them: the agents of F&NY-PAD wouldn't buckle in the face of capture.

He glanced around the gallery. The *West Coast (,) Man* abomination stood close to an enormous cube-like structure at the apex of the obtusely angled hall, with paintings and informative displays filling the exhibit down either side. Right now he was standing in a CCTV blind spot, having taken out the camera covering this area, and the entrances at either end were locked off. No-one could see him, and it was still possible no-one knew he was there, so if he could find somewhere to hide, then maybe he'd get out of this after all. He'd have one hell of a scoop, too, though his 'source' would, of course, have to remain anonymous.

Taking a step closer to the windows, he noticed that there was a large, double-wide doorway built into the wall next to the exit furthest from where they'd come in. He ran towards it, barely daring to hope, but found it to be locked, a 'Museum Staff Access Only' sticker warning him off.

'Dash it.'

But who was he to be put off by a sticker? He was a man of action now, with a hammer and a chisel. This called for some Positive Action Direct.

He took the chisel from his sock, then looked back to

where he had left his hammer on the floor, which was when he noticed that the cube-structure had an entrance on one side.

'Hold your horses,' he muttered to himself. 'This could be the very dab.'

Walter had a look through the gap. There was a blank TV screen on one wall, and a long raised bench arrangement opposite. When he took a pace inside, the interior became brightly lit, which seemed to puncture any notion of hiding in there until he noticed the white panelling beneath the bench, intended to blend it geometrically with the rest of the cube. His heart accelerating again, he crouched down and forced the chisel between the top of the panel and the underside of the bench. It came away easily, revealing a crawlspace accessing several power points, cables and a coaxial hub.

Sanctuary.

This, he decided, really was covert operative stuff. Discovering secret compartments, improvising on the spot and taking steel-nerved action to evade capture at the hands of the state. Fear and dread were turning back into excitement, the hollow feeling in his stomach back into a sense of physical enlivening that ran all throughout his body. *All* throughout.

He tried the space for size, pulling the panel back into place. He could fit but it was quite a squeeze, not helped by one part of his body traitorously attempting to take up far more space than usual. That said, he'd have to admit the sensation wasn't entirely unpleasant, and helped distract him from other discomforts.

The alarms continued to ring despite the cessation of the sirens, but he suddenly heard another sound from right beside him, a rather disconcerting moaning that had him almost bursting from his niche in fright. As it persisted, he realised from the accompanying static hiss that it must be coming from a speaker inside the cube. He rolled out of the crawlspace to investigate, and saw that the TV screen was no longer blank, instead now showing a man and a woman, naked and locked in an embrace.

'Goodness.'

Of all the stupid luck – he'd holed himself up inside the pornographic exhibit. His first thought was to flee, but reason told him he was low on alternatives. His entry had triggered the lights and the videotape, but if it was off when he arrived, then presumably it ran a finite loop. If he bided his time, with any luck it would be in a state of apparently deserted darkness again by the time anyone came to investigate.

Just for peace of mind, he had a quick peak outside and confirmed that the doors were still down. Time – and perhaps not a little smart thinking – were on his side. On the downside, he'd have to bundle himself back under the bench or sit there and endure this filth until it stopped. Well, so be it, he thought. He was a grown-up, it couldn't harm him, no matter how unpalatable. He was stronger than that, and anyway, maybe it was a worthwhile exercise in knowing your enemy. It wasn't like it had a mystical power he ought to be afraid of, for goodness sake. Those made of sterner stuff wouldn't be affected by it, though that didn't make it harmless; you certainly couldn't let just anybody see this sort of thing.

If he was supposed to be shocked, then the so-called artist had failed. It wasn't shocking at all. He'd seen worse things on Channel Four. In fact, there really oughtn't to be anything about the human form that did shock a civilised adult, but that didn't make it right for people to cheapen it by acts of exploitation such as this. Let's face it, we all knew what a woman's breasts looked like, so we didn't need anything like this to goodness gracious, she really was rather beautiful, wasn't she? Admittedly, in the art world there had always been a place for the aesthetic appreciation of the female nude, from the busts of Aphrodite through the pre-Raphaelite my God, she was . . . she was . . . or rather he was, around her erect nipple with the end of his . . . and she was . . . oh surely not oh surely not oh sweet Heaven she was, with her mouth.

Walter was feeling dizzy, the alarms fading in his head against a rushing sound as his pace heightened and his, his, *it* swelled and strained against the inside of his trousers.

Calm down, for goodness sake. Just a lot of nonsense, puerile and vulgar, getting all confused with the excitement of good Lord he was actually going to put his tongue in her, her . . . he *was* putting his tongue in sweet Heaven sweet Jesus and oh she likes it, she really likes it, and no wonder, the little minx was . . .

Walter's hands seemed to be acting of their own accord, unzipping his fly and taking hold of, of, the old chap. It was the only way, a voice was telling him. Crucial to the mission. Have to dispel this tension, clear your head, can't afford distraction. Anyway, no-one can see, no-one will know, and mother of Christ she was magnificent, she was glorious, she couldn't get enough oh yes she liked it, she liked that oh God yes and in that position too, Jesus this *was* art oh yes turn her over that's it she wants that she likes that oh yes oh no don't stop oh no don't take it out oh Jesus surely he wasn't but yes he was oh good Christ Lord almighty he was actually going to stick it in her aaaaaaaaaaaaaaaaaaaaaaaaaaaaaaaaaaaaaaaaa . . .

. . . aaaaall over the TV monitor: violent, copious, endless. 'Limitless, limpid jets of love, hot and enormous.' Now he knew what Walt Whitman had been going on about.

Oh Jesus. Oh God. Oh. Oh.

Oh bloody hell.

It was like waking from hypnosis to find yourself naked onstage. Walter looked down at his already shrinking penis, then at the floor and finally at the dripping monitor.

'Mother.'

Walter lunged forward and tried to wipe it away with his hand, but succeeded only in spreading it across a wider expanse of glass, as well as leaving a plethora of sticky fingerprints.

'Bugger.'

He pulled his sleeve down over his fist and drew the material across the screen, scrubbing so hard that it squeaked. This was slightly more successful, in that his jumper absorbed much of the moisture but covered the entire screen in an amorphous film. At least the fingerprints would be gone, though it wouldn't go unnoticed that the porn video was now in permanent soft focus. He was in the act of pulling down his other sleeve for a second attempt when he heard a rumbling, whining electrical noise, and realised with a hollow chill that it could only be the sound of the shutters reopening.

'Oh please God no.'

Less than a second later, the videotape ended and the cube's interior suddenly returned to darkness. It was a Godsend, quite undoubtedly: clemency and succour for a faithful servant only trying to do what was right. Walter wasted no time. He crawled into his niche and pulled the panel back into place. The message was clear: his

363

indiscretion, like his transgression against the law, were immediately understood and forgiven. He was hidden from sight, delivered from his enemies. The Lord protects his own.

# nothing in this hand

'We've just got the one so far, sir,' said the voice on Shaw's radio. 'He had a replica pistol, but he dropped it pretty sharpish when he saw we were carrying the real thing. We're sure there were more, though. It was hard to see.'

Shaw and Angelique pulled up last, behind the two vans, whose passengers had quickly dispersed to points inside and around the building. One of the thieves had been apprehended by the undercover officers before anyone else could get there, a development announced over the airwaves as they approached the gates to the park surrounding the museum. Instead of the usual elation, Angelique was reminded of how she felt when she was on duty and heard Richard Gordon reveal that there'd been a goal for the away team at Ibrox. The excitement and undisguised pleasure in the voice on the radio was entirely at odds with the impact on she the listener.

They walked swiftly towards the entrance, where a uniformed officer held the door open for them.

'What do you mean it was hard to see? That Horsburgh Gallery was supposed to be lit up like Blackpool. What went wrong?'

'They weren't in the Horsburgh Collection, sir. They were in the South Hall. Hawkins thinks he saw three on the monitors, but they made for the centre of the hall, where it bends, and shot out the camera. That's what triggered the alarms.'

Shaw and Angelique looked at each other, asking the same unspoken question: what were they doing in the South Hall?

'I'm at the front door,' Shaw said.

'We'll bring him to—'

'No, stay where you are. I'll come to you. All units, any further suspects?'

Shaw rolled his eyes at the growing silence. It was broken eventually by Anderson, Hawkins' undercover partner.

'Sir, the security shutters came down automatically when they tripped the system. Chances are they're still inside. We're having a bit of bother getting them to open again, but the guy here says he'll have them up in a minute.'

'Okay. And when he's done, can you ask him if there's any danger of turning these fuckin' alarms off?'

'Yes, sir.'

Shaw strode briskly through the lobby, heading for the South Hall. Angelique trailed a couple of paces behind, but it wasn't just his gait that was putting distance between them. The sight of Zal in cuffs was one she now knew for sure she was in no hurry to see.

Shaw turned the corner first, into the South Hall's glass-roofed vestibule area.

'Is this it?' she heard him ask.

'Yes, sir. He's saying nothing. Don't want us to hear that accent, do you?' taunted Hawkins.

Angelique walked into the vestibule to see Shaw standing over a cuffed but defiant prisoner, his face cast in the stony expression of the seasoned arrestee. Her first glance was cursory, sufficient to the primary concern of identifying him as someone other than Zal. Upon a second inspection, however, she realised she recognised him.

'When this wee ned does speak, the accent won't be

366

American,' she told them. 'It's Liam McGhee. He's the chief Fanny.'

'The what?' asked Shaw.

'Family and Natural Youth, sir. It won't have registered down south. He used to be a small-time crook but he discovered the Big Man in the Big Hoose and started his own bampot Christian pressure group. What you doin' in here, Liam? Or did you see the light on the road to Damascus and convert back to thievery?'

Still he remained silent, staring into space, demonstrably ignoring her.

'It's a wee while since you've been lifted, isn't it, Liam? Right to silence has gone, you know.'

'Hawkins, bring him up to date on his rights,' Shaw ordered.

'Yes, sir.'

'This is a legitimate protest,' McGhee suddenly blurted. 'As Christians and parents we have the right to take action against council money being spent on filth and immorality. If the authorities won't protect our children against pornography, then we have no choice but to act.'

'You don't have children, Liam,' Angelique pointed out.

'All children are our responsibility.'

Up ahead, the security shutters clunked lethargically into action. Shaw and Angelique made for them immediately. Angelique took hold of her radio, unsure if Shaw shared her knowledge of the building.

'South Hall doors are opening. We're at the west entrance. Somebody get to the east sharpish.'

Shaw nodded acknowledgement, then ducked under the rising door.

'Can we get some lights in here?' he asked his radio.

'Yes, sir.'

367

Angelique bowed down and followed him into the gallery.

'A protest against pornography?' he asked her.

'Usual shit, sir. A bit more dramatic than placards and hysterics, but the agenda's the same.'

'Never mind the agenda, it's the fucking timing that's pissing me off. These arseholes will have blown the whole thing.' He sighed wearily, looking like he was seriously considering punching a hole in the nearest painting. 'Oh well, let's huckle the rest of them and have done with it. Any of you useless buggers found a body yet?'

'Sir,' came a response. 'PC Keir here, outside. There's a vehicle round the back at the loading bay. Shit, sorry, forget that. It's a cooncil van, up on bricks.'

'Marvellous,' Shaw grumbled. 'Mind an' gie's a shout if you find any abandoned shoppin' trolleys, eh?'

'Sorry, sir.'

'Fuckin' muppet.'

They made their way through the gallery to the apex, where they met up with three officers approaching from the opposite end, conspicuously suspect-free.

'Surely it wasnae just that one wee scrote?'

'I would doubt it, sir,' Angelique assured him. 'He said "we".'

'Aye, but these pompous bastards always say "we".'

Shaw seemed to suddenly notice the statue they were gathered around. He had a long, barely credulous look at it, before breaking into a small chuckle despite himself. 'Is this what the God Squad are up in arms aboot, then?'

'Afraid so. The big fella here seems to have upset them.'

'I wouldnae exactly cry it pornography, though.'

'No, the pornography is inside—'

Angelique was about to direct his attention to the *Voyeur* cube, but the installation beat her to it, its exterior video screens suddenly flickering into life. Within moments, all four of its walls were showing a ruddy-faced and rather agitated man staring towards the camera.

Shaw regarded the screen with a wry expression.

'It's a while since I've worked Vice, but I cannae see them linin' up for this doon Soho. Oh here, hang on.'

The man in the image then proceeded to pull out his erect penis. All five police officers looked on in appalled silence as he began to masturbate feverishly, pounding away with a tortured, twisted expression until he ejaculated messily, the emission arcing towards the screen.

'Good thing it's no in 3D, eh?' one of them observed.

'It's called *Voyeur*,' Angelique said. 'There's a porno tape showing inside, but the gag is that while you're inside watching it, there's actually a camera . . .' She stopped dead, realising.

'What?'

'He's still in there.'

Shaw looked back to the cube. Wanking Man was wiping at the screen with his sleeve, then they watched him climb under the bench and pull a white panel into place in front.

'Get him,' Shaw ordered.

'I'm not bloody touching him,' Angelique replied. 'He's covered in jizz.'

Moments later, the quivering moral activist was dragged from the cube between two officers.

'Talk about coming to a sticky end,' Angelique observed.

'This is a legi . . . I . . . as a member of . . .'

'Hing on, you look familiar,' said one of the uniforms. 'Did you no used to have a column in *The Post*? With a big photie, opposite the editorials?'

If Wanking Man could have turned any whiter he'd have been ultra-violet.

'Aye,' said another. 'Now you mention it. Didnae buy it myself, but the wife . . . Thorn, isn't it? In the flesh!'

'I . . . look, this isn't what it . . . Okay. I'm a journalist. I'm under-cover. I infiltrated the . . . I had to go along with it, I had no choice.'

He began weeping, instinctively wiping his face with his sleeve and inadvertently smearing it with semen.

'None of this was my idea. It was the American.'

'American?' Shaw and Angelique both asked.

'Yes. Masterton. Ask him, he's the ring-leader. He's the one who . . .'

But neither of them were listening.

'Why do I feel I'm running the wrong way down Buchanan Street again?' Angelique asked.

Shaw grabbed his radio, anger visibly rippling through him, even to his fingers as they tightened around the plastic.

'Have we arrested anybody else? An American?'

Silence.

'Fuck. Well, can somebody at least turn off these fucking alarms?'

'Sir?' came a voice eventually.

'Yes. What?'

'We've got reports of a fire, possibly an explosion at a sub-station in Argyle Street, Dumbarton Road end. Close to the Kelvingrove Museum and Art Gallery.'

'Jesus bastardin' fuck. But we . . . I mean, what's in there that you could sell?' he asked Angelique. 'Apart from stuffed animals and thon big Dali?'

'Treasures of the Aztecs,' said one of the uniforms. 'My wee yin's dyin' tae see it.'

'Doesnae open until January,' Shaw told him. 'It's on show in London the noo. They're still installing the security system.'

370

'Aye, but sure they're behind schedule puttin' it in. It closed in London end of October and was meant to open here at the start of this month.'

'You mean the actual stuff is on-site?'

'Aye, down in the vault in the basement.'

'Tell me this isnae happening,' he implored Angelique. She couldn't.

'Mexican gold. Mexican gangsters.'

'And we're all scratchin' our arses on the wrang side of the fuckin' river.'

Shaw began running, gesturing the others to get moving, too.

'All units from Shaw. Proceed to the Kelvingrove Art Gallery immediately. Robbery in progress. Repeat, robbery in progress.'

He released the button and ceased transmitting, turning to Angelique as they ran for the door. 'Who am I kidding? Robbery all over, by the time we get there.'

They climbed into his car and took off at speed, the rear of the vehicle slewing on gravel as Shaw gunned the accelerator. Behind them the vans were filling up, sirens were blaring and the Dalriada's alarms stubbornly continued to sound.

'I must be gettin' too old for this malarkey,' he said. 'You told me to keep an open mind, but I just decided this was the place.'

'You were spot-on about one thing though, sir. Tonight was the night.'

'Aye, but the Neil Young song should have been *Why Do I Keep Fuckin' Up*.'

Zal's eyes remained on his phone, the dim glow of the LCD display and the light from Karl's laptop screen the only

371

illumination in the crowded cramp of the van. He was waiting for a text message, but it was as good a place as any to be looking when you were sharing such a tight space with four other people and the tension had had three hours to build. It wasn't just the silent wait and the magnitude of what was at stake that made the atmosphere uncomfortable, either. Nobody could speak, but nobody had to say it anyway. Karl and Leo had been in the back of another van once, waiting silently and nervously, before being locked in there by Zal when the action was supposed to start.

Added to all of that was the unwelcome presence of their appointed interloper, Dominguez. It had always been a strictly non-negotiable term of the arrangement that a 'representative' of the Estobals be in the presence of the goods from theft to handover, to make sure there was no opportunity for any costly interference. The idea of Zal being in unmonitored possession of such valuables was not one Alessandro had been remotely comfortable with, even if he did hold the leverage of Parnell's life, and this concern was understandably reinforced in light of how Hannigan's gimp had been stiffed at the bank. Thus, they had Rico Dominguez, a cousin of Alessandro's, along for the ride. Fortunately, he had at least assured them that he *could* handle an electric spanner.

The final message flashed up on Zal's phone.

'Okay,' he whispered. 'Green light from Jerome: he's ready and in position. Just waiting for . . . yep, there it is. Confirmation: the sub-station is down. The lights are out on Kelvingrove.'

'Time to get Alessandro his Christmas present,' said Dominguez.

'Not quite yet,' Zal warned him. 'Give it a moment.'

Dominguez made to speak, but Zal held a finger to his

lips. A few seconds later, the sound of sirens joined that of the constant, howling alarm.

'Karl?'

Karl turned his laptop around for Zal to see the screen. It showed the front entrance to the museum, via one of three miniature cameras Zal had secreted outside on the day he went there to meet Angelique. The police vehicles had all left, with only a couple of uniformed officers milling around the lobby in discussion with museum staff, including the recently arrived curator. Satisfied, he gave the order.

'Gentlemen? Let's practise our art.'

The four of them climbed out quickly and silently, each carrying a wheel and an electric spanner. They took position around the vehicle, kneeling down to quietly remove four piles of bricks whose true purpose was not to support the van, but to conceal the bolted-on hydraulic jacks that were. These were Leo's weighty adjustments, fitted out the week before in a garage in Newcastle, and could be deployed at the flick of one switch to take the vehicle's weight in seconds, allowing swift removal or replacement of the wheels.

They had driven up and stopped at the loading bay shortly before the museum closed. It was a time when the road through the park was busy with departing cars, obstructing the view from the museum of the approach of a solitary vehicle that was anyway inconspicuous to the point of invisible, bearing as it did the Glasgow City Council Parks and Recreation Department livery. Once in place, Karl's laptop monitored the approaches from cameras either side, to ensure all was clear when they rendered the vehicle conspicuously and unsuspiciously immobile.

The sound of the alarms covered the noise of their

Daytona-speed wheel refit, which was task priority number one: ready the getaway vehicle before you even think about anything else.

The museum staff would be upstairs still trying to figure why they couldn't get the system to shut off, unaware that Jerome had cooked the electrics at a maintenance panel in the basement storage area. Right now the system was responding to a general fault, which would register in the control room as such but which they were undoubtedly attributing to the destruction of a CCTV camera during the raid. It would then most probably be put down to a general malfunction when the South Hall's security doors came down a second time, but even if it wasn't, at that point nobody would be able to get in anyway: not the night staff, not the uniformed cops, and not the two embarrassingly obvious under-cover guys who were guarding the Horsburgh Hoard.

The vehicle now back on four wheels, Leo got into the driver's seat while Karl hopped back into the rear to monitor the perimeter on his laptop. Leo turned the van around and backed it down the slope towards the loading bay's servo-assisted metal doors, which were in the process of sliding open. Jerome stepped from the widening gap and ushered them inside.

'You know, I find robbing a museum so much easier with a full set of staff keys,' he said, jangling the said items with a grinning flourish.

'How did you get those?' Dominguez asked.

'Trade secret,' Zal told him, shooting Jerome a chastising glare for treading on fragile ground. Jerome acknowledged it with a gulp.

'I trust the Lord's work went well?' Zal asked, covering the unspoken exchange.

'Oh, a mighty blow was struck for decency tonight. I just hope those assholes enjoy jail as much as I did. Come on, we've an appointment with a big ugly cocksucker.' He looked at Dominguez. 'Oh yeah, and before that we've gotta steal a statue for him, too.'

'*Pendejo.*'

'Bite me.'

Jerome led them into the double-wide lift, inside of which he had already placed the hydraulic pallet-lifter that the museum staff used for moving heavy and outsize items. It took about twenty seconds to ascend to the South Hall. Jerome unlocked the double doors using one of his colour-coded keys, and they emerged at the east end of the History of Allegory exhibition.

Jerome stayed with the lift while Zal and Dominguez proceeded to the centre of the gallery, where they loaded Pepe Nunez's *West Coast (,) Man* on to the pallet-lifter. Zal used a pair of wire-cutters to free the statue from its electronic mooring, causing the security doors to come down as planned and preventing any rapid discovery or even investigation of their activities.

# hindu shuffle

They were halfway through the Clyde Tunnel, Angelique holding on to the door-grip as Shaw swerved back and forth across the double white lines, weaving between the lanes. He had the siren going, blue lights flashing, pedal to the metal, the car approaching Dianacide velocity in Shaw's desperate haste to get to Kelvingrove. And that was when it hit her.

'Fuck. We're doing it again.'

'Doing what again?'

'Running in the wrong direction. Turn around.'

'I cannae turn around, I'm in the Clyde fuckin' Tunnel.'

'Aye, and on the wrong side. We should be in the south-bound tunnel. It's a double bluff.'

'Hawkins and Anderson are still coverin' the Horsburgh Collection. There's nae double bluff about it. And we've got the Kelvingrove in darkness. We cannae ignore that.'

'You're right, sir, because we *have to do our job* – like he's *relying on us* to.'

'Aw, shite fuck pish bollocks,' Shaw said, which she took to be concurrence.

'Trust me on this. Let the rest of them check out the Kelvingrove, but I want another look back there.'

Shaw executed a hand-brake turn as soon as they exited the northbound tunnel, swinging the car across the inter-change and powering back down under the river. Angelique picked up the radio handset and hailed Hawkins, who didn't share her animated concern.

'There's nothing happening, except for the fucking alarms still going off. Oh, and the doors to the South Hall have apparently shut again, I'm told. I'd turn the bloody thing off at the mains if I could find the plug.'

The South Hall. Exactly where Zal had taken her.

'Get in there, now.'

'In where?'

'The South Hall. Get those doors open, or go in the fucking window, but get in there.'

'Yes, ma'am.'

They were back at the Dalriada inside ten minutes, Shaw's engine-punishing haste not even diminished by the narrow road through the park.

'Go round the back,' Angelique told him as they approached the building. He slowed to a less terrifying pace and turned right at the fork marked by a sign admitting 'Authorised vehicles only beyond this point'.

'There,' Angelique said, pointing to the loading bay at the building's rear.

'What? I don't see anything.'

'That's the point. PC Keir said there was a van up on bricks at the back.'

Shaw eyed the whole load of nothing that was sitting there now.

'You know, I'm actually glad we're no gaunny catch this bastard,' he said.

'Why?'

'Because ex-polis get a hard time in the jail, and that's where I'd end up once I'd battered his melt in.'

Driving on a few yards, they could see into the South Hall, where there was an ominous gathering of museum and police personnel. Angelique couldn't wait until she got inside to find out what was going on. She grabbed the radio again.

'We've just got the doors open,' Hawkins reported, a worryingly apologetic tone to his voice.

'And?'

'It's the statue, the big wan of, hingmy, you know, the boy suckin' his ain boabby. It's gone.'

Shaw butted the steering wheel, adding the sustained parp of his horn to the unending howl of the museum's alarms. He lifted his head after a few seconds and looked across to the passenger seat. When he spoke, it was with admirable calm, though the quietness was surely a sign of uneasily restrained fury.

'A number of questions come to mind, Officer de Xavia, in light of this new development. Too many to list, in fact, at this moment, but the chief among them must undoubtedly be *JUST WHAT THE FUCK IS ALL THIS SHIT ABOUT?*'


Leo turned the van left into an industrial estate and pulled into the carpark behind a large furniture showroom, where he killed the engine. There was another van already waiting there, similar in size but a different model and colour. Zal got out from the passenger seat and immediately peeled off the Parks and Rec livery, revealing that of 'FAC Courier Services – We Deliver' underneath. Leo did likewise on the driver's side as Zal opened the doors at the rear.

Dominguez looked predictably perturbed, particularly when he saw the second van.

'Hey, what is this bullshit? This isn't the rendezvous. What are you assholes trying to pull?'

'Nothing,' Zal assured him. 'Just . . . call me cynical if

you will, but I had this paranoid inkling that your boss might have something unpleasant lined up for me once I've outlived my usefulness.'

'I wouldn't know about that, but he's sure got something unpleasant lined up for your amigo Parnell if you don't get him his shit.'

'Oh, I'm gonna deliver. But the handover's gonna happen on my terms, not Alessandro's.'

'That's what you think,' Dominguez said, pulling out a handgun and taking a pace back so that he had an angle on all four of them where they stood on the tarmac. 'You and I are getting back in that fucking van, right now, and going to the rendezvous, *comprende*?'

'Or what? You won't get all four of us before we get you.'

'Don't put it to the test. Get in the goddamn van.'

'Go fuck yourself,' Zal told him.

Dominguez pulled the trigger, which locked tight against the stock, as happens when you're out of bullets. Zal punched him in the throat, following through with all he had. Dominguez dropped to the ground, clutching his neck, his gun clattering beside him.

Zal held a cupped hand over him and let a fistful of bullets rain down on Dominguez's head, tinkling as they rolled on to the pavement. Such tricks were easiest done with playing cards and coins, but the more practised hand could manage far heavier and more awkward objects. He had picked the asshole's pocket within moments of collecting him for the job, then replaced the empty weapon while they were loading the statue back at the museum.

'Now, as I was saying, the handover's gonna be on my terms.'

'I'm not going anywhere . . . without the statue,' Dominguez croaked. 'That's the deal.'

'It sure is, and that's why you're gonna stay in the back of the van with it until delivery. See, you're not just here to make sure I don't fuck with the statue, you're also here as my witness that I didn't. I'm only interested in Parnell, okay? And I'm not gonna give Alessandro any excuse to kill him.'

'Where are you going?' he asked, as Zal walked towards the second van.

'To the rendezvous. Where else?'

Zal got there inside twenty minutes. As anticipated, the address turned out to be not a warehouse or lock-up, but a wasteground, where a single car was parked in wait. Two men got out as soon as he pulled up. One was Paco Gomez, another of Alessandro's Praetorian guard; the second looked like one of Hannigan's Brotherhood of Versace. They approached on either side, cutting off Zal's exits from the van, both drawing weapons.

'I don't see Alessandro,' Zal said. 'That was the arrangement. I hand over to him and him only.'

'You hand over to us or we blow your fuckin' brains out,' Gomez told him.

'Just get oot the van and leave us the keys,' grunted the other.

Zal climbed out, his hands in the air. 'Have it your way,' he told them. 'But you better not forget about your buddy Dominguez.'

'Go let him out,' Gomez told Versace. He turned to face Zal again. 'And he better have marked you a good report card.'

'Don't worry about that. I'm the one honouring his end of the deal.'

'He isnae here,' announced Versace angrily from the rear. 'The fuckin' van's empty.'

Gomez nodded, smiling bitterly, not particularly surprised.

'Alessandro warned us, you're a regular box of tricks.'

'Like I said, I hand over to Alessandro only.' Zal pulled out his phone. 'Now, how about you put the guns away, tell me where the real rendezvous is, and get back in your fucking car. *Then* I'll call my buddy and get him to bring Dominguez and the statue right there.'

Gomez shook his head. 'You're gonna call your buddy, and you're gonna get in this fucking car with us. Alessandro will want to thank you personally.'

'I didn't doubt it for a second. But I ain't getting in that fucking car. I said I hand over to Alessandro and Alessandro only. No guns, no gangsters.'

Gomez raised his weapon and pointed it between Zal's eyes.

'Get in the fucking car and make the phone call.'

'You pull that trigger, you'll never see the statue again. If I don't show up back in one piece, my friends will drop Dominguez and disappear the statue forever.'

'Your friends, huh? Well how about this? I pull this trigger and then we go pick up your friend Karl later at number six, Botanic Crescent, where he's been staying the past four nights. We take him someplace quiet with a load of power tools and a blow-torch, and we torture him for a few hours. Then, just before he loses the power of speech, we offer to finish him off quick if he tells us where the statue is.

'You ain't the only one who thinks ahead, asshole. Make the call.'

## just what the fuck all this shit is about

The place looked like it was fitted out pretty good for a massacre, Harry thought, or a particularly messy torture session. Plastic sheeting covering practically every square foot of the warehouse floor, oxy-acetylene burner ready to rock 'n' roll, and wall-to-wall hoods, most of them packing. Hannigan's entourage looked like they were auditioning for parts in a gangster movie, trying too hard to look like the real thing. They were a bunch of fucking nobodies, just white trash tough guys; the baddest kids on the block, no doubt, but it was a real small block. Back home, there were flatbed trucks bigger than this city. They were strutting their stuff, flexing their muscles, part territorial pissing and part subconscious compensation for feeling inferior now that the real thing was in town. The fact that there was two million pounds of their boss's money in two briefcases on the floor was, admittedly, another factor in their bristling postures.

Hannigan at least had the nous and the perspective to see this whole deal for what it really was: a gift from the gods, a happy quirk of fate, and not proof that he had arrived on some greater stage. The Man would have approved of Bud, Harry was sure. Hannigan was ambitious but pragmatic, knew the realistic limitations of his situation, but knew also how to make the best of what he had. This deal would consolidate his position and give him a new edge on the competition, but it didn't mean he was

382

now some kind of fucking international player.

And what about Alessandro, was he the real thing? He sure as shit wasn't an international player, whether he was here in Europe tonight or not. The Estobals were the real thing, no question, but the kid was more like Hannigan's wannabes, playing at being a gangster. Innez called it right: he might have his hands on the tiller and the crew at his command, but that didn't mean he knew how to steer the fucking boat. He was standing there next to Hannigan, smiling and trying to look like he was used to this kind of shit being calmly under his control, just another multi-million-dollar deal. A closer look would reveal his nails bitten to the quick and his whole body tingling with nerves, that so-near-and-yet-so-far anxiety as the moment drew ever closer when he could finally get out of the hole he'd dug himself into.

There were lean times in every business. People thought organised crime was just in permanent boom, but they had their own peaks and recessions like any other sector. Things had been getting tough for the Estobals even before The Man passed, because there were factors that no calibre of leadership could control, even if he did anticipate them. In such times, you needed a steady hand at the wheel, a decision-maker who could guide the organisation through the darker days so that it was in good shape when the sun shone again. Alessandro, needless to say, did not fit the bill.

The Man wasn't entirely deluded about the kid. He had a lot of qualities that given time would shine through, as experience and a few harsh lessons pared down his rasher instincts. If Alessandro had become boss at a stronger time for the organisation, his energy and even his impulsive-ness might have been the driving forces behind success

383

and expansion; at the very least the cost of his mistakes would have been more easily absorbed. But he had come in during a period of comparative austerity, and not only did he lack the character to deal with that, he didn't even have the brains to fucking see it. He thought it was party time, his dreams come true, which meant he was too busy *playing* at being a gangster to get on with the reality of it.

Miguel was there to advise and consent, but while executive power remained with Alessandro, there was only so much he could do, especially when Alessandro was inclined to go against Miguel's advice, purely as a demonstration of his autonomy and a reminder of who was boss.

The border was tightening all the time, and the law of natural selection dictated that those who didn't adapt would die out. Supply chains were breaking down and matters of infrastructure needed to be addressed. Quite simply, their business relied on getting cocaine into southern California from Mexico, and if they didn't find new ways to do that, they were history. Their stocks were fast running out north of the border, while down south it was piling up uselessly like a defunct currency.

Miguel was considering a number of options, but preparing everybody for the unavoidable realities that came with each. The new methods would necessarily mean a slower and smaller supply, at least for a while, with obvious knock-on effects on revenue further up the chain. Plus, in the meantime they would have to consider the possibility of selling the surplus south of the border at a massively reduced price, against the risk of losing it for nothing in the event of a bust, either by police or competitors, both of whom were bound to know about it sooner or later.

Alessandro, however, had a better idea.

He knew about this guy, Pepe Nunez, who was making

a big name for himself as a sculptor, working in Mexico but exhibiting in the US. Nunez worked with metals, notably lead, which as well as being easily malleable, had the tangential advantage of being entirely resistant to x-rays. Alessandro's brilliant idea was to get Nunez to make a trojan horse for his stockpiled cocaine: Nunez would pack it inside a hollow lead statue, which would be 'bought' by a gallery owner in LA and exported for exhibition. The shit would be sealed in tight and the statue hose-blasted to remove all traces on the exterior, but as insurance and kind of a double bluff, Alessandro insisted that the statue should be of a guy doing a line of coke.

Nunez already having such a high profile, it was easy to get a reporter and a photographer down there, resulting in an article in the *LA Times* about this controversial new piece ahead of its export. Letters were written, complaints were made, and despite the protestations of appalled liberals horrified at this adulteration of his vision, Nunez gave the cops an assurance that real coke would be substituted by baby powder when the thing went on show in LA. This, however, would mean that if the dogs *did* smell something when it went through customs, there would be a well-known and documented explanation. Sure they can smell traces of coke, there was coke on the statue, but it's all gone now, and besides, Officer, can't you see it's *art*?

Pretty fuckin' ingenious, apart from the fact that Alessandro was threatening to kill Nunez instead of making it worth his while in other ways, and you can't trust a desperate man. Not that Alessandro did trust Nunez: he had him working naked and under constant supervision until the statue was complete, and a rota of guards watching over the thing thereafter. Unfortunately, the guards were only on the lookout for Nunez (or anyone else) fucking with the statue; not for Nunez fucking with *them*.

The sneaky son-of-a-bitch Mickey-Finned the jerkoff on duty one night, slipping something into his beer. When the poor schmuck woke up, Nunez was gone and so was the fuckin' statue. Next anyone knew about it, he'd sold it to a museum in the UK, where it cleared customs without any trouble thanks to the local press picking up on the background from the *LA Times*. That the artist himself had disappeared from the face of the earth merely added to the mystique.

So instead of arriving in LA, in a gallery that's just a front for the Estobals, it goes to fuckin' Glasgow, to a public museum where it will be under all the security and supervision as if it was the *Mona* fuckin' *Lisa*. Alessandro has put all his eggs in one basket and the basket's now halfway around the world, on show to the fuckin' tourists.

Alessandro, in his desperation, figures on the one guy he believes is capable of boosting the statue: Innez. He's also the last guy on the planet Alessandro should be resting his hopes on, but the kid's short on alternatives. But even with Innez roped into the deal, he's still looking at a best-case scenario of having five million bucks worth of coke 3,000 miles from where he can sell it. So he has to find a local buyer, someone who can not only move that much shit, but with the ready cash to pay for it up front. Step forward Bud Hannigan.

Hannigan's built his operation principally on heroin, but has the network to move whatever else happens to come into his hands. That, of late, has not included much coke, as a cartel of competitors have been freezing him out of that market so that they can get a better foothold of their own in the city. Alessandro's precarious situation means that

386

Hannigan can suddenly get a massive supply at a bargain rate, which is just simple economics, but it's what he plans to do with it that would have pleased The Man. Hannigan intends to flood the local market with cheap product and thus drive down the price, reducing the profits of his competitors and destabilising their entire operation.

Everybody wins. Hannigan gets five million bucks' worth of pure for a little over half its value. Alessandro redeems his fuck-up and, despite the fire sale, brings in a better return than the more cautious Miguel's plans would have earned over the same period. The hare beats the tortoise and the good ship Estobal sails ever on.

But only if Innez delivered the statue, and didn't find some way of fucking them in the process, which was why Alessandro was as jumpy as a shithouse rat. They had Parnell for insurance, but despite that, even Alessandro had the brains to worry that Innez's insistence on him being present looked a lot like a trap. That was why the kid had gone to Miguel and for once actually sought his advice on the matter.

Miguel sanctioned the trip on the tripartite grounds that first, a trap was only a trap if you didn't see it coming; second, that as they were beholden to Innez's expertise then they didn't have any fucking alternative; and third, that having to spend Christmas on the wrong side of the Atlantic would teach Alessandro about the consequences of making a deal that gives your enemy the whip hand. This last he naturally shared only with Harry, as well as a few choice words of advice regards contingencies.

*West Coast (,) Man* was already unloaded on the floor of the warehouse when Zal was led in by Gomez and Versace. Dominguez had driven it there, the guys having surrendered him the keys and walked away after Zal made his call. They had a car hidden just around the corner from the carpark, and would already be out of the city by now, heading south for flights out of Manchester in the morning. He had shared Gomez's suggestions regarding the power tools, just in case anybody felt like sticking around. There was no need for stupid gestures: they all knew they had done their parts and it was out of their hands now.

The room was full of Hannigan's assholes, all in the regulation uniform apart from the guy manning the blow-torch, who was wearing a boiler suit and a protective mask. Hannigan was watching the operation with keen interest, standing beside the two briefcases he was there to hand over in exchange for *West Coast (,) Man*'s innards. American Harry was there too, hovering less conspicuously in the background.

Alessandro greeted Zal with two exaggeratedly open arms and a beaming smile.

'Señor Innez, how good of you to come. Thank you for your work. Sterling effort, truly. About two million sterling, in fact.'

'I said I'd hand the statue over to you and you alone.'

'And here I am, as good as my word.'

'Not exactly alone, though, are you?'

'No, I wasn't really comfortable with that part.' Alessandro gripped Zal's hair and pulled his head back viciously. 'I had this crazy idea that maybe you'd try to fuck me. Oh yeah, you need me to fly all the way over here and meet me one-on-one for the exchange to happen.' He let go of Zal's hair and took a step back. 'You think I'm fucking stupid?'

'You came, didn't you? And I know you're fucking stupid, Sandy.'

388

Alessandro punched Zal in the mouth, Gomez immediately grabbing his arms from behind to facilitate further beating. He had a few more shots at Zal's face and body before his rage subsided. It hurt, but Zal had known a lot worse. The guy was a pussy, always had been. He wouldn't last a day in the joint, and not because he wasn't tough enough, but because he didn't even realise that.

'You're the stupid one if you thought you could fuck with me. What were you gonna do? Get me alone and shoot me? Hand me over to the cops?'

'I'm not trying to fuck anybody,' Zal told him. 'I'm only interested in Parnell. If all I wanted to do was take a shot at you, why would I come all the way over here and go through all this shit? Huh?'

Alessandro thought about it. You could almost hear the logic counters clunking into place. He looked like his lips would move when he read a book, if he'd ever read a fucking book.

'You honoured your end of the deal, I'll honour mine. Parnell will be okay. I only care about my business. Unfortunately, that means you won't get to see him again. All this polythene isn't just to catch the powder. Soon as our business is concluded here, *your* business will be concluded here, finally.'

'Waste of a valuable resource, is it not?'

'The second we get that coke is the second you become a liability, not a resource. Can't have that scheming little mind of yours on the loose, can I? That really would be *stupid*.' He backhanded Zal across the face to underline the point. 'No, I'm gonna hand you over to my local associate Mr Merkland over here. I'm told you guys go way back.'

Zal looked to his right. Merkland waved at him with the pistol he was holding, then drew a finger across his neck.

'Gonna cut my throat with a handgun. Still a born fuckin' genius, aren't you, Athena?'

'Aye, very funny. What was your other line? Oh aye, I'm wan brain short of bein' able tae fuck with you. Well in aboot two minutes, pal, you'll be wan brain short of bein' able tae dae anythin' but bleed.'

Zal looked away, back towards the statue. They were on the far side of it from the guy with the burner, but the sound of the flame shutting off alerted them that a panel had been successfully cut away. Merkland tapped his watch, smiling. Alessandro just folded his arms and looked on.

The guy in the boiler suit coughed and spluttered, then stepped back and straightened up, pulling off his mask to reveal an expression of distaste.

'It's full o' shite.'

Alessandro wore a nervously quizzical look. Dominguez reassured him.

'He means shit. They say shite.'

'Good shite, yeah?' Alessandro said, offering Hannigan a winning smile. 'Real good shite.'

'Naw, I mean shite shite. Shite, as in keech, as in toley, as in jobbie, as in *shite*.'

He held up a brown hand to illustrate. Alessandro and Hannigan both immediately walked around to investigate, with the rest of the goons leaning in to have a look too.

'What the hell . . . ?'

'Aw, Jesus.'

'Fuck me.'

'That's giein' me the boak.'

'It *is* full of shite,' Hannigan said in an accusatory tone, putting a hand up to cover his mouth and nose.

'This is impossible. Dominguez . . .'

'I was with it the whole time, boss. Nobody touched it.'

'Well somebody fuckin' must have,' Hannigan said. 'You cannae make a barrowload of coke disappear as if by magic.'

'Alakazammy, stairheid rammy,' Zal said quietly.

Alessandro almost hurdled the statue in his desperation to grab Zal.

'Where's my coke, you fucking cocksucker?' he shouted, shoving a gun in Zal's face.

'Like I told your boy Paco back at the wasteground, kill me and you'll never find out. My friends are long gone, and I'm the only one who knows where it's hidden anyway.'

'Your friend Parnell will die screaming, motherfucker.'

'Not if you want your coke, shithead. The deal's still on the table, Sandy, but the hand-over's got to be on my terms, because I knew you'd try to kill me as soon as you had what you wanted. I just want to save my friend, I don't want your fucking coke. Like I said, I'll hand it over to you and to you alone. No guns, no goons, just you and I. That way, I can walk away safe when we're through.'

'Do it,' Hannigan advised sternly.

'There you are,' Zal said. 'Mr Hannigan knows this is just business. You drop your gun, we walk out of here, we get in your car and I take you to the stuff. Or you can have Mr Merkland drill me with two million pounds' worth of bullet. Your call.'

Alessandro looked at the two briefcases sitting on the floor, suddenly a lot further away from his grasp than they'd been two minutes ago.

# watch you burn

There was a solitary figure moving swiftly beneath the sodium and neon, exiting the warehouse and making for one of several cars parked in the lot outside.

'They're bailing out,' Bob Hogg whispered. 'Let's get in there before it's too late.'

'Shut the fuck up,' Shaw hissed, holding up a clenched fist both as a gesture to stay put and a threat of what would happen if anyone didn't.

The figure stopped and looked around, perhaps having heard something. Collective breaths were held, none more anxiously than Hogg's for having broken the silence. The man resumed walking, climbed into a blue BMW and drove away, but stopped and killed his lights only a hundred yards down the street.

'What's he up to?' Hogg asked impatiently.

'Why don't you go doon there and ask him?'

'If you'd bloody let me, I would. What are we waiting for?'

'I'll tell you when I see it.'

They were lying face-down at the top of a grass embankment, overlooking a warehouse in Port Dundas, less than a mile from the snooker club in St George's Cross from which Hannigan ran his operations. Out of sight in the surrounding streets were several vans full of Kevlar-kitted armed officers, ready to move in upon Shaw's signal. What they were waiting for was Zal to leave the building with

392

Alessandro, though precisely why remained a matter of some conjecture.

Angelique had received a call on her mobile back at the Dalriada, while Shaw was threatening to take one of F&NY's hammers to the South Hall's exhibits as an outlet for his frustrations. Happily, she was able to offer him Hannigan's head as an alternative.

The call was from Karl, Zal's oldest partner in crime, giving her the address of the warehouse where the stolen statue was being taken. They would find Hannigan and his men there, along with two million pounds in hard cash. However, in a phrase that bore Zal's hallmark, Karl insisted that the cops 'would have nothing until they had everything'. They couldn't move in until Zal left the building with Alessandro, heading for a location Zal would only provide once he got there. 'If you go in before that, all you'll have on Hannigan is receiving stolen goods, and with all respect to Pepe Nunez, that statue ain't worth two million.'

Given his current frame of mind, Angelique couldn't see Shaw abiding by this without some serious persuasion, and possibly therapy, but instead he merely nodded, like some deeper understanding was setting in.

'It sounds like shite to me, sir,' was Anderson's perspective, but Shaw's demeanour had been transformed.

'We're gaunny dae exactly as Innez tells us,' he stated. 'The guy was away clean. He doesn't *need* to be doing this for us, and that tells me he's doing it for him. Bottom line is, he's gaunny give us Bud Hannigan, and after the calibre of our policework tonight, that's a lot more than we deserve.'

There were voices from inside the warehouse: shouting, anger, arguments. The words were unintelligible, but the tension was unmistakable. Shaw and Angelique exchanged some anxious looks, no doubt thinking the same thing. Something was wrong, very wrong, and Zal was inside there. She was about to implore Shaw to just give the command when a door opened and Zal and Alessandro walked out of the building as predicted.

They got into an ostentatious red Merc sports model with rental plates, and drove off. The blue BMW waited a few seconds after they had passed, then turned its lights back on and pulled away in pursuit.

Shaw stood up and took hold of his radio. 'Go go go. All units move in.'

The vans sped in without sirens, though the squeal of their tyres and the sudden roar of engines was warning and identification enough to the trained ears of their targets. The police vehicles slewed across the carriageway and pavement, cutting off vehicular access, while the armed officers swarmed into the building on three sides.

They were making their way briskly down the embankment when Angelique saw a loading hatch burst open at the rear of the building. A man barrelled through it, firing randomly with a pistol as he emerged into the concreted passage at the foot of the grass slope. All three of them dived for the floor, but while Shaw and Hogg bit the turf, Angelique executed a practised roll to come up in a crouching position. Resting on one knee, she fired four shots with her Walther, throwing the gunman back against the wall as his weapon spun off into the darkness.

'Fuck,' she said.

'What?' Shaw inquired. 'You got him.'

'I know, but it occurred to me a wee while back that I've killed more men than I've slept with. I thought I'd scored the equaliser recently, but that's me back in deficit.'

'Depends how soon the ambulance gets here,' Shaw said. 'But I'm grateful your concern didnae slow your trigger finger.'

'That *was* slow, sir. You should see me when I've *not* had a man for a while.'

Angelique helped Shaw to his feet while Hogg radioed for an ambulance. There had been no shots from inside, so it sounded optimistically like they'd only need the one.

'I'll stay with this one,' Hogg offered, crouching beside the injured man. 'Looks like you're slipping, Agent X. Only three hits: right arm, shoulder, leg. He'll live.'

'Ya fuckin' bitch,' the man grunted. 'You're fuckin' deid, I'm tellin' you. Fuckin' polis cunt.'

'Mr Athena! How lovely to hear your charming voice again. Haven't seen you since Innez ripped the pish out of you at the bank.'

'This guy was the fifth man?' Shaw asked. 'The mug?'

'Aye. Falling into place, isn't it?'

'I'll tell you that once we've seen what's inside.'

What was inside turned out to be an all-star night for Glasgow gangland's A-team. Hannigan was standing with his hands behind his head, in the similarly postured company of half a dozen known associates and Alessandro Estebol's two travelling companions. Around them were close to twenty armed cops, and in the middle was *West Coast (,) Man*, who appeared to be in the process of being disembowelled.

'Is there anything I can assist you with, Officer,' Hannigan said as Shaw entered the room. That was Hannigan all the way: he only ever spoke to the officer in charge, and when he did, it was with a calm, butter-wouldn't-melt decorum. Even with his hands behind his head and an arsenal pointed at him, he acted like they were meeting over tea and scones. To give the guy his due, this was also why no bloodbath had ensued, despite the number of guns in the room. Hannigan was the kind of crook who always reckoned he could beat the rap, mainly because he so often had. There was absolutely no reason to get into an against-the-odds shooting match as long as there were still lawyers left in the world, so he'd pleaded for a calm surrender when he realised what was happening. Clearly not everybody had been listening, or just didn't have the sense to hear, but Athena's Butch and Sundance bid aside, the police were offered no resistance.

Shaw took a walk around the statue on his way towards Hannigan.

'I see we're torturin' statues noo. Waste of time, Bud. This wan'll never talk. No' wi' his walloper in his mooth, anyway.'

'Jock Shaw. Long time no see. What brings you back to these parts?'

'Ach, nostalgia, really. I thought I'd arrest your arse again, just for old time's sake.'

'What for?'

'Eh, well, to be perfectly honest, I'm no entirely sure yet. But tell you what, we'll start with receiving stolen goods and work our way fae there.'

'These cases are both hoachin' with serious money, sir,' one of the cops informed him.

'Aye. Two million, if my sources are correct. Which has me a wee bit confused, Bud. See, I'm sure I read in the paper that this statue cost the museum whit? Aboot twenty, thirty grand?'

'That's art for you, Mr Shaw. One day a picture's not worth the canvas it's painted on, the next it's going for three million at Sotheby's.'

'Aye, well, hard to see how this would be rendered more valuable by cutting it open, especially as it seems to be full of farmyard manure. Unless, of course, you were expecting to find something else inside. Drugs, perhaps. What do you reckon, DI de Xavia?'

'Drugs, sir? Bud Hannigan? And two senior delegates of the Estobal family? Nooooo. And certainly not two million worth. For goodness sake, that could put a man in jail for twenty years.'

'As much as that, Angelique? Dear, dear, dear.'

'Aye,' Hannigan said. 'So it's a shame all you've got is a big pile o' shite.'

'This is it here. Pull over,' Zal said as the Mercedes approached the alleyway. The studio was at the end, constructed of two lock-ups knocked through into one. Alessandro stopped the car and looked suspiciously at the dark passage.

'Anything happens to me and Parnell loses,' he warned.

'Yeah, thanks for the heads-up, Sandy. That had almost slipped my mind. Come on, let's get this shit over with.'

They walked briskly between the two rows of facing doors, their footsteps quiet on the concrete. A light rain had started to fall, with a biting wind in the air that threatened snow.

'Could be a white Christmas,' Zal remarked. 'I've never seen snow for real.'

'It goddamn better be a white Christmas, or else you die like that asshole Nunez died. You ever seen the crazy shit a junkie'll do if you keep him from his drugs? Multiply that by a thousand and you've got an Estobal.'

Zal produced a key and opened the door, beckoning Alessandro to enter.

'You first,' Alessandro ordered. 'No tricks. And turn the goddamn lights on.'

Zal complied. Alessandro followed him into the narrow passage that functioned as an ante-room and supply cupboard, its walls lined with shelves bearing the artist proprietor's materials. Zal then opened the door to the studio proper and flicked another lightswitch. It revealed a cluttered room, the bottoms of the walls spattered with paint in a thousand colours and shades where the grey plaster was visible. Where it was not, this was because it was obscured by drapes, great linen sheets hung like white banners because the temporary resident artist preferred to work inside what he called 'a blank space of the mind'. The environment should have been confusingly, ominously familiar to Alessandro, as should the style of a number of works in progress positioned about the floor. However, little Sandy was predictably oblivious, his albeit baffled attention commanded slavishly and exclusively by what sat, in pride of place, at the centre of the room: *West Coast (,) Man*, identical and unadulterated.

'What the fuck? What the fuck? I don't get it.'

'The original, as promised.'

'You switched them. That asshole Dominguez wasn't paying attention and you switched them.'

'No, he was paying full attention to what we stole from the museum. But the original was never in the museum.'

'So where, I mean how . . . what the fuck?'

'You know, my old man taught me . . . you remember my old man? Guy you had killed just to prove a point? Yeah. Well, he taught me that whether it's a street-corner card trick or a grand-scale illusion, the guy in *your* seat never knows who else is in on it, or how many. Maybe there's one plant in the audience, or maybe he was the blindfolded volunteer and *everybody* but him is in on the gag.'

'I don't know what you're bullshitting about. How did you switch the fucking statues? And where did you get the other one? It's completely identical, right down to the goddamn signature in his ass. How did you copy it?'

'I didn't.'

'*I* did.'

Alessandro turned around to see a figure emerge from behind one of the drapes, and found himself standing face to face with Pepe Nunez.

'*Ola.*'

'*Chinga. Madre mia*, Jesus.'

Alessandro reeled away from Pepe as though struck, stepping backwards and tumbling over the statue to the floor.

'Pepe and I go way back. We were at art school together. Guess you didn't know that. Karl too, and a guy name of Cream-T. 'Course, these days he has to go by the more formal Thomas White, what with being curator of the Dalriada Museum and all.'

Alessandro picked himself off the floor. The wheels were whirring, but he still hadn't worked out the ramifications, far less the imminent consequences. Maybe if he had another month and a lot of paper to write down his working.

'Yeah great, so you art-fags are real tight and real clever. But you're also gonna be real dead if my coke ain't inside that statue.'

'Of course it's there, Alessandro. It has to be, for when the cops arrive to arrest your ass.'

'The cops? Bullshit,' he said, but the fear was writ large.

'Bullshit? Take a look at that.' Zal held up his phone, showing him the pre-keyed text message that he'd sent

Angelique, having hit the Send button in his pocket the second they entered the studio.

Alessandro made to run, but Zal halted him with a fist to the stomach, letting him fall choking at his feet.

'Get a rope,' he told Pepe.

'My pleasure.'

'We're gonna tie you to this statue, one cocksucker to another, and then the cops are gonna stick you in jail for so long, the Lakers franchise will have moved to the moon by the time you get out.'

'That's not gonna happen,' said a low, growling voice.

Every head turned towards the doorway leading to the ante-room, in which American Harry was now standing, gun in hand.

'Fuck.'

'Shit.'

'Step away from Mr Estobal,' he ordered.

Alessandro climbed to his feet once again.

'Hey, the not-so-late Mr Nunez. You're looking better than before.'

'I clean up pretty good, don't I,' Pepe said, by way of bravado.

'Where the fuck did you get to?' Alessandro demanded.

'Something I learned from your Uncle Hector, Alessandro. If something don't feel right, it ain't right. Soon as I saw what was comin' out of that statue, I bailed. Thought I'd take a back seat and see what was in the wind. Good thing I did, huh.'

'Yeah? You're so goddamn smart, how come fucking Nunez is still alive?'

'I told you what I saw. Showed you the pictures. Guess none of us looked close enough. How'd you do it?' he asked Pepe.

'Animal meat. Goats.'

'And the head? Oh yeah, you're a sculptor.'

'That's right. I can work with more than metal.'

'Yeah, real cute,' said Alessandro. 'Now let's kill these assholes and get the merchandise out of here.'

'Too late for the statue,' Harry told him. 'The cops are on their way and we can't move it. Mr Innez has fucked us up pretty good, just like I warned you. Not all your fault, though. Hell of a coincidence you should go to Nunez with your big idea and he should turn out to be Innez's buddy. Can't legislate for that kinda bad luck. *Hell* of a coincidence.'

'Let's just get out of here,' Alessandro said. 'I fucking hate this town. And I want you to know, Innez, before you're even cold tonight, I'll have made the call on Parnell. Then after that I'm gonna track down every last one of your art-fag buddies and I'm gonna kill them too.'

He spat in Zal's face, then turned to Harry.

'Do it.'

Harry raised the gun and cocked the hammer. Zal looked him in the eye.

'Let's see you magic your way out of this one,' Alessandro sneered.

'Nothing personal, kid,' Harry told him. 'This is just business.'

Harry swung his arm thirty degrees and shot Alessandro through the middle of the forehead. The bullet zinged right through into the statue, from which cocaine started to bleed.

He looked back at Zal, still pointing the gun.

'I killed your old man, kid. I want you to hear that from me. But this means we're square. No comebacks.'

Zal swallowed, too many emotions to cope with flooding in at once. Pragmatic survival instinct took over.

401

'No comebacks,' he confirmed.

Harry turned to Pepe.

'It was your idea, wasn't it? You came to Alessandro with the plan and he made out it was the other way round.'

'I came to Alessandro,' Pepe confirmed. 'But the plan was all Zal's idea.'

'You cooked up this whole thing from way back?'

'Yeah,' Zal said. 'It's amazing what you can come up with when you've got three years and nothing to do but plan your revenge.'

'Yeah, well like I said, we're square. But you gotta disappear, and I mean forever. You did this, you understand? Not me. You fucked the Estobals, and I got here too late to stop you killin' Alessandro.'

'I fucked the Estobals, but you ain't telling me this wasn't sanctioned. You guys are using me to cover up an internal coup.'

'You're smart, Innez. Way too smart. That's why you can't come back to LA. We've got a business to run, and right now we need stability. Everybody knew Alessandro was gonna get himself killed eventually. We gave him the chance to make amends, but . . . It's easier for everybody to deal with if we can put the blame on an outsider. Don't make me regret not killing you.'

'What about Parnell?'

'Miguel's gonna be in charge from now on. He's a businessman. Parnell ain't his business.'

'Okay.'

Zal began walking towards the door.

'Hey kid?' Harry called.

'Yeah?'

'Hannigan busted?'

'Oh yeah.'

'Shit. I mean, that's what I figured, but . . .'

'What?'

'Don't suppose you know where I can get a decent blow-job in this town?'

# encore

Angelique walked out of the pub's smoky, raucous hubbub into the quiet night of a rain-washed street. She couldn't stay. Everyone was insisting otherwise and lining up drinks for her, but she knew she had to be somewhere else. She'd slipped away on the pretext of going to the Ladies, and just didn't come back.

It was a celebration, but she didn't feel much like she shared the mood, bearing emotions more appropriate for a wake. They'd got Hannigan. Hip, hip, hooray. Two million in cash and a stolen statue, identical to another one packed with Charlie and sporting a single, blood-rimmed bullet-hole. No Alessandro, but nothing was ever perfect, and nobody was complaining. It was a hell of a result for a night otherwise distinguished only by poor judgment and serial ineptitude, dropped into their laps by someone she now realised was gone for good.

She'd always known that this was how it had to end, but only when she saw that second statue in the otherwise deserted lock-up did it truly hit home that it *had*. Everything had ended, everything, and her colleagues wanted her to celebrate.

In significant contrast to the aftermath of Dubh Ardrain, everyone was toasting her as the hero of the hour, with Shaw the principal cheerleader. Ironically, this made her feel all the more that she needed to get out. After all those years of isolation and defiance, it was their efforts to make her feel she belonged that most confirmed she didn't.

Christmas was the time of miracles, they said. She wasn't a believer, but she was grateful to accept when the word 'TAXI' appeared in yellow light on this least likely night of the year. She hailed it and jumped in, leaning back deep into her seat as the cab moved off. It felt like a getaway. She stared out of the window as the taxi drove through the rainy night, staring at buildings, parks, statues, landmarks; the places of a city as familiar as her face in the mirror, but just as intangibly distant as that inverse world behind the glass.

She had a decision to make. Well, no, that wasn't really true. What she had to do was acknowledge to herself that the decision had been made some time back. All that was left was for her to pass it on.

The cab dropped her off at her flat, where she climbed the stairs to the accompaniment of music from at least four parties in progress elsewhere in the close.

'Merry Christmas.'

She looked up as she reached her landing. Zal was sitting on her doormat, arms around his knees, damp and slightly shivering.

'I thought you'd gone.'

'I should be. My flight sure is. I had to see you again, even if it's just to say goodbye.'

'I could arrest you. You know that, don't you?'

'You can make this my Gethsemane if you want, Angelique. It would be worth it for the kiss.'

She didn't kiss him, and she didn't arrest him, either. Instead she opened her door and led him inside. They sat in her living room, where she poured them both a single malt to warm up.

'Alessandro. He's dead isn't he?' she asked.

Zal nodded.

'You killed him? Is that what all this was about? Revenge?'

'I didn't kill him. American Harry killed him.'

'Who?'

'The Estobals' primary enforcer. It was a coup, an internal thing. But you got one part right. Revenge was entirely what this was about.'

Zal explained it all as they sipped their malt, from initial inception to final sting.

'I had other plans, other schemes,' he added. 'But this was the one the parts fell into place for. We were gonna pull it in Canada at first, but when Tom got his new job last year, it looked a lot like fate was dealing a hand. I was going to Glasgow, like I was always supposed to.'

Nothing would be provable against Thomas White, Zal cautioned, and with Nunez already having made a third statue (as well as those very cute fake guns), the museum wouldn't have to miss a beat. The only losers were the gangsters and the poor dopes of F&NY, whom White had identified as viable patsies from the moment they showed up protesting outside his gallery.

It had all been a massive illusion, planned to the final detail and executed, with immaculate precision, only once all the necessary pieces – and players – were in place. Which was what had been troubling Angelique since she saw the *fait accompli* that was the scene in the lock-up.

'Alessandro wasn't supposed to die, was he?' she asked. 'He was your bargaining chip to get protection for Parnell from the authorities.'

'Exactly as we agreed. Like Parnell would need it. Dexter's tight with some bigger players than Alessandro, but you have to be sure, so I needed the deal.'

'Except, you were always going to make that deal with somebody; with whoever. You just got me to offer it, same as you got me to chase everyone out of the bank. And if I hadn't happened along, someone else would have filled the same part.'

Zal said nothing. Angelique felt tears welling up. She didn't want him to see her cry, but she knew it was unavoidable. 'That's all I was. Just another sucker, another volunteer from the audience.'

'That's not true.'

'Of course it's true. You drew me in and played me from start to finish, like you played everybody else. Christ, you took me for a mug once, and that's understandable, but at least I didn't have to go to bed with you the first time.'

It was way too late to stop the tears now; they were in full flow. Zal knelt down in front of her and took her hand, but she batted it away.

'Leave me alone.'

He sat back down.

'I think you should go now,' she told him.

Zal stood up, but didn't make for the door.

'Did I lie to you?' he asked quietly.

'You deceived me.'

'Did I lie, at any time? Did I really spin you a load of bullshit to make you do things you didn't want? Make up some phoney backstory, play a part? *This* is who I am, Angelique, right here. You got it all, undiluted. Making you part of this was the only way I could afford to get close to you. And once I saw you in that bank, believe me, I knew I had to get close to you. Even if it was just for a while.'

Angelique looked at him through the tears. Perhaps for the first time, there was a weakness about him, an undisguised pleading in those otherwise formidable blue orbs.

But what other way was there left for him to fool her? She got up, had to stand her ground.

'You had a thing for a police officer and couldn't let a little matter like her being on your case get in the way?'

'It was a little more than a *thing*. And Jesus, you *know* that. I didn't mean this to happen, any more than you. It just did. Christ, it's not like I couldn't have done without it at a time like this, but that's how it worked out. And what about you, Officer? When I called you on the phone, did you figure: "I know, I'll hook up with a bank robber – me being a cop, that sounds like a stable long-term relationship in the making"? You knew it couldn't last – maybe that was the attraction.'

Angelique sighed. Nothing hurt like the truth. It had been easier during that brief spell when she didn't believe him.

'Maybe that was the attraction,' she said quietly. 'But attraction is only what happens at the start. It's what comes next that you can't anticipate.'

'Ain't that the truth.'

She took hold of both his hands and looked up into his eyes.

'Stay,' she said.

'I can't. You know that. I have to disappear. It's what I do.'

'I'll find you,' she told him. 'That's what I do. Wherever you go, I'll track you down and I'll find you.'

'I'm counting on it. But I still gotta disappear.'

'Not yet.'

Angelique lay awake in the darkness, her head on Zal's chest as he slept. The sounds of the parties had gradually diminished, though she could hear people singing as they staggered and slalomed drunkenly home along the street outside. She thought of Andie MacDowell and Bill Murray in *Groundhog Day*, trying to stay awake because once they fell asleep, this magic that they had between them would be gone in the morning. Her eyes were closing, she knew, her resistance fading. It would be over soon. But not yet.

She was woken by the ringing of her doorbell.

It took a few moments for her to come to sufficiently to suss what the sound was, longer to recall what was expected of her in response. She staggered groggily out of bed, and had made it almost to her bedroom door before she realised she was naked. That was when she remembered what had happened the night before and reality came flooding in mob-handed.

She turned around to see an empty bed, then nodded to herself.

Quickly pulling on a T-shirt, back-to-front as it turned out, she made for the front door and opened it to find a large, rectangular parcel wrapped in Christmas paper. She brought it inside the flat and ran to the window, looking down on to the street. There was a man getting into a car just outside the close. She only caught a glimpse, but she was sure she'd seen him at the Dalriada the night before: the Canadian curator, Thomas White.

Knowing no further progress could be achieved without stimulants, Angelique made herself a cup of coffee and brought it into the bedroom, along with the parcel. She had a couple of essential caffeine hits then unwrapped it, laying its contents against the fireplace once denuded of the red and gold foil.

It was a painting of herself, recognisable despite the indulgences of the artist's flattery. She had never looked

409

that pretty – not even her mother would say she'd ever looked that pretty (okay, well, maybe) – but it was definitely her, nonetheless.

She was standing in a gallery in front of what she recognised as a painting by Monet. Her head was turned so that she was in profile, her eye looking to one side as though waiting for someone. Above her was a glass ceiling, undoubtedly of allegorical import but also confirming her location as the Musée D'Orsay. In her left hand she held a greetings card, which upon close inspection read '*Bonne Anniversaire*'.

Further up her arm, her wrist displayed a watch, its hands palmed at midday.

Tipping her head back to swallow another mouthful of coffee, she noticed that there was a curious, unfocused shape towards the bottom left-hand corner. She put her cup down and placed the painting on the mantelpiece, then knelt on the floor a couple of feet to the side.

Angelique smiled and nodded again as the skewed image revealed itself. It was the seven of diamonds.

She picked up the phone and dialled. It rang out for a long time, but she knew that this was one place that would still be open on Christmas Day. They had to transfer her around a few times, but eventually she got put through on his home number, where a woman's voice answered.

'*Allo?*'

'*Bonjour*,' Angelique said. '*Je voudrais parler avec Monsieur Dougnac, s'il vous plaît.*'